REAPER

GHOST TARGET

ALSO BY NICHOLAS IRVING

The Reaper

Way of the Reaper

ALSO BY A. J. TATA

THE CAPTAIN JAKE MAHEGAN SERIES

Foreign and Domestic

Three Minutes to Midnight

Besieged

Direct Fire

THE THREAT SERIES

Sudden Threat

Rogue Threat

Hidden Threat

Mortal Threat

REAPER

GHOST TARGET

A SNIPER NOVEL

NICHOLAS IRVING

WITH A. J. TATA

St. Martin's Paperbacks

Published in the United States by St. Martin's Paperbacks, an imprint of St. Martin's Publishing Group.

REAPER: GHOST TARGET

Copyright © 2018 by Nicholas Irving.
Excerpt from *Reaper: Threat Zero* copyright © 2019 by Nicholas Irving.

For information, address St. Martin's Publishing Group, 120 Broadway, New York, NY 10271.

www.stmartins.com

ISBN: 978-1-250-21125-5

Our books may be purchased in bulk for promotional, educational, or business use. Please contact your local bookseller or the Macmillan Corporate and Premium Sales Department at 1-800-221-7945, ext. 5442, or by email at MacmillanSpecial Markets@macmillan.com.

Printed in the United States of America

St. Martin's Press hardcover edition / June 2018
St. Martin's Paperbacks edition / August 2019

10   9   8   7   6   5   4   3   2   1

To all who have supported along the way, to those whose life has been changed, to the men and women of our armed forces past, present, future, and those who will see war no more. Most important, my family. RLTW!

NICHOLAS IRVING

Dedicated to Michael and Dr. Hanna Haskett, two of my dearest friends.

A. J. TATA

ACKNOWLEDGMENTS

It is a privilege to work with Nick Irving on this exciting new fiction spin-off series of his *New York Times* bestselling autobiography, *The Reaper*. From our first conversation and throughout our continuous collaboration, Nick has proven himself to be a true professional, and I want to thank him for the opportunity to partner in entertaining readers through the lens of Vick Harwood. When we first discussed the idea of a fiction story based upon his autobiography, we riffed on ideas, plots, character development, and even our common bond as soldiers in combat, not realizing that two hours had passed when we were done talking. Nick is an American hero, and I'm proud to be teamed with him in this endeavor.

This collaboration would not have been possible without the hard work of our mutual agent, Scott Miller, and his fantastic team at Trident Media Group. Scott and Trident continue to demonstrate why they are the best in the business. They invest time and energy in their authors and build careers. Simply the best.

The driver of this story has been our editor, Marc Resnick, who from the very beginning has demonstrated a high level of enthusiasm for the Reaper fiction series. Marc's unwavering support, endless enthusiasm, and detailed reviews not only made *Reaper: Ghost Target* a better book, but also made me a better writer.

Jaime Coyne has done a fabulous job editing *Reaper: Ghost Target,* and the countless hours she and her team have invested in the story made it the best it could possibly be. Like Marc, her positive outlook under the most demanding deadlines makes everything seem like it will be just fine—which it usually turns out to be.

If there are mistakes or errors, those are mine, and I accept responsibility. To the extent you enjoy the story, you have Nick, Scott, Marc, and Jaime (and a host of others in the chain) to thank.

PROLOGUE

September 12, 2010

Khasan Basayev, the Chechen, stood in the open bomb bay of a prototype Russian PAK-DA stealth bomber flying at thirty-five thousand feet above sea level just twelve miles off the coast of Savannah, Georgia. Strapped to the front of his parachute harness were a nuclear weapon the size of a briefcase and a small rucksack with essential supplies.

Three men from the Russian army, his watchers, stared at him from their respective bomb bays. The four men were kitted up with ballistic helmets, blackened face shields, oxygen masks and tanks, Nomex jump suits, and high-altitude skydiving parachutes to help them survive the nearly seven-mile drop.

The bomb bay light switched from red to green and Basayev dove headfirst into the night from the high-tech, experimental aircraft, which was similar to the American B-1 bomber.

Basayev looked at his GPS watch and altimeter as

he stabilized his aerodynamic flight path toward the east coast of Georgia. At twenty-five thousand feet, he deployed his parachute, which popped open and slowed his descent. The toggles fell in front of his face and he maneuvered them to catch the wind and glide as far west as possible. His goal was to land in a small estuary south of Hunter Army Airfield.

Already the bright lights of Savannah's riverfront were glistening off the Savannah River three miles below him. Just south, the runway lights of Hunter Army Airfield provided him the beacon necessary to guide his flight to the watery landing zone. From there he would lead his handlers, if they could keep up, to the electrical power plant and complete his mission.

He landed with a splash in the estuary, the water warm and soothing for the short period of time he was in it. He pulled the risers of his parachute until the nylon canopy was wadded in his hands, sidestroked to the bank, trudged into the underbrush, and finally reached a dry location. He placed his gear and the canopy on the matted pine straw as he removed his parachute harness. Unlatching the RA-115 case from the harness, Basayev inspected the seal. It seemed secure enough. He had slowed his descent sufficiently to prevent any significant seepage into the case from impact.

Basayev removed the small rucksack from the harness, then changed from his wet jumpsuit to dry clothes: black cargo pants, tactical shirt, and boots. After stuffing the jumpsuit and parachute into his rucksack, he shouldered the pack. Behind him, he heard the soft splashes of his handlers landing in the estuary. With no time to waste, he picked up the suitcase-sized device and carried it as if he were a businessman on a morning walk to work. His handlers were several minutes behind him. It was better this way. He knew how to find the electrical power grid and he knew how to connect the nuclear device to keep it active, ready for detonation.

Basayev didn't hate America; rather, in addition to enjoying the buzz of combat, he loved being rich. The promised payday was fifty million dollars, of which he had already received five. Ten percent down payment on a mission this size was his going rate.

He would receive the remaining forty-five million when the bomb detonated near the Port of Savannah and Hunter Army Airfield, home of the First Ranger Battalion and Third Battalion of the U.S. Army's Special Operations Aviation Regiment.

In the meantime, he would enjoy tasting real combat again. This time in Syria or Afghanistan. With the Arab Spring around the corner, there would be plenty of opportunities.

CHAPTER 1

Present Day

Vick Harwood's mission was to kill the Chechen, but complications arose quickly as two Taliban riflemen appeared on the ridge above their hide position.

It was a tough enough shot without the Taliban factor. Harwood and his spotter were in a dusty hide position. The tan-and-black Kandahar Mountains leaned over them like a pissed-off drill sergeant, hot, smelly, and overbearing. The Chechen was holed up eight hundred meters away. Below Harwood, poppy farmers scraped resin into burlap sacks. Red and white poppy flowers framed the brown waters of the Helmand River and its valley until the horizon met the setting sun. Harwood and his spotter smelled like unwashed week-old gym socks.

But Harwood could make the shot. He'd done it before. Thirty-three times in the last three months, to be exact. Harwood was a sniper. Not just any sniper, but the deadliest sniper in the U.S. Army. He seemed to always be there. Providing cover. Knocking down the guy that was about to kill friendlies. Picking off the mujahedin about to shoot the rocket-propelled grenade. Always there. His buddies had nicknamed him the Reaper. A nom de guerre was a badge of honor among warriors. "Reaper" left no doubt about Harwood's specialty: killing the enemy.

With harvesting the next kill on their mind, Harwood and Corporal Sammie Samuelson—too new to have a Ranger nickname—homed in on the Chechen's domain.

"We've still got movement on the ridge," Samuelson whispered. "Two hundred meters. Muj. Still heading our way. AK-47s. And we've got a convoy closing in on Sangin village a mile in the other direction." Sangin was a small hamlet of adobe huts on the Helmand River and was the nexus of Afghanistan's poppy trade.

"No way the muj knows about us. We're solid," Harwood said under his breath. It was a judgment call. Over the past two days since their insertion, shepherds and wanderers had drifted within fifty meters of their nearly invisible position. They looked like rocks in their tattered ghillie suits.

"You're the boss," Samuelson grunted.

"What's up with the convoy?"

"Three Hilux pickup trucks. Prob Taliban poppy dudes coming in to check the stash."

Clumsy footsteps on the far ridge echoed. Boots scraped on shale. Rocks broke free and rolled hundreds of feet down the sheer cliffs. The Taliban were getting close, but only one kill mattered now—the Chechen—not two Taliban riflemen and not the convoy of small pickup trucks. The sun had the Chechen's hide site—a U-shaped rock formation—spotlighted perfectly.

"Muj closing in, boss. On the ridge."

"Roger," Harwood said.

The Chechen's lightly bearded face briefly filled the crosshairs of Harwood's Leupold scope, which was mounted on his SR-25 sniper rifle, then disappeared.

Harwood had nicknamed his rifle "Lindsay" after a foster sister. Lindsay had been older and kind to him. Cooked for him. Gave him advice. Took care of him and the others. Told him to run as far as he could when the time was right—when things turned bad on the farm. But he hadn't run. He had stayed to fight. To protect Lindsay. To make sure she made it out, too. But he had failed her.

He carried Lindsay with him everywhere he went now. For Harwood, it was all about keeping the memory alive. He didn't have much to treasure from his childhood, but Lindsay was someone, a sister of sorts, he would honor his entire life. Lindsay—the rifle—still took care of him, in her own way. She was outfitted with a ballistic sound suppressor on the muzzle. The suppressor wasn't perfectly quiet, wasn't meant to be, but it was better than the alternative. Most importantly, Lindsay was effective.

Thirty-three kills in ninety days.

The setting sun dialed back the heat incrementally, like turning down the flame of a gas stove. In a matter of minutes, the temperature would swing to cold. The sweat would transition from useful and cooling to damp and irritating. But they were Rangers. Conditions didn't matter. Only the mission.

"Confirm friendlies clear," Harwood said. "Sun is

spotlighting his shadow. Might help us predict when he comes out."

"Roger, boss. No friendlies in the AO, but those two muj are sniffing now about a hundred meters away," Samuelson muttered. "AO" was army acronym parlance for area of operations.

"Chechen's moving a lot. Shadow looks like he's on his radio," Harwood said.

"Roger, watching," Samuelson replied. Samuelson was less than five feet from Harwood, observing through his spotter's scope. The standard was to always be within arm's reach of your Ranger buddy. Three weeks ago Harwood's former spotter, Joe LaBoeuf, had been that close when the Chechen's sniper shot found LaBoeuf's forehead. The bulk of LaBoeuf's brains had splattered onto Harwood's face.

"Roger. Ignore the muj for now. Focus on Basayev," Harwood directed.

After LaBoeuf's death, the Ranger intelligence officer had provided Harwood with a full dossier on the Chechen. His name was Khasan Basayev. Considered the number-one threat to U.S. soldiers other than roadside bombs, Basayev was a mercenary. The report indicated that the Taliban and Pakistani intelligence paid nicely to kill American soldiers in Helmand Province. Basayev was mainly protecting supply trains moving between Iran and Pakistan. The Ranger operations officer had briefed Harwood and Samuelson, telling them that their mission was to kill the Chechen so that the Rangers could raid the convoys and interdict the weapons and drugs.

And now, the duel between the Reaper and the Chechen.

Harwood shifted his scope to the town of Sangin, a short half mile beyond the Chechen's position. The three-vehicle convoy Samuelson mentioned consisted of identical tan Hilux pickup trucks with toppers. They skidded to a stop in front of some adobe homes—qalats. Switching back to Basayev's hide, Harwood noticed Basayev's shadow. The Chechen was gesturing with his arms in an agitated manner.

"Check out what has him so freaked, Sammie," Harwood directed his spotter.

Samuelson was nineteen years old and relatively new to the Rangers. He had passed Ranger training and was an apprentice sniper. The corporal had to have some mettle to get through Ranger School. Even more, Ranger Command Sergeant Major Murdoch must have thought something of him to put him on the path to sniper.

"Roger. Three guys out of the trucks now and . . . holy shit."

"What?"

"They're dragging two women wearing burqas from one of the compounds. They're handcuffed. Now I see a third woman. She's fighting like a banshee."

"Maybe the Chechen knows them," Harwood said, remaining focused. The Chechen's outline danced against the khaki-colored rock formation like a shadow performance.

With no shot on Basayev, he shifted his scope again to the action Samuelson was describing. He twisted the focus dial with his fingers protruding from cut olive-and-black gloves. The silky sheen of long, raven hair caught his eye. *No burqa*.

The men were dressed in traditional Afghan outer

garments that loosely covered the torso and leg, and the Peshawari turban, a sweat-stained white sheet wrapped around the head a few times with the remainder left to hang like a ponytail. The captors had dark beards dyed with henna. Two men lifted one woman into each truck. A third man pulled the long black hair of the lady without the burqa. They scrambled. The man slapped her hard. Her face turned toward Harwood, as if she were looking at the scope from a mile away, perhaps wishing for him to shoot her, knowing what torturous fate lay ahead.

The sun cast an orange glow that made the small village of adobe huts look like center stage in a spaghetti Western. Harwood switched back to Basayev, whose shadow showed he was shouting into a mobile radio or phone as he stared at the village.

Having no loyalties was the mercenary's maxim. Fight for money, not country or anything else. A pure cash transaction, devoid of emotion. The thin gruel of intelligence on Basayev identified that he had married a French woman. There had been just one picture in the Ranger intelligence officer's target folder, showing the Chechen with an attractive, black-haired woman with ropy muscles. The photo showed her wearing a black sleeveless dress, him a gray pin-striped suit with white shirt open at the collar. The background appeared to be a hotel casino.

Was that Basayev's wife in the village? Harwood wondered.

Briefly, the Chechen's head popped out and his ice-blue eyes flashed at their position. It appeared to be a random, unknowing glance.

Samuelson noticed it, too. "Think he saw us?"

"No chance," Harwood said. "We look like rocks. What do you have up on the ridge?"

"They're scanning. Still in the open. I think we're good."

"They connected to what's happening in the village?"

"Don't know. Be weird if they were."

From their perch, the poppy fields were no different from the farms Harwood worked as a foster child in rural Maryland. A reputation as a hardworking kid had stopped a series of pass-arounds for young Vick Harwood when a cattle rancher had seen him carrying a bale of hay in each hand as if they were briefcases on a morning commute to work.

"What's holding you up, bro?" Samuelson asked. "Thinking about that USO babe?"

"Watch it, Sammie," Harwood replied. His lips were dry and dusty as he spoke. The truth was that the "USO babe" made him feel good. Most of the men had swooned over the blond hair and freckles of Jackie Colt, the Olympic air rifle gold medalist they had met a few weeks ago.

"Just remember, bros before hos," Samuelson said. "That's our code."

Harwood smiled. The informal code of placing your battle buddy first was ingrained in every Ranger's mind. It always came down to that in the end. Ranger buddies first and forever. Harwood sniffed and could smell himself, or maybe it was Samuelson. By now it didn't matter. They both stank, sweat stains dried into their combat uniforms, leaving the white salt residue that was a badge of honor when returning to the forward operating base.

"Trucks packing up. Like a kidnap team or something. I'll call it in after we cap the Chechen," Samuelson reported. "Muj on the ridge at fifty meters. Looking this way. Moving this way." His whispered words tumbled over each other as the adrenaline surged.

Harwood shifted his scope and rifle. Three trucks were snaking out of the village.

"What'd they get? Three women?"

"Roger that. Back on the Chechen. Check it out," Samuelson said. Before Harwood moved his scope, one of the men in a passenger seat pulled out his binoculars and scanned in their general direction.

He shifted back to the Chechen. "I've got him. He's looking right at us. It's not possible for them to know where we are unless someone's talking to him," Harwood said. "What's on the ridge?"

"*They're* looking right at us," Samuelson said. The men in the village, the Chechen, and the Taliban on the ridge were all looking in their direction. Not good.

Basayev carried an SV-98 rifle known for its accuracy and enhanced penetration rounds, but not its distance. Similarly, Harwood's SR-25 was known for its versatility and accuracy at shorter distances. While the advertised maximum effective range of the weapon was something less than a mile, Harwood knew it all came down to the sniper. His Ranger Regiment command sergeant major had always told him, "It's the archer, not the arrow."

"Here he comes," Samuelson said.

"I've got him," Harwood replied. He tightened his finger on the trigger, ready to do to Basayev as the Chechen had done to LaBoeuf. Harwood stayed in the zone, ready to fire. His sight picture was good. A few wisps of dust shot across his scope lens but nothing serious enough to obscure the shot.

The Chechen was shouting into a personal handheld radio and had completely diverted his attention from taking cover behind his hide position to standing and beginning to run toward the village. The trucks pivoted and kicked up clouds of dust as Basayev stopped and stared.

He was perfectly still.

Harwood steadied his rifle, had the man's head in the crosshairs, saw the emotion on his face. Something terrible had happened to him. Not his concern. The shot was there.

He took it.

Basayev dove back behind his rock pile. The bullet missed, smacking harmlessly into the shale, a dust cloud in its wake. It was now nothing more than a warning to Basayev. Perhaps he had known all along that he was under surveillance.

"Shit," Harwood said.

"What's he doing now?" Samuelson asked.

A piece of cardboard the size of a combat ration box, two feet by two feet, emerged from behind the rock.

It's a damn message! Harwood thought. *Written in black camo stick!*

Bring her back! Trade?

"Oh, man," Harwood said. "We're burned. Bring her back? Trade? WTF?"

The high-pitched whine of mortar or artillery rounds whistled overhead. Oddly, the distinctive noises were not coming from the direction of the Chechen, the men on the ridge, or the Taliban hideout of Sangin.

Basayev must have offset the indirect fire team. Based upon the whistling sound, the rounds were coming from behind and only a few seconds away.

Explosions rocked their position. Shrapnel and rocks flew everywhere. Debris whipped past them like a hive of angry hornets. Harwood tried to move, but the deafening thunder of mortar rounds bursting around their position immobilized him.

"Sammie!" he shouted. Harwood reached out with his hand only to have it raked by supersonic shrapnel and rocks. Samuelson wasn't there. Lindsay, the sniper rifle, jumped in front of him, bucked with the ground as the shale beneath him buckled and gave way like a California mud slide in heavy rains. The sensation of plunging into a rock pile was worsened by every sniper's worst fear: losing his spotter.

Harwood landed somewhere, he wasn't quite certain. His mind was reeling. Rocks pounded relentlessly into his body, like Mike Tyson body punches.

Bring her back! Trade? spiraled through his mind before blackness consumed him. Pinging in the darkness, like sonar, was the final echoing thought: *Bring who back? And what did he have to offer in trade?*

CHAPTER 2

Khasan Basayev stood in his sniper hide as the two men approached. They placed a wounded man and a rifle on the ground in front of him. A quick glance confirmed this was not Harwood. He looked up, shaking his head.

"Go back and get me the Reaper," he said to his two Taliban spotters. "This is not him."

After a pause, the leader asked, "How much?" They knew the risk of American helicopters arriving soon. It was only their proximity to the mortar fire that had allowed them to secure the one injured American and a rifle.

"One thousand dollars for each of you," Basayev promised. It was a hollow gesture. The men would die tonight.

They nodded and began running the half mile along a mountain-ridge goat trail to the American hide position. Prior to executing any mission, Basayev spent two days scouting potential enemy reconnaissance locations, pencil-sketching them at the angle from which he expected to be observing. Having studied Vick Harwood, the black Ranger sniper, Basayev admired the man's tradecraft. It was just one rock angled slightly askew that had tipped him off. Even with his preparation, though, he never had a shot at Harwood or his spotter.

Now as his two pawns closed on the position again, the search-and-rescue helicopters—a UH-60 Black Hawk medical evacuation aircraft and an AH-64 Apache gunship—arrived and struggled with the high winds that had predictably appeared with the change of temperature as darkness arrived. The two men found cover and fired on the helicopters. Rifle shots echoed down the Helmand Valley. The Apache gunship spit Hughes M230 chain-gun rounds at his two men, most likely dead now. Better that than captured.

The Black Hawk medevac hovered over a deep ravine next to the Reaper's hide position. A pararescue medic sat atop a T-bar connected to a wire cable as the crew lowered him into the crevice using a hoist. After a minute, he reappeared with a body strapped to his chest, presumably Harwood. For thirty minutes the search-and-rescue team continued the fruitless hunt for Harwood's spotter. More rifle shots echoed in the Helmand Valley, pushing away the vulnerable helicopters.

As the helicopters fled the random gunfire, Basayev looked at the American and the rifle the two men had delivered. The man was barely alive, having suffered a severe head injury either from shrapnel or falling debris.

He created a makeshift litter to drag his newly acquired captive, shouldered his rucksack, and then pulled behind him the heavy weight of his bounty. Stepping onto the treacherous trail, he moved quickly to his vehicle, which was parked a mile away.

With the helicopters off station, Basayev had to assume that a Predator drone was still overhead, scanning the area. Persistent and lethal, the drones were handicapped in that they could view only a specific area. Their mission would be to continue to search the area for a second body and to do battle-damage assessment on the Taliban.

His window was now.

A company of Rangers would soon ferry in from Lashkar Gah and begin to expand outward in ever-increasing circles until they found his hide site.

Moving quickly along the rocky path, Basayev did his best to protect the injured head of his captive. He reached the valley floor after a dozen steeply inclined switchbacks that challenged even his muscular, well-conditioned body. Before this mission, he had backed his Hilux pickup truck into a small cave. His was the four-door version and he opened the rear door, carefully lifting the man into the rear seat. Basayev was glad to find a pulse. The man had survived the treacherous descent. Using an enhanced medical kit from his pickup bed, he went to work on the soldier. Keeping the vehicle dome light off, he wore a medical headlamp to help him further discern the extent of the man's injuries.

The crusty cave floor crunched beneath Basayev's boots. The man's skull appeared mangled on the right half. He used a canteen of water followed by a bottle of Betadine to flush the wound. A flap of skin lay back, revealing white bone. Fractures in the skull looked like a broken but barely intact eggshell. More flushing and antiseptic were followed by gauze and pressure, to stem the marginal bleeding. Moving from the most severe wound to inspect the rest of the body, he saw the man's face littered with shrapnel marks, like freshly oozing acne. He used a cloth to apply antiseptic and clean the wounds, followed by an application of antibiotic cream. He inspected the rest of the man's body by looking for tears or punctures in the sniper's ghillie suit, a tan-and-black-flecked outfit that provided him concealment in the mountains. He found no other injuries serious enough on which to waste any more time. He looked in the man's eyes, noticing their dilation, a sure sign of concussion, perhaps even coma.

He carefully belted the man into a supine position in the backseat after laying a blanket over him. Wanting to keep his neck and head stable, Basayev placed a rolled blanket around the man's head and tightened a seat belt across his forehead. He tested his work and found the body secure enough to withstand the bumpy ride to Kandahar.

He took the rifle that the two men had brought back with the wounded man and disassembled it. Placing the weapon in his rucksack, Basayev retrieved a Sig Sauer pistol and an Uzi machine gun, which would be more useful during the drive.

Certain that he had done all he could, he began the three-hour drive to Kandahar. He needed to get the soldier to a qualified physician. Thinking about what had transpired earlier in the day in the village, he had listened to the shrieks of the women as the kidnap team took them. This had been going on for some time now, and Basayev knew it was a mistake to have his wife, Nina Moreau, with him in the village.

Looking at the man hanging on to life by a thin fiber in the back of his truck, he bounced along the ruddy trail toward Kandahar thinking that, while he had more to trade, the captive was now his best bargaining chip.

Resolute, Basayev found the blacktop road and sped toward a doctor in Kandahar, knowing that locating Nina was now the most important mission of his life.

That night, Harwood was in the emergency room, doctors milling around, barking orders. Morphine running through his veins. *Funny,* he thought, *I'm supposed to stop opium movement, not live high on the juice.*

Footsteps entered the plywood operating room in Kandahar. Three shadows were backlit against the light green curtain that had been pulled around his operating table. Harwood shifted his eyes left and right, trying to find Samuelson, but saw only the three dark outlines and a cluster of medical personnel leaning over him.

"Close your eyes," a nurse admonished. He did, listening as the men talked and the heart monitors beeped.

"All the coffins loaded?" one man said beyond the screen.

"They're called transfer cases, but yes, sir, they're all loaded," another responded.

"He going to make it?"

"Not sure. Going to be close. Head wounds," a new voice commented.

Soon Harwood lost the voices and the beeps of the machinery. His mind swam to a peaceful place where he and Jackie Colt, the Olympic champion, were dining in a fancy restaurant. He had showered and shaved and his hand was reaching across the table holding hers as they clinked glasses and toasted to his winning of their shooting bet in Kandahar.

"But the coffins," she said in his dream. "Why so many coffins?"

And then he blacked out again for the second time in a single day.

CHAPTER 3

One week after Vick Harwood had been evacuated from Afghanistan, he was lying in a bed with crisp white sheets. Dutiful nurses scurried about efficiently. He was in a hospital, but wasn't sure precisely where or why.

It was a challenge to get outside of his own head. He was trapped like a caged animal. Thoughts were not maturing fully.

He wondered, though, about Samuelson. He remembered the mission to kill the Chechen. The pickup trucks in the village. The two men on the ridge. The Chechen going crazy and screaming into his radio or phone. Then the mortars. Then no Samuelson. Samuelson and LaBoeuf. Gone, forever.

Like Lindsay, his foster sister.

Gone forever.

Couldn't he take care of anyone? Guilt ricocheted in his mind like a rubber ball bouncing aimlessly and endlessly.

Then another thought, one he didn't deserve. Jackie Colt, the Olympic champion. He remembered their contest in the Ranger compound at Kandahar Airfield.

A group of Olympic champions and entertainers had swept through Afghanistan to meet with the troops. One was Jackson "Jackie" Colt, the female gold medalist for the air rifle competition. She and Harwood had established a rapport, talking about angles, deflections, clicks, and scopes, but Harwood had a difficult time taking her seriously until she said, "All right, cowboy, let's use your weapons and loser buys the other dinner the next time you're home from this garden spot." Jackie had smiled, tossed her golden hair over her shoulders, and scrunched her freckled nose at him. If he hadn't been smelly, sweaty, and just plain nasty, he might have thought she was flirting with him. They held the shoot-out, Harwood beating her by a hair on the last shot. He wasn't sure if she had intentionally missed or not. She was good, he had to admit.

"Damn, you just beat an Olympic gold medalist," Jackie said. "Must be why they call you the Reaper." She leaned over, pulled the gold medal from her pocket, held it up, and took a selfie of her face next to his, gold medal beneath their chins. She was smiling. Others would describe his expression as dumbfounded.

Harwood *was* flustered. A beautiful woman and Olympic champion knew his nickname. "How do you know who I am?" he asked.

"You're a legend," she said, bumping him with her shoulder before they turned toward the small group that had followed them to the firing range. "But even legends need to bathe," she whispered in his ear. She wrinkled her nose and sniffed. "So, clean up before I take you to dinner when you get back home."

He couldn't remember how long ago that was, but the vision was clear. And he remembered the soft voice, a throaty whispering melody that matched her smile perfectly.

"Reaper," she said.

He smiled. He could see her deep in the recesses of his mind.

"Reaper, wake up," she said, again.

For the first time in a week, Harwood opened his eyes. He was staring at Jackie Colt's smiling face. Two doctors in light green scrubs hovered behind her. She clasped his hand. White against brown. It was warm, like he imagined the rest of her to be.

"Reaper, you're okay," she said. "I'm here with you."

The doctors tried to move around her, but she didn't move. She stared at him with a knowing smile. She pointed at something across the room, but he couldn't turn his head.

"I'll be right there," she said.

She stepped back and let the doctors move forward. One shined a flashlight into his eyes. The other said something, but he was still focused on Jackie. She was here, for him.

"Still not out of the woods," one doctor said.

"Vick, can you feel this?"

The doctor was pressing something against his feet. He wanted to say yes, but he couldn't get the word out. He wanted to nod his head, but he couldn't move his neck. He pulled against the restraint on his forehead. His neck muscles flared with hot pain.

"Don't try to move. Blink your eyes twice if you can feel this, Vick."

He blinked. He could do that. He was an Army Ranger sniper and former high school athlete and the best he could do was blink his freaking eyes. Great.

"That's a good sign, son," the doctor said.

The doctors wrote something on the clipboard, looked at each other, and then looked across his bed, presumably at Jackie.

"He's improving."

They walked out of the room, and his mind spiraled into sleep, exhausted by that little bit of activity.

While the Reaper was opening his eyes in Washington, D.C., Khasan Basayev glanced at his smartphone's Instagram feed with disappointment. Nothing yet. He lifted his eyes to consider his prisoner. They were on the outskirts of Kandahar. The man had improved thanks to the help of Dr. Mohammed Nijrabi. Lying on the single wide mattress, the man was still motionless.

Basayev decided to name the man Abrek, an ode to his own Chechen and Circassian heritage. The term meant "warrior" or "brave man" in the tortured languages of his homeland. After all, the man was a soldier. A warrior. A U.S. Army Ranger. He had the skills. Now Basayev needed to test the malleability of the young man as he healed.

"I've done everything I can do," Dr. Nijrabi said. "He will survive, but I'm not sure about his mental capacity." Nijrabi was dressed in standard Afghan clothing, the long white outer garment covered with a brown vest. A stethoscope hung around his neck, the ear tips and diaphragm meeting just below his long black beard. He smelled of antiseptic and soap.

"That's actually not a bad thing, as long as he is physically capable," Basayev said.

The doctor paused. "What do you have planned?"

"The less you know the better, as always. I've paid you well."

"I have an oath," Nijrabi said. "To do no harm."

"And you've done none. Quite the opposite. You've worked a miracle. I didn't think he would live."

"You did well preserving the wound. I've stitched his scalp. He's got the skull fracture which appears to be healing, but it will heal deformed. I'll leave it up to you on whether you shave all of his hair."

The doctor had shaved the right side of the man's head, flushed the wound multiple times, and then stitched the scalp back into place. After a week, bristles of hair were poking around the row of stitches, which looked like a long black centipede embedded in the man's scalp.

"He's beyond getting an infection now so I'm declaring him your patient, Khasan," the doctor said. After a pause, he whispered, "I'm sorry about Nina."

Basayev nodded. The doctor had met Nina briefly prior to Basayev's mission in Helmand Province.

"Thank you," Basayev said. "Be safe in your travels."

"*Inshallah.*" *God willing.*

Basayev closed and locked the door behind the doctor. The doctor wasn't the best at his practice, but he was reliable and trustworthy. The trade-off was necessary.

His temporary residence was a small outbuilding on Nazim Ghul's forty-acre vineyard and water-bottling operation. The Taliban paid Ghul well to allow Basayev unfettered access, and Ghul knew better than to ever question Basayev. The two men rarely saw one another other than from afar. Surrounded by tall West Himalayan firs, the compound was secure enough. An additional benefit was that Ghul's son was an interpreter for the Americans at the military compound on Kandahar Airfield. On more than one occasion Basayev had wedged himself in the false bottom of Tariq Ghul's pickup truck to gain access to the base.

Having separated the two twin beds, which he had previously placed together for himself and Nina, Basayev sat on the bed opposite the man he called Abrek. The man breathed steadily, his torso rhythmically lifting the gray wool blanket. The scabs on his face were healing. About fifteen or so pockmarks would scar, as if he'd been blasted in the face by a shotgun. Basayev's initial inspection had proven mostly accurate. Other than some bruises, the head injury was the only meaningful wound the soldier had sustained.

Night had fallen and through the window opening came the clarion hunting call of the Eurasian eagle owl, a distinctive hoot. The sounds were those of two owls communicating prior to their nightly prowl. The hedgehogs that scampered through the vineyards were a favorite of the owls. Through the square glassless opening, the cool night air seeped in, bringing with it the syrupy smell of fir trees. A brilliant array of stars swirled above the evergreens. The muted television cast flickers of light that contrasted with the beauty and stillness outside.

"The b-birds."

For a moment, the words didn't register with Ba-

sayev. The night was utterly silent save for the owls'
nefarious melody.

He turned toward Abrek and looked at the injured
soldier.

"Yes," Basayev said. "What about the birds?"

Abrek opened his eyes and directed them at the
voice.

"Do they m-mean I'm alive?"

Basayev had a week to think about this moment. If
the soldier was going to wake, how would he approach
him? What would he say? After several permutations,
he had developed a plan.

"Yes. I saved you, Abrek."

"Abrek," the man said, as if trying on a new shoe.

Basayev paused, allowing the name to soak into his
wounded brain.

"I-Is that my name?"

"It is now, my friend."

"A-Abrek."

A long moment of silence endured, interrupted only
by the fluttering of wings and the gnashing of talons
and flesh.

"Y-You're my friend?"

"The only friend you have, Abrek."

"I d-don't remember," the soldier said.

"You were wounded. The Americans left you behind," Basayev said. This was the tricky part. He had
cut away and burned the man's uniform the night he
had returned to the compound. Abrek was now dressed
in traditional mujahedin tactical garments of black
pants and shirt with an empty outer tactical vest.

"Left me?"

"You were part of a kidnap team that was ambushed."

"K-Kidnap team?"

"Yes. Your teammate left you behind. Saved himself. I came to your rescue."

Abrek lifted his head and stared at the blanket covering him. Basayev moved swiftly to his side.

"Careful, brother. You were wounded badly."

Abrek's eyes searched Basayev's, looking for recognition. Basayev held the gaze, imprinting his face into Abrek's memory, like creating a permanent photo to be kept on the hard drive or in the cloud. Always there. The first one there. The most enduring.

He brought water and soup to the soldier, who drank and ate sloppily at first, but with Basayev's help, managed to get most of the fluids into his system.

"B-Brother," Abrek said.

Eyes locked again. Soup clung to the newly forming strands of beard on the soldier's face. Basayev held Abrek's eyes until the man looked away.

"We're brothers?" the soldier asked.

"Like brothers. Brothers in combat," Basayev said. "You were wounded badly by Americans." Basayev lifted Abrek's hand and placed it against his shaved scalp. "Go lightly. The wound is fresh." Abrek's hand recoiled at the touch of the stitches.

After another long silence, the soldier asked, "Where?"

This was another tricky juncture for Basayev. Did he go with Afghanistan or some other location? Deciding it might be too risky to try to make him associate with another country, Basayev determined that he would tell him the truth.

"Kandahar. We are in a safe house."

"Safe house."

"It is dangerous. The Americans are looking for you. They know you kidnapped the women."

Silence.

"Women?"

"Yes." Basayev let the soldier's mind churn. Abrek's face was pinched in frustration.

Then finally: "Women in trucks."

It was a statement, not a question. A moment of recognition.

"Yes. Women in trucks." Basayev paused. Where would his captive's mind go next?

"Burqas," Abrek said.

"Yes. Afghan women in burqas. You were part of the team."

His captive nodded. Watery eyes locked on to his gaze.

"Brothers?"

Basayev was interested in the speech pattern. Sometimes there was a stutter and other times there wasn't. He wondered if that meant anything. Perhaps the doctor could tell him.

"Yes. Brothers in war. I saved you. The Americans wounded you." The repetition would build the memory, like a foundation.

"Yes. Rockets. B-Bombs."

"I got to you as soon as I could. Then brought you here to a doctor." He segued quickly from the attack to something far more personal to test the man's memory. "Do you know what your name means?"

"Means?" he asked as if he wasn't sure. "You told me my name is Abrek."

"Yes. Abrek means brave warrior."

The man nodded slightly, whispering, "Warrior. Abrek. Wounded."

"Yes, and you're tired now, Abrek. You must rest. I'm taking care of you. The Americans left you."

"Left me? Why? Who? N-Not right?"

Abrek's temperament had reached the right pitch. "Yes. Not right. Please rest, brother. Warrior."

"Yes. Tired." After a pause, his captive said, "Thank you, brother."

Basayev pulled the blanket tight around Abrek and walked to the window. The owls were quiet, their kill bagged for the night.

He turned and walked to the television. After a few minutes, CNN International showed an attractive young blond woman pushing a black man in a wheelchair. Cameras flashed and reporters were shouting questions. The woman was wearing a red, white, and blue jacket with five interlocking rings. The Olympic symbol. Basayev unmuted the sound and listened, keeping the volume low so as to not disturb Abrek . . . or spark an unwanted memory. A male reporter wearing a dark suit spoke into a camera.

". . . Olympic gold medalist Jackie Colt escorts wounded Army Ranger sniper Sergeant Vick Harwood at Walter Reed National Military Medical Center in Washington, D.C. . . . Harwood is the cover story in the current issue of *Rolling Stone*. They call him 'The Reaper.' One sharpshooter taking care of another. An Olympic champion and a combat hero. A story made for Hollywood . . ."

The image switched from the reporter to a cover of *Rolling Stone* magazine with a picture of Harwood below the title "The Reaper." Quickly, the picture faded to a television commercial. Basayev stared at the screen and couldn't believe what he was seeing. The same woman who was pushing the wheelchair was now running in her Olympic outfit and sweating as she gulped down a red-colored sports drink. She smiled and held up her gold medal as the commercial ended.

He lifted the smartphone. Still nothing on Instagram. He walked to the window and stared at the distant rectangle of Nazim Ghul's water-bottling plant. Then he turned around and watched his prisoner sleep and continue to heal. His eyes flicked to the damaged weapon in the corner. Then he thought of the high altitude jump in 2010. *Indeed, I do have something to trade.*

Basayev smiled. He called Dr. Nijrabi for one more favor. He would be ready when he got the message.

CHAPTER 4

Three months after Vick Harwood had been evacuated from a rock pile in Afghanistan, he stretched outside of the enlisted visitors' quarters at Fort Bragg, North Carolina. His medical journey had taken him from Walter Reed National Military Medical Center, in Washington, D.C., to Brooke Army Medical Center, in San Antonio, Texas. The last phase of his rehab included reintegration into the force as a trainer of snipers and today had been a full day.

He chugged a sports drink that Jackie Colt was now sponsoring. She had given him two cases of the stuff. He felt the sweat bead on his arms in the North Carolina humidity. Wearing formfitting Under Amour activewear and Nike running shoes, he worked the tightness out of the shrapnel scars from the mortar attack that had left him unconscious and wounded. He didn't remember much from that day and was still struggling with bouts of memory loss on a routine basis.

Two things had stuck with him, though, ever since he'd woken up. First, the army had listed his spotter, Samuelson, as DUSTWUN, army abbreviation for "duty status—whereabouts unknown." Samuelson could be a prisoner in a Taliban dungeon somewhere in Pakistan or dead and buried in a forgotten grave. Second, his platoon sergeant had told him that the search-and-rescue team reported finding no sniper rifle at his location. The only weapon they recovered was the nine-millimeter Beretta Harwood he'd carried on his hip. Apparently that had remained in place beneath the rubble. The crew chief from the SAR team had admitted their search was cut short by the intense enemy fire they received while conducting the evacuation.

Lindsay was missing.

Harwood finished lengthening his ropy muscles, working out the kinks. At six feet two inches, he was broad and well-muscled. A self-professed gym rat, Harwood had hit the weights even harder after his injuries. Shrapnel to the back and face were the most severe, the ghillie suit having saved him from further harm. The doctors had told him the fall had been just as damaging as any shrapnel that had hit him. His broken left arm had healed nicely, and the torn rotator cuff on his right shoulder still bit at him every time he did a pull-up, but he still did pull-ups every day. He was powering through the injuries and using his skills to train U.S. military special forces and scout snipers around the country.

On his fifth and final night here at Fort Bragg in August, he was already sweating as he stood and shouldered his rucksack. Harwood always ran with a black rucksack full of fluids, meds, and other things he probably shouldn't have carried. But he'd taken mortar rounds for his country and he wasn't exactly in the mood to be complying with all the rules. There were viable targets on the home front that necessitated taking every precaution.

Stepping into his pace, he followed his usual route along the golf course, through the officer housing, past the headquarters, through the generals' brand-new mansions, and to the sawdust pit that had pull-up, dip, sit-up, rope, and Pilates platforms. Passing an attractive female soldier running in the opposite direction, Harwood nodded at her with respect at the size of her rucksack and she returned the gesture as she continued her gait. Harwood stopped, off-loaded his rucksack, and turned when he saw General Sampson, the commander of the JFK Special Warfare Center, pull into his driveway about a quarter mile away.

"Son of a bitch," Harwood muttered. Sampson was a sanctimonious asshole. Harwood didn't know or care much about generals, but this one had dressed him down on his first day of training the special operations snipers. Harwood jumped up and started knocking out pull-ups, his injuries screaming at him the entire time.

Sampson. His mind rewound back to five days ago when he had reported for duty to begin training the snipers in the special forces school.

"No charity here, Harwood," Sampson had said.

"Don't expect any, sir." Harwood's "sir" had been a tad late, like a missed musical note. The general picked up on it right away.

"Got a problem with authority, soldier?"

No, just pricks like you, he wanted to say, but went

with the safer "No, sir." The "sir" had been tightly connected to the "no" this time.

"I got guys that can outshoot you, Harwood. I understand the army is trying to rehab you, but this ain't the time or the place for the disabled list. This is major-league ball here, son. And none of that Reaper bullshit around here, understand?"

The general verbally railed him for about fifteen minutes as Harwood stood at attention, his shoulders, arms, and neck tightening into one metal knot. When the general dismissed him, Harwood uncoiled from his position of attention, stumbled as his muscles refused to lengthen, the scar tissue fighting every move he tried to make. Then he heard the general mutter, "Reaper, my ass," as he stepped into the large anteroom that housed an executive assistant, an aide-de-camp, an enlisted aide, and a host of other soldiers. How many people did it take to manage a general? he wondered.

Like most times he went deep into a memory, his mind spiraled. Dizzy. Other memories crept in, took over. Emotions flared from the dormant images that flashed in his brain. He jumped down from the pull-up bars, breathing hard, panting practically, and leaned over, hands on his knees.

His eyes moved to his rucksack, his mind spinning. Spiraling down the hole, he felt himself slipping into the abyss. Was it the exercise? He didn't think so. Was it seeing General Sampson? Maybe. He never knew what the catalyst might be, but it was there . . . and the spiral was hard to stop once it started.

Harwood had talked to his therapist about these episodes, but she didn't seem to understand.

"Your mind spirals and you think about what?" she would ask.

Frustrated, Harwood would say, "I can't think about anything!" But that was a lie, he knew. He thought about the Chechen and how that foe had beaten him. Harwood wasn't a prideful man—he was humble almost to a fault—but losing to the Chechen had done something to him. Changed him. Altered his wiring. He'd lost in an epic match on the world stage for all to see.

The Chechen. His nemesis. Harwood's fight-or-flight instinct amped up as if he were a kid playing a video game for four hours. He was spiking.

The damn Chechen.

Harwood needed to forget the Chechen, but how could he? Did he have alternatives? Could he prove himself again? He was certain that General Sampson had ridiculed him precisely because he had lost the duel with the Chechen.

Rangers never quit. They never lose, either.

What could he do? he wondered. The spiral was taking him deep into his darkest fears and emotions, some of which he had no idea he harbored. Nefarious ones. Murderous. Maybe even a death wish, common among PTSD survivors.

The Chechen. The spiral. They were one and the same.

He stood, leaned against the dip bars. Had he done any dips? Feeling the ache of the rotator cuff, Harwood watched Sampson.

Then his eyes flitted back to his rucksack. Then back to the general.

Light-headed, Harwood swooned, as if he were in a faint, but not completely out of it. He struggled to regain his balance as he knelt in the sawdust pit.

The sniper watched General Sampson through the scope of a sniper rifle from a wooded area that the soldiers at Fort Bragg used for infantry training and testing.

The expert sniper had scouted this spot on the first night after securing the rifle. The rifle was key to everything. There it had been, exactly where it was supposed to be. Every day for the past five days, the sniper made some microadjustments to the lair, but was satisfied that this was the best location for the mission. Not only did the infantry train here, but there was a small workout facility about twenty meters away. It was the perfect place for fifteen minutes of climbing ropes, doing push-ups on incline benches, using the pull-up bar, and finishing off with some dips.

The trick for the sniper was the timing.

The sniper moved the sight of the rifle scope to General Sampson's driveway. The sun was setting and the patterns of life were those of an army base settling in for the night. Parents tucking kids in, soldiers cleaning their gear, and a few doing physical training here and there, but mostly there, because the sniper had found the perfect spot.

General Sampson was sitting in the seat of his brand-new 2018 dark green Mercedes-Benz in the driveway. It was a warm August night, and the general had chosen to drive with the top down. He appeared to be texting. The general's head was down and his hands were working a small device, probably a smartphone. Sampson was either issuing orders or locking down a hookup with his girlfriend before he went inside to kiss the wife.

The car was about four hundred meters away. Easy shot.

The sniper lined up the crosshairs on the back of the general's head, saw the white hair full in the scope, and began to pull back on the trigger, no lateral drift, just perfectly smooth pressure against the spring. While this rifle was beat-up and damaged, the sniper had done everything necessary to make it fully operational again. Multiple test fires had proven that the weapon had been restored to its full operational splendor.

The general continued to look down, his arms moving with the rhythm of his texting, but importantly to the sniper, his head was a perfectly still oval situated dead between the crosshairs.

Under the pressure of the sniper's finger the trigger gave way and a slight cough erupted from the weapon. In the scope, the sniper watched the general's head explode onto the front windshield of his car. In the periphery, there remained a stillness in the small copse of trees. It didn't appear that anyone had heard the barely audible whisper of the weapon, but it wouldn't be long before General Sampson's wife or one of his aides-de-camp would find the general's brain matter on the windshield.

Time to get moving!

The sniper gave it two minutes, eyed the ejected casing, let it lay where it had landed, broke down the weapon, slid it quietly into the rucksack, and low-crawled, then stood, then walked, then ran into the night.

Harwood was running again, resurfacing from a memory blackout as bad as anything he'd ever had. He was a swimmer augering as fast as he could for the surface. Couldn't breathe, but trying to suck in fresh air. The humidity was thick, and he coughed as he ran along a dark, unlit path ten yards off the main road.

Military police cars raced toward him from all directions. Passing him, they headed toward the beautiful brick Georgian mansions in which the Fort Bragg generals lived. Blue lights bounced off everything: the pine trees to his right, the golf course to his left, the random warehouses and headquarters buildings. A military police car set up a cordon in front of him near an iconic statue of a paratrooper. He jumped up on the sidewalk and continued his run, oblivious of what had transpired.

Vick Harwood was a survivor. But he was also suffering from traumatic brain injury, known as TBI. The mortars that bombarded his hide position had caused an avalanche of rocks to nearly crush him, including his unprotected head. As a sniper, he rarely wore his helmet when shooting.

Whether it was the foster homes and foster farms of Maryland or the U.S. Army Ranger School's toughest tests, Harwood pushed through it all. As he sucked in the thick humidity and blew out his frustrations with every step of his run, he thought about the last three months with Jackie the Olympian. She had come to visit him in the hospital at both Walter Reed and Brooke. She had been there for his rehab, helping him every step of the way when she wasn't out doing television commercials to capitalize on her fame.

Now she met him at the different army posts where he was training special forces and airborne snipers. Jackie was good for him, he thought, as he came within one hundred meters of the police car with spinning blue lights. The police shined a spotlight in his direction. The golf course was to his left, so he avoided the entire roadblock and ran along the cart paths. As he jumped onto the asphalt path, the military police shouted something, but they couldn't be talking to him.

His thoughts shifted from Jackie the Olympian to Samuelson, his spotter. Survivor's guilt was a yoke around his neck every day. He didn't know what had happened to Samuelson and neither did the army. While the young corporal had been a newbie, he was a fellow Ranger and they lived by the creed of leaving no man behind. The fact that he couldn't find him, go get him, save him, or all of the above, ate away at Harwood's psyche.

Plus, the rocks to the head caused his mind to have memory lapses, like a skipping record. He'd just jump to the next thought, leaving behind an entire train of logic. Jackie the Olympian. Samuelson the spotter. Now what? Did he have the opportunity to save Samuelson, did he try, was he able? He couldn't remember. Sometimes all he knew was what was right in front of him.

Like right now: the military police.

The blue lights had gotten brighter and two military policemen shouted at him, "Freeze!"

But he was already two hundred yards down the path. Instead of freezing or slowing down, he sped up. He had no part in whatever the police were doing, so he just kept running.

The spotlight shined on him from a distance, its powerful beam weakening the farther away he ran. He sensed that his direction was off a bit, so he angled through the woods, found a minor trail, and powered past branches that slapped him in the face, as if he deserved punishment.

Harwood just wanted to get back to his enlisted quarters on the base and see Jackie. Sweating, Harwood emerged on the far side of the golf course, spotted his building, and then saw Jackie in the parking lot. He sprinted up the hill and onto the pavement, catching some movement in a car parked away from one of the security lights. A bearded man with a baseball cap watched him. Probably just another guy waiting to get Jackie's signature. As a sniper, he was accustomed to observing and absorbing his surroundings. He never wanted to be a long-rifle guy in a short-weapon fight, so his radar was constantly spinning. The sight of Jackie placing a black bag in the trunk of her car near the side entrance to the building consumed him quickly and the bearded man was forgotten.

"Hey," he said.

She turned and smiled a frozen grin, almost fake, which he had never seen on her before.

"Hey, yourself." She quickly closed the trunk lid and stepped forward to give him a hug.

"You're sweating," Harwood said, smiling.

"Good workout. You're sweating, too. Love it," she said. Jackie was wearing workout clothes, also. She had some twigs and leaves stuck to her sports bra and spandex running pants.

"Wished I'd known. Would've waited for you."

"I can't keep up with you, Reaper. I'm just trying to stay in shape. You're getting back into Ranger condition." She led him by the arm to the back entrance of the enlisted quarters.

"Back door?"

"I don't feel like signing autographs tonight," she said. Ever since she won the Olympic gold and signed multiple endorsement deals with the National Rifle Association and weapons manufacturers, Jackie had become a rock star in the military community. "Plus, I think we can work up another sweat." She gave him her best seductive smile, kissed him fully. Her lips were sweet with salt. Jackie usually welcomed the attention and always gave her full devotion to her fans. But tonight, she seemed intent on one thing.

They snuck in the back way and vanished inside Harwood's room. Something had Jackie jazzed and she was on top of him, her long blond hair tossing in the dim light like thousands of golden whips, brushing his face, caressing his chest, covering his ankles when she leaned back in an acrobatic move.

Afterward, they lay on the bed panting, her Nordic white skin against his ebony frame.

"Needed that," she said. "Gets better every time."

"Agree," he muttered, breathless. Jackie nuzzled up to him, their sweat and fluids all mixing together to create a pungent aroma. She traced his eight-pack with her fingers.

"You're one fine physical specimen, Reaper," she said.

He ran his hand down her back, looped his finger around her bull's-eye tattoo just above the crack in her ass. Coolest tramp stamp he'd ever seen.

"Feels nice," Jackie whispered into Harwood's chest.

"Yeah. Feels good. You make me feel almost normal," he said.

"That's the plan," she said. "Want you healthy and whole."

Harwood pulled her closer and said, "I appreciate everything you've done."

"You mean like put my life on hold for this guy I met four months ago in Afghanistan?"

"Yeah, basically that."

"Well, you're worth it."

Harwood nodded, felt his chest flutter at that pronouncement, and then pulled her closer.

"Once I get through this rehab, I'd like to talk long-term strategy with you," he said.

"You mean like planning a war campaign?" she teased him.

"No, you know . . . it's just how I talk. What I know," he replied.

"I know. It's one of the many, many things I adore about my guy, the Reaper. I want us to make some sharpshooting little athletes."

Harwood's chest fluttered again.

"You mean get pregnant?"

"Yes, as in knocked up. I'm ready," she said.

"I'd like to talk to your father first. Ask him. Do it right. Give you your wedding day. Our wedding day. I don't have a ring yet. Haven't really approached the subject yet, to be truthful." He felt like a Ranger about to go on a combat mission without having planned or developed a packing list.

"I know, Vick. We'll work it out. I'm just telling you that I love you. And that I'm ready, whenever you are. You're an amazing man. I'm proud of you. Proud of us. I think we've got something here."

Harwood was speechless. He settled into the bed, pulled her with him, and said, "Yes, we do. Only thing I disagree with is that you're the amazing one, not me."

CHAPTER 5

The next morning, Harwood rolled over to find an empty warm spot next to him. Like most nights, his dreams had haunted him. Samuelson danced in his mind like a leering jack-o'-lantern, saying, "Leave no soldier behind? Yeah right, Ranger *buddy*. You're a buddy, all right, a buddy *fucker*. Just call you Bravo Foxtrot."

But it was his own voice talking to him. While he didn't know Samuelson very well when the mortars had rained down on them, it was illogical for Samuelson to blame him for his current DUSTWUN status. Harwood had been unconscious. One minute they were lying within five feet of one another about to take the shot on the Chechen and the next minute they were hearing the whistles of incoming bombs. With only a fraction of a second to prepare, neither had the opportunity to seek more cover. They just sucked it up and endured the fusillade.

But that wasn't how survivor's guilt worked. For

whatever reason, Harwood was the one who had come out okay, or at least alive. Scarred, tattered, psychologically damaged, but still breathing. Still pulling in oxygen and blowing out carbon dioxide. Heart still pumping. But the brain, maybe not back all the way. *Definitely* not back all the way.

Somehow, though, he sometimes managed to sleep through the nightmares, perhaps held down by the weight of his emotions, lost in the haze of his brain injury. Like a dazed motorist wandering through a foggy night after a single car crash on a winding country road, Harwood stumbled through each day. He mustered the courage to instruct snipers that the military was counting upon to kill his nation's enemies. The assignment was part sympathy from the army and part tapping into his vast knowledge and experience as the army's deadliest sniper.

The Reaper.

What did Harwood feel about those thirty-three enemy commanders he had killed? Nothing but satisfaction. He was glad they were dead and that he had killed them. One less bad guy to do the country harm, to Harwood, equaled five soldiers in a Humvee that didn't get their legs blown off. That was Harwood's math. The end justified the means.

He flipped his legs over the bed, stretched tightened muscles, ripped some more scar tissue, grimaced, and then stood. His small quarters at Fort Bragg had a sliding glass door and a balcony about two feet wide. He was in his boxers as he stepped into the morning humidity. He could hear the distant call of cadence coming from paratrooper units conducting physical training.

"C-130 rolling down the strip, airborne daddy gonna take a little trip . . ."

How many times had Harwood sung that cadence? Too many to count. Memories flashed like lightning in his mind. Formation runs. Buddies on his left and right. Joking in the ranks. Sergeants yelling at them to shut up. Then he was a sergeant, leading the physical training.

Stepping back into the room, he spotted a note from Jackie on the desk.

Vick, had to run to do some promo. Ugh. Can't wait to see you in Savannah! Love, J

While he was disappointed that Jackie had left quietly in the night, he couldn't complain. This was the first time that she had done so and he counted his blessings every time he looked at her. A gorgeous blonde who loved him, her country, and her guns. What could be better?

He flipped on the television, scanned a few channels, and landed on the local news, which had a young brunette reporter standing outside of General's Row at Fort Bragg. The small mansions were in the background as she spoke. He punched up the volume.

". . . and we're learning that General Sampson was a target of Islamic extremists. As the special forces training commander, he sent many soldiers overseas to fight and kill members of ISIS and Al Qaeda. The latest edition of the Al Qaeda magazine, *Inspire,* contained an article calling for a 'fatwa' on the heads of certain commanders of military units and chief executive officers of private companies such as Microsoft and Apple. That means there is a monetary reward for killing the military and business leaders."

An anchor in a studio appeared on the screen. His face was set with the appropriate amount of grim melancholy as he asked the reporter, "Do the police have any leads, Monica?"

"Yes, in fact, Bill, the military police and Fayetteville police are working jointly. Already they say they have discovered the spent casing that once housed the bullet that killed General Sampson. Likewise, my sources tell me that the actual bullet has been recovered and may hold some clues as well. The police are scouring the area for anyone who might have been in this vicinity at approximately seven P.M. last night."

The reporter poked toward the ground as she spoke. The camera followed her as she turned. In the background was a small copse of trees next to the workout station with the climbing ropes, pull-up bars, and dip bars.

"Let's hope it does and that we find this killer soon. Monica Johnson from Fort Bragg, thank you."

Harwood stared at the television and punched the remote vigorously until the picture went away. A lightning bolt struck in his mind, illuminating something from last night, a brief image. The trees. The physical-training station.

His rucksack. General Sampson.

Sitting down on the bed, Harwood rubbed his eyes with the heels of his hands, grinding away, trying to stitch together one continuous memory or thought process, but unable to do so. What had he seen or heard?

Or done?

As was his practice, Harwood quickly transitioned from self-doubt to action. Never one to suffer the sorrows of others, he certainly wasn't going to wallow in his own angst. He just wanted to be normal, whatever that meant. He looked at the note from Jackie again and remembered that he needed to get on the road to Hunter Army Airfield near Savannah, Georgia, home of the First Ranger Battalion, where he had served his first tour as a private. While he had served primarily in the Third Battalion, in Fort Benning, Georgia, he still had many friends in First Battalion.

He jammed what little dirty laundry he had in a plastic bag, gathered bottles of the sports drink Jackie had given him, zipped his duffel tight, and hefted his rucksack onto his back. He walked out the back door of the enlisted guest quarters, loaded his extended-cab pickup truck, and pulled out of the parking lot.

The flashing blue lights of the military police cars blinked in his rearview mirror as three sedans shot to the front door of the large rectangular enlisted-quarters building. Pulling onto the All American Freeway in Fayetteville and then onto I-95 south, Harwood gunned his truck toward Savannah.

CHAPTER 6

Deke Bronson smacked his lips as he studied the grainy video footage of a man running past the golf course with a rucksack on his back.

"Strong candidate right there," Bronson said. He was speaking to his "go team" of agents in a nondescript office building near the Newport News, Virginia, airport. Bronson and his team of four had been assigned the task of monitoring extremist activity within the United States, including everything from white-supremacist militias predicting the overthrow of the government to the Black Lives Matter movement.

An African American himself, Special Agent Bronson was pro–law enforcement and a believer in all things American. Every morning he ran five to ten miles, depending on his mood, did a circuit of upper-body and abdominal exercises, showered, checked his ten to twenty Match.com profile hits, shaved his head, manscaped, and then dressed in a two-thousand-dollar

Zegna suit, usually navy blue. A confirmed bachelor, Bronson enjoyed looking good and feeling good. He used online dating as a time-saving tool to broaden his reach in finding the perfect partner. He had served as a marine in Fallujah, used the GI Bill to finish his undergraduate degree at Howard University, and then obtained his law degree from Georgetown. After ten years with the FBI, he had been rewarded with command of his own task force in charge of hunting domestic terrorists. Pushing thirty-five years old, Bronson felt good about his station in life. Things were black-and-white for him. You were either a good guy or a bad guy. There was no in-between. Purgatory didn't exist.

"Angel, can we review the entire video and capture a still frame that gives us the best image of his face?"

Angel Rojas smiled and brushed her hair out of her eyes.

"Roger that, boss man," Angel said.

"Thanks, you're the best," Bronson said.

He turned from the fifty-five-inch high-definition television screen and looked at Max Corent, the ballistics expert for the team. Ever since the shootings of multiple policemen in several cities, Bronson had asked for and received his own ballistics expert, which gave him direct connectivity to the lab in Quantico. More rapid processing times led to better, more efficient decision making. Instead of spinning his wheels in one direction, he could now wait a few hours and make a better, more informed decision based upon the evidence. Sure, Bronson had gut instincts, and good ones at that, but he was hardwired to trust the facts, leaving as little as possible to doubt and using his judgment to fill in the rest. Their headquarters sat on a twenty-terabyte secure information hub that provided lightning-fast relays of high-density files such as fingerprints and ballistics matches.

Corent was looking at him with anticipation. His light brown hair reached down his neck to the blue Death Cab for Cutie T-shirt. He wore shorts and flip-flops and usually had earbuds planted inside his ear canals. Younger than Bronson, Corent was a techie who could perform a broad range of functions, from cybertracking criminals to conducting rifling tests on spent ammunition and hammer-impression tests on expelled cartridges. With one arm completely covered in a tat sleeve, Corent had mentioned to Bronson that he was waiting for the right inspiration to design the other arm. Bronson had shrugged. He had just one tat on his left arm: "Semper Fidelis."

Always faithful.

"Yes, young Mr. Corent," Bronson said. "What do you have for me today? A treat?"

Corent smiled and said, "You know it sounds weird calling you 'boss' when you're only a few years older than me. But we're not buddies or friends, so I can't call you 'pal' or anything like that. So, you know, I guess I'll just leave off the salutation."

"Whatever you do next time," Bronson said, "make it shorter than what you just did."

Corent smiled again. "Gotcha. So anyway, this is weird. You know how we use the Integrated Ballistics Identification System to match weapons and ammo to actual criminal activity?"

"Yes, Max, I'm very familiar with the process. What's your point? You have a match already?"

Corent paused and then said, "Well, yes."

"What?" Bronson asked. He looked at his watch. It wasn't even ten o'clock the morning after the shooting of General Sampson.

"Yes, I do. But it's not possible," Corent said.

"What's not possible? That you have a match? Or that the match doesn't make sense?"

"That one," Corent said. He stood from his chair in his bullpen cube and pointed at the fifty-five-inch screen where he had transferred the image of the cartridge the military police had found at the suspected shooter's location. "Here is the picture of where the firing pin struck the casing. It's as distinctive as a fingerprint."

He switched images by leaning over and pressing a button on his MacBook. "Here is the seven-point-six-two-millimeter piece of lead fired from the preceding cartridge. It penetrated the rear of General Sampson's skull, bored through his brain, exited through the front of his skull, and, having lost velocity, bounced off the windshield and tumbled onto the dashboard where the police found it. These rifling marks are also as distinctive as fingerprints."

"So we have two points of confirmation. Do the firing pin and barrel markings match something in our system?" Bronson asked.

"Yes and no," Corent said.

"Don't give me that. You know how I hate fuzzy stuff. It either does or it doesn't," Bronson said.

"Well then it does. But here's the catch. Remember several months ago when we were in Kandahar working a connective lead between Al Qaeda and that train-derailment plan in Philadelphia?"

"Yeah. What about it?" Bronson asked. He was proud of that mission. They had interrogated an Al Qaeda detainee who had coughed up not only blood but enough information for Bronson and his team to stop a planned attack on the Acela Amtrak line between Washington, D.C., and New York City.

"Well, the Rangers and the Green Berets were in a pissing contest about who was killing more bad guys and they had me look at a few rounds that had passed through the gray matter of Taliban commanders. You know me. I logged it all in, even though it was on the down low. Didn't get any names—you know how those guys are—but got the unit. Rangers."

"Rangers? As in Army Rangers? Badass, kickass, God-and-country, U.S. Army Rangers?"

"Yes, those guys," Corent said, sitting down again at his desk. "Turns out, the same rifle that killed a bunch of Taliban just killed General Sampson."

Bronson worked through that tidbit of information as he loosened the Windsor knot of his teal Hermès tie and opened the neck of his white Boss shirt with its English spread collar. He rolled up his sleeves so that they were flawless and perfectly aligned on each muscled forearm and then leaned forward on Corent's desk. "Say that again," he said, staring the man in the eyes. "Because if I heard you correctly, you are asking me to go up against some nobility that will fight back hard."

"You heard me right. It's the same rifle. I checked five times. There's no doubt. I wouldn't have mentioned it to you if there was."

Bronson stood upright and turned to look at the HD screen again. He saw the cartridge and the mangled lead bullet side by side now.

"Did you get a serial number of the weapon?"

"They didn't give me any of that. Like I said. It was on the down low. But we've got the date and the time that I performed the tests. Gives us a starting point," Corent said.

"Narrows it down to about two hundred Rangers," Bronson said.

"Well, actually, it narrows it quite a bit more," Randy White said. White was the team's intelligence expert. Like Bronson, he had served in the military. A former military intelligence officer in Bagram, Afghanistan, White had operated with conventional and special operations forces. White was a large man, who had put on a few too many pounds at the Bagram dining facility during his tours. As a workaholic, he made excuses to skip workouts, while at the same time creating products of record that led to the kill or capture of over one hundred Taliban commanders. He kept his head shaved and had chosen to use his combat pay to buy a single diamond stud earring, which he wore in his left ear.

"Talk to me," Bronson said.

"We're forgetting this guy's a sniper. It's a sniper rifle, right, Max?"

Corent looked down and then up. "Yes, of course. In my excitement, and confusion, I left out that important piece of information. It's a sniper rifle and the striations show it most likely to be an SR-25 at that."

"So, how many Army Ranger snipers were in theater on the specific day? I'm guessing no more than ten, twenty if you count their spotters," White pointed out. "And of those teams, how many used an SR-25?"

"Just a sec, Randy. Remind me. The striations?" Bronson asked.

"The grooves and lands, the flat parts between the grooves, leave spiraling on the lead of the bullet. All that combined is called striations."

"Got it. Now to Randy's point. That's at least a ninety percent reduction in the field of possibilities right there," Bronson said. "Good work. Now the hard part starts."

"What's that?"

"Penetrating the Rangers. Be easier to get inside Al Qaeda. That's a real brotherhood there," Bronson said.

"Oh and the Marines would just cough up the information?" White countered.

"Touché. No, we wouldn't. But we have to start somewhere so let's go straight to the Special Operations commander. One of his generals was just killed and it looks like one of his guys might have done it. Keep it in-house; they're more likely to provide the information if we go directly to them."

Bronson turned to the fifth member of his team, Faye Wilde, and said, "Get me General Taylor, Special Operations Command commander in Tampa. We'll start there."

Wilde was fresh out of Liberty University with her political science degree, and Bronson thought it would be good to have a young, eager worker bee on the team to do things like look for impossible-to-find phone numbers. But Wilde was good and after five minutes said, "Sir, General Taylor is waiting for you."

Bronson walked into his office, shut the door, picked up the landline phone, and said into the handset, "General, this is Special Agent in Charge Deke Bronson. I'm heading the task force dissecting the information on General Sampson's murder. Can I have five minutes of your time, sir?"

Bronson listened as the general coughed and said, "You can have all day long if you catch that son of a bitch for us."

"I've got some sensitive information, sir, and it sounds like I'm on speakerphone. Can we go point-to-point?"

Bronson paced in his office, stared outside at the parking lot full of cars and trucks, windshields winking in the sun.

"All right, son, what you got?"

"Sir, we've got a ballistics match to a sniper rifle," Bronson said.

"Go on," Taylor said.

"We have positively identified the weapon as belonging to an Army Ranger sniper team that was in Afghanistan four months ago. Your guys asked us to do some ballistic and rifling checks," Bronson continued. He provided the exact dates and then said, "Our firearms forensics expert doesn't have the name of the individual. He only knows that the rifle belonged to the Ranger unit in Kandahar at the time."

After a long pause, Taylor said, "That's impossible."

"No, sir, I'm afraid not. My guy is the best there is. Handpicked because of the Dallas shootings. We were in Kandahar. Some guys came in with some lead they'd plucked from dead Taliban commanders' heads and asked for my guy to identify the weapon. They wanted to know who had the most kills."

Bronson listened to the faint static of the phone line, wondering if Taylor was asleep.

"Shit," the general said. "What do you need?"

"I need access to the unit that was there. Talk to the commander and some of the others. Find out if this is a rogue shooter, a missing weapon, whatever," Bronson said.

The general perked up at the mention of a missing weapon.

"Roger that, Agent. I'll bet you your paycheck that the weapon was missing or even discarded in combat."

"That could be, General. We have this lead and we're running with it as fast as you'll let us."

Bronson's subtle dig—that the only thing that would make them move slowly in finding the general's killer was another general getting in the way—was not lost on Taylor.

"I'm not slowing you down, son. We've been on the phone less than five minutes. Make sure you log that in. Now, the Ranger regimental commander's name is Colonel Bart Owens. Bart's a reasonable guy. I'll call him and give him a heads-up. The only problem is that several of the people you want to talk to have probably rotated out of the Rangers or are currently in combat. I'll do everything I can to help you get the access you need to solve this crime."

"Thank you, sir." Bronson figured the general was speaking as if he were recording the conversation, which he wasn't. Not prone to political bullshit, Bronson was focused on mission accomplishment, not racking up evidence in case he needed it. He didn't have the bandwidth to purposefully gather information on a neutral party on the off chance that they might become a foe. He knew people who did that sort of thing, and every ounce of energy they put toward that collection effort was a unit of measure they could not put toward finding a solution or accomplishing the mission.

Taylor gave him the number for the Ranger commander, whom he called, which led to another call, to a captain, and soon they were in a van headed toward the hangar where Bronson's government Gulfstream jet awaited.

"What are we putting on the back burner as we focus on this new mission?" Bronson asked Wilde.

"Sir, we've still got three unsolved police murders in Wichita, Des Moines, and Phoenix."

Bronson nodded as the vehicle stopped on the tarmac next to the airplane. "This is priority, then." Climbing up the steps of the aircraft, Bronson leaned in between the two pilots in the cockpit and said, "All set for Fort Benning?"

"Roger that, Agent. Be there in less than two hours."

Bronson hung up his Zegna suit coat, stowed his go bag full of clothes, checked his personal phone for text messages from women—there were two—and then sat in the big leather chair. The rest of his team filed past him to the comfortable seats beyond the main cabin.

Faye Wilde was the last to board, her strawberry-blond hair bouncing off her shoulders as she hustled up the steps.

"Good work, sir. Less than twenty-four hours and we've got a major break," she said.

"Be good to solve this today. Be good for all of us," Bronson said. He smiled at his young apprentice as she stared at him. "Anything else?"

"Oh, yes, sir," she said. Faye lifted her smartphone and showed him the screen. "I had an algorithm scan every significant activity report in Afghanistan over the past year using the word 'sniper.' Got nothing. Then I Googled 'Afghanistan' and 'sniper' and got a

Rolling Stone article about an Army Ranger. He was called the Reaper."

"The Reaper?"

"Yes. Thirty-three scalps in ninety days. Apparently he was a killing machine."

Bronson thought for a moment, looked out the window, and said, "Or still is."

CHAPTER 7

Vick Harwood checked into the enlisted visiting quarters at Hunter Army Airfield, where he unpacked his duffel bag, changed into his running gear, chugged one of Jackie's sports drinks, shouldered his rucksack, and immediately took off for a run to Forsyth Park in the Victorian District of Savannah.

Harwood wore a thin plastic wallet hung loosely around his neck with his army identification card visible through the window. He nodded at the security guard at the gate as he jogged through the personnel portal with metal rotating bars like an old-time amusement park entrance. Once on the busy street, Harwood found the dilapidated sidewalk and did his best to avoid turning an ankle.

During his drive, he had stopped for gas and texted with Jackie, who was staying downtown and doing some publicity tours her agent had set up for her. Harwood was proud to be dating not only a beautiful woman but also a bestselling author. Jackie had parlayed her Olympic

gold medal into a nonfiction book about a woman per-
severing in a man's world. *Guns, Girls, Gold, and Guts,*
she had titled it, and the book was a page-turning best-
seller that was in its fifth week on the *New York Times*
bestsellers list. Jackie was a self-described martial-arts
expert, but weapons were not her only forte. During
their three-month relationship, she had shown Harwood
steadfast support despite his bouts of memory loss and
post-traumatic stress.

As he ran along Bull Street and crossed Victory
Drive, he dodged a twenty-year-old Buick that the
owner had spray-painted black and gray. The driver—a
white man with a beard and wearing a baseball cap
low on his forehead—was unapologetic. He was riding
low in his seat with Jay Z blasting from heavy bass
woofers in the back. The driver's eyes locked onto his.
Harwood had a flash of recognition, as if he'd been eye
to eye with the man previously. The beard seemed off,
though. Harwood struggled to recall the face, the
image, something from somewhere recent. Regardless,
the car blew down the street and was a diminishing
speck before he could think any more about it. He just
nodded and kept powering along on his run, feeling
the ligaments stretch a bit more each time he exer-
cised. The rucksack was heavy, but he intended it to
be. Not only did it carry necessary equipment, tools of
his trade, but it was a physical reminder of the mental
load he carried every day. The fifty-pound rucksack
was a metaphor for the fact that he had left his spotter on the battlefield. Unconscious or not, Samuelson
had been his responsibility. Newbie or not, Samuelson
was still an American soldier whom the army and the
Rangers had entrusted to him. One month as a team-

mate or not, he still had learned that Samuelson had a seventeen-year-old sister who adored him and school-teacher parents who loved God and country.

Samuelson's tight-knit family was something that Harwood never had to begin with. The irony was that he survived, with no survivors, and that Samuelson, while not technically declared killed in action, was most likely dead, with his sister and parents as his survivors.

Yes, that rucksack pulling his shoulders straight back was loaded with more than fifty pounds of gear. Stuffed inside was a dense mass of guilt, a black hole of culpability so heavy that sometimes it was all he could do to put one foot in front of the other.

Harwood narrowly avoided getting run over again. This time by a zipping Porsche that had the right-of-way. An attractive, black-haired female was driving the car and she glanced at him as he performed a spin move to keep from being run over. This time it was the hair that seemed familiar. A lightning bolt in his mind flashed with a memory. Swishing black hair, like that of a horse's mane. The runner he had passed yesterday at Fort Bragg during his workout? He tried, but couldn't hold the image long enough to discern. Two cars. Two faces. Did he recognize them? Should he? Or was his mind so damaged that he was reliving his last moments in Afghanistan: the Chechen's panic, Samuelson's calm demeanor, and the kidnapped woman's hair swirling as she was smacked?

"Check your shit," Harwood muttered to himself. He felt the sweat running down his face and focused on the reality in front of him as opposed to the anxiety of his shame. He zeroed in on the Lil Wayne music he had playing in his earbuds—"Hot Revolver"—and saw he had missed a text from Jackie on his iPhone.

Here. Staying downtown. Let me know when you're avail. Hugs, J

Jackie gave Harwood something positive on which to focus. Instead of being weighed down by the past, maybe he could start a new life, one that gave him a foundation upon which to build and gain forward momentum. One that would empty the rucksack.

But still. Samuelson. How could he let him go?

Harwood approached Forsyth Park, in the middle of the Victorian District of Savannah. Million-dollar homes lined the streets. American flags hung limp in the August humidity. Some porches displayed the red Georgia Bulldog flags in honor of the approaching college football season. During Harwood's first year at the University of Maryland, the fighting Terrapins were looking for an outside linebacker, and he was on the cut bubble. The memory flashed and disappeared. Suddenly, he was a couple hundred meters into the park. He flexed his pecs and growled, frustrated that his mind was choppy, like a windblown ocean. Different memories popping up and going down, tossed about by the rips and currents of electrons surging through his brain.

He approached a grove of trees and decided to walk for a bit, having run nearly six miles, although that was not much of a workout for him. As he strode, he gained some balance, some sense of where he was and why he was there. He was going to train some First Ranger Battalion snipers tomorrow and the next day before moving on to the Seattle-Tacoma area to train Second Ranger Battalion snipers. He was a consultant of sorts, best of breed. Thirty-three kills in three months. Eleven a month. One every three days. Truth be told, he killed every time he was in position. And he was deadly accurate, whether from fifty meters or eight hundred meters.

He was the Reaper.

The enemy had come to fear him in Afghanistan, Iraq, and Syria. Once Harwood was in position, he eliminated targets, packed his gear, and moved on to the next target. And that was a little bit like what he was doing now. Base to base. Trainees to trainees.

But the killing. Had he enjoyed it or was it just a job? Did he relish watching the head explode into the fabled pink mist—it was actually more white and gray than anything—or did it repulse him? He honestly wasn't sure anymore. He'd killed, and saved American lives. He was good with that.

But the Chechen had lived. And the Chechen continued to kill. And the Chechen was in that rucksack right next to Samuelson, because the Chechen had beaten him.

"Hey!" someone called out.

Harwood looked up and saw that he had walked straight into a couple walking hand in hand through the small wooded section of the park.

"Sorry," Harwood said.

"Watch it, bro," the man said, puffing up for his girlfriend.

"No need, man. Seriously. I'm sorry. Lost in my thoughts," Harwood said. The white man with the goatee and his girlfriend with the nose ring looked like a nice couple just out for a walk.

"Cool. Just pay attention," the guy said.

Harwood nodded and placed his hands on his knees as he leaned over, breathing hard. His mind began to spin, but he pushed off his knees, stood upright, and walked to the edge of the low-hanging live oaks, where he saw a large Victorian home about fifty meters away across Drayton Street. A man stood on the covered porch of the home, beneath a rounded corner tower that was topped off with a third-story turret that looked like a witch's hat. He had a wizened face and gray hair shaved close in a crew cut like the one Harwood's high school gym teacher had worn. The man was dressed in an untucked checked button down shirt atop olive shorts. He wore boat shoes and carried a tumbler full of gold liquid, most likely Scotch, in one hand and a cell phone pressed to his ear in the other.

"Holy shit," Harwood said to himself. "That's General Dillman."

Mike Dillman was a retired two-star general, who was now the chief executive officer of Military Logistics and Quality Manpower, which Harwood knew had the unfortunate NASDAQ stock ticker symbol of MLQM. Many of the active-duty army soldiers had nicknamed the private military contracting company "Milk 'Em." Dillman was a former special operations soldier and intelligence officer, who first had moved up the ranks as an infantryman and then was assigned to the military intelligence branch by the military human resources command. But now Dillman was worth hundreds of millions of dollars, as his company had blossomed and profited during the Iraq, Afghanistan, and ISIS wars. That gravy train was coming to an end, though, as American presence overseas had dwindled.

There was movement in the third-story tower of the Victorian-era home. A wrought-iron balcony protruded from a small doorway that had sheer curtains fluttering outward like escaping ghosts.

More like Norman Bates, Harwood found himself thinking.

A woman with olive skin and black hair stood just inside the open doors. Her set jaw, pressed lips, and distant eyes combined into a terrified look. Quickly, she turned back inside, as if she was breaking a rule by stepping onto the balcony. Wearing a long, flowing dress, the woman appeared out of place in every way. A young, ethnic woman on an old white man's balcony. A long dress in the heat of summer. A distant look of remorse etched onto her otherwise striking face.

Harwood had not expected to see the recently retired general on this run, much less a Middle Eastern beauty on the general's balcony. Vaguely he recalled that he knew that the general lived in Savannah, but truly he was having a hard time remembering what he had for breakfast, so some random general's residence was not on his radar.

But then again, Dillman wasn't a random general. His company, MLQM, had provided to the war efforts dining facilities, power generators, embassy security, and even contract hit teams for high-value targets on occasion. Harwood had crossed paths with some of the MLQM contractors. Most were good dudes, he thought, but he had encountered a few douche bags. Dillman was a first-class douche bag. The general had flown on his private jet to Kandahar to check on his troops. Harwood recalled landing in a Chinook helicopter after killing number eight of his thirty-three confirmed scalps early in his three-month tour. He was sweaty and dusty, hadn't bathed for three days. He stepped off the chopper carrying his rucksack and his SR-25 and eyed the glistening Gulfstream V with the oversized jets on the back. He was wondering, *WTF, is the president here or something?*

The retired general looked pissed off, and as if he had a mission. Harwood stopped walking and nudged his former spotter LaBoeuf as he pointed at Dillman.

"What kind of rod does that guy have up his ass?" Harwood had said. "Just floated in here on a jet with pole dancers and booze. He's got nothing to bitch about."

"Got that right," LaBoeuf had said. "Wait a sec. That dude was the speaker at my basic training graduation. Dillard. Dillweed. Something like that."

Harwood remembered looking at LaBoeuf and saying, "Shit, dude, you remember your basic grad?"

"Well, wasn't that long ago, old-timer."

Dillman had been yelling at the pilots and shouting at crewmen putting the chocks beneath the wheels. He spun and yelled at Harwood and the Rangers.

"What are you assholes looking at?"

"Back at you," LaBoeuf shouted.

Dillman was running toward them when one of his private contractors blocked him about ten meters out.

Harwood and LaBoeuf looked at each other and shrugged. Harwood said, "Next time I'll cap his ass for you." LaBoeuf had smiled.

Back in the moment now, Harwood was thinking of LaBoeuf as he looked over his shoulder. He was deep in the wooded section of the park. His mind spun as he dropped to do some push-ups. He was in a thick grove of mature live oaks, their branches low to the ground and providing cover and concealment as the sun was setting.

He looked at Dillman again, confirmed it was him, nodded, then unshouldered his rucksack. Looked at the general one more time, his mind spinning.

Then Harwood went back to his rucksack.

The sniper watched through the scope, seeing General Dillman standing on his porch with a glass of booze. Knowing the sins of this man, the sniper had no remorse leveling the crosshairs of the banged-up Leupold scope on the general's head. It wasn't a long-distance shot, maybe fifty to one hundred meters. It was a simple distance for an expert such as the sniper.

With a score to settle, the sniper went through the mental calculations of the shot. Distance was not a problem. Therefore, wind and altitude were not an issue. This was more like what the sniper imagined combat to be. The short-range kill.

In fact, it was combat. Dillman was number two on the kill sheet. General Sampson was number one and that shot could not have been more perfectly executed. The goal was to have the same type of success this evening. The park was sparsely populated. The heat was driving everyone indoors, except General Dillman, who continued to sip the gold liquid from the glass tumbler and talk on the phone.

A peaceful look on his face, Dillman appeared about as satisfied and happy as a man could be, which meant to the sniper that it was a perfect time to kill him. The angle was good. The sniper saw the man's head in the scope as big as a full moon. Behind the man's head was the soft pine of the porch, which would welcome the lead that was about to pass through General Dillman's brain.

Why did Dillman deserve to die?

Sins against humanity. The terrified woman in the turret was why. She was just one of many. The sniper's finger tightened against the trigger mechanism, the movement nearly autonomous from years of practice, training, studying, and actual field craft.

With steady, unflinching aim, the sniper felt the trigger give, the firing pin snap forward, the bullet release, and weapon buck. The scope jumped marginally, but never lost sight of the head of General Dillman, which exploded in a gruesome eruption of gray and pink matter. The glass tumbler hung for just a second in the general's hand before his grip loosened and the glass shattered on the concrete porch. The phone landed in the broken shards. The general's head was mostly gone. Mission accomplished.

The sniper checked the ejected shell casing, left it where it was, disassembled the rifle, repacked it, and moved quickly away from the scene. After the murder of General Sampson in Fort Bragg, the sniper knew that things were about to get interesting.

Night had fallen completely as Harwood left Forsyth Park and ran toward the hotel where Jackie had mentioned she was staying. His heart was racing beyond its normal rhythm. Whenever he went into memory-loss mode, he became anxious and his fight-or-flight instinct kicked in. Why couldn't he remember what happened even a few minutes ago? He had no problem recalling the starting line up from his high school football team. Could even see their faces.

He turned down a side street toward the hotel and slowed to a walk. Gathering himself, he retrieved his phone from his armband, removed his earbuds, and opened the Wickr app, which Jackie had encouraged him to use.

At the hotel, he typed.

She replied quickly. *Ok Room 814 ;)*

He navigated past the registration desk, nodded at the two female clerks, who smiled at him, and found the elevator bank. Harwood stepped into the elevator and the doors began to close. He pressed number eight on the keypad and the doors suddenly retreated open again. In stepped a man about his size and age. Dark blond/light brown hair, ice-blue eyes, tailored Canali suit, checked shirt with an open collar. Dark stubble highlighted the outline of the man's prominent jawline and chin. The man had combed his hair back in Wall Street greaser style and the length in the back reached the collar of his suit coat. He reached a long arm across the elevator and slid his key card into the reader, then pressed the button for the top floor.

Harwood recognized something about the man, but couldn't place him. Most likely a television commercial, he thought. There were several television shows and commercials filmed in Savannah and the surrounding areas.

"Hello," the man said, returning Harwood's stare.

"Hi." Harwood nodded. He was still sweating. As in his combat days, he was the filthy field soldier to so many others who were well-groomed.

"Good workout?" the man asked, eyeing Harwood's sweating face and his dirty, sweat-stained shirt and shorts. Harwood checked himself out in the reflective elevator doors. There were leaves clinging to him from his push-ups.

"Roger that," Harwood said. Then, to change the topic, he countered, "Nice suit."

The man smiled, as if he understood that Harwood didn't want to talk about himself. "Thank you. Just business. Would much rather be working out. Forsyth Park, I presume?"

The ball had been lobbed back at him. However, the chime rang and the doors began to open for the eighth floor. There was an inflection to the man's voice that wasn't of American origin, but Harwood couldn't quite place it.

"Have a good day," Harwood said, always reluctant to offer more information than anyone needed. He stepped out of the elevator. The doors began to close behind him.

"You do the same, Reaper."

The doors snapped shut. Harwood stopped. Turned around. The elevator was shooting to the top, the protected floor for VIP guests. How did the man know who he was? And why did he look so familiar?

Standing in front of the four closed elevator doors, two on each side, Harwood remained motionless. He struggled to remember the face. It was familiar. A face from a different time and place? Or one from television or the cyber world? He couldn't be sure. After the *Rolling Stone* article crowning him as the Reaper, he knew that some may recognize him. Perhaps it was just a fan. But fans usually asked for autographs or made the connection immediately, not with elevator doors closing and no chance of retort. The man's comment seemed almost like a taunt, a challenge.

You do the same, Reaper.

Harwood found Jackie's room, knocked, and saw that she had left the bolt in the door to keep it open for him. He stepped in and saw the back of her sports bra and her well-toned legs covered only by running shorts. She was still in her running shoes and her blond hair was in a ponytail. She was texting on her phone, it appeared. He walked up behind her and kissed her neck. He saw her blank the screen and toss the phone on the bed with the flick of her wrist.

She turned and kissed him fully, leading him to the bed. She ripped the Under Armour shirt off his muscled frame and yanked down his running shorts. Soon they were tangled in the sheets, making love with vigor.

Done, sweating, and breathing heavy, raspy breaths, Harwood looked at Jackie.

"Missed me?" He smiled.

"Always," she purred. Her head was on his bronze chest, her hair having burst free from the elastic band and now fanned out across his pecs. She looked up at him, his head propped on a pillow. "You have a good run? I've got you more of that sports drink."

"Thanks. Good run. Been getting dizzy some, though," Harwood replied. He pulled her closer, liked the feel of her warmth right up on him. She traced letters absently on his abs, running her slender fingers along the ridges. "Thanks for the liquids. Staying hydrated has been an issue, I think."

"Make sure you drink enough before you run," she

added. "That's probably what's causing your dizzy spells. It's a million degrees outside with the humidity."

"Roger that," he said. His chest heaved with every breath. The fan of blond hair looked like an exotic sea coral spread against his pectorals.

A moment passed before Jackie looked up at him.

"Did I scare you yesterday with the baby talk?"

There was something in her voice. Maybe a question, maybe some doubt, he wasn't sure. He looked at her.

"Nah," Harwood said. "You know my background. Orphan. Foster kid. You don't think I want that? This?" He waved his hand between her face and his.

Her blue eyes flicked away and then locked with his again. "Vick, I want this with you. I like that we're both strong and have made something of ourselves. I may have had a head start, but you've blown past me."

"Jackie, you're an Olympic champion. I haven't blown past anything."

"So I can shoot a BB gun better than most. Big deal. You've been protecting our country. I couldn't even protect my little brother."

"Hey, Jack. Don't be so hard on yourself. People can hide stuff and trick you. You never had a chance to protect him from the way you tell it."

Jackie sniffed and a tear slid onto Harwood's chest, then another. He pulled her closer. As Jackie had described it, her brother, Richard, had died eighteen months ago of an opium overdose. Richard's body had been found at Fort Benning's Airborne School near Columbus, Georgia. Columbus was the city just outside the main gate of Fort Benning where Rangers, paratroopers, and basic trainees all trained for combat. There was a seedy underbelly at the seam of the base and the town, though. Growing up in Columbus, Jackie and Richard had gone to school with the children of soldiers all their lives. Given her father's status as the president of the Chamber of Commerce, she and her brother interacted with the senior officers' children frequently.

"I should have seen the difference in him. I was too busy training. Too self-absorbed."

"You're being hard on yourself. You tell me to stop it when I beat myself up about Samuelson and LaBoeuf. So let's just agree that neither of us is perfect. We've both lost people close to us. No, those two soldiers weren't my blood brothers, but they were brothers-in-arms. Warriors."

Jackie stiffened when he said the word "warriors." Her fingernails dug into his side. Her biceps flexed and she pulled deeper into his chest.

"He told me things," Jackie said. "That a year before he died kids around Fort Benning were scoring uncut opium. Pure poppy resin. Everyone assumed it was from Mexico, but Richard told me there was a pipeline coming in through the military bases."

"You never know," Harwood said. And he didn't know. He lived in the world of privates and sergeants, not generals and colonels.

"He said some generals were running a ring. That one of the generals' sons was the distributor." Her fingernail dug deeper into his skin as she spoke, the emotions of sibling loss surging. Harwood did the math. He had met Jackie about four months ago. She had lost her brother over a year ago. In the last couple of years, she had won an Olympic gold medal, had dedicated it to her brother, and was a last-minute addition to the USO trip, which consisted mostly of entertainers. Her presence made sense. She was a national icon. Not a hero, but certainly a marketer's dream.

Across the room, the mirror reflected into a halfway-open closet where her rucksack sat with its drawstring loose and open.

A rifle barrel poked upward from the opening like a small black smokestack.

CHAPTER 8

FBI Special Agent Deke Bronson rode in the black Suburban next to Faye Wilde as they traveled from Fort Benning's Lawson Army Airfield to the commanding general's quarters on the main base. White and Corent were sitting behind them in the rear seats. Night approached with the static buzz of cicadas as the shadows from the tall pines lining the road blended with the graying twilight.

"Checking Match?" Faye asked, smiling.

"Big-time," Bronson said. "Need you to respond to Samantha and Amelia after work hours, of course. Delete the rest."

Faye helped manage Bronson's Match.com account as a "consultant" for a fee of one hundred dollars a month. Bronson figured she enjoyed the inside look at his psyche and playing matchmaker. Faye was tech-savvy and knew how to position Bronson's profile best, using "click bait" one-liners such as "I promise not to handcuff you," which of course, given the popularity of

Fifty Shades of Grey, drove huge numbers of women his way. Once they saw his picture, they lingered. Once they saw his background, Marines, FBI, loved musicals, the gym, and national parks, they emailed him.

"Really, Samantha? The redhead?" Wilde asked. "Thought you'd go for Syrah, the Egyptian fashion maven from Tysons Corner."

"Liked her. So okay, don't delete that one yet. Keep her in the bullpen."

"Knew you'd like Amelia. She's a big Teddy Roosevelt fan, so you guys have the park thing going. Was going to put you down for this Saturday with her at Virginia Beach Oceanfront. Walk and a picnic?"

Bronson smiled. "That's perfect. Then dinner with Samantha at someplace trendy. You pick it."

Wilde rolled her eyes and smiled. Two dates in one day, she must have been thinking. Whatever, she'd get used to it eventually.

"Roger that, Romeo." Wilde smiled.

In the rear of the Suburban, Corent and White seemed bored until they pulled in front of the general's home.

"You've got to be kidding me," White said.

"The brass knows how to treat themselves," Bronson said. "Have to visit this dude first, according to protocol."

The compound had a home with antebellum pillars, live oaks with strings of moss, a grove of magnolia trees, and an out-of-place guard shack with two riflemen manning their weapons. Bright lights illuminated the entire façade, as if the home were on display. Two late-model Corvettes sat in the driveway, like twin brats ready to wreak havoc somewhere.

From the driver's seat, the agent from the Atlanta field office rolled his window down and flashed his creds to one soldier while the other used a mirror to inspect under their vehicle.

"General Bishop is expecting you," the private said once the inspection was complete.

They drove along a gravel driveway to the front of the covered porch, where Bronson got out and directed his team to stay on the porch.

"They've got these nice rockers out here," he said, pointing out a row of rocking chairs.

He entered the home as an enlisted aide opened the door and ushered him into the general's anteroom. General Frank Bishop was a two-star general and had the privilege of leading the troops at one of the country's largest training bases. As Bronson was studying the assortment of plaques and awards displayed on the wall, a disheveled teenage boy walked through, hands stuffed in his jeans pockets, hair covering his eyes, black long-sleeved T-shirt hiding a skinny frame.

"Hey, dude. You a cop?" the kid asked.

"Something like that," Bronson replied. "What's your name?"

"Why you asking?"

The kid stood there as if he owned the place. Perhaps he did. This was probably the general's son.

"Brice?" Bronson guessed.

"Dude. Stay out of my shit, okay?"

So it was him. The kid looked like a burnout, nothing he would expect a general's son or daughter to appear to be. General Bishop walked in and sat down in a large leather chair.

"Brice, what are you doing here?" the general asked

his son. There was no loving tone in the question. It was nearly a rebuke. Restraint, coupled with anger.

"Nothing, man." And the kid was gone, like a phantom. He disappeared through the doors and into the bowels of the historical home. In his wake was a mile of emotional distance between father and son that anyone could plainly see.

"Kids today. So stuck in their phones and Snapchat it's hard to get them outside to play sports."

General Bishop didn't appear to be the athletic sort, but perhaps he was into golf. Bronson said nothing.

"Please," Bishop said, waving his hand at a less prominent chair opposite him. Bronson sat and looked at the general.

"You're saying a Ranger did this or a Ranger's rifle did this?" General Bishop asked. Bronson had done his homework. Bishop had served four tours in Iraq, mostly as a mechanized infantryman. The bulk of his career was spent rotating between Germany, Fort Hood, Texas, and the Republic of Korea. He had a wife and two sons, one in college now, at Georgia Tech, in Atlanta, and Brice, who attended high school in nearby Columbus. He wore the new army camouflage uniform that Bronson understood was pretty much roundly disliked by the troops, though the general seemed comfortable. The two black stars stood out prominently on the front of his uniform as he rocked in a black and gold West Point rocking chair. He wore a high and tight haircut, and what little hair the general had on top was gray. He puckered his lips as he sipped some tea, squinted his eyes as if he couldn't believe he was even having this conversation, and looked at Bronson.

"Sir, we don't know if both of those are true, but

we know the rifle that killed some Taliban commanders killed General Sampson last night, almost exactly twenty-four hours ago," Bronson said, realizing it felt good to be in front of the curve. He felt the momentum, hoping this general would release him so he could talk to the Ranger unit members who had been in Afghanistan at the time that his weapons tech, Corent, had inspected the lead and identified the rifle as one used by the Rangers.

"And we know this how?" General Bishop said. He quit rocking and leveled his eyes on Bronson. The general wore oval rimless glasses that made his eyes seem larger than they were. Bronson detected an air of arrogance about the man. He had seen aloof generals before, never ones to muddy their boots or get their hands dirty, figuratively or literally. Bishop seemed like the kind of officer who always kept someone between him and the problem. Good for career advancement, but bad for the men and women who labored beneath him.

"Sir, I explained all of this to General Taylor, and his team actually authorized me to speak with the Rangers who were in Afghanistan. We are burning daylight, as the saying goes, and every minute we spend rehashing everything is a minute that we don't spend catching the murderer of a general."

Just then Wilde came barreling into the room, opening the French doors with a rushed flurry. "Sir, I need to speak with you," she said.

"Talking to me, young lady?" General Bishop asked. "I'm the only 'sir' in this room, mind you."

Wilde stood motionless until Bronson smiled and covered for her.

"General, we have a similar protocol in the FBI. Nothing to get spun up about. Excuse me a second."

"I say who is excused and not excused, Agent," Bishop said, standing, as if to block Bronson from colluding with Wilde. Bishop was a small, thin man. A bookworm. Bronson's physique dominated the room and General Bishop. He stepped past the general, avoiding contact, and walked with his assistant onto the covered porch of the antebellum home.

"Another general has been killed. Savannah. About thirty minutes ago. Same MO. Head shot. Police pulled a seven-point-six-two slug from the wall. It flattened out, but there might be something there. Found the casing, too. Just like yesterday," she said.

Bronson looked up, took in the tranquil surroundings, listened to the birds chirping in the magnolia trees. He looked over his shoulder through the parlor's single-pane windows, which were sweating from the humidity clashing with the air-conditioning.

"Okay, thanks," he said to his executive assistant. "Hang on a sec." He walked back into the house, where the general's aide was blocking the parlor door.

"General's on the phone, sir," the aide said.

Bronson bulked up, leveled his marine's steel gaze on the aide, and said, "Move, son, before you get hurt."

The aide reluctantly moved, Bronson opened the door, and the general stood up and evidently shut down his phone in the same motion.

"Do you disobey every rule, Agent?" General Bishop barked.

"Not disobeying anything, General. Just telling you I'm leaving and heading to the Ranger headquarters. General Dillman, U.S. Army retired—"

"I know who General Dillman is!" General Bishop's neck was turning red, his carotid artery pulsing. What about his presence in the general's home would elicit such a reaction? Bronson wondered.

"Then I'm sure you know his head just exploded in the proverbial spray of pink mist about an hour ago?"

Bishop stared at him, perhaps a second too long.

"Oh, so you do know?" Bronson asked. He could see Bishop's mind spinning.

"Word travels fast, Agent. Now how can I help the investigation?"

"You mean after you've obstructed justice?"

"Don't push it with me. I know people," General Bishop said.

"People who can blow my head off? Let's have a seat, then," Bronson said, moving toward a chair.

"Enough! Colonel Rogers is expecting you. He will give you access to whatever you need."

Bronson turned on his heel and sped out of the door, collected Faye Wilde, Max Corent, and Randy White, jumped in the black Suburban, and zipped across Fort Benning with blue lights flashing. They stopped in front of the colonel's headquarters and saw that they had a welcome party of soldiers wearing digitized-camouflage uniforms and tan berets, the distinctive Ranger headgear.

"Colonel," Bronson said, as he exited the Suburban and walked through the phalanx of Rangers. Rogers met him halfway down the sidewalk, shook his hand, and escorted him into his drab office.

"Special Agent Bronson, thanks for coming. We're here to do whatever we can. I didn't know Dillman at all. Knew some of my guys who left the service went and worked for Milk 'Em, but I didn't know Dillman. I did know Sampson. Not a bad guy. Not a good guy. Just another guy. Made general. Maybe a little full of himself. If we have a weapon connected to these crimes, I want to help. Have a seat."

Bronson stepped back and held his hands up. "Whoa. You have already been more helpful than anyone I've talked to about this thing. If the level of cooperation goes up as I go down in rank, let me at some privates right now," Bronson joked.

"In time." Rogers smiled. "Show me what you've got."

Corent, Wilde, and White had all walked in with him. They hovered in the back of the office near the door, eyeing the plaques and mementos that bespoke a heralded military career. Corent came forward with a packet of documents, which included pictures of the casing and lead from Fort Bragg and the earlier work he had done several months ago in Afghanistan.

They walked the colonel through the analysis.

"Seems legit to me," Rogers said. "Carlsen!"

A Ranger lieutenant came barreling into the office. The stocky, fit young man looked like a heavyweight wrestler from Minnesota, with his large frame, translucent white skin, and blond Mohawk haircut.

"Carlsen here works in my operations shop. He pulled the names of our sniper teams in country during the window of time you're talking about," Rogers said. "It's eight teams of two. So that gives you sixteen people to check out. We've already checked them out, of course. Three of the sixteen are KIA, two are in Walter Reed, one is DUSTWUN. Of the remaining

ten, six are still in the service and four have transitioned out. Five of the six are still with the Rangers."

"That's some good, fast work there, Colonel. Thank
you," Bronson said.

"Like I said, we're here to help. I don't know General Bishop very well, but I imagine you didn't have
much fun visiting with him. I do, however, know
General Taylor in Tampa very well. He called and said
to help. So I'm helping."

Rogers handed the list to Bronson, but kept his hand
on it until Bronson looked him in the eyes.

"I love my soldiers, Special Agent. Fuck with them,
you fuck with me. So be sure of what you're doing
before you start this," Roger said.

"I appreciate the sentiment more than you know,"
Bronson said. "I was a marine. Didn't have patience
for commanders who didn't have the stones to say
what you just said. Total respect. And will proceed
with due care."

Rogers released the list of names and nodded.
"Roger that. Now I've got my five waiting for you outside the conference room. Carlsen here will send them
in one at a time. I've asked him to sit in on the briefings."

Bronson paused. It was unusual to allow non-FBI
personnel in the interview of a potential subject, but
given the circumstances and the trust Colonel Rogers
had placed in him, he relented.

"No problem," he said.

Carlsen and his massive frame escorted them to the
conference room, which was surprisingly more high-
tech than he anticipated. There were two flat-screen

television monitors on either end of the room, perched high up on the wall. An odd-looking device with telescoping and recessed cameras sat in the middle of the long conference table. It was a twenty-thousand-dollar secure Polycom 360-degree videoconferencing unit. Whiteboards and maps of Iraq, Syria, and Afghanistan dotted every square inch of the walls. He took a middle seat and his team sat behind him in what was a secondary row of chairs.

"Okay, let's bring in . . . Corporal Irving Jacobson," Bronson said.

Lieutenant Carlsen leaned into the hallway and barked, "Jake. In here, now."

A stout, short soldier walked into the conference room and took the seat directly across from Bronson, as if the Rangers had rehearsed the interviews. Perhaps they had? Bronson wondered.

"Have a seat, soldier," Bronson said.

The young man sat down across from Bronson with his back erect, his hands on his knees, and his face expressionless.

"Are you a sniper or a spotter, Ranger Jacobson?"

"Sniper, sir," Jacobson said. His response was crisp.

"What type of rifle did you use?"

"I have an M24 Remington, sir. Use seven-point-six-two-by-fifty-one match-grade, sir. I'm old-school," Jacobson said. He offered a thin smile.

"You're maybe twenty years old, but you're old-school?"

"Roger that. Born with a rifle in my hand, my daddy said. Hunted badgers in Wisconsin as a kid. Best shot in the unit now."

"Now?"

"Well, I was third. Behind Samuelson and Harwood, but they're gone now. And Samuelson was a spotter."

"Where did they go?" Bronson asked.

"Samuelson most likely was KIA, sir, but no one really knows. The Reaper? He's dinged up pretty bad and training unit snipers now."

"The Reaper?"

"Yes, sir. Mortar attack about three months ago damn near killed him. That's when Sammie went missing."

Bronson leaned back in his chair, thinking, *Interesting*. He looked over his shoulder at Corent and asked, "What type of rifle are we looking for again?"

"SR-25," Corent said.

"That'd be either the Reaper and Sammie or Mickey Child and his spotter Brad Steele," Jacobson said. "They used the SR-25. We all got to pick our poison."

Bronson looked at Lieutenant Carlsen. "Are any of these men available?"

"Child is. Steele rotated out a few months ago. But Child's in the waiting room."

Looking back at Jacobson, Bronson said, "You've been very helpful. Just to make things formal, where have you been for the past two days?"

"Right here. Training. Doing PT. Lifting. Shooting. Watching movies at night. Maybe some Xbox. That's about it," Jacobson said.

Bronson looked at Carlsen, who nodded and said, "I can confirm that. He's the *Call of Duty* champion around here."

"Thanks, Ranger Jacobson." Then to Carlsen, "Can we get Child in here?"

Jacobson stood, performed a textbook about-face, and exited about the same time Sergeant Mickey Child walked in with a scowl on his face as if he would rather be a target on a live-fire range than be in a conference room with some suit from Virginia.

"Sergeant," Bronson nodded. "Please have a seat."

"Gonna take long?" Child sat down in the wooden chair. He was a big man whose uniform seemed grossly oversized, as if they had to go up two extra sizes just to make it fit in all the right places.

"Tighten up, Ranger," Carlsen ordered.

Child sneered at Bronson and looked at the lieutenant with a mix of curiosity and mirth.

"Roger that, sir. Do I need a lawyer?" Child asked.

"I don't know. Do you?" Bronson said, offering the oldest line in the book.

Child looked at Bronson with narrow eyes, half lidded, like a lizard's.

"What's your game, Special Agent? We've all been told to cooperate with you. Want me to rat out a fellow Ranger? Not going to happen."

"Well that would be obstructing justice if you actually know something useful, which seems doubtful," Bronson said. As he expected, Child was offended.

"What the hell does that mean? I know a lot of stuff," Child said.

"Oh really? Then let's hear it. Did you have an SR-25 in Afghanistan and if so where is that weapon right now? And if so, did you have it checked by FBI ballistics in Kandahar to determine kill counts?"

Until Bronson had asked him the last question about the ballistics check, Child had reverted back to being an uninterested party. Now, his eyes were level with Bronson's.

"What's this about?" Child asked. "We didn't do nothing wrong over there. Just asked some guy to confirm who shot who."

Bronson wanted to correct his grammar, but skipped the lesson and pressed on.

"So you had your rifle checked by my man Corent here," he said, hooking a thumb over his shoulder. "Where is that rifle now?"

"Got pretty dinged up in the 'Stan so had to trade it in for a new one. Then they put me on the Barrett. Ever see one of those, Agent? Make your head explode like a watermelon dropped on pavement from two stories up."

"Thanks for the visual, Sergeant. I know what a Barrett is. I'm interested in your SR-25."

"Turned it in to the armorer in Kandahar after your dude there confirmed who shot who. The lieutenant here can help you with that." Child pushed away from the table and began to stand.

"Sergeant, where have you been the last couple of days?"

"None of your fucking business is where I've been. If you need to know, it's a small town called Up Your Ass. I ain't done nothing wrong." Child stood, knocking his chair over, and walked dead into Command Sergeant Major John Murdoch, the esteemed long-time Ranger Regiment command sergeant major, who served as the senior enlisted advisor to Colonel Rogers.

In the information packet on the Rangers, Murdoch was listed as a four-gold-star combat-jump veteran of

Afghanistan, Iraq, Syria, and Panama, to include seeing action in just about every conflict in which the nation had engaged over the past thirty-five years of his
career. Having turned down advancements to higher-
level units, Command Sergeant Major Murdoch was
an icon in the Rangers. Lieutenants stood at parade
rest when in his presence and sergeants trembled in
their boots as he walked past, often carrying his M4
rifle in one hand and a box of ammo in the other. He
was single, never married, and lived in a special room
in the barracks that the commander several years ago
had built for him using Murdoch's money. How legal
it was, no one knew, but there weren't any inquiries
into Murdoch's presence in the barracks twenty-four/
seven. Ranger morale was high and discipline was
good. Murdoch lived by the ethos that he was committed to doing one thing right in this world and that was
leading Rangers. Of all the bios Bronson read during
the plane flight, Murdoch's was the most interesting,
by far. The man had a shaved head and carried the
muscled presence of a heavyweight wrestler, which he
had been in college. Turning down a stint at the World
Wrestling Federation, Murdoch enlisted in 1989 and
later that year jumped into Panama for his first combat
action. Today, he led the most elite fighting force in
the world. Bronson thought, *That is doing something
with your life.*

"Going somewhere?" Murdoch asked. He was toe-
to-toe with the petulant sergeant, but had a hundred
pounds of muscle and almost a foot of height on the
six-foot-tall sniper.

Child immediately shifted from defensive to professional.

"No, Sergeant Major. I just feel insulted that I'm being questioned by the FBI."

"Then sit back down and be a man, Ranger Child. If you've done nothing wrong, then there's nothing to be afraid of. After all, you're an airborne Ranger in the U.S. Army. You going to let a shiny-headed dude in a suit get you all flustered?" Murdoch asked, smiling. He winked at Bronson. "Now turn around and sit your ass back down and answer the man's questions. Or you can answer mine in my office later . . . which you may still have to do."

Child spun around in a professional about-face movement and sat down, this time with an erect back and palms downward on each thigh.

"Sir, I was on leave for the past week. Home in Florence, South Carolina. My ma can account for my whereabouts," Child said.

"Thank you, Sergeant. Now about your weapon."

"Got the receipt in my room, sir. Turned it in to the armorer in Afghanistan."

Bronson looked at Command Sergeant Major Murdoch.

"I can help there. I vaguely remember that. Something about a firing-pin issue. Got him an M24 as a replacement, then we needed someone on the Barrett. Ranger Child is a big guy and can haul that hunk of metal around better than most."

"Can we talk to the armorer?" Bronson asked. All the while, it felt like a hollow lead, but still, he needed to check it out. He wanted to press the button on his phone to check the time—he didn't wear a watch unless he was on a dinner date—and felt that he was losing momentum. The other sniper team using an

SR-25 might bear more fruit. Missing soldier and missing weapon. Was that too much of a coincidence? Nonetheless, he pursued Child's angle.

"He's rotated out, but we can check to see if he filed a disposition form to destroy or sell the weapon," the sergeant major said.

"If the weapon was sold," Bronson replied, looking over his shoulder at White for reassurance, "there would be an ATF form on that, right?"

"That's right, Special Agent. ATF form thirty-three ten," White said, leaning forward, referring to the Bureau of Alcohol, Tobacco, Firearms, and Explosives nomenclature for a weapons-disposition document.

"Well, that's a paper trail we need to check," Bronson said. He looked at Child. "You've been very helpful. Thank you. We will give your mother a call, just FYI."

"Be nice to her. She don't feel well most the time," Child said.

"You're dismissed," Bronson said, standing. To the sergeant major, he said, "Can I have a private audience with you in your office?"

"Roger that."

"There was one thing," Child said as he stood.

Bronson was already on to the next item, but glanced at Child and twirled his hand in a motion that said, "Go ahead, already."

"I was on the SAR team security. I did some crater analysis back when I was in Iraq," Child said, as if that war was of a different era. "No way those mortars came from Sangin. The spall was toward the enemy, not away from them."

"That's good to know, Sergeant. Thank you,"

Bronson said. Turning to the sergeant major, he said, "Ready?"

Child departed with a quick about-face. Bronson waved his staff off and followed the large man into an office filled with headshots of fresh-faced rangers wearing tan and sometimes black berets.

"All my KIA," Murdoch said when he caught him looking at the pictures on the far wall. "Reminds me that my job is never done. Now how can I help?"

The two men sat at opposite ends of the same sofa, which was situated below the rows of pictures, as if the spirits of the warriors were watching them. Bronson figured that was probably part of the sergeant major's purpose. Youthful eyes keeping him honest. Keeping his nose to the grindstone. Making him never forget.

"What do you know about your missing Ranger and Ranger Harwood?"

"Lots. Harwood is like a son to me. He was a foster child, came to the army because he had nowhere else to go. I have spies in basic training that tip me off to the hard chargers. Harwood was a hard charger from day one. Had something to prove to everyone. We get a lot of kids like that, but Harwood was a cut above. More physically fit and more deadly with a rifle. Ranger material right away. I recruited him into the unit and put him in Third Battalion here in Fort Benning so I could keep an eye on him. I stay in the barracks and so did he, of course. While the others were playing Xbox, I was helping Harwood with his shooting and other skills, especially mixed martial arts."

"What happened to him? And to Samuelson?"

"Well, I know Samuelson, of course, but not as well as I know Harwood. Sammie was new and Harwood had just lost his spotter. He was on a roll. The men were calling him the Reaper. I let it stick, because I think Harwood kind of liked the nickname. And let's face it. You get a nickname, that usually means you're accepted. The guys without nicknames are usually the ones who never fully integrate. I was worried about Harwood at first, but then he started performing like a machine, killing every bad guy. That rifling check you're asking about? We'd pulled some bullets out of some dead Taliban in the surrounding areas after we had to conduct a damned investigation because someone said we had killed a civilian. Well, turns out we didn't, but still, we had all these dead Taliban commanders and Harwood knows they're his kills. A Ranger doesn't ask for much, but he will want credit for how much safety and security he has provided his teammates and, by extension, our country. So Harwood was concerned when a special forces A-team claimed credit for those kills. Of course, they did so only after the investigation cleared us of killing a civilian. The armorer that rotated out was the guy who took the lead and some of the casings in to your guy."

Bronson soaked in the information, processed it.

"Sounds like we might be looking for Harwood's rifle. Any of those rounds come from Child's SR-25?"

The Sergeant Major paused then nodded.

"Maybe. I approved their little clandestine mission to take the bullets over to your guys. May seem petty or stupid, but when you're holed up in Kandahar and you're out there getting your ass shot off every day, a little bit of feedback and affirmation that you're making a difference goes a long way."

"Doesn't seem petty or stupid. We were glad to do

it." Bronson processed the irony that his current mission had come full circle from that day in Afghanistan.

"So I guess you want to know about Harwood?"

"Well, him and Samuelson."

"The search-and-rescue team found an SR, which we assumed to be Harwood's. It was pretty banged up. At the time, we were more concerned about finding Samuelson. The SR got shipped back to the states with Harwood and the rest of his gear. Just how we do it. Ranger and his equipment. Now, you're going to ask me where that rifle is, and I checked when I heard about all of this. It's not in the arms room, and the armorer has no record of it."

"Just a second, sergeant major. The SR-25 you recoverd. We don't know whose it was or where it is?"

Murdoch paused and nodded. "That's right. We've essentially got two missing weapons. Samuelson carried as SR, also. This was a screwup by the armorer. He should have logged in the serial number and so forth. Instead, it was bedlam. The SAR team came under some fire as they were doing the aerial medevac of Harwood. I was waiting for them at the hospital in Kandahar. But it was just Vick. He's lucky to be alive. We got Harwood back, the docs stabilized him for a few hours in Kandahar, and then we put him and all his equipment on the C-17 to Germany. Then we sent raids all over Helmand Province, that's southern Afghanistan, looking for Samuelson. That's his picture over there on the wall."

Bronson thought about the missing weapon and drew the conclusion that Harwood was a solid candidate for the shooter. He looked at the photograph of the young man. High and tight haircut. Tan beret.

Fresh face. Not on the dead wall. Somewhere else. Like purgatory. Where was he? Captive? Dead and blended with the earth in Afghanistan? Alive and roaming around? Shooting generals?

"Did either Harwood or Samuelson have authority issues?"

"None whatsoever. Harwood respected authority. Wanted it. Needed it. Samuelson was your average Ranger, which is better than ninety-nine percent of humanity, mind you."

"So we don't know where Samuelson is, but we do know about Harwood, right?"

"Yes. I got him a job training snipers for JSOC and other units. Don't know exactly where he is right now since he's freelancing it as a temporary duty soldier on loan from Walter Reed, where he is presently assigned. We try to integrate soldiers back into the force gradually until they're ready for combat again. Harwood has been working out like a fiend. Need to get him back on the range though. He's a sniper. The Reaper. That's what he knows."

"Can you find him for me? Just so I can talk to him?" Bronson asked. He softened his voice, as if he were sympathetic to the sergeant major's connection with Harwood. Murdoch's face twitched just a bit, a microexpression. Bronson understood, given Murdoch's and Harwood's close relationship. The man would want to be as protective as possible with his protégé.

"Sure. Might take me a few phone calls."

"Any chance he's in Savannah?"

"Where that retired general just got his head blown off? Heard about that. Our First Battalion of Rangers is down that way, so it's possible."

"Thank you, Sergeant Major. I'll take my team into our Suburban and we'll huddle and compare notes, knock out some emails, and when you've got a bead on Harwood, can you just send a runner out to let us know."

Murdoch nodded. "Roger that."

Bronson shook Murdoch's giant catcher's mitt of a hand and departed the sergeant major's office, collected his team, and piled into the Suburban under the watchful eyes of dozens of tan beret–wearing Rangers collecting around the headquarters wondering what was happening. Night had fallen and streetlights dotted the road. Spotlights lit up the fence behind the headquarters to keep intruders at bay. They were in the heart of the most elite unit in the military. The place thrummed with professionalism and no-nonsense commitment to duty. Rangers moved smartly about the area, carrying weapons, issuing orders, and preparing for the next day.

Ten minutes later, Murdoch walked up to the SUV. Bronson powered down his shaded window.

"Harwood checked into the Hunter Army Airfield enlisted quarters a few hours ago. Then he went for a run, according to the clerk." After a pause, the sergeant major looked away and then back at Bronson. "But he's not your guy. I guarantee you that."

Bronson nodded. "Thank you, Sergeant Major."

"And remember. You mess with him, you mess with me. Not a threat. If he's done no wrong and you put the squeeze on him for no good reason, expect some blowback. That's how I roll. Up-front and direct."

"Someone might say that you *are* threatening a federal agent, Sergeant Major. I thought we were getting along just fine?" Bronson said.

"You didn't listen to me very well. I'm obligated to give you the truth and every bit of information I have. That's the code we live by. Help allies, help law enforcement, help the good guys. You turn out to be a bad guy? You're toast. Trust me on that."

Bronson nodded, somewhat impressed with Murdoch's spine. Most leaders should have been this passionate about their charges.

"I understand," Bronson said.

"For your sake, I pray that you do."

Bronson buzzed the window up as the driver pulled away slowly. He turned to Faye Wilde and said, "Call the pilots and tell them to file a flight plan for Hunter Army Airfield immediately."

CHAPTER 9

Harwood normally slept soundly, but awoke to Jackie's movement. She slipped out of bed, sheets ruffling and some body part banging into the lamp in the unfamiliar hotel room. He watched through one sleepy eye as she packed her bags, flipped on the bathroom light, and dressed in the pale glow by the hotel room door.

She came back to the nightstand, spotted what she was looking for, and reached out for a rubberized flotation device. It had a small chain through it with a few keys, some large and some small. As she shined her iPhone light on the nightstand he saw the words "Ten Meter Lady"—her nickname with the Olympic team—printed on the rubber key chain. Beneath that were the words "River City Marina" in small, italicized print.

"What's going on?" Harwood asked.

"Got a text," she said. "I need to get to an event in Atlanta that I totally spaced on."

"Atlanta? It's . . ." He checked the hotel clock. "It's after midnight. Can't you just go in the morning?"

"It's an early appearance. A signing, I think," she said.

"You think? You don't even know what it is and you're bugging out like this?"

"Vick, I love you. I'm with you as much as I possibly can be, but I've been so focused on you, us," she said, waving her hand between them, "I've got a calendar glitch. It's no biggie. I'll catch up with you in Seattle in a few days. You were supposed to teach one class here and then head out, right? We'll catch up when you hit Second Ranger Battalion."

He leaned up, flicked on the light. Something wasn't right. He had spent enough time with Jackie by now that he knew her voice tones. Her speech carried an unfamiliar octave, an inflection of nervousness.

"What's wrong?" he asked. He stood and walked over to her. She was standing in the rectangle of light cast from the bathroom. She was dressed in denim jeans, a dark gray T-shirt, running shoes, and a black windbreaker that had the five-ring Olympic logo and the letters "USA" embroidered on the left breast.

She stepped toward him and placed her hands on his shoulders, looked up at him with her wide blue eyes, and said, "Nothing, Vick. Nothing other than me freaking out over my schedule and not fulfilling my obligations. You've become my world and I still have obligations, you know?"

Harwood brushed some hair away from her forehead and kissed her first there and then on the lips.

"I understand. Let me help you with your stuff."

"No, really. I'm feeling guilty enough as it is by waking you up. You should leave soon, too, but I've got this," she said. Jackie lifted her rucksack, slung it over her shoulder, tugged on the four-wheel roller suitcase, kissed him again, and then walked out of the room. "I left you a few more bottles of your new favorite sports drink," she said over her shoulder. Jackie winked and smiled.

She stood in front of the elevator door, tapping her thumb on the opposite wrist, her impatience cue. She had somewhere to be. Driving to Atlanta from Savannah at one in the morning was not wise, but if she had a commitment, who was he to stop her? And she was right. She had been there for him the past three months. Not every day, but most days. Completely smitten with her, Harwood had begun to envision a lifelong future with the Olympic sharpshooter. Their children *would* be expert marksmen.

The elevator doors opened with a chime. Jackie looked over her shoulder, blew him a kiss, and stepped into the car. The doors snapped shut and she was gone.

Harwood shut the door, flicked off the bathroom light, and lay back in bed, trying to sleep with his head propped against the fluffy pillows. Restless, he grabbed the remote and turned on the television. The news channels were all running with the story of two generals killed in twenty-four hours. One at Fort Bragg and one in Savannah. He paused on one channel with a reporter standing outside of Fort Benning's main gate.

Interested, he turned up the volume and absently pulled apart the plastic wrap sealing a six-pack of Jackie's sports drinks. He lifted the octagonal plastic bottle and raised it to his mouth.

Then stopped.

Removing his eyes from the television, he rolled

off the bed, walked across the room, knelt, and pawed through his rucksack. He retrieved a round bottle with a similar label of Jackie smiling and holding her Olympic gold medal. Walking into the bathroom, he studied the two bottles. The name of a major soda manufacturer was stamped on the base of the octagonal bottle. The round bottle had tiny characters from Arabic or a Middle Eastern language in the exact same spot. The bottles had identical labels. He looked in the mirror and said, "What the hell?"

Is someone spiking my drinks?

He turned his head when he heard a reporter on the television.

"An inside source tells us that the FBI is already here at Fort Benning, Georgia, interviewing Army Rangers and not only that, Dave, but Army Ranger snipers. We saw a government plane land at Fort Benning's Lawson Army Airfield, so there is evidence that the FBI is here. Also, my sources tell me that there has been a match between the ammunition that killed the two generals and a sniper rifle used in Afghanistan. They're looking for an SR-25 sniper rifle."

Harwood walked slowly from the bathroom and stood in front of the television. The image showed a man holding a microphone standing in front of the military police checkpoint at the main gate of Fort Benning. His mind spun. He placed the two sports drinks on the bureau. He stared at them as if he were looking at fraternal twins, one evil, the other not. The television kept crawling with the news and the leads. Images flashed in his mind. At Fort Bragg, sucking down a sports drink from a round bottle. General Sampson arriving in his driveway. Him passing out in the workout pit. The police sirens afterward. Running. Then at Hunter Army Airfield sucking down another drink from a round bottle, the run, General Dillman on the porch. Him fainting. And now here he was in Jackie's room. She had mysteriously left at 1 A.M.

Was it all too good to be true? Was someone trying to say that he shot the generals?

As if to add accent to his last thought, blue lights flashed against the window of Jackie's eighth-floor hotel room.

The television reporter said, "And, Dave, I've just been told that the government airplane left here about an hour ago headed to Hunter Army Airfield in Savannah, a short forty-five-minute flight away. My source tells me that a main person of interest in this investigation is this man."

The reporter was holding a copy of *Rolling Stone* magazine. Harwood stared out from the television, eyes dim, checked scarf around his neck, salt-stained uniform clinging to his muscular frame, Lindsay cradled in his arms. The average viewer would think he was a menacing figure.

"He's obviously armed and dangerous. The question law enforcement officials are debating right now, I'm told, is whether this man can be taken alive."

"Serious stuff, John Bledsoe. We're fortunate to have you on the ground at Fort Benning and we will be back to John soon."

Taken alive? Was there a shoot-to-kill order on him? Who was feeding information to the reporter? Harwood wondered. The FBI had talked to Rangers in Fort Benning and now were on the way to Hunter Army Airfield. But the reporter had what seemed like real-time information. Harwood's heart raced. He ran through everything again, his memory faltering like a sputtering boat engine. Two dead generals. Both killed when he was less than a couple of hundred meters away. Sports drinks that made him dizzy.

Blue lights continued to spin outside. Anxiety welled in his throat. *What to do?*

It was almost two in the morning as he pulled on his shorts and top, slipped on his socks and shoes, and hefted his rucksack. He took one glance around the room, looked out the window again, and saw a SWAT vehicle bouncing into the parking lot.

He didn't want to get within a mile of the police, especially if they were on a manhunt carrying his *Rolling Stone* cover photo. He was acutely aware of the heightened racial tensions begotten by media sensationalism of law enforcement clashes with the African American communities.

The flashing lights hypnotically grazed his retinas. Alarm bells were ringing in his mind. As his vision retreated from the light show outside, he focused on his own dark reflection in the window. Studying his face, he zeroed in on his eyes, soulful and searching. In the window, he believed he saw flashes of Jackie's face, then Samuelson's, then Command Sergeant Major Murdoch's, and then that of the Chechen, bearded and grimy in the crosshairs.

Then the elevator. The slick businessman.

Then the Chechen.

The contours of the jawline, the broad planes of his face, the height of the man all seemed to fit together, as if he had placed tracing paper over the businessman's face and penciled in the beard, the dirt, and the pakol.

Could the Chechen be here in America? Stalking him?

Framing him? Calling the reporter?

If the shooter was leaving behind spent casings, that would be either stupid or intentional. Harwood went with intentional. The Chechen wasn't stupid.

Footsteps thundered toward his room. Thumping on the door. His door.

Was it the police? Was it the Chechen?

He retrieved his nine-millimeter Beretta pistol from the outer pouch of his rucksack, jacked the slide to chamber a round, and wished he were wearing boots. When he heard a battering ram against the door, he paused. Heard it again. Paused again. Then, on the third loud bang with the ram, he fired a single shot into the deadbolt of the door leading to the adjoining room. He aimed at an extreme downward angle, so as not to injure any occupants.

The door and jamb splintered as he shouldered his way into the next room. A quick scan showed a pristinely made bed, no switched-on lights, and no luggage. The room was unoccupied. The hall door to Jackie's room gave way and footsteps pounded into the room. He vaulted over the corner of the king-size bed and carefully opened the door from the unoccupied room to the hallway. Leading with his pistol, he peeked around the corner and saw no one in the hall. He dashed the ten yards to the fire stairwell and began bounding down the concrete steps four at a time, the rucksack on his back heavy and cumbersome.

The galloping footsteps rumbled into the same stairwell two floors above him and began cycling down the stairs in his direction. As he reached the second floor, the ground-floor door opened with a bang. Black-helmeted SWAT members began filing inside the base of the fire stairwell, preparing to assault upward.

Who was chasing him from above?

He wasted no time and dashed into the second floor, which was filled with a workout room, pool, conference rooms, and an open stairwell down to the lobby. To his right was an opening to the rear of the hotel. The stairs went in both directions. On the fly, Harwood made a quick decision to go through the front of the hotel, thinking the police had used the rear parking lot as a rally point. If they were just marshaling in the stairwell, perhaps they had not blocked the front entrance yet.

He flew down the carpeted stairs—maybe twenty of them—and dashed past the registration desk, where a clerk was seated in a chair, watching a movie on the television. As he flew past the desk, the young clerk stood up and shouted, "Hey!"

Footsteps were still behind him, thundering along the carpeted hallway he had just navigated. He pressed the spring-loaded bar, which unlocked the door, and provided him access to the sidewalk on the sparsely populated street. He saw a newspaper delivery truck passing by slowly and ran quickly into the street, leapt up onto the rear bumper, and grabbed the cargo-door handle. The driver must not have noticed, because Harwood felt no change in momentum. No acceleration or deceleration. Steady as she went. He looked over his shoulder and saw a man running out the front door. Harwood flashed back to his earlier run and thought about the man who had almost hit him with the old Buick. Was it the same man? Hard to tell from nearly two hundred yards away.

The baseball hat looked the same. The beard. A thin but wiry guy wearing dungarees and Doc Martens boots. Just like the silhouetted man in the parking lot at Fort Bragg. The man stood at the door to the hotel and watched him vanish into the night on the rear bumper of a panel van filled with newspapers.

Harwood took a deep breath.

He pounded the door of the van in frustration, forgetting that the driver had no clue he was hitching a ride. Turning his head toward the rear door, he noticed two vertical rectangular windows. Newspapers were stacked to about midway. On the front page, he saw the headline SECOND GENERAL KILLED BY SNIPER IN TWO DAYS.

The subtitle read, FORSYTH PARK SHOOTING POSSIBLY LINKED TO ARMY RANGER.

Further confirmation that someone might be trying to frame him.

The van made a turn onto a major thoroughfare and began to accelerate. Harwood leapt off the bumper and ran as fast as he could to prevent stumbling with the forward throw of the vehicle's momentum.

Hooking a right onto the next road, he entered a grouping of warehouses. In the air hung the unmistakable musty scent of fish spawning and silt churning with the ebb and flow of the river and the ocean tide. The van had taken him in the opposite direction of Hunter Army Airfield—toward the river—where his duffel bag full of clothes was in his room. A distant tug belched, confirmation that Harwood was near the

Savannah River and its burgeoning port. Lots of ships and lots of places he could go.

Harwood jogged a block to the south and turned left toward the river, a natural barrier. He slowed to a walk, the river sounds taking over. Tumbling water. Engines churning brown silt. Shouts of dockworkers preparing for a long day, or perhaps closing out a long night. When a ship came in to port, stevedores worked until it was unloaded. Same for when the reverse was occurring. The loading process was nonstop.

Harwood stared at the Riverwalk, spotlights every fifty yards. He stood alone in the shadow of a warehouse at the intersection of River Street and Martin Luther King Jr. Boulevard. He thought briefly about what the civil rights icon had meant to him as an African American. For Harwood to reflect at all about race, politics, or religion was unusual. The heft of the pistol in his hand reminded him that he was a soldier. He had a mission. He killed bad guys so the good guys could live in freedom. There was no need to make it any more complicated than that.

But he realized that his life today was quite different than if he had lived thirty or forty years ago. Men such as Martin Luther King Jr. had helped pave the way for men such as him. He didn't make too much of that and he didn't discount it. Just as Harwood believed that General Dave Grange, the famous Army Ranger, and General James Gavin, the renowned World War II paratrooper, were icons in the military community, he didn't make too much of them, either. He appreciated their example, but wanted to make his own way.

He was the Reaper. He'd done his duty and was all

about carrying his own weight and carving out his own niche in history.

The gray Buick spun around the corner and barreled directly at him, then fishtailed into a perfect 180-degree Rockford turn so that the passenger door was two feet from him. The car was pinning him to the warehouse wall, its nose almost touching the sheet metal and its trunk close to the brick porch that jutted out from the building. The Buick was the long leg of a triangle that blocked Harwood's exit unless he wanted to leap over the hood, which was an option.

Until he looked up.

The bearded man with the baseball cap was leveling a pistol at his chest.

"Reaper, get in the damned car now," the man said.

The interior of the car was dark. The driver's facial features were a theater mask, half in the shadow and half in the dim glow of a distant streetlight. A reddish-brown beard, unevenly cut hair, and familiar voice.

"Lower the pistol and I'll do it, Sammie," Harwood said.

"Sammie? My name's Abrek. Now, I'll make this easy," Samuelson said. "You may have left me behind, but I damn sure ain't leaving you behind. Now get in the car before I shoot you."

The Reaper lifted his pistol slowly and tucked it away as he slid his rucksack off his shoulder. "Abrek? You're Sammie." Harwood stared, certain it was his former spotter. "I've been worried, man. I blamed myself. Thought you were dead. And all this time you're . . . where the hell have you been?"

"It's Abrek to you, Reaper. Cops are coming. Let's

go." Samuelson's excited voice gave Harwood incentive. He was stuck.

"Not before you tell me where you've been. I don't have anything to hide from the cops. And it's Sammie, not Abrek or any other bullshit name," Harwood said.

"Maybe *I've* got something to hide. Want to jack me over twice in one year? Leave me dead on the battlefield and now let the cops haul my ass in?"

Samuelson played the guilt card effectively. Harwood nodded and said, "Okay, you win. I owe you this. I don't know what you've done, or who Abrek is, but I owe you. I know that much."

When he opened the back door to toss his rucksack into the rear seat, there was a banged-up SR-25 lying exposed on the floor of the car.

"Yeah, that's a sniper rifle. Now get your ass in the car," Samuelson said.

"You kill those generals?" Harwood asked, sliding into the front seat.

Samuelson stared at Harwood with a furrowed brow, a true look of puzzlement on his face. "Seriously?" he asked. "You don't know?"

A police cruiser sped past them on a perpendicular road, most likely going to the hotel, Harwood thought.

Blue lights bounced off Samuelson's windshield. Harwood turned and stared at the man with the beard, who called himself "Abrek." This was Samuelson. Not Abrek. The same blunt nose, crooked teeth, unibrow, and deep set brown eyes. His stringy brown hair, however, was longer on one side than the other.

"Did you leave anything at Hunter you need?" Samuelson asked.

"My duffel bag and shaving kit. Why?"

"They're looking for you, Reaper. The cops." Samuelson kept driving, turned onto Interstate 516, and kept within the speed limit. "I'll grab your stuff."

Samuelson's stony gaze remained fixed forward. His sentences were clipped, as if rehearsed. Harwood was still thinking about the name, "Abrek." He had no idea what it meant, but guessed that perhaps the Taliban had recovered him and nursed him back to health. Stockholm syndrome. Harwood's mind spun to the obvious question.

"How did you know what room I was in, Sammie?" Harwood asked.

After a pause Samuelson said, "You d-don't know what's going on, do you?"

"Damn it, quit being so cryptic and just tell me," Harwood demanded. *A stutter?*

"L-Let's just say: Your thirty-three kills in the 'Stan?"

"What about them?" Harwood was thinking, *keep him talking.*

"T-Twenty women went missing from Helmand and Kandahar Provinces. D-During your missions."

"Our missions," Harwood corrected.

"You and LaBoeuf. I didn't come on till later."

As red taillights flashed in front of them, Harwood felt cheated. He had always visualized his reunion with his spotter to be a celebratory affair, not a middle-of-the-night escape from Alcatraz with a man who called himself Abrek.

"What does that even mean?"

"Everything, m-man. Everything." After a pause, Samuelson said with more precision this time, "Khasan wants his wife back."

"Khasan? As in Basayev?"

"Khasan saved my life."

Harwood stared at Samuelson. His former spotter reminded him of a cultist, with his distant stare and cryptic answers.

"He brainwashed you, Sammie. Listen to me," Harwood said.

Samuelson began rocking back and forth in the driver's seat.

"N-Not like that."

"It's exactly like that!" Harwood barked. "Snap out of it. He's using you. You're Sammie Samuelson. Not Abrek!"

Harwood stared at Samuelson, who remained silent for the next five minutes as they rode along the interstate, took the ramp to Hunter Army Airfield, and pulled into a vacant, abandoned gas station. The cinder-block building's windows were shattered, jagged edges poking up in hard triangles. The lot was dark. Samuelson shook his head like a dog drying off from a swim.

"Okay, Reaper. We'll stop here for a minute while I get my shit together."

"Wake up, Sammie. You're better than this."

"Don't pull rank on me, Reaper. Now, give me your room key and wait for me here," Samuelson said.

"You've got a rifle in the backseat of your car. You're not getting on the airfield," Harwood said. "I'll walk from here and get my own stuff."

"See that?" Samuelson said, pointing a quarter mile up the road at a dark silhouette of a vehicle. "C-Cops. Ambush. Waiting for you."

Harwood looked at Samuelson, confirming again

that this was his long-lost spotter. The man had literally manifested out of nowhere to now commandeer him allegedly away from trouble.

"Sammie, what do you know about these generals."

"Reaper. Go."

"Who's framing me?"

"Just leave me for dead and here I am *helping* you. Give me your key and get the fuck out of my car."

Harwood felt his mind race three months back, memories fluttering like bats alighting from a cave. The mortars, the Taliban on the ridge, the kidnapped women, and the Chechen. He took a deep breath, sighed.

"Roger that. You're my spotter. You call the target."

"Target is getting your ass out of my car. I'll find you."

"How?"

Samuelson nodded at the iPhone secured in Harwood's armband. "Smart enough to stay alive in the 'Stan. Smart enough to let me find you."

Harwood understood. Snagging his rucksack from the backseat, he spotted the sniper rifle again. Didn't know what to think, but decided to give Samuelson the benefit of the doubt. With his ruck slung over his shoulder he walked around to the driver's window. Harwood looked at the run-down, defunct convenience store and gas station, the gravel lot and the woods behind the shuttered building.

"I'll be back there. Flash your lights three times when you pull in so I know it's you. You're not the only one packing. I've been praying I'd find you, now hurry up and get back here, Sammie. You hear?"

"Roger that, Reaper." The words were hollow,

without eye contact. He gripped the steering wheel and stared straight ahead at the police a quarter mile away.

Samuelson gunned the engine, the Buick's tires spit gravel, and the car leapt onto the pavement. Samuelson drove the speed limit, tapped his brakes, red lights flashing briefly, and then continued past the gate to Hunter Army Airfield without turning in to the base.

Once the vehicle was out of sight, Harwood moved quickly behind the building and walked into the woods, using the flashlight function of his iPhone to find a relatively cleared area upon which to camp until Samuelson returned. He pressed one knee into the soft pine straw, cleared some low shrub branches out of the way, and shut off the phone light.

The time was almost 5 A.M. The sun would be rising soon. While it was pitch dark where he was in the woods, there were some streetlights near the road where it fronted the gravel parking lot. He was about 150 meters from the road.

Samuelson was alive. Just now the notion was sinking into his mind, his heart. Having felt like a failure on the battlefield, he now could at least feel some relief that he had not left a fallen soldier behind to die. During the rehabilitation months after the mortar attack, the army psychiatrist at Walter Reed continued to emphasize that Harwood had not left behind a fallen comrade. That he, too, had fallen and had been rescued.

Little good that did for a soldier who had been mentored by the toughest of them all, Command Sergeant Major Murdoch, who had once told him, "You decide to leave a fallen comrade you might as well suck the end of your pistol."

But that was the psychiatrist's point. Harwood hadn't *decided* anything. He had been unconscious from his own traumatic brain injuries. But still, what had happened to Samuelson? Where had he been? Apparently, the Chechen had rescued him? Named him Abrek? Brainwashed him?

About thirty minutes later, two cars pulled into the gravel lot where Samuelson had dropped him off. They were standard police cruisers with light racks, white cars with writing on the side. One looked like a Crown Victoria and the other a new Dodge Charger.

Harwood put his other knee into the pine straw to steady himself, his mind still swooning from the lack of sleep and the activities of the last several hours. Steadying himself, he placed his hands on the soft matting. Sounds of animals rutting in the woods to his flanks filtered through the dizziness.

Car doors slammed with hollow thunks. Two uniformed officers spoke with each other across the hood of one car. Nearby to the east were the metallic and gravelly sounds of digging. Rhythmic.

Chop, lift, toss, scrape.

Harwood retrieved his thermal spotter's scope from his rucksack and looked through the dense foliage. A figure about three hundred yards away from him and the police, like the third point of a triangle, was digging with a shovel. Beyond the digger was a mini power substation about twenty yards to the east.

Chop, lift, toss, scrape.

The police were looking in that direction, almost impatiently, it seemed.

Mind swimming, Harwood looked at his rucksack. He needed what he carried. Was he addicted? He didn't want to be, but that was what an addict was all about, right? Not being able to help himself.

He looked toward the police officers, then at his rucksack.

The sniper was feeling good, with a nice soft spot in the woods and clear fields of fire. There was even a decent escape route. These were important kills, at the nexus of everything happening. The sniper waited for the sounds that were expected.

While police officers were always a good possibility, they were a risky placement on the kill list. Given the tensions in the country today, killing a police officer or two would create a firestorm. The sniper smiled. Yes, killing two police officers would create a bigger mess than killing two generals. *How about that,* the sniper mused.

The rifle felt cool in the sniper's hands. After all, it had been fired, broken down, cleaned, packed, reassembled, and now loaded.

The sniper heard the noises. Chop, lift, toss, scrape. Those were reassuring sounds. The mission was advancing. Waiting for the sound of metal striking metal, the sniper dialed in the scope. There it was.

Clank.

Followed by another probe that produced a distinctive ping that hummed liked a tuning fork.

"Sounds like a treasure hunt," the sniper heard one officer say.

"Well, it kind of is, supposedly," the other said.

"We're just supposed to help him on the base, that's it, right?"

"That's all I've been told. Not originally part of the

deal. I thought we was just looking the other way on the planes coming in."

"This is different. Sneaking someone in. Not sure I'm down with that."

"We could leave. I'm good with bailing on the deal."

But the sniper wasn't good with them bailing on the deal. There was no bailing. They were either in or they were dead. Honestly, they were dead either way. The sniper just disliked ending their usefulness so early.

With the possible defection of the police officers, the sniper placed the crosshairs on the head of one officer and practiced the one-two timing rhythm required to kill both officers. Killing just one would absolutely be no good. A radio call would ensue quickly, followed by a rapid response probably including dogs. No. Now, both cops needed to go down immediately.

One-two.

The sniper focused on the officer to the left, head as big as a basketball in the Armasight Zeus Pro 640 thermal scope, which the sniper had chosen instead of the Leupold during reassembly. Using hot black, the warm items were dark, cooler items were white. The engines of the cars were shimmering black, while the trees and leaves across the street were a perfect background of white, highlighting the ninety-eight-point-six-degree blackness of officer number one's brain.

The trigger gave way under the sniper's practiced pull and the weapon coughed slightly. In the thermal sight, officer one's head exploded in a black mass, like a canful of black paint a modern artist might throw against a white canvas. The sniper was quickly on officer two, who stood there one second too long before figuring out what had happened. His head exploded also, but with more of a backward spray. The sniper had overcompensated and, instead of hitting center mass, had torn a rear chunk of the brain off the back of the officer's head. It was a fatal shot, nonetheless.

The sniper put the thermal scope back on the digger near the substation. The figure was up and moving toward the cars. The sniper saw it all. The police officers were sized up. One was selected and stripped. Clothes were changed. The freshly unearthed object was placed in the trunk. The car was driven toward the main gate.

Casings in the pine straw. Clues left behind. Rifle disassembled. Rucksack packed. The sniper was on the move.

Harwood came out of his spiraling memory as he cinched his rucksack. He saw the two police officers fall as if puppet strings had been cut. Thought about being framed.

What was going on?

There was rustling in the woods, animals moving through the forest. In less than half an hour the area would be swarming with cops, probably dogs. A figure moved toward one of the police cars. An engine rumbled. The nearest police car cranked and headed toward Hunter Army Airfield. Harwood needed to move.

He shouldered his rucksack and moved west, away from the scene, hoping that Samuelson would be able to find him again.

CHAPTER 10

Harwood's phone showed no messages from anyone. It was midmorning and he had been on the run through the woods, hitched a ride in the back of a pickup truck, and made it to Statesboro, where the driver worked maintenance at Georgia Southern University. Hopping out of the back of the truck, Harwood nodded at the man, who said, "Always gotta help a brother out."

"Roger that. Thanks, man," Harwood said.

He walked two blocks, found a Burger King, bought two breakfast sandwiches and two large Powerade drinks, carried them across the street, dodged traffic, and found a wooded area where he could eat, hide, and think. Any number of people had seen him. But he looked like just another college kid around here and he had already noticed on his short walk that there were plenty of black males to confuse him with, if someone were looking for him.

Harwood sat in a copse of trees. Behind him was a baseball field about one hundred yards away. The street hummed with traffic fifty yards to his front. Secure for the moment, he processed the last day. Instead of hiding, he should have been training snipers today. But now, he was wondering if he was being framed and if Samuelson had picked up his gear.

As Harwood chewed on the breakfast sandwiches, his strength returned. A solid workout, then sex with Jackie, and then up all night fleeing Savannah—Harwood was famished. He inhaled both sandwiches and sucked down one bottle of the power drink. Stashing the other bottle in his rucksack, Harwood took inventory of his equipment. Everything he needed was in there, though if he was ever stopped by the police, he was done.

The hiss of heavy traffic on the road continued. The air smelled of pine straw and sap in the thicket of tall pines. Pulling his phone from his pocket, he found that he had four bars of connectivity. He tapped Google and connected to CNN to read the top stories. He used his thumb to scroll through the links on the Syrian civil war, the new president's latest conflict with Congress, and a story about a mall shooting in Chicago. The fourth URL had a picture of an SR-25 sniper rifle and a photo of Vick Harwood. It was a full-body photo of himself dressed in his nasty uniform, cradling his SR-25 sniper rifle—Lindsay—like a baby, and staring directly into the camera, giving the viewers of the photo a clear image of his face. The picture was maybe seven or eight months old and had been snapped by a fellow Ranger, who had posted it on Facebook after they had rotated back from Afghanistan. Either the Ranger had coughed up the picture or he had an open Facebook page where anyone could pull the picture into their photo files. Regardless, the entire world knew he was the prime suspect in these murders. This wasn't some local news show. It was international.

Damn.

Harwood was lucky to have made it this far. He read the story, which basically said that he was a key person of interest in the killing of two police officers and two generals, one retired and one active duty. The article also said that the FBI had a special task force on the case, meaning the pressure on him would increase.

Part of his rehabilitation had been to attempt to return to his self-sufficient, driven self. Relying on others had never been Harwood's strong suit, yet here he was being buffeted about by forces out of his control.

"When in charge, be in charge," Harwood muttered to himself, a maxim taught to him by Command Sergeant Major Murdoch. He needed to find his moorings. Now was as good a time as any.

Not now, but soon, he needed to contact Murdoch, the man responsible for his current assignment as an instructor. If nothing else, he would let the senior enlisted Ranger know that he was not intentionally AWOL and that he also was not responsible for the murders.

Knowing the capabilities of the intelligence community, though, Harwood needed to shut down his communications sooner rather than later. Law enforcement agencies were no doubt tracking him at this moment, or at least about to be, once they could gather his information and home in on all his email, phone, and text messaging.

Still, despite the security that being off the grid would provide, there was a trade-off in situational awareness. He would have to go old-school by watching television where he could and finding Web news when possible.

Before shutting down, though, he checked social media. Twitter already had a hashtag that appeared to be generated by the Black Lives Matter movement: #HeroHarwood. He winced. He did not believe killing noncombatants made anyone a hero. As a black man, sure, he'd had his share of scrapes with others, but that only drove him harder to prove to everyone else what he already knew: that he was the best and his skin color didn't matter. He looked at the hashtag stream on Twitter and saw it scrolling with epitaphs such as *Cap some more #HeroHarwood #BLM . . . revolution has begun thanks to #HeroHarwood #BLM . . . rally around our new leader #HeroHarwood . . . We've got our own army now #HeroHarwood.* And the tweets kept scrolling as thousands of Twitter users voiced their opinions.

Next, he checked Instagram, and it was more of the same, only his photograph had been cropped, zooming on his face so that it was right there for all to see. Soulful brown eyes, strong jawline, curly black hair, lips together but angled in a slight smirk. Harwood had once liked that picture, but now he hated it, wished it didn't exist. He had lived by the Ranger creed for the past six years of his enlistment: . . . *Readily will I display the intestinal fortitude required to fight on to the Ranger objective and complete the mission, though I be the lone survivor.*

Today, at this moment, Harwood was alone and had to fight on to defend not only his good name, but that of the Ranger Regiment and all the men who had fought for freedom. Though he truthfully could not remember much about the past two days, he knew— *believed*—in his heart that he had not committed those murders.

He opened the flap of his well-worn black rucksack and looked at the red, white, and blue American flag stitched on the inside, a reminder of home when he was in combat and now a reminder to him that he was a loyal patriot.

Not a murderer.

He snapped a picture of the flag. Pressing his thumb lightly against the picture, he inserted the photo into an iMessage and typed Jackie's name into the address window. In the text field he typed, *Love you, RLTW.* He waited for a full minute to see if Jackie replied, which she usually did immediately. In fact, a minute later, the message turned green instead of the typical iMessage blue. Sent as a text message, his phone reported. He tried again with the Wickr app, to no effect. Either her phone was off or her battery was dead. Perhaps she was on a phone call, but typically that didn't turn his messages green. They seemed to go through. Interesting.

After no response, he used Google to search for mentions of Jackie's appearance to see how it might have gone. Instead of reports, there were multiple articles referencing the fact that Jackie had missed an appearance in the Buckhead area of Atlanta this morning. Checking his iMessages again, he saw that she had still not responded. Instead of being reassured, Harwood was concerned, but there was nothing he could do.

Harwood powered down his iPhone. Retrieving a small pin from his rucksack, he slid the fine point into the SIM-card slot and popped the card out. He replaced the pin in a small pouch along with the SIM card and safely tucked the pouch into the rucksack.

The FBI and all the other intelligence agencies could track his last text and knew the nearest cell phone tower that had processed that message. He needed to move, but where? And how?

Atlanta was his first option, but that was a long way up the road. Plus, Jackie apparently wasn't there. Command Sergeant Major Murdoch was equally as far on the other side of the state at Fort Benning. Samuelson would not be able to find him with his phone powered off.

Ever since the mortar attack that had knocked him unconscious, Harwood had been reliant upon medics, doctors, nurses, physical therapists, and others such as Jackie and Murdoch. His sojourn through the foster-care system of Maryland had made him self-reliant almost to a fault. He had shifted from one end of the spectrum to the other. And now, he found himself fighting a riptide of uncertainty.

Being reliant on others did not suit Harwood. And now that he knew Samuelson was at least alive, he removed the self-emplaced yoke of guilt from his neck. With that lightening, a sense of freedom of maneuver and thought appeared. Decision time.

He retrieved a baseball cap from her rucksack and pulled it tight over his forehead; then he cinched the rucksack as he performed a 360-degree analysis of his environment. Forest in every direction, but it was a thin layer of insulation from the cold, hard world that was now searching for him. It was possible that if he stepped into the open, people would recognize him and the social media universe would collapse on him, tracking his every move.

Shouldering his ruck, Harwood walked a mile through the woods until he came to a road that afforded him a view of Georgia Southern University. The school had a good football reputation at the small-college level and he saw the stadium on the far side of the campus.

In his physical-fitness clothing, he emerged from the trees and began a jog in that direction, as if he were an ordinary student either late for class or doing a workout.

As he scooted through the parking lots, passed academic buildings, and dashed through a series of sports complexes, the fight-or-flight instinct shot adrenaline into his gut.

Spotting a road beyond a stand of trees, he saw five students standing in a circle about thirty yards across the parking lot. Wearing backpacks smaller than his, they joked as they looked at their phones. They wore an assortment of jeans, hoodies, and baseball caps, all bearing some symbol of the bald eagle, the Georgia Southern mascot.

One of the young men in a hoodie turned and stared at Harwood, then spun around and looked at his phone. The student glanced at the others in his group and they all looked at him.

"That's him!" one of them shouted.

CHAPTER 11

At eight thirty in the morning Mountain time, retired air force general Buzz Markham stood at the window of his hunting lodge on the outskirts of Glenwood Springs, Colorado.

He held a steaming cup of coffee in one hand and used his other hand to point a trigger finger at two mule deer standing one hundred yards away on the sloping plain outside his compound. The deer were perfectly spotlighted by the sun nosing over the horizon as they grazed in the blissful ignorance of the threat that might one day be posed by Markham and his hunting buddies.

Hooked onto his left ear was a wireless earpiece that purred with his anticipated call.

"Talk to me," Markham said.

On the other line was the president of MLQM Private Military Contracting Company, Derwood Griffin, a former Department of Defense civilian contracting officer, who retired at fifty years old with a two-hundred-thousand-dollar-a-year pension and now collected his one-million-dollar annual salary for securing contracts with the government. For his part, Markham was the CEO of a major hedge fund that held over two billion dollars in assets. He had parlayed his four-star rank into a fortune by sitting on corporate boards, investing wisely, and staying married to the same woman for forty years. A former chief of staff of the air force, Markham was living his dream and he was the chairman of the board of Corporate Leaders Employing Veterans and Retired, or CLEVER. Essentially their group was a gang of loosely knit chief executive officers of both private and public companies whose stated mission was to help veterans find jobs. They also often met to discuss and choose which foreign-policy initiatives they might want to influence.

Griffin's MLQM was a portfolio asset of Markham's wealth-management holdings. Markham mentored other retiring senior flag officers and civilians, coaching them on how not just to get rich, but to build wealth. The two were as different as night and day, Markham would tell his transitioning peers. You could have the nice home on the golf course or even the beach and be debt free, or you could own multiple homes in several countries, have your own aircraft for personal and business travel, and be a player on the world stage of international and national politics. A talking head for several television news programs, Markham was also sought out by sitting presidents, senators, and business executives for counsel on wars, trade, and leadership.

He had it all.

That was, until now. He had an empty feeling in his gut that Derwood Griffin did not have good news.

"Dillman was shot and killed last night. Head blown off by a close-range sniper shot," Griffin said to Markham.

"Saw that on the news. Surprised you didn't call me sooner," Markham admonished. "Same as Sampson?"

After a pause Griffin said, "Yes. By coincidence, I was there. Learned he had brought one home. I parked out back, came over, he made us some drinks, and I went up to check on her. He evidently walked onto the porch to take a call, and that's when he got shot. There was a lot to clean up before the police arrived."

"Did you clean it up?"

"Of course. As much as possible. Cops were on it pretty quickly."

"Police forensics are pretty good nowadays as are eavesdropping capabilities, my friend," Markham said.

"Everything is fine. Operations are continuing. We are on secure phones and I'm in some random diner," Griffin said. "Noisy as hell in here."

"Anything else?" Markham asked.

"Two cops were shot by the same rifle that killed Dillman and General Sampson at Fort Bragg. Four dead. One rifle. My sources tell me they're tracing it to an Army Ranger."

"Keep bird-dogging that. Sampson and Dillman were our guys. The cops?"

"Ours, too," Griffin said. "No way for anyone to know that. They were our customs guys. What they were doing at five in the morning in a random parking lot near Hunter, I don't know," Griffin said.

"Do we have more customs guys?" Markham asked, looking to the future.

"I can find some, I'm sure, for the right price. These guys were perfect. I don't know how any of this could be connected, though. No one knows about any of this," Griffin said.

"Assume someone knows. Assume our killer is after all of us and take appropriate measures."

"That's what you used to say to me when we were in Afghanistan," Griffin said. Griffin had deployed as a high-level civilian working directly for Markham when the general commanded the air component of the joint task force. Because the coalition was rebuilding the runways and air force accommodations, Markham had deployed Griffin to lead the construction and contracting effort. Griffin's role had grown over time to include handling the dark side of Markham's business dealings. To keep Griffin under his thumb, Markham had made the competent bureaucrat wealthy.

"And that's what I'm saying to you now. What about the coffins?"

"The only ones we've got are for spare parts stuffed in the back of our hangar from the last two flights. We don't have the personnel to empty all of them right now. Was next on my to-do list, but these shootings are bothersome."

"Take the personnel ones to a junkyard, have them crushed and sanitized. The ones with 'parts,' as you call them, get the parts on the street and then do the same to those."

"Roger that," Griffin said.

Markham pressed the button on his earpiece and heard an audible beep, indicating that the call had been terminated. He sat in a soft chair that afforded him a view of Lookout Mountain to the east. Beyond that was Interstate 70 and the White River National Forest, some of the best elk and mule deer hunting grounds in the world. He had just ordered Griffin to destroy any evidence of the personnel shipment containers, known as transfer cases, used by the military for repatriation of human remains. Dead bodies.

Annually Markham brought his top five investors, all part of the CLEVER network, to the mountains or the beach, or both. His palatial mountain compound was rustic, with bronze eaves and faux-wood exteriors. The well-crafted home, though, was state-of-the-art in every aspect. The security fence provided two miles of cameras and sensors that Markham's on-site muscle monitored twenty-four hours a day, seven days a week from a bunkered outbuilding with firing ports, monitors, slew-to-cue technology, thermal imaging, and infrared sights. Forty-million-candlepower searchlights and spotlights were set back from the fence, which was lined all the way around with a warning track where the security team could look for any intruding footprints and easily drive the interior.

Markham had the security personnel place a bank of monitors in his control room off his study, where he sat now. Leather sofas sat in a U shape fronting a tall open wood-burning fireplace big enough to handle tree trunks.

He sat in the leather sofa facing the fireplace and pressed the speed dial button on his MLQM secure smartphone, routing the call through his earpiece.

"Roger," a male voice said crisp and clear.

"We need something official shadowing our government friends," Markham said. "You know I don't like not knowing what's going on."

"Roger that. Just returned from the sandbox, but I'm in the AO. I'll report back. Moving now," the man said. The area of operations for now was Savannah, Georgia.

Markham had hired former CIA Ground Branch operative Ramsey Xanadu, who had been discharged from service for misconduct. Xanadu, though, was good at what Markham wanted him to do. He had proven that time and again in Afghanistan and Iraq as he executed Markham's missions. Markham invested millions in MLQM and received in exchange the opportunity to insert his own teams . . . and his own agenda.

"And, Xanadu?"

"Yes, sir," he said.

"If this is who I think it is, this person is not someone we need back. I'm having to deal with this now because it wasn't cleaned up earlier. Clear?"

"Crystal, sir."

"Roger, out," Markham said.

He took a sip of his coffee and pressed a different speed dial button on his phone. This time a female voice answered.

"Yes, sir?" she said.

"Be ready in thirty minutes. It's that time of the morning," Markham said. The wealth manager liked to start his mornings with pre-stress relief, as he called it. Why wait until the stress builds? That was his motto. Bust a nut first thing, maybe follow it with a short nap, and then go cap a few unsuspecting deer. This was what retirement life was all about: enough money to buy a yacht and a Gulfstream jet and an endless train of fresh, exotic women to accompany him.

"Yes, sir," she replied.

"How are my guests being treated?"

"They all seem very . . . happy," she said. As he listened to the voice, he conjured the image of the eighteen-year-old Afghan beauty. She was the oldest of the lot, in some cases by several years, so he had given her management responsibilities. She had eyes the color of copper pennies, toned legs and breasts, and full lips. Markham had to admit that he had been surprised by what was hiding behind those burqas. The Afghan and Arabic women cleaned up well.

He finished his coffee as he popped a blue pill. Letting it course through his system for thirty minutes, he wondered who could be hunting his people and whether the hunter ultimately would come after him? Probably, but that was of little concern to Markham. He had a private jet, private runway, private cars, private yacht, private concubines, and private security.

He even had a compound on Tybee Island, near Savannah, similar to this one.

No issues. He could pretty much go wherever he needed and do whatever he wanted.

He stood, feeling renewed vigor, and walked into the basement where Mehrangez awaited him. Mehrangez's mother had named her daughter after the Afghan vocalist who had managed to escape the shackles of her native culture. Lucky for him, *his* Mehrangez had not escaped.

As he approached her, she was sitting on the bed wearing fishnet stockings, stilettos, no top, and her long brown hair mussed just enough with pouty lips painted red. He stood before her and she undid his belt buckle. While her task might not have been her first choice for a career, Markham thought, her path was certainly better than what he did with the discards.

As her brown doe eyes looked up at him, he thought about the first time he had seen her on the airplane. It was nighttime in Afghanistan and she had been wearing an orange jumpsuit and a burlap hood.

Just like all the others.

Xanadu clicked off the call. He was standing in the MLQM warehouse that had a back gate connecting to Hunter Army Airfield in Savannah. A high school dropout from Santa Cruz, California, Xanadu had been involved in an escalating series of criminal enterprises that had landed him in front of a judge who said, "Either join the army or I'm sending you to San Quentin."

The army had been good for Xanadu, given him structure and showed him mostly how to operate around the system, not within it. He had been a member of Seventh Special Forces Group in Afghanistan, and then the CIA recruited him because he had special skill sets. He was fluent in Pashto and Dari, the two primary languages spoken in Afghanistan.

Some sketchy expense-report submissions and reports of domestic abuse resulted in his dismissal from Ground Branch. MLQM was eager to hire him, paying a handsome two hundred thousand dollars a year—mostly tax-free—for operating between Afghanistan and Savannah.

When Markham learned that Xanadu was working with MLQM, the general developed a relationship with the former special forces soldier. As trust grew between the two men, Xanadu proposed to Markham how to increase MLQM's bottom line in the face of severe cutbacks in the military contracting world. Markham had listened and said nothing, which Xanadu had taken as a green light. He understood that Markham might have been suspicious that Xanadu was recording the conversation, which he was. Regardless, the first delivery included opium, weapons, and two women that he had kidnapped as part of a raid he was conducting in Helmand Province with his three-man team.

They had entered the building on a tip that it contained a week's worth of poppy-resin harvest. Xanadu's team had shot two guards in the head using their night vision goggle advantage, and then Xanadu had checked the team's fire as they cleared the last two rooms, one of which had two fifteen-year-old Afghan girls in it. The moral dilemma he faced was whether he should kill them or let them live. Killing them seemed . . . excessive. Letting them live seemed . . . stupid. So he kidnapped them, which turned into a new business line.

In the truck, he had two transfer cases, military coffins, that he was using to disguise the opium shipment home. He put the drugs in one case and the women—it was a tight fit—in the other case. First, he had bound and gagged them. When he got back to Kandahar and the MLQM private compound, he quickly loaded the two transfer cases on the MLQM 737-900ER that flew the weekly route to Savannah and back. Having led the mission, he personally escorted the two transfer cases back to Hunter Army Airfield, where he had them moved to the MLQM private compound just beyond the gate. The customs officials rarely inspected the transfer cases, given the sensitivity of combat deaths, the American flags draped on top, and the human remains that were supposed to be contained inside.

Xanadu took full advantage of that. Once in a private warehouse by himself with the two transfer cases, he stored the opium-filled case with about twenty other empty cases at the back of the fifty-thousand-square-foot dry-storage area. The cases were on a palletized rack system, stacked vertically.

He opened the case with the women, hoping they had survived the shipment time with no food or water. They had. He led them to the locker room and had them shower in front of him. He liked what he saw. Dark hair; smooth, young bodies; and big almond eyes. He became aroused. They were embarrassed and resisted, of course, but Xanadu hatched his plan right there.

He raped both girls, one right after the other, at gunpoint on the locker room benches. He kept one tied up while he forced himself on the other and then reversed the situation. One he had to "dust off," meaning she was a virgin. The other had been penetrated previously.

He bound and gagged them afterward and called Markham, explained his plan, and Markham said nothing.

Which meant the general gave a green light to the plan. While planning his second opium-house raid he discreetly researched the human intelligence where there might also be attractive young women or girls. Each raid was a near-instant replay of the other until the fifth time out, when he actually got into hand-to-hand combat with a woman, who turned out to be French and married, at that.

Still, she was a looker, and to Xanadu, a keeper. He kept the rare French beauty to himself in a container yard at Kandahar for two months and three weeks, not unlike the undocumented detainees—the ghost prisoners—they had snatched early in the wars. He would come back from a mission, send the transfer cases to Hunter Army Airfield, rape the French woman, make sure she was fed and watered, and then go on his missions. Not bad duty.

That was exactly three months ago and he'd operated on the principal of five to seven a month, which had seemed to work out so far. He hadn't run across any other non-Afghan women, though, which was fine by him. The French woman was . . . perfect. The entire enterprise had paid off in many ways, but General Markham had been the genius behind the big-time payoff. Had taken it to another level.

Now, just off the phone with the general, he looked at that stack of containers inside the warehouse just outside the gate of Hunter Army Airfield. He had one special case to open. A week ago, he had moved his French woman to the United States. Planned to keep her. She'd been in storage for a week, bringing her total time in captivity to three months.

He walked to the rack storing system, fired up the forklift, elevated it to the seventh level, plucked the transfer case, and lowered it to the ground. He returned the forklift to its proper position in the warehouse and came back to the transfer case.

As he ran a rough-hewn hand over the metallic casket lid, he visualized her beautiful raven hair and green eyes. Slender body with legs all the way up to her neck. He had given her a box of combat rations and water bottles as he had left for another run to Afghanistan last week. There wasn't much room to move around in those coffins, but she would be hungry and thirsty enough to figure it out. She seemed like a survivor.

Using his key, he unlocked the hasps and opened the container.

It was empty.

Save for a note that read, *Find me.*

Which was laid neatly atop a metal briefcase covered in mud and dirt.

Xanadu wasn't an expert in improvised explosive devices, but he did know enough to believe that this could be one. He checked it for IED-related triggers or sensors and didn't see anything immediately, other than two wires connected to a battery, which was obviously a sign that whatever was inside required power. It occurred to him to simply disconnect the wires from the battery, but he knew about anti-handling devices. They were hidden and tricky and he wanted nothing to do with being at ground zero of a stupid IED.

He quickly shut the transfer case, ran outside of the warehouse, and puked onto the concrete apron of the runway, thinking, *How the hell did she escape?*

CHAPTER 12

Khasan Basayev, the Chechen, stared at the Savannah River through the window of his hotel room in Savannah, Georgia, wisps of fog appearing like lost souls escaping confinement. The excitement of the morning had given way to late afternoon. Thunderstorms had rolled through, pounding their way across the Savannah River until they were out at sea. Basayev had come face-to-face with the Reaper, who didn't even recognize him. He had tracked his every move, stalked him like the prey that he was, and was tightening the circle of pressure around the Reaper like a boa constrictor, slow and steady.

He *needed* the police chasing Harwood.

Basayev's muddy boots sat in the closet of the hotel room. He had worked hard through the night. The shoveling. Finding the right-size police uniform. Driving onto Hunter Army Airfield. And ultimately working his way into MLQM and finding the right transfer case. Just about anything was possible with a police uniform.

He had not been surprised to find the device he had parachuted into America and planted years ago. The Russians had hesitated on activating the weapon, and then in 2014 their economy began to collapse, leaving his employers with no ability to pay. Basayev did not work for free. But now, with the geopolitical winds swirling, apparently, they had found the money.

The police had arrived at the hotel based upon his "anonymous" call that he had seen "a sniper" in Forsyth Park. In fact, he had seen more than one, which excited him. This game would be fun for Basayev if it weren't so deadly serious. While he was a true mercenary gun for hire, and had worked for many countries and organizations, he was also a human being. He had his own set of hopes and dreams forged in the aftermath of constant conflict in his home country.

He wrote poetry with the same economy of force with which he could slit the throat of a target. He had fended for himself in the lawless days of Russian dominance in the years surrounding the 9/11 terrorist attacks in America. Those attacks were barely a blip on the screen for Chechen rebels such as himself. Basayev vaguely recalled that he was holed up in a remote hide position awaiting a column of Russian infantry soldiers, who usually marched with their heads down, unaware of the threats that lurked two hundred yards away. With the Russians trudging to reinforce an embattled city, Basayev killed ten men including the commander of the unit. Sniper fire followed by a mortar attack was his trademark maneuver for breaking contact and evading capture or retaliation. It had worked in Chechnya and it worked in Afghanistan.

His journal entries had turned from dark and humorous—*Heads upon a spike? Shall I drive them into the ground or take a selfie and give them a "like"*—to uplifting and hopeful—*I've found my one true love, hear the voices from heaven, Nina is my white-winged dove*—once he transferred to Afghanistan in 2017.

Nina Moreau.

As a giant merchant ship glided along the Savannah River, Basayev thought of Nina and their not-so-random meeting in Saint-Tropez, France.

He had been gambling. She had been watching. Having just returned from a good payday working for the Turks killing infiltrating Kurds in the mountainous regions of Turkey, Basayev had been on rest-and-relaxation time. Not total R&R, though, because a cutout for the Russian government had contacted him asking to meet in Saint-Tropez.

He was running the baccarat table and had piles of euros and stacks of chips in front of him. Nina had smiled from across the room and he instantly knew it wasn't an "I like your money" smile. There was a deep soulfulness to her eyes that told him they were kindred spirits. Wanderers. Perhaps warriors. And that maybe she was his contact.

With the reach of one of his long arms, he swept the cash and chips into a Louis Vuitton day-travel bag without breaking her gaze. He walked to the elevator of the hotel. She placed her drink on a linen-covered round high-top table and followed him. He was vaguely aware of the dome camera as she strode into the elevator. They didn't speak a word on the ascent.

Entering Basayev's room, she took one look and said, "Drop the bag."

Basayev stared into her emerald eyes, studied the flowing raven locks, gauged her lithe frame, and came back to the eyes. He nodded and dropped the bag in the foyer of his luxury room. She clasped his hand and said, "Follow me."

They left her room and reentered the elevator. She held a fob against the reader on the panel of floor numbers and pressed "PH."

After a rapid climb, the elevator stopped, the doors opened, and two guards said, "Good evening, Miss Moreau."

She smiled and nodded. "Good evening, Jacques, Henri. You gentlemen may take the rest of the evening off."

The two men departed and Nina led Basayev by the hand to the balcony, which provided a spectacular view of the Côte d'Azur and town of Saint-Maxime across the Mediterranean Sea. On a small table was a bottle of Goût de Diamants, which Basayev knew was most likely the most expensive champagne in the world.

"*Ma mère était une Chapuy d'Oger,*" she said. Her French accent was smooth and buttery. "*Ne crois pas que je vais acheter ces bouteilles. J'en obtiens deux par an.*"

My mother was a Chapuy from Oger. Don't think I buy these. I get two bottles a year.

"At a million euros a bottle, that's a good trust fund," Basayev said.

"Please," she said, switching to English. "I drink the champagne, but make my own money."

Basayev nodded in admiration. "I've learned that nothing in life is free, especially unearned money."

He removed the bottle from her hands, popped the cork, and poured the fizzing champagne into the two glasses.

"You are correct, sir. And before we drink. Your name?"

"Khasan Basayev." He raised his glass.

"Nina Moreau."

"And your occupation, Miss Moreau?" he asked.

"I think you know, but I fight . . . for what is right," she said. "And you?"

"I fight," he said, paused, and then finished, "to live."

"*Battre pour vivre,*" she toasted. *Fight to live.*

They clinked glasses, looking each other in the eyes, and took long sips from the crystal stemware.

She placed her glass on the table. He looked above her head at the sea, heard the waves crashing into the shore, and felt his heart, for once, open like a flower sensing spring.

"I think we are in the same business," she whispered, as if sensing his reluctance.

"Are we?" he asked. "If so, perhaps we could combine our talents for the biggest payday of all."

From that night, he and Nina had become both lovers and business partners. To get to Savannah, she said, required them to first go through Afghanistan. She had intelligence on a sex-slave operation that her French DGSE handlers required her to investigate.

His entry to Afghanistan had been as a businessman wearing the very same suit he had worn last night in the elevator with Harwood. Over the course of his first month in country he had established his bona fides as a banker and wealth manager, which was a growth industry in the prosperous upper crust of Kabul. In preparation for one business meeting he had flown in Nina as his business associate. Nina had proven to be resourceful in her ability not only to travel, but to disguise herself. While her features were dark, she sometimes chose to wear the burqa, which had proven useful in smuggling certain supplies. This versatility allowed her to appear at one moment a businesswoman and the next a submissive Afghan woman following the directives of her husband.

After riding from Kabul to Kandahar, Basayev proposed in the middle of the barren landscape that would be their home for the next few days. Nina smiled and said, "Yes." A local Taliban imam married them in the town of Panjwai on the Arghandab River, known for its pomegranates and grapes. They were wed in the arboretum surrounded by a Taliban warlord's vineyards, where he produced grapes and raisins for export along with the occasional bootleg case of wine, strictly against the law. The warlord, Nazim Ghul, was Basayev's main employer, as well. At the wedding, Nina was dressed in customary Afghan tribal regalia while Basayev wore a different suit. They honeymooned in the mountains near Tarin Kowt, him finding a happiness he never believed possible and believing that she was content, as well. There they sighted six of the eleven species of hawks found in Afghanistan. The lesser and common kestrel, the rare Amur falcon, the merlin, the peregrine, and the prize of them all, the gyrfalcon.

"En général, les oiseaux nous aident à rêver. Cependant, les faucons permettent à nos rêves de

s'envoler," Nina whispered in his ear one dewy morning in the middle of the valley. A hawk soared above them like a black cross gliding in circles.

Birds in general help us dream. Falcons make our dreams take flight.

"Ils soulèvent nos âmes à chaque fois qu'ils s'envolent, parce que nous aussi, nous pensons que nous sommes dans les airs avec eux," he replied.

They lift our souls every time they fly, because we believe that we, too, are up there with them.

"Oui," she said softly. Her voice was like velvet. And her words were inspirational to an earthbound infantryman like him. He had never thought about it before, but ever since she had made that observation, his spirit soared just a bit each time he saw a bird, especially a falcon, in flight.

They left the Arghandab River valley and moved by camel to Sangin, where he would begin his mission as part of Ghul's opium protection force in the Helmand River valley. There had never been a question of whether Nina would come; he always knew she would and frankly he wanted her there with him. She was, after all, a trained French DGSE agent who could shoot a rifle nearly as well as he could. Her legend was as a nurse, whose duties she could perform also. As he departed for the mission three months ago in the foothills of the mountains of northern Helmand Province, she had stayed in Sangin in a small hut Guhl had provided them.

"Come back to me, Khasan," she had said. "Come to me." She had given him a small medallion of an Amur falcon. "For you," she said. "The Amur is only here temporarily. It migrates from China to Africa every year, passing through Afghanistan on each trip. That's what I'm asking you to do. Be like the Amur. We are only here temporarily, passing through. When you are done, we will leave and grow our family."

"I will," Basayev said. "I promise. Be here when I return and we will do as you say, Nina."

Nina had used her sniper rifle to cover his movement out of the village. He had driven his pickup truck, loaded with his rifle and rucksack, determined to kill Vick Harwood, the man they called the Reaper. The dossier his employer had given Basayev detailed Harwood's personal life, his operating style, and his crimes against humanity. The information indicated that Harwood had killed over two dozen high-level enemy commanders, which Basayev couldn't care less about. But what interested him was that during Harwood's two and a half months on the ground, nearly twenty women had gone missing, suspected kidnappings, each on a day that Harwood had killed a Taliban commander. The link analysis conducted by the Taliban intelligence officer who built the dossier indicated that each of the women was in some way connected to Harwood's kills, that in fact Harwood was operating off a kill sheet to eliminate the tribal elders and family patriarchs so that these women—*young* women, from fifteen to twenty-five—were made vulnerable and ripe for kidnap teams.

That—and the money—was enough to motivate Basayev to quickly kill Harwood and return to Nina. But as he waited in his lair to kill the Reaper, he had received an alert on his secure satellite phone from one of Ghul's lieutenants that the three pickup trucks were steaming toward Sangin. He had watched helplessly as the kidnap unfolded before him in the valley below—less than a mile away, but an eternity in the Afghan terrain. He had known that he was being watched by Harwood and that if he left his position he stood no chance of rescuing Nina even if he was able to reach the village before the kidnap team retreated. He had been trapped.

Nina had been kidnapped on his watch. He had wondered if he would ever see her again.

Then the Instagram photo tag had come a week ago. In the image an Amur falcon was soaring high above the Savannah skyline, free. *Free as a bird*, as the saying went. The picture had a sign with a name and he knew that the game was afoot. The large payday was within reach. He only needed to leave a package behind and had done so. Until yesterday, he had no idea whether it had been retrieved.

Basayev snapped out of his reverie when he felt the tear sliding along his face. *Nina*. He thumbed the Amur falcon on the silver chain. His sorrow quickly gave way to anticipation.

He walked over to his laptop, checked the tracking device he had slipped into Harwood's rucksack in the elevator as the man had exited the yawning doors. Punching the trackpad, he saw the map pop up and scan west, stopping in the middle of Georgia, showing a blue dot speeding along Interstate 76. Apparently, the Reaper had hitched a ride. He was proving to be a resourceful infantryman.

But still, the Chechen believed his skills to be superior to the Reaper's. Case in point, he could have kidnapped him last night, but did not want to give up his cover just yet. Knowing that police would be descend-

de the convenience store. It was about time to
 own wheels so that he could take charge of
situation. Stop the spiral.

d from between the two tractors and bounced
 pavement. Dark shades of gray preceded
 as he jogged away from the filling station.
d hooked a left into a neighborhood filled with
950s-era brick homes that had devolved into
lum, crack, or vacant housing. Most likely a
ation of all three. Yards were overgrown with
ree feet high. Rusty chain-link fences framed
ot. Some homes were shuttered and boarded
 in expectation of a hurricane. Lights flickered
 the windows of a few homes. Mostly, though,
ses appeared as if they were uninhabited. Five
 in on the left side of the road was a house with
 windows, no lights, no car in the oil-stained
ay, and absolutely no sign of life. He jogged up
carport, found a dark recess, and was motion-
eathing hard, pulling in oxygen, refreshing his
 It was all about the basics. Physical condition-
always been important to Harwood and he had
ushing himself through rehab. Physical rehab
er been the issue; that would come. It was the
ogical piece that confounded him.

is heart rate steadied, a sense of control began
his logic train. Break into this apparently aban-
ouse and wait for darkness. Steal a car and get to
 The Google report had mentioned a Barnes &
 Buckhead where Jackie was supposed to have
. He could find that, maybe find her manager at
 hotel, and work from there.

ood slid deeper into the carport, found that

ing on Savannah quickly, Basayev wanted to give Harwood running rope. The chase was important.

The sound of pounding on the door, as if with the butt of a hand, boomed in the hotel room. Basayev walked over, peeked through the hole, then opened the door, and Samuelson brushed past him.

"I g-got his stuff just in time," Samuelson said, holding Harwood's duffel bag and shaving kit. "And I didn't kill him, like you asked. Even though he left me for dead."

Samuelson spit out the words "left me for dead" as if they were foul-tasting food.

"Good work, Abrek. Yes, we will kill him, for you, but not yet. He needs to lead us to Nina."

That was the indoctrination narrative. Harwood had to stay alive until they found Nina. Every day for the last three months Basayev had been planning and prepping the mission while brainwashing Samuelson that Harwood had intentionally left him for dead. During physical training and shooting drills in Kandahar, he had also taught Samuelson breathing exercises to minimize the distracting stutter.

"He's just west of a town called Statesboro. He found a ride," Basayev said. "Probably headed to Atlanta."

Samuelson looked at him and nodded.

"To link up with J-Jackie?" Samuelson asked.

"That's what I'm hoping. She is key to the entire operation," Basayev replied.

He placed a hand on Samuelson's shoulder, thinking he didn't want to kill the young man yet, but that day would come. The months of indoctrination had created a faux bond between Samuelson and Basayev.

"You did well," Basayev said.

Samuelson smiled, a distant look in his eyes.

"We will save Nina," Samuelson said.

"Yes, Abrek. The Reaper kidnapped her."

Basayev walked out of the hotel room with his own duffel bag and suitcase. Samuelson followed, carrying a small gym bag. Basayev had found a used car lot, purchased a Hummer H2 with cash, the king of all languages, and parked it two blocks away from the hotel. They walked through the misty streets, fog rolling off the river like dry ice at a rock concert. He cranked the Hummer, pushed the button placing it into gear, snapped his smartphone with tracking device into its cradle, and sped out of the parking lot toward Statesboro.

"Rifle loaded?" Basayev asked.

"Always," Samuelson replied.

CHAPTER 1

Harwood had managed to find two ride with a trucker, who seemed o thing except texting with his girlfrie miles. They drove through some thr the first chance Harwood ditched t a few hours in the woods behind he found a second ride on the bac trailer driven by a group of Hispa little English. He wedged himself ing lawnmowers and lay down, rear wheels of the tractors. Despi the rattle of rakes, chain saws, a Harwood managed to fall asleep didn't know, but based on the l was maybe an hour, two at the m

He awoke when the vehicle sl heard the rapid-fire talking of th sign for a popular gas station loc of the men was filling up the g

went ins
snare hi
his own
He s
onto th
nightfa
Harwo
small
either
combi
grass t
every
up, as
beyon
the ho
house
board
drivev
to the
less, b
system
ing ha
been
had ne
psycho
As
to feed
doned
Atlanta
Noble i
appeare
a nearb
Har

the storm door was hanging by one hinge. He used his Leatherman to remove the remaining hinge and set the door aside, leaning it against the brick exterior. The wooden door was chipped and peeling paint where he pressed his shoulder into it. He slid the Leatherman's knife blade between the latch and the jamb and fractionally opened the door. He leaned back against the brick wall and used his hand and wrist to flip the door backward, opening it to a ratty kitchen floor. Leading with his Beretta pistol, he entered the barren kitchen and moved swiftly to the dining and living room area, which was also empty. The house smelled of urine, fried food, and mold. Someone had used the house recently. There was no furniture. The windows were boarded with plywood, but dull gray twilight seeped around the poorly aligned edges, allowing him to visually inspect the premises.

Taking long strides down the narrow hallway, he cleared the one bathroom, which had dry brown water stains on the floor and cracked plaster falling from the ceiling. Visions of dead bodies in the tub danced in his mind, but he shuttered them with newfound purpose. Flashes of clearing a house in Kandahar or Baghdad or some nameless village in Syria popped like lightning strikes, leaving behind the photonegative image, but he shunted those, too, and forged ahead.

Keeping his back to the door, he slid into the hall, thinking he heard a noise coming from the back bedroom. The hallway was like a spine, bathroom and bedroom on the right-hand side and one bedroom on the left-hand side. Harwood slid along the wall to the nearest door, spun into it, and found some old gray blankets scattered on the floor along with some water bottles. The closet doors were missing and there was a rumpled sleeping bag running the length of the closet.

He had happened into a transient homeless shelter. Moving to the interior wall, he trained his listening skills on the far room. Deep breaths. And whispering.

Two people. Or one person talking to himself? But he could make out two distinct octaves. A conversation going back and forth.

Moving into the hallway, Harwood lifted his pistol and spun through the last door on the left. Two children and an elderly man sat huddled in the corner. They were on a blanket, water bottles scattered around them. He kept his pistol trained away as he visually inspected them. No weapons, just the unmistakable detritus of squalor. The children were maybe twelve years old, malnourished. The elderly man looked over eighty, bright white hair contrasting with his dark skin and wizened face. He held the two children with long thin arms as if protecting them under his wings.

"We ain't got nothing to give you, son," the man said. "'Cept maybe a bottle of water."

Harwood glanced at the closet, which had two doors closed tight. He looked back at the man and said, "Anyone in the closet?"

After a pause, the man said, "Now you come in here with a handgun scaring my grandchildren and start asking *me* questions?"

"I'll take that as a yes," Harwood said as he instinctively moved against the far wall that was opposite the hallway. "You don't look like the lying type, so just tell me what's on the other side of that door, please."

He was looking at two solid panel doors that were in much better repair than anything else he had seen in the house. New hinges on both sides at all four points: top right, bottom right, top left, and bottom left. The door fit flush at every angle and joint. Harwood remembered the long hallway and the two rooms on the right and just the one on the left. Could this set of doors lead to another room?

He caught the children staring at the doors when he glanced quickly in their direction. The looks on their faces were practically screaming *"Please don't look in there!"* Harwood had no interest in any of this now other than his personal safety. He was in the house, which he originally saw as a sanctuary, but which now contained a possible threat.

"From one brother to another," the grandfather said. "Please don't go in there. You look like you might be law enforcement. And you're right, I don't lie, particularly in front of my grandchildren. So, whatever your purpose here is, we have no quarrel with you, nor you with us. I kindly ask you to leave us alone."

Before Harwood could respond, the doors opened. He lifted his pistol in pure combat mode, crouching into a shooter's stance. A young man stepped toward him, maybe close to his age, wearing a Falcons jersey, cargo pants, and high-top white sneakers.

And aiming a pistol at him.

"We could both just shoot each other right here, homes," the young man said.

"Jermaine, don't do this," the grandfather said.

"I got this, Pops," he said. "Whatchu doin' here? This is our turf, dude."

"Honestly," Harwood said, lowering his pistol just a bit, trying to indicate he wasn't a threat. "I was just looking for a place to crash. Question is, what are you doing hiding in that closet and using kids and your grandfather as a human shield?"

"Not doing that," Jermaine said. His inflection of cockiness dropped a note. Beyond Jermaine was an entire room filled with televisions, smartphones, and computers, all still in the box. This was a fence house for stolen goods. There were four single beds with fresh linens. The grandfather and children were props, buffers, which pissed off Harwood. He'd seen enough abuse and misuse of children in his foster youth that this situation triggered immediate anger.

"Exactly what you're doing, Jermaine," Harwood said. He lifted the pistol back up, aiming it at the thief. "Whatever operation you're running here, don't involve the kids in it. Grandpa? He can make up his own mind. But not the kids."

"I know who you are, Reaper," Jermaine said. "Stared at you through the crack in the door. I follow Black Lives Matter every day. Twitter feed. Facebook. You name it. You can judge me as a gangbanger or whatever, but I do what I have to do to provide." He held up a smartphone, indicating his source of information. "So, here you are. A hero to the movement. And you're threatening me?"

"Not threatening you. Just disapprove of kids being used."

Only seeking temporary respite until he could get to Atlanta, he was now oddly confronted with the might-have-been version of himself. Was there a way to turn this situation to everyone's advantage? "We're on the same team here," Harwood said.

"Are we?" Jermaine shot back. His knuckles tightened around the grip of the gun, which Harwood saw was a Ruger American Pistol, noting its Picatinny rail and dual magazine release. It was a good nine-millimeter weapon that had set Jermaine back some coin. Between the product in the back room, the smartphone and social media capabilities, and the up-scale armament, it was obvious Jermaine had a net-work. Networks could be useful. They could also be loose-lipped liabilities.

"Yes. I see what you've got here. I'm not judging. Kids and the elderly need protecting, not the other way around. I'm no threat to you. Maybe we could help each other."

"Cops are all over your ass. No threat to me? Us? They could come busting in here any minute," Jermaine said.

"Give me some credit. I wasn't followed."

"Police around here ain't what I'm worried about. You must not be following social media. People track-ing you everywhere. I give us five minutes before you get us busted." He paused, looked at his kids and grandfather, and said, "We're going to do this. I'm go-ing to wand your ass for microbugs and then we're go-ing to sneak out the back and . . ."

The unmistakable sound of helicopter blades snapped through the air in forward pitch, pushing the aircraft at high speed toward a known destination.

"Yeah, we're done here," Jermaine said. "Follow me."

Harwood followed Jermaine through the two "closet" doors into a room filled with boxed goods and a single computer and monitor, which showed an eBay auction for a fifty-five-inch LG flat-screen televi-sion, probably the one he nearly tripped over as they fled into the backyard. They scurried beneath a cordon of oak trees into a vacant lot where a black Dodge Challenger waited. The eBay business must be decent, Harwood thought. Jermaine punched the remote; no lights flashed, but he heard the door locks snick open.

"I'm getting you and whatever tracking device you're wearing to a safe place. And then I'm going to redirect social media away from you. Ain't cool what you did coming in there and threatening me and my family. Those are my kids. We struggling. Ain't proud of what I'm doing, but I'm doing. Know what I mean?"

Jermaine started the car. Harwood held his rucksack in his lap in case he needed to open the door and do a barrel roll out at high speed.

"Roger," Harwood said.

"Roger? My name's Jermaine. Ain't no Roger. We're going a mile. I'm stripping your ass down. We find the bug and then I'm taking you somewhere else."

"Hadn't thought about a tracker. Have some memory lapses from Afghanistan. So, I apologize if your family felt threatened."

Jermaine paused. "No need. Never apologize. You're doing what you need to do. I read your background on Wikipedia. You and me, we're not too far apart. I'd probably be a sniper or some shit if I'd joined the army. Now, me? I'm capping people who need it here in the U.S. You? You're capping people who need it somewhere else."

Harwood didn't necessarily agree with the "capping" logic, but Jermaine's predicament did resonate with him as he had previously thought. The young man was a father and a son and Harwood wished he could help him find a legal path to providing for his family.

After ten minutes, Jermaine fishtailed into a vacant lot somewhere in east Macon near Interstate 16. Harwood had been getting his bearings and now he knew exactly where he was.

"City Park," Jermaine said.

"About an hour up to Atlanta. Give me a ride?"

"Ain't no Uber here, Reaper man. First things first," Jermaine said.

Harwood stepped out of the car and set his rucksack on the gravel of the parking lot. In the distance the helicopter blades sliced the night sky. Jermaine came around the corner holding something in his hand. For a brief second, Harwood thought it might be a pistol and began to reach for his own, but stopped when he saw he was holding a small multichannel bug detector with two stub antennae. He began moving the device slowly around Harwood and then the rucksack, where it immediately alighted on the lower back left rear pocket.

"Bingo," Jermaine said.

Harwood reached his hand into the pocket and found a small, circular black tracking device that looked like a coin. It was magnetic and had attached itself to a spare knife that Harwood carried in the back of his ruck.

"Don't throw it away. Let's go," Jermaine said.

Harwood knew what the play was, but couldn't go through with it if it meant putting innocent lives at risk. Placing this device on another car could jeopardize the safety of people riding in the car. A train rumbled in the distance, the tracks thirty yards to his front. The Ocmulgee River flowed just beyond.

"I've got an idea," Harwood said. "What do you have in your trunk?"

Wasting no time, Jermaine popped his trunk, which was filled with more brand-new items, including a box of GoPros, chest and surfboard mounts, and backdoor flotation devices.

Harwood grabbed his ruck and jogged to the river, picked his way through the slight wood line, found the bank where the eerie glow of the industrial lighting above highlighted the dark brown river. The water rolled south toward Savannah and he figured this was his best option. He looked up. The rotor wash of a helicopter and roar of a train competed for the night's attention.

He stepped into the murky river and hoped for the best.

CHAPTER 14

Ramsey Xanadu leaned outside of the fifteen-million-dollar black Sikorsky S-97 Raider prototype helicopter that his boss General Buzz Markham had secured for their stateside operations.

The wind slipped effortlessly across his shaved head as he searched the horizon with night vision goggles, looking for a pulsing infrared beacon on the tracking device Basayev had placed in the Reaper's rucksack. Xanadu had been able to hack the Chechen's primitive device, realizing it might not have been a coincidence that he had gained access so easily.

After receiving the call from Markham, which was essentially an order to kill Vick Harwood, Xanadu had directed the Raider into operation from Hunter Army Airfield, where the private military contracting company MLQM leased space for its air fleet. The advanced blade concept aircraft created a lower audible signature than most other helicopters and provided a more stable firing platform from the rear cargo hatch.

The sleek, angular design was perfect for slipping quietly through the night—the proverbial black helicopter—on clandestine missions.

The pilots, both MLQM employees, were homing in on the tracking device, where Xanadu would take the easy shot on an unsuspecting Harwood. They buzzed along the Ocmulgee River, a feeder to the Savannah River. The pilots kept low, between the trees, which also helped with deadening the noise beyond the sparsely populated river basin.

Xanadu thought about the Reaper, his interactions with him in Afghanistan and Iraq, and how he was now chasing him in the United States, of all places, the three-million-dollar bonus sufficient incentive. He had a nice home on Edisto Island and a condo above one of the more popular nightclubs in the Battery of Charleston. He scored easily in the Charleston pickup scene and enjoyed the escape to the ocean. He wanted a larger boat, which usually impressed the types of women he was pursuing. Not looking for anything but casual sex, Xanadu spent a great deal of time honing his body in the gym, pumping iron, climbing ropes, and boxing. He had modeled for a few romance-novel covers because his six-pack was really an eight-pack. And while he was desirable to men and women, Xanadu had a temper. Hauled in three times for beating women, he had a record as a domestic abuser, which, when coupled with his financial misdeeds, had ultimately resulted in his dismissal from the CIA. For a short period, he was disappointed, but then MLQM called him seeking a man with his skill set. He was an expert marksman with everything from a pistol to a fifty-caliber Garand to an eighty-one-millimeter mortar. Xanadu had been the consummate infantryman to special operator, which included an ability to make radios, computers, and cell phones perform in the most austere conditions.

He had led teams of three to four men in Iraq and Afghanistan in efforts to secure MLQM's forward operating and logistics bases. Believing in active patrols as opposed to static defenses, Xanadu used his Hispanic/Persian heritage—though he was born and raised in Pittsburgh, Pennsylvania—to blend with the local populations in Iraq and Afghanistan. His Persian mother had taught him both Arabic and Farsi, which came in handy in the two U.S. combat zones.

His father had beat his mother, so he had learned that habit from his dad, though one day he had come home and his mother was aiming a pistol at his father, smoke wafting from the barrel, his dad dead on the floor. She had trained the pistol on him, and Xanadu had backed away and left, never to see his mother again. His take-away: If you're going to beat women, don't let them hang around long enough for them to shoot you.

When the alarm beeped that they had a signal on the tracking device, he chambered a belt of 7.62 mm linked ammunition in the minigun mounted on a gyro-stabilized firing platform on the starboard side of the aircraft. The platform was similar to the stabilized fire control system of an Abrams tank, which could be driving forty miles per hour along the bumpy desert but giving the gunner a solid, stable view of its target.

As the helicopter slowed, Xanadu looked through his night vision goggles. The ping from the tracking device was coming from the west bank of the river, which put him on the wrong side.

"Go past and loop around," Xanadu said into his headset to pilot Stu Benton.

"Roger, that's the plan."

The pilots kept low and powered forward for another half mile, then lifted above the trees, the lights of Macon blinding Xanadu's night vision goggles momentarily. They lowered back into the riverbed and now had the machine gun aiming to the west as the helicopter flew south, coincident with the river.

"Up ahead four hundred meters," Benton said.

"Roger that. I'm ready. Once I'm done, we keep flying. Pedal to the metal. Understand?"

"You got it."

The audible ping increased in speed as they got closer to the tracking device. Through his goggles, the infrared beacon flashed brightly every few seconds.

Xanadu drew a bead on Harwood and began to aim, realizing he probably had one chance to kill the sniper this easily.

Tightening his grip on the trigger housing, he fired. The miniguns spat a fusillade of lead that raked the water.

Basayev, the Chechen, drove the Land Rover as if it were a European sports car. Samuelson was hanging on to the grab handles with white knuckles. Basayev powered along Interstate 16 at ninety miles per hour, not caring if any cops were tracking him. In the passenger seat, Samuelson stared blankly out of the window.

Basayev's meeting with a man named Xanadu in a Sangin safe house had confirmed for him that Harwood, the Reaper, was at the helm of a sex-slave ring operated out of Kandahar using blacked-out airplanes at night. Xanadu had told Basayev that his mission was to capture the Reaper and find all the missing women, to include Nina, who he assured him was still alive. Basayev and Xanadu knew they could not openly work together, but they could use cutouts and open-source technology when it made sense, as in the case of the tracking device Basayev bought at RadioShack.

The device was emitting a strong signal as they approached from a few miles away.

"It's right there," Samuelson said, pointing at the iPhone. It displayed a map of Macon, the river, and the road on which they were traveling. With each flash of the tracking device, the red dot moved fractionally downriver, as if Harwood were floating. It would be a moving target, but he had always been superb at picking off those. He looked up at Samuelson, whose stony-eyed gaze was distant, as if the young man was having a flashback.

"Find anything good in Harwood's bag?" Basayev asked Samuelson.

"N-Not really," Samuelson stuttered. While nursing the young man back to health, Basayev had thoroughly indoctrinated Samuelson; though there was always the chance that the spotter's memory could come rushing back. Basayev needed to finish his mission before that happened.

"So that means he's got all of his equipment still. We need to be careful. Do you understand me, Abrek?"

"Careful," Samuelson said. "Yes."

Letting him pick up Harwood had been a calculated risk. How much would he remember? Would seeing Harwood live and up close trigger a memory that would give up Basayev and his plan? It was a testament to

Basayev's skills at brainwashing that Samuelson had returned to him, mission accomplished.

"The beacon's just across the river," Samuelson said.

"I see a good spot over here. Let's park there and look," Basayev said. He pulled off Interstate 16, made a left underneath the highway, passed a couple of gas stations, and found a small access road that led to the river. Parking along a gravel turnout, he had a clear view across the river and into the park.

"Okay, let's get set up," Basayev said. A helicopter whooshed through the middle of the river moving from south to north, pulled up, banked, and then slid over them in a hovering crawl south. Basayev didn't know if this was a police helicopter or perhaps even something Xanadu was orchestrating. Many people wanted the Reaper killed or captured, depending on who was doing the killing or capturing.

The noise dissipated as the helicopter crabbed downriver. They dismounted from the Hummer and found a spot with clear observation across the river. "Okay, the ping is coming from that direction," Basayev said, pointing to the south. "Spot for me."

Samuelson lay on the ground and sighted through his infrared spotting scope, and immediately told Basayev he noticed the bright flash of white.

"There," Samuelson said. "It's f-flashing and moving slowly downriver. About fifty meters. Just sort of d-drifting away. Want me to call out to him? He can just swim to us."

Basayev looked through his own scope and found the flash, but something didn't seem quite right. He internalized his thoughts. Could this be a diversion?

If the tracker was going south, was Harwood going north? Or was the tracker still on Harwood as he floated downriver? It was impossible to tell. The thermal scope did not show a warm body mass connected to the tracker, but the cool river water could be blocking the thermal signature of Harwood's body. It would be a sign of excellent tradecraft if this was Harwood's play. To confirm his normally solid instincts, Basayev said, "Keep an eye on the tracker. I'm checking something out."

He stood and leaned across the warm hood of his Hummer. Staring through the thermal scope, he switched from hot white to hot black and back to hot white, checking to see which thermal mode worked best with the ambient backlighting from streetlights and automobile headlights.

On one sweep of the scope, Basayev saw a figure with a rucksack running beneath a bridge north of Central City Park. There were too many trees and structures to be certain, but his gut told him that it was Harwood.

"Reaper," he whispered. "I've got you on the run."

For Basayev, that was good enough for now.

CHAPTER 15

Harwood had put the tracking device on a GoPro mount attached to an orange flotation device from Jermaine's stash of pirated goods.

He had tossed the device into the south-flowing river and run north. A helicopter was sliding quietly through the night. It wasn't a Black Hawk; he knew that sound well from many combat missions. These rotors were like whispers compared with the Black Hawk's thundering report. He was huddled against the back of a bridge that abutted the Ocmulgee River. The helicopter cycled north of him and then turned south, presumably following the floating beacon. Of course, that meant it wouldn't be long before his pursuers figured out that it was just that, a GoPro floaty with the tracker on it.

A truck across the river rumbled as it skidded to a halt. Doors opened and closed. Voices echoed across the water. With all this activity, it was time to move. He stood and began jogging north along an asphalt trail.

Harwood wondered, who was framing him, and why?

As he jogged, he didn't want to think about the un-thinkable: Had he actually committed the shootings? That thought, like a penny dropped in a large cone, began to circle slowly toward the abyss of his mind, the black hole of memory. He was unable to reach in there and find what he was looking for. Was it the pos-sibly spiked sports drinks? Or had the mortar attack dislodged something, shaken his brain, and kept him from stringing together the logic in events? He was trying his best to find a guidepost or grounding around which he could stabilize his freefall. After running a good mile to the north along the riverfront, he was in downtown Macon running along Dempsey Park, having turned to the west.

He emerged into a clearing populated with hun-dreds of people. They were all facing a stage with spotlights. The scene reminded him of a football-game tailgate party. He stumbled through a parking lot, recognizing a sports car and a dark-haired woman. A group of rowdies started yelling before he could connect the dots. He kept moving around the back side of the throng, headed to the far wood line. A voice echoed over a loudspeaker system, talking about a new tomorrow and how the establishment politicians were stemming the tide of technology such as artifi-cial intelligence and driverless cars.

"And we should be able to buy a car directly from the manufacturer without having to go to a dealer!" the politician shouted, to the resounding applause of his hundreds of supporters.

"It's time to take back America from those who have stolen it from us, those who husband the power like it is theirs alone; and only issue out bits and morsels while they fly around in their private jets and sail along in their sleek yachts!"

More applause. The Reaper took a knee, winded. His memory reeling. Where had he seen this man before? He was a politician. Perhaps a visit in Afghanistan? Politicians were always coming there to "touch the magic," as they called it.

The penny in the cone began to spiral more rapidly. The crowd was in a frenzy. Harwood backed away and knelt in an isolated area apart from the crowd. Then, he unshouldered his rucksack.

The sniper felt fortunate to have been in position to take the shot on the former CEO of a major soft-drink manufacturer turned politician. Here the man was talking to a group of about five hundred people, peddling lies and bullshit.

The sniper didn't care, because this man's background was unimpressive. What was more, the sniper knew things about this man that no one else did. Julian Assange and Anonymous were probably better hackers than the sniper, but not by much.

The politician's name was Senator Tyler Kraft, a man born with a silver spoon in his mouth and one who had never done an honest day's work in his life. He had been placed in a high-level position at his father's soft-drink company and then migrated to the CEO position by pure gravitational force. The U.S. Senate was a downgrade in pay, but an upgrade in power. The sniper guessed that when Kraft breathed, a mirror somewhere fogged up and that made him qualified for the job.

The sniper had to take these opportunities when

they presented themselves. The kill sheet included just ten names, and the sniper had killed four so far. The fifth was about to be added to the list. There was no order in which they needed to be killed; the only requirement was that they wind up dead.

With a full FBI manhunt on the trail of the Reaper, the sniper knew that the leaders of MLQM were also probably hot on the Reaper's trail, too. There was a thin veneer between what they had been doing in Afghanistan and Iraq and what people believed they were doing.

The sniper lined up the crosshairs from a kneeling position, one of the more difficult sniper shot positions. Nonetheless, the sniper drew a solid bead on the head of the politician. Dark hair with flecks of gray shone in the spotlighted stage. Shirtsleeves rolled up to show he was a man of the people. Khaki pants and loafers to speak to the preppie, regular-guy crowd as well as to soccer moms. MLQM owned him and that was all the sniper needed to know.

The sniper's index finger began a light tug on the trigger. The sight picture held steady. The man was standing at the microphone motionless as the trigger spring collapsed, the 7.62 mm match round cut through the humid night air, the sound suppressor no more than coughed, and Senator Tyler Kraft's head exploded as he tumbled backward into a small rock band that had been playing "Eye of the Tiger."

The sniper liked that song and was sorry that it had to end, but then again, everything had to at one time or another.

CHAPTER 16

FBI Special Agent Deke Bronson looked at the map on the fifty-five-inch HD monitor inside the Hunter Army Airfield makeshift command post and said to Faye Wilde, "Given all the local intersections here, can you get the police chief on his way in, please?"

"I already gave him a heads-up. Should be here in a few minutes."

Bronson smiled and shook his head. "What was that helicopter that took off about an hour ago from the other side of the airfield?"

"Saw that. I inquired. No flight plan. Probably a Ranger training mission."

"No. First of all," Bronson said, "the army doesn't do single-aircraft missions. Remember that *Top Gun* movie where Iceman says, 'Never, ever leave your wingman'?"

"Not really. All I remember is the white T-shirts and the volleyball scene." She smirked.

"Okay, well follow up on that heli—"

Before he could finish his thought, Wilde's phone dinged again. She pushed her chair back and stood. "Oh my God. That politician. The soft-drink guy. Kraft."

Bronson looked at her and knew before he asked. "Dead?"

"Sniper bullet to the head during a campaign rally. Just now."

"Location?" Bronson asked.

"Macon, just west of Statesboro. Man, this has got to be our guy," Wilde said.

"Maybe," Corent chimed in. "We've got Harwood and Colt as potentials. Remember, she can shoot."

"She's also an Olympic champion with her own sports drink and about to be on a Wheaties box. But, okay. Five dead now in less than seventy-two hours. I agree, we've got to consider everyone," Bronson said.

"Really about forty-eight. This is going to break huge on the national news in about fifteen minutes. Kraft was a huge deal in Georgia. Kind of a moron but his political party loved him for some reason," Wilde said. She flipped her hair behind her ears, exposing the freckles on her cheeks.

"Moron is right," said a new voice. It was the police chief. He was a beefy, tall man who could have been a defensive end for the University of Georgia back in his day. But he had gone soft. Pink jowls hung like a bulldog's above a fleshy throat. Four stars sat on each shoulder epaulet of his navy-blue uniform. He spoke with a deep baritone voice that commanded respect. "But he was my moron, so we'll have some respect, please."

"Sorry, Chief. We're all a little punch-drunk," Bronson said.

"Well then, don't drive," he joked. "I've got two nuggets for y'all, but first, I'd like to know why this pretty lady called me down here."

"Special Agent Wilde did so at my request," Bronson said. "We just wanted to keep you up to date given that there's so much happening in your city."

"I'm Chief Frank Harvey, by the way. We lost two men yesterday. I thought they were good men, but I'm hearing about this opium. Hard to believe, honestly, but I've been around enough that I reckon nothing should surprise me anymore."

"We're sorry for your loss, Chief."

While the chief was overweight, Bronson thought, he was young to be a police chief. He'd gotten a big promotion somehow. Jumped the line. Maybe he *was* a Georgia football star.

"Thank you. I see you looking at me and my stars wondering how I can be not even forty years old and police chief."

"Well, we work with a lot of police departments. You're probably the youngest chief I've seen," Bronson said.

"No magic to it. Local boy. Played a little football at Georgia Southern. Won a national championship. Served in the infantry for my three years. Came home. Then lucked out and caught them Russian spetsnaz."

"Spetsnaz?"

"Yeah, Russian special forces—"

"I know what spetsnaz are, Chief. You caught them here? Not Afghanistan or overseas?"

"Yeah, here. It was a huge national story. A little disappointed big-leaguers like you guys don't know about it."

"I do," Wilde said. Bronson rolled his eyes and guessed that Wilde had discreetly used her Apple watch to scan the story.

"Two thousand and ten," she said, "you were a lieutenant, three years back from the war. You see four guys walking down the road with shovels and rucksacks. Haul them in and they don't speak English."

"Oh, they spoke English. Just wasn't very good. Two were Russian, one from Kazakhstan, and we never did find the fourth guy. They all sounded like bad actors in an Arnold Schwarzenegger movie and one ran through the woods and escaped. The others we drew down on hard."

"Where was this?" Bronson asked.

"That's the bitch of it," Chief Harvey said. "Apologies, ma'am." He nodded at Wilde, who waved him off. "It was right close to where my two men were murdered."

"What were they doing? Where were they coming from?" Bronson asked.

"Wouldn't say. We scanned the woods all over the place. The shovels had been used. They were sweaty and tired. I found them near their car. It was pulled over on the side of the road. Probably better to say I found the car first, backed off, and let them come to it."

"You're lucky you didn't get in a firefight," Bronson said.

"I had my partner and my assault rifle. No worries there."

"What would four Russians be burying in Savannah, Georgia? Or digging up?" Bronson asked.

"We had a rash of missing-persons cases. We figured

it was dead bodies. Why we sent the cadaver dogs out. The Rangers even joined in the hunt. All the First Battalion guys."

"But no bomb-sniffing dogs?" Wilde asked.

"By the time we got to that point, you feds had taken over," Chief Harvey said. "We drove on with our regular business and then it just faded away."

Bronson nodded. "You said you had two nuggets?"

"Roger that. First, we've got the pictures from the hotel. Got your Reaper. Got your Olympic champion. And got your basic terrorist, we believe."

"Terrorist?"

"We ran everyone's photos past the government's no-fly-list's facial-recognition software. Got a hit on an individual named Khasan Basayev. He's a mercenary."

"I know who Basayev is," Bronson said. "Interpol, everyone, wants this guy."

"Well, he's here in my city. I intend to find him."

"What's the second nugget?"

"The DNA in that red room in General Dillman's house? There's some evidence that there was a woman in there. My team found four pairs of handcuffs in between the mattress and box springs. All had blood. DNA shows young woman—teens—either Pakistani or Afghani descent. And you know about the message etched into the hardwood floor beneath the bed. *Help me.*"

The room fell silent.

Before Bronson could crystallize his thoughts, Wilde's phone rang. It was lying in the middle of the table and it buzzed with an incoming call. The caller ID revealed, "Unknown."

"This is Faye," she answered.

"This is your boss's boss, Faye."

"Hi Director Stein, how are you this evening? You're on speaker by the way with Agents Bronson, White, and Corent and Police Chief Harvey. We're doing interagency coordination."

"Good, because you all need to hear me very clearly. Two dead generals. Two dead police officers. And a dead politician," FBI Deputy Director Stein barked into the phone. "And Chief, sorry for your loss."

"Sir, we've got a plausible theory, multiple persons of interest, and solid leads. We haven't slept for two days and we are pressing ahead at full speed."

"Well find something that goes faster," Stein said. "That politician was a personal friend of the president and vice president and they gave me twenty-four hours to solve this thing."

"And my senator," Chief Harvey said.

"The president? He's getting involved?" Bronson asked.

"No. He's already involved. The call came from him personally," Stein said.

Bronson paused. "Okay. Twenty-four hours. We'll do our best, sir."

"You'll do better than that, Deke. Or you and your task force will be a footnote in history. If you can't solve this one, then what can you solve? We've got an obvious disgruntled veteran who is an expert marksman and is in every one of the exact locations that these murders are taking place. Let's try to remember that these are not random kills. He has a kill sheet. The question is, who is he going after next? If you can't figure that out, you'll all be walking back to Virginia to pack your shit and find another job."

"Sir, I get the veteran thing. But as we were just discussing, it's not that easy—"

Stein cut off Bronson before he could speak any more.

"Then make it that easy." Stein hung up the phone.

Bronson turned to his team and said, "Helicopter. Macon. Now."

"I'll catch you guys later," Chief Harvey said.

Bronson and his team raced through the door, Director Stein's words nipping at their heels.

CHAPTER 17

A throng of people raced directly toward Harwood and then beyond him. Hundreds of attendees at the political rally hurtled past him as if the shooter were still active, capping people as they ran. Perhaps he was, Harwood thought.

Hoisting his rucksack on his shoulder, he began running with the crowd. Shouts and screams of panic permeated the night. After a hundred yards, he veered into the parking lot and found a man with a duffel bag fumbling with his keys.

"Damn it!" the man grumbled. He looked at Harwood, as if he were too incapacitated to find the right key.

"Hey, can I give you a hand?" Harwood asked the man, secretly hoping for a ride. The man was white, about six feet tall, wearing a black windbreaker over blue dungarees, and a long-sleeved shirt beneath the light jacket. The duffel bag was an aviator's kit bag that zipped up the middle.

The man stared at him a moment and said, "Sure, man. Just lift that into the trunk for me. This place is a shitstorm."

He pressed a key fob and the lights to a blue late-model Ford Mustang flashed, as if it were awaiting its owner and ready to race. The trunk popped open and Harwood hefted the bag into the cavity with one arm. It wasn't so much heavy as it was bulky.

"Be careful," the man said. "Important shit, there. Just hurt my arm running through this wild crowd."

People swam past them like a river surging around a rock.

"No problem," Harwood said. He turned to walk away, reconsidering his need for a ride.

"Hey, dude. You want to get out of here in a hurry, this bitch hauls ass."

Harwood stopped, thought, and, knowing that the police in the area were looking for him, accepted the ride. Sitting in the front bucket seat of the Mustang, he kept his rucksack in his lap as they drove. They dodged traffic and the driver seemed to have an agenda to escape the scene just as quickly.

"I'm Lanny," the man said.

"Vick," Harwood responded. Lanny was a stocky man, well built, authoritarian, as if he might have been law enforcement. The driver studied him when he wasn't steering around confused people. Finally, they were on a major road, up on a bridge and crossing the span. Where there was a roadblock setting up. The bridge was chaos. Cars were careening into the bridge railings, but Lanny found a path.

At least four police cars had responded to the shooting and were spinning blue lights as they began to get in position to block all traffic and close off the crime scene.

"Get ready," his driver said. "Hang on."

Lanny sped the Mustang through the incomplete roadblock, getting air as they flew over the apex of the bridge. Wasting no time, he gunned the Mustang to one hundred miles per hour as they raced away. Lanny downshifted the manual transmission and fishtailed onto a dirt road, shut his lights, and sped along what must have been a familiar road, because Lanny was negotiating it like a professional race-car driver.

Lanny had a double-lightning-bolt tattoo on his forearm, and while there was no sound coming from the muted speakers, the digital display showed *Chaos 88,* which was a white-supremacist rock band.

Lanny caught Harwood staring at the radio display and grinned.

"Nothing for you to worry about, boy," Lanny said.

Harwood's hand quietly slid his Blackhawk knife from the outer pouch where he kept it on the right side of his rucksack, which was out of Lanny's view.

"You can drop me off anytime now," Harwood said.

Lanny laughed. "Yeah, right. I got me the Reaper right here in my car. The number-one wanted suspect in all these murders going down. A true *African American.*" Lanny said the last two words with scorn, as if they weren't part of the English language. "A little too close for you to use your sniper rifle on me, dumbass. Plus, I was at that rally to firebomb that bitch, but thanks to you, the sumbitch is dead. He was all about affirmative action and diversity and all that happy horseshit."

The car hurtled along the unlit gravel road to an

unknown destination. Lanny punched a button on his steering wheel, his Bluetooth kicked in, and a phone began to ring. Harwood saw that the name appearing in the dash display read *Stoner*.

"Hey, Lanny, whatcha got?" a voice said, most likely Stoner.

"Stoner man. You ain't going to believe what I've got. I'm almost at the lodge. You pick up the girl?"

Lanny clicked off Bluetooth and held the phone to his ear, driving with one hand. Harwood now couldn't hear Stoner, but Lanny replied with, "What? Damn straight. Keep working her, save some for me. I've got a new plan. By the way, someone else did Kraft for us." He punched off the smartphone and grabbed the steering wheel again with both hands.

Lodge. Five minutes. Harwood calculated that his odds were one on one, right now, especially with Lanny's hands on the steering wheel. Might be two on one in five minutes. Infinity on one any time after five minutes. And there was a woman—a girl—involved somehow.

Keep working her.

He carefully slid the knife into his waistband, freeing his hand to go for his pistol, which he kept in the inner flap of his rucksack. It was a harder grab than the knife, but seemed like the better choice, given his predicament.

Lanny quickly had a pistol aimed at Harwood's face. It was a Sig Sauer Tribal nine millimeter, the same kind that a highly trained former Special Mission Unit operator named Jake Mahegan carried when he and Harwood worked together in Afghanistan. The main difference was that Mahegan was a patriot and a friend and would never turn his pistol on him or any right-living American.

"See your mind working there, Reaper. Don't you know you're the most popular person on television right now?" The word came out *tel-ee-vision*. "All over that Twitter thang and the Facebook. And here you are in the front seat of my car with my pistol *in your face*! Yeah, buddy!" The emphasis on the last few words—"*in your face*"—told Harwood that Lanny might be on some type of amphetamine. He'd seen it before with Afghani, Iraqi, and Syrian fighters chewing qat or spaced out on morphine, one to make them more aggressive, the other to deaden the pain of what they were about to do. Combined, the two were a potent mix that led to polarized swings in personalities.

The car fishtailed, spit gravel, and gunned up a ruddy washboard of a dirt road. In the distance was a cabin with a single light burning inside. If it weren't for the mention of the girl, Harwood would take his chances at bailing from the vehicle, rolling, grabbing his pistol, and coming up shooting, betting that he was a better shot than Lanny.

But the girl. What about her? And what were they doing to her that made Lanny ask Stoner to "save some for me"?

He rode it out to the very end of the driveway with Lanny's pistol pointed at his face across the short expanse from the driver's seat to the passenger's seat. In fact, it was a challenge for Lanny to drive and aim properly at Harwood's face. The pistol was jumping around and Harwood presumed that Lanny would have more than a fifty-fifty chance of missing him even at such a short distance. He braked hard in the driveway, causing Harwood to press into his rucksack that was in his lap. Lanny flung his door wide open and was up and out of the car, saying, "Okay, Reaper man. Get your black ass out of my car."

Harwood left his rucksack in the front seat, because he fully intended to return to it shortly. He removed his hand from his waistband, having just placed a tool of his trade in the tight, stretch material. His physical-training running shirt hung loose over his shorts.

"Leave that pack in the car and follow me," Lanny said, gun pointed with one hand, turned sideways gangster style. A single light shone in the cabin through a window with sheer drapes. One dark shadow was moving back and forth, walking, as if the person was doing something on one side of an object and then doing the same thing on the other side of the object.

"I'm following you," Harwood said. He kept his voice calm and steady, avoiding any provocation before he was ready to act. He needed to see who was inside and then determine the best way to resolve the issue. He had noticed that the Mustang had three-quarters of a tank of fuel, enough to get to Atlanta and find Jackie. His mind was kicking into high gear, combat mode. He liked it. The rush of having a loaded pistol in his face catalyzed something deep inside of him, perhaps even began to dominate whatever was causing his memory loss.

Because at this moment, he remembered his hand-to-hand combat skills, stalking techniques, and close-quarters combat as if he had trained on them yesterday. Adrenaline surged through his veins. Coursing through him were the catalysts that empowered him to think, act, and remember. Previously, he had been stumbling along trying to keep pace with rapidly moving events, figure them out, and react.

React.

That word had never been in his vocabulary. He was proactive. Stalk. Position. Hide. Shoot. Escape. Evade.

The look in Harwood's eyes must have taken on a new measure, one that spoke of his inner strength and training. A countenance that communicated: *Danger.* Lanny's eyes narrowed as Harwood walked toward him, around the front end of the automobile and toward the house.

"That's right, keep walking, boy. Up the steps and remember I've got this gun aimed at the back of that big, nappy head of yours."

Harwood felt Lanny's rhythm behind him. With every step Harwood took, Lanny made a similar step, keeping a safe distance. Harwood could have attacked at any moment, but he had decided he wasn't doing anything until he knew who was inside.

The gun barrel pressed against the back of his skull as he stepped through the threshold of the doorway, pushing the wide pine board door inward. As if he were clearing a room not with a stack of four Rangers, but by himself alone, Harwood checked the hard-left corner: two sofas and a fireplace, but no threat; the diagonal left corner: a kitchen and breakfast nook, but no threat; the diagonal right corner: two twin beds, but no threat.

To his hard-right was the leading edge of the door and the same shadow dancing back and forth around something.

Threat.

"Keep moving," Lanny said, pressing the pistol into the back of his head.

"Lanny, I've just about got her rigged for us," Stoner said. The voice was the same one from the phone call in the car.

Lanny and Stoner.

To Harwood's right was a third person.

She was tied to a four-poster bed naked. A black cloth gag ran through her mouth. She was a light-skinned African American woman, maybe even a girl. Discerning her age was nearly impossible because Stoner had tied her facedown and slid a pillow under her stomach, making her ass lift off the bed, receptive. Her head was facing Harwood, eyes wide with fear and perhaps hope. A new person had entered the cabin, and like her, was perhaps not there of his own volition. He gave an imperceptible nod to her before he lifted his head and fixed his gaze on Stoner.

"What you looking at, boy?" Stoner said. "This fine piece of meat right here?" Stoner was holding a squeeze bottle of K-Y jelly. "You ain't getting none of this. Telling you that much."

Stoner was wearing jeans that hung low around his waist, a T-shirt that said EAT LOCALS, and some type of basic work boots, which most likely had steel toes in them.

"Here's my plan, Stoner. This here is the Reaper. Every TV station in the country has his picture on it. He's wanted for four maybe five murders. I've got his equipment in the car. We use condoms, bust our nut, then kill the bitch, and then act like we almost rescued her and captured the fugitive."

"That's a hell of a plan, Lanny, if you hadn't just

spelled it out for him right here and now. Plus, I don't feel like using no condom. Drill this bitch and dump her ass in the swamp with the gators. Fuck it."

"I say we do it my way," Lanny said, trying to assert some authority over the steadfast Stoner. Lanny was a bigger man than Stoner and could certainly hold his own in a fight. Harwood was going to have to kill both men, or at the very least, incapacitate them. He could still feel the fire flowing through his veins, knew it was adrenaline, but an extra dose that hyperfocused him like a laser on his task at hand. This zone was like stalking prey as a sniper. He stood there, almost feeling invisible because he was seeing the action unfold before him. Something in the back of his mind reminded him that this was the old Vick Harwood, the combat-hardened killer.

The Reaper.

Sensing the pistol barrel in the center of his skull, Harwood listened to Lanny and Stoner argue about who was going to rape the young girl first, not realizing neither of them were going to live long enough to accomplish their bucket-list item. He played the rhythm of their conversation back and forth, like music. Stoner would riff for a few seconds about the brilliance of his plan, then Lanny would say what a genius he was. The more they focused on each other, the closer Harwood came to executing.

But he didn't flinch, because the timing wasn't right just yet. The pistol was beginning to jump with the increased inflection in Lanny's voice, wearing a spot in the back of his hair. He could feel it sliding. Left then right, then left again.

Stoner said, "Fuck this. You do what you want with him. I'm busting my nut."

"You get your DNA in there and you're in prison for the rest of your life!"

When Lanny said "life!" the pistol barrel slid hard to the right, clearing Harwood's skull but maybe not his ear. Lanny was talking with his hands. In a swift hand-to-hand combat move, Harwood dipped his right shoulder, turned his head left, reached up with both hands and controlled Lanny's shooting hand while he shifted his hips sufficiently to give him leverage to flip Lanny over his back onto the floor. During this quick action, he snapped Lanny's wrist with his powerful forearms and swept the pistol into his palm. While his running shoes were not the preferred close-quarters-combat footwear, they did afford him traction as he lowered his right heel into Lanny's windpipe and aimed the Tribal pistol at Stoner.

Unfortunately for Stoner, he had already lowered his jeans around his ankles, so as he tried to rush Harwood, the Reaper had time to lower the pistol, secure his knife, flip the blade open, and slash it across the stumbling Stoner's throat. Stoner fell on top of Lanny as Harwood stepped back to avoid the blood. Some of the spray from Stoner's carotid artery spotted his running shoes. Also, the sharp edge of the knife had nicked the small finger of his right hand, which was bleeding.

He knelt and checked for a pulse on Lanny, who was still wheezing through his collapsed windpipe. With Stoner draped across Lanny's legs, Harwood lifted Lanny's torso enough to brace his back with his knee and then use one hand on the back of the head and one on the chin to snap his neck cleanly. A quick, violent twist, and Lanny was gone.

With both men dead, Harwood moved quickly to the sink, washed his hands, wrapped the cut finger in a paper towel, scrounged and found some black electrical tape to secure it tight. Washing the knife in the sink, he cleaned the blade before he walked over to the twin beds, removed a sheet from the unoccupied bed, and covered the young woman. She was no more than sixteen years old, if that. He quickly cut her ropes and then leaned over as he gently pulled on her shoulders.

"I am on your side. I just killed two men to keep you from being raped. You need to come with me to get away from here and then we can figure out how we get you back to where you belong."

The girl looked him in the eyes.

"I don't belong nowhere, mister. I hook on the internet. This was a job gone bad, that's all. I can take care of myself."

"The internet?"

"Ha. Like you don't know how to find girls like me."

She must have seen the blank look on Harwood's face.

"Gawd. You have no idea, do you? There's websites for men who want to have sex. I was supposed to get four hundred dollars to have sex with both of them. They didn't mention anything about tying me up, though."

She sat up, wrapped the sheet around her tighter.

A simple thank-you would have been sufficient. He said, "They were going to kill you. You understand that, right?"

She turned large brown irises up at him, batting eyelashes, making him wonder if she was even fifteen years old. "Yeah, I heard that. I guess I owe you something." Her hand reached out for him.

He stopped her progress and said, "You owe me nothing. Get dressed and we're leaving in two minutes."

While she pulled on some jeans, a long-sleeved black shirt, and high-top black PRO-Keds, Harwood hurried into the kitchen area and looked at the windows. Wire-mesh screens covered each window. Not the normal bug screens, these were steel gauge to keep animals out of the fishing or hunting cabin, whatever it was. Maybe it was just a place these two men brought women, who knew? But the metal screens gave him an idea.

He did what he needed to do in the kitchen. When he returned, the girl had rifled both dead men's wallets and pulled about six hundred dollars in twenties; she stuffed the bills in her pockets and looked at him.

"Just bidness, that's all," she said.

"Okay, I don't have a problem with you taking their money, but you have to help me here. Lift the fat guy first. There," he said pointing at the man's arm.

"No fucking way!" she said, backing up. "Not touching me no dead man."

"Hey. Watch your mouth. Okay, then go get the ropes from the bed," Harwood said. She seemed to have no problem with that as Harwood dragged Stoner to the kitchen table and hefted him into the chair. He looked at the window then back at the chair and figured that was good enough. He did the same with Lanny, putting him opposite Stoner, as if they were eating dinner or having a conversation. The blood issue became more complicated, but his plan had evolved.

"Here," she said. Harwood grabbed the ropes and looped them around the chest of each man, securing them upright to the backs of the wooden chairs. He even pulled one of the ropes under Lanny's chin so that his dead eyes were staring directly at Stoner's slumped head. Nothing he could do about Stoner with his neck cut to the bone, but he had placed Stoner so that his back was to the window.

"Smell something," the girl said.

"Don't worry about it. Let's move," Harwood said. He ushered her to Lanny's Mustang, removed his ruck-sack, and placed it in the backseat. He kept Lanny's Sig Sauer Tribal and stowed his Beretta in the ruck-sack. He kept the knife in the pocket of his running shorts, vowing that his next stop would be to get some suitable clothing for the mission ahead.

He was thinking about the bag Lanny had asked him to place in the trunk of the car. Was it a bomb? A rifle? He didn't know. But as he transitioned from hunted to hunter, he knew he would need resources. Whatever was in the bag might be helpful. Sirens wailed in the distance. No time to check out the bag. Backing out, he peeled north, away from the sirens and the site of the political rally. The Mustang had muscle.

"Where we going, pardner?" the young girl asked.

"First of all, you're not my partner," Harwood said, steering the car through a series of washboard cuts in the road. "What's your name?"

"Monisha. Who are you?"

"I'm Vick. Where do you live?" Harwood asked.

"I stay in Atlanta mostly, but spend a week in Macon every month doing jobs down here."

"You don't go to school?"

Monisha cackled. "That's a good one. I ain't got no momma or nothing and so I have to fend for myself. This money right here? That's a pretty good take. That'll get me through the next week or so."

Harwood shook his head. "How old are you?"

"Seventeen," she huffed.

Harwood gave her a stern look, one he often used on his Ranger subordinates. Monisha's icy confidence melted immediately.

"Fourteen," she admitted.

"Fourteen? And you're selling your body for sex?"

"Hey! You just killed two dudes. Who are you to talk?" The brash confidence reemerged.

Harwood was driving north on the gravel road. The car had a map function and it appeared that he would hit a secondary road in about a mile, which would lead to Interstate 75 north.

"Put your seat belt on," Harwood ordered. Laden now with a fourteen-year-old prostitute, he began churning through his options. His last-known location for Jackie was a Barnes & Noble in Buckhead, Atlanta, so that was where he was headed.

But then he thought, no, that was wrong. His last-known location for Jackie was in Savannah.

"Go with what you know, Vick," he whispered to himself.

"Oh great. A murderer who talks to himself," Monisha said, rolling her eyes.

"First of all, I'm not a murderer. I killed those men in self-defense. You heard them talking about killing me and you," Harwood said. He maneuvered the car onto the secondary road and was quickly heading south on Interstate 75.

"Yeah, better get our story straight," Monisha said. Then, "Hey! This ain't no way to Atlanta."

"I know. We're going to Savannah. I'll turn you over to child services once we get there."

"Like hell you will. You ain't the only one who can kill somebody." Monisha brandished a small pocket-knife.

Harwood laughed and said, "Go for it. We're doing seventy miles an hour on the interstate. How do you think you're going wind up if we wreck? You've got to start using your head, young lady."

Monisha put away the pocketknife and paused, pensive, Harwood thought. "What's in Savannah? Your woman?"

"Yeah, my woman," Harwood said.

"Figures. Good-looking guy like you had to be taken."

"Listen, Monisha. You're fourteen. You may be all tough on the outside, but you're just a fourteen-year-old girl, so act like one, will you?"

Monisha stared straight ahead and remained silent. She pulled out her smartphone and started playing with it.

For the first time in a long time, Harwood felt okay, as if he was moving closer to his normal self, away from the trauma and nightmares and toward the Vick Harwood action figure he knew himself to be. He felt his adrenaline spiking even higher. His instincts were coming back. He'd just performed two close kills. That felt good, perhaps better than it ought to, but they were in danger and he had solved the problem efficiently. His training was right there where he'd left it.

"Don't be texting anyone," he said to Monisha.

She turned her head and smiled, teeth bared, lips pulled back.

"Ain't texting," she said. "Just reading about you on Twitter. Hot damn. They was right. You're the Reaper! This is going to be fun!"

He shook his head and aimed the car toward Savannah, while trying to maintain the speed limit.

CHAPTER 18

Ramsey Xanadu never subscribed to the notion that it was better to be lucky than good, but he had to admit that it was his good fortune to intercept a police-band radio call of the Reaper getting into a late-model dark blue Ford Mustang with an accomplice.

Someone had snapped a picture of Vick Harwood placing a heavy kit bag into the trunk of the car. The picture had made its way to the Macon police, who immediately shared it with the FBI, which meant Xanadu had immediate access, also.

Markham's main concern was to kill Harwood before the Reaper remembered what had happened in Kandahar and Helmand Provinces.

"We will have a bead on this car in a few minutes," the pilot, Chief Warrant Officer Stu Benton, told Xanadu.

"In a few minutes he can kill a few more politicians," Xanadu said.

"Fine by me. I'll slow-roll the info to you then," Benton said, chuckling through the microphone.

"Don't be a smartass, Benton."

They hovered slowly above the park, watching the mayhem, looking for clues that possibly Vick Harwood had escaped and evaded detection even after the camera had snapped a picture of him.

"Bingo," Benton said.

"What you got?"

"My intel inside the FBI room tells me that it's a 2016 Ford Mustang and they're working a warrant for tracking its GPS. Address associated with the car is about twenty miles from here in the country. Some cabin on a farm. I've got the address. That's all they'll give us."

"Perfect place to hole up," Xanadu said.

"FBI is going to beat us there. I say we wait until we've got a lock on the car and then we just nuke it," Benton said.

"Not a bad idea, but if they're at the cabin and the FBI gets to him first, that's not good for us. So let's hit the cabin. FBI's still in Savannah. They're just now spinning rotors so let's go," Xanadu said.

"Roger that," Benton replied.

The experimental helicopter pivoted midair and raced to the programmed grid coordinate that led them to the cabin in less than ten minutes.

"No car," Benton said.

"There's a garage. Probably parked in there," Xanadu said.

Xanadu was back in the monkey harness leaning out of the helicopter with his rifle at the ready. Looking through his thermal scope, he saw through the window the heat signatures of two human outlines seated at the table.

Put a cap in their ass. Never know what hit them, Xanadu thought.

"Going to hit the two dudes at the table," Xanadu said.

"Don't have confirmed ID and the car is not confirmed in the garage," Benton warned.

"Best case, it's Harwood. Worst case, well, it's collateral damage," Xanadu said.

"Can you tell if it's a white guy, black guy, anything?"

"Thermal just gives me body heat," Xanadu said. "They're both glowing in my scope. Just sitting there. How far out are we?"

"Quarter mile," Benton said.

"Okay, here we go," Xanadu replied. He adjusted his scope, and put the crosshairs on the smaller of the two men, because he didn't think Harwood had put on fifty pounds since getting out of Walter Reed. If anything, he'd lost weight on all that hospital food.

"Hold steady, Stu," Xanadu said. He leaned fully outside of the aircraft, pulling the nylon strap taut so that if it were to break, which would be nearly impossible unless it was cut, he would fall several hundred feet straight down. The smaller man's head was perfectly still in the crosshairs. Xanadu was known more for his shoot first, ask questions later policy, and true to form he held steady in the hovering aircraft as he squeezed the trigger on the rifle. The sound suppressor muffled the shot and the whispering rotor blades muted any noise from the rifle. Xanadu watched his shot pierce the protective metal mesh on the windows, saw a spark, and said, "Oh, shit."

He never had time to determine if his shot was on target, because an enormous fireball erupted from the house.

"Hang on!" Benton shouted into the microphone.

"Hanging. What the hell was that?"

"Think the Reaper mind-fucked you, bro. That was a propane gas explosion."

Xanadu thought about the unmoving bodies. Something had happened in that house and Harwood had been there. The Reaper wanted the evidence destroyed. Xanadu gave the man credit for thinking through the problem set.

Being outwitted by Harwood meant the sniper's memory was coming back. Not a good thing for MLQM or him, personally. Xanadu reached back with his large hand and used his muscled forearm to pull himself into the racing aircraft.

"Where we going?" Xanadu asked once he was back inside.

"Away from this nuclear explosion," Benton replied.

Xanadu looked out the port-side cargo opening and saw the billowing orange ball that would have every county and city police officer in a fifty-mile radius racing to it.

"FBI is waving off, too. They boarded but now are returning to Hunter," Benton said.

"That's unusual."

"Only chatter I'm getting from those guys is that the police chief talked to them about evidence found in Dillman's house."

"Oh shit. Thought that was cleaned," Xanadu said.

"Evidently not."

The helicopter nosed over and sped toward Hunter

Army Airfield, small-town lights slipping beneath them.

Harwood parked Lanny's Ford Mustang in the parking lot of the Breakfast Club on Tybee Island. Monisha had dozed off in the front seat and had eventually woken before crawling into the backseat, where she was now sound asleep. The Atlantic Ocean, beyond the diner, showed the first edges of before-morning nautical twilight appearing. Muted gray tones pushed against the black horizon with the slightest lick of orange.

During the drive, Harwood had done the battlefield geometry. While it was not a wise decision to put himself on an island with only one way out, he was about four hours ahead of the FBI and everyone else that wanted him dead or captured.

When Monisha had slipped between the bucket seats into the backseat, she'd left her purse on the floor of the passenger side. Harwood leaned over and retrieved Monisha's smartphone from her purse and saw on the locked screen multiple text messages asking about her "availability." Apparently, she was quite popular as a fourteen-year-old call girl, and that made Harwood sad. His foster parents had pimped out the girls and boys with whom he had been placed. That memory surged through his mind like a freight train.

He had turned, lightly grasped Monisha's hand, and pressed her right thumb against the home button, which recognized her thumbprint. The phone came to life and he dialed the one number he knew from memory. The phone rang three times before being answered.

"Command Sergeant Major Murdoch, this line is unsecured," Murdoch said.

"Rangers lead the way," Harwood replied.

After a long pause, Murdoch said, "Indeed they do, son. I understand the training is a little tough right now?"

Murdoch's pause and redirect to his official duties indicated to Harwood that Murdoch knew he was in trouble.

"A little rough, Sergeant Major, but I think I know how to fix it," Harwood said.

"Do tell, Ranger."

"Crater analysis and blue force tracker. As I'm teaching these snipers I just realized that they need to be aware of the location of *all* friendly elements on the battlefield, private and military, especially if crater analysis is involved afterward."

Another long pause. "That's an excellent point, Ranger. I'll have some of the ops folks make note of that and send you any updated teaching points on that topic."

"I would appreciate that, Sergeant Major," Harwood said.

"I assume you need it soon?"

"Well, I'm in the middle of a session right now."

"Roger that. Keep your head down and school 'em, but don't milk 'em," Murdoch said, and ended the call.

"Roger, out," Harwood whispered into the phone.

He had called the one man he believed he could rely on to keep the faith and help him. Speaking in partial code, he had communicated to the sergeant major to check out which other friendly forces might have been on the battlefield the day of the mortar attack on his position. He remembered that day three months ago in pieces.

School 'em but don't milk 'em?

What the hell was the sergeant major talking about? He wondered.

Milk 'Em? MLQM? It had to be a clue. Murdoch said nothing without purpose.

Fragmented images danced in his mind. He now realized that one sliver came back to him when he saw Monisha tied up on the bed by Lanny and Stoner, now dead. Like a jagged puzzle piece, the memory of the three men "escorting" three women from adobe huts in Sangin moments before the mortar attack came hurtling into place. He positioned that puzzle piece next to the fact that the mortars had come from behind him after one of the men had scanned the terrain with binoculars. But really, the only way to get a direct hit on his and Samuelson's position would have been for someone to have a ten-digit grid coordinate locked into their mortar ballistic computer. And there were only one or two ways that could happen. Someone could have checked the blue force tracker data before heading out on a mission with the express purpose of firing on his position, or someone could have been one-in-a-trillion lucky and guessed correctly.

Harwood didn't believe in luck or those kinds of odds.

Milk 'em. MLQM.

His conversation with the sergeant major hinted that MLQM was one of the groups that was chasing him. Harwood finally decided to disconnect the GPS on Lanny's car. He reached into the glove box, removed the owner's manual, found the fuse-box display, opened the box beneath the steering wheel, and removed the panel that controlled the GPS. It was a calculated risk to wait this long, but he was tired of being chased and wanted those chasing him, the ones that wanted him dead, to know he was in their domain. Then he had driven to Tybee Island.

He was now hunting them.

A flock of pelicans glided low along the ocean's surface. The orange-tipped leading edge of the sun was painting the morning sky. Someone dressed in cook whites flipped a cardboard sign on the front door from CLOSED to OPEN. Monisha twisted in the backseat and mumbled, "Where we at?"

"Beach," Harwood said. "We're going to eat breakfast and leave."

"Why come all this way if we can't stay for a bit? Love the beach," Monisha said, more awake now.

"Want to talk to you about all those texts on your phone," Harwood said.

"You been in my phone!"

"Yes. Needed to make a call. And I'm hanging on to it for the time being."

"The hell you are," Monisha said.

"I've got social services on speed dial here. Either play by my rules or they come get you," Harwood said.

"Ain't nobody from the gov'ment awake right now, so I know that's bullshit," Monisha said.

Smart girl, Harwood thought to himself, but he pressed her.

"They have a twenty-four-hour hotline. We do this my way, okay? We go in, eat breakfast. I go for a short run. You enjoy the beach. Then we leave."

"Run? Where you running to?"

"Just for exercise," Harwood said. He looked at her in the rearview mirror, caught her eyes. She was processing everything he was saying.

"I'm hungry," she said. "And a little scared."

"You should be, but I'm going to make sure you're okay. I did it last night and will continue to do so. Understand?"

"Yeah, I guess," she said.

"All right then, let's eat."

They got out of the car and were the first customers to the restaurant. The salty air felt good. He sucked it in and felt his mind clear even more. Harwood figured he had maybe another three hours before he had to be off the island. While breakfast was being prepared—he ordered the farmer's special and she ordered blueberry pancakes—Harwood asked Monisha to sit in the booth next to him and help him navigate her phone.

"This here's Twitter. Hit the hashtag for Black Lives Matter. That's where you're the hero," she said. Just as before at Georgia Southern, the tweet stream was collapsing every second with new tweets about how Harwood had shot Senator Kraft, whom some believed to be a law-and-order racist. *Harwood is taking it to the man! #BLM!!* Or *Vegas placing odds on next victim of #HeroHarwood!*

"Who you gonna shoot next?" Monisha asked.

He looked at her and said, "I haven't shot anyone."

"Please. I saw you kill those two men like it was nothing."

"I killed them because they were going to kill us. For being different than them. Just because they could. Or thought they could."

"Well, excuse me for having a hard time believing that you didn't kill them others. They saying it was your rifle and everything."

"I'm sure it was my rifle. I'm trying to figure some things out, okay?"

Their breakfast came. Monisha stayed next to Harwood despite her spoken concerns. He sensed she felt safer with him and even next to him. She was a scared child forced to live in an adult world well before she should have been. They devoured their breakfasts and walked back to the car after Harwood left thirty dollars in cash for a twenty-dollar breakfast. He retrieved his rucksack from the car and shouldered it as he popped the trunk and dug through Lanny's kit bag, pleasantly surprised by what he found.

"That where you keep your rifle? In there?" Monisha asked.

"I keep a lot of things in here, little girl. Now you see that bench? Go sit on that for about half an hour. I'm going for a run." He pocketed the keys and pointed at a bench in the dunes that afforded a view of the ocean and a pier that jutted into the water.

"Can I have my phone?"

"No. I need it to take some pictures."

"Don't be looking at my photo stream," she said.

"I won't. Just need to take a few pictures," Harwood said. He locked the car and began jogging. He looked over his shoulder and saw Monisha staring at him, her arms crossed and her black long-sleeved shirt and blue jeans making her look out of place at the beach in August. It wouldn't be long before beachcombers showed up and noticed her.

He crossed the street and ran along side streets until

he found the Tybee Creek beach, the work out feeling good, but having little to do with why he was running. After about a mile, he saw what he was looking for. The sun was above the horizon and he was glad that he had chosen the westerly approach, preventing him from being silhouetted against the flaming ball. He found a few sand dunes and unshouldered his rucksack. He retrieved a spotter's scope from one of the pockets and dug its tripod into the sand. Invisible sand fleas bit at his arms and legs, but he concentrated on his mission.

Through his lens, he saw the compound of the chairman of the board of what most soldiers knew as "Milk 'em," or the MLQM contracting company. After his conversation with Murdoch, he'd used Monisha's phone to search MLQM and had pressed on the "Leadership" icon. At the top of the page was General "Buzz" Markham's picture, chairman of the board. A quick internet search showed him as the owner of a "home" on Tybee Island.

MLQM's private military contractors were in Afghanistan when Harwood was wounded. Ramsey Xanadu had been one of the malcontents unhappy that Harwood was getting some attention for killing so many Taliban commanders. Harwood recalled that Xanadu had begun leaving the wire of Kandahar operating base within hours of his team every time they would scoot out in their Humvees or in an MH-60 helicopter. These memories were reappearing in his mind, like a lost patrol of soldiers emerging from the forest. Perhaps rescuing Monisha was healing for him. Helped his mind reboot and reset to its original formatting; maybe even upgrade, like a broken bone growing back stronger.

He studied the fortress through the scope. That was exactly what General Buzz Markham's Tybee Island home was: a three-acre fortress. It had high walls on the north end with two guard towers on the east and west sides. He noticed two guards staring into the early morning with binoculars. They had AR-15s hanging from their outer tactical vests held in place by snap links attached to two-point slings. He was a good four hundred yards away and so far, he believed he had been undetected.

Where the concrete wall ended, razor wire tapered off into the ocean on the east and the sound on the west. Most likely, there were underwater sensors, as well. He used Monisha's phone to snap several pictures, though their efficacy was doubtful once he blew them up and developed a target folder. The sun continued its ascent. Two boats bobbed in the distance, fishermen most likely. Final assessment: The compound was a formidable fortress with high walls, sharp razor wire, alert sentries, and one canalized route of entry.

The sniper was in perfect position to shoot General Markham—the worst offender of them all—if the dumbass would just step outside his fortress. Scanning, waiting, and scanning some more, the sniper continued to come up empty. The only targets were the two guards.

Shoot them? Why not? They were pawns protecting the king. By now the king knew that he was in trouble. Might as well start taking his pieces off the board more quickly and send a clear message the noose was tightening.

The sniper leveled the crosshairs on the guard furthest away. These were tough shots, but not the toughest the sniper had ever made. The image of a young military age male staring through binoculars to the west swayed in the retina display. Thinking, anticipating, and timing the shot, the sniper squeezed the trigger, sending a bullet into the temple of the guard, who folded straight down inside his turret.

Quickly moving the rifle aim to the nearest guard, the sniper dealt with the sway, did the same anticipating and timing. The guard had turned his head toward the western turret. The guard towers were maybe one hundred yards apart. He'd heard his comrade fall. As the guard was intuitively turning back in the direction from which the shot must have come, the sniper's crosshairs were a fraction to the left of the guard. It wasn't perfect, but the shot sliced through the guard's neck, causing him to spin and fall halfway out of the tower.

Time to move. The ejected casings would probably not be found anytime soon, but they were clues left behind nonetheless.

Having seen what he needed to see, Harwood packed his bag and shouldered his ruck while he was still in the prone position. The sound of two coughs skidded inland from the tranquil ocean.

A boat roared in the distance as Harwood prepared to depart. Thinking he could use the noise as good cover, he stopped when he saw a black spot low on the north-facing side of the estate. Instead of evading away from the compound, he dipped below the sand dunes and jogged along the wall of the sand, eventually reaching the razor wire. Acting boldly, he retrieved some wire cutters and snipped his way through the thin layer of defense, certain that cameras were monitoring him. He refused to care; he'd come too far. Harwood approached the dark cavern on the side of the mansion where water ran from Tybee Creek into an arched passageway. Wading knee-deep in the murky water, he felt ebbing tide rush against his legs.

He reached the cavern and saw a cigarette boat on a lift.

Be One Bomber.

Had to be Markham's boat, Harwood thought. It was blue and silver, air force colors. Its sleek, long design befit the former fighter pilot. An escape avenue or a play toy? Harwood wondered. He cut through some more wires, this time setting off an alarm inside the building. Harwood climbed into the boat, found the console, reached into his rucksack, and—thanks to Lanny's supplies—took about three minutes to do what he believed needed to be done.

He waited a moment, looked at his handiwork, and was satisfied. Footsteps were racing above, as if through the front door. A door opened above him, about twenty yards away. As he was jumping into the water, a light came on and a voice called out, "Who's there?"

He retraced his route through the cut wires and then began jogging the beach back to the north. As he was running, he looked up at the guard towers he had seen on his initial recon. The western tower looked empty. The eastern tower had a man slumped halfway out of the tower, evidently shot. He cut up onto the peninsula and crossed the main street, where he found Monisha waiting impatiently. He was sweating heavily as he pulled up to the bench where Monisha was swinging her legs like the fourteen-year-old she should have been. She smiled and asked, "Kill anyone?"

"No. Let's go," Harwood said. They had been on the island for two and a half hours. The good trackers would find him in thirty more minutes. The lousy ones another hour and a half.

They jumped in the car as the parking lot was filling up with customers. Monisha snatched her phone from Harwood's pocket as he used both hands to maneuver the car.

"Hey," Harwood said.

"Just checking to make sure you weren't looking at my pictures," she said.

"Wasn't. Now give me the phone back."

He was heading north toward the turn for the bridge back to Savannah.

"Hot damn," she said. "You took some pictures of a mansion. That's who you're going to kill next."

"No, it's not," Harwood said with little conviction.

"Oh, shit," Monisha said.

"What?"

"Twitter. Damn that shit moves out," she said.

Harwood followed Route 80, racing toward the bridge over the Wilmington River, trying to get back into Savannah. From the bridge, he could see a string of police cars with lights flashing about two miles away.

"I knew it," Monisha said. "You just killed them two guards. We're just like Bonnie and Clyde!"

CHAPTER 19

"I didn't kill those guards," Harwood said. "Don't even know what you're talking about."

"Not what it's looking like," Monisha shot back. "Internet's got you pegged as the killer. Latest CNN poll says eighty-four percent of the people think you're guilty."

"At least I've got sixteen on my side," Harwood quipped.

"Not really. They the same bunch that don't know who's president."

Harwood had parked the Mustang under a low-hanging live oak tree about fifty yards from a warehouse at the north end of the Port of Savannah. A dirt road led to a sixty-acre wooded site that was up for lease, commanding top dollar because of its river frontage and relatively new warehouse. There was a boat ramp and a small pier with two center-console boats moored at the dock. The open lot seemed like prime land for a shipping business that wanted to be close to the port. The morning sun had risen. It was about 8 A.M. and Harwood figured that unless there was a showing of this property in the next couple of hours, they should be okay here. The car was completely out of view from overhead surveillance and only marginally visible from ground level. They remained seated in the bucket seats.

"Take a nap, Monisha. It's going to be a long day. I've got to figure out what to do with you after I make a few phone calls with your phone."

"Hey, we got a deal if we do a quick Snapchat I can send out. Then I want a two-minute video I'm gonna upload to YouTube and it'll make me a millionaire."

Harwood thought for a moment. What better journalist to cover his story than someone who wasn't a journalist? Monisha was just a lost fourteen-year-old child who needed some grounding. Of course, the whole thing could backfire on him. The mainstream media could allege he had taken liberties with the child, and for that matter, so could she. He needed to protect himself, and the best way to do that was to get some of their interaction on digital video.

But first, the call he had been waiting for came through.

"Just a sec, Monisha. We've got a deal. You'll be famous under one condition and that's you stop this internet hooking you're doing."

She paused. "Okay. It's a deal." She held out her slender hand and they shook. "Better take that call."

"Roger," Harwood said as he answered the phone.

"Ranger, you have good instincts as we've always known," Command Sergeant Major Murdoch said. "What's more, you should train your students that

Q-36 radars are good at confirming those instincts and crater analysis. I just looked at a few reports." A Q-36 radar was a ballistic-intercept radar that could track mortar rounds or incoming Scud missiles.

"If I'm to properly train these students, Sergeant Major, I want to be able to tell them that sometimes blue-on-blue action can occur, no matter how many precautions you take," Harwood said. "Blue-on-blue" meant friendly fire. "Blue-on-green" meant U.S. fire on Afghan forces. "Blue-on-red" meant U.S. fire on enemy forces.

"Indeed. What's even more important for your trainees to know, Sergeant, is that blue-on-blue doesn't necessarily mean you're dealing with military forces. There are other types of blue forces as well."

Just as he thought. MLQM had a raid team conducting missions in Kandahar Province. Sometimes they provided security to dignitaries and sometimes they had independent missions, such as securing critical targets like cell-phone towers, schools, or water reservoirs. Ninety-nine percent of the military contractors Harwood had served alongside were true professionals with the same mission and goals as him and his Ranger teammates. There were a few, such as Xanadu, that had given him a bad vibe.

"My advice to you, Ranger, is to wrap up this training as quickly as possible so that you can Charlie Mike with the Ranger mission."

"Roger that, Sergeant Major. One last mentorship question."

"Make it quick," the sergeant major said.

"Why would an enemy ultimately want to kill a sniper?" Harwood asked.

"Always the same reason. To take an enemy's most

effective operator off the chessboard in preparation for the big finale."

The line went blank. The sergeant major had given him everything he had, filled in some gaps, though some questions remained.

"Get what you need?" Monisha asked. She was looking at him with big eyes and a wry grin. "I got good ears, but I didn't understand none of that."

"Yeah. I know what to do," he said. The sergeant major had confirmed for him that MLQM forces had fired the mortar rounds at him. He wondered if it was MLQM private military contractors conducting the kidnap raid in Sangin that he and Samuelson saw directly before the mortar attack.

Bring her back! the Chechen had messaged. Then: *Trade?* Was his adversary making a legitimate request? Could the MLQM contractors have kidnapped or killed someone the Chechen knew? It was a possibility. But what did the Chechen have to trade?

"So that means my phone's going to be famous and shit, right? Sell it on eBay?"

"Not if you keep talking like that. For all practical purposes now you're my kid sister." Harwood thought of Lindsay, his foster sister, the one he didn't save. Was he being offered redemption? Perhaps.

"So you do what I say and pay attention. Things could get dangerous. But I don't know where to take you where you just won't get lost in the system and get jammed up like I did."

"Like you did?" Monisha asked. Harwood nodded. Monisha looked away. She wiped away a tear and looked back at him.

"Here you were a loser like me and you at least

made something out of your life. Killed some dudes in war."

"You're not a loser, Monisha. Just obey me and we'll get out of this. I'll get you somewhere safe and finish my mission."

"I don't want to be somewhere else," she said. "I want to stay with you. Like you said. You're my big brother now. Never had that."

"Well, pay attention to me like I'm your brother then," Harwood said.

She paused. "I'll do that as long as we keep our deal."

"You got it," Harwood said. Monisha smiled and leaned back in the bucket seat.

"Me and the Reaper. Gonna write a book one day."

"Yeah, well, in the meantime understand this. Your phone has probably been intercepted by now, so we need to shut it off until I need it again."

"You're in charge," she said.

They sat silent in the car a moment, watching a large merchant vessel slide quietly along the river.

"Who do you think killed those people in the guard towers I was reading about?" Monisha asked. "Because I believe you now, *bro*."

Harwood heard the innocence in her voice and the newfound belief in him that he had not done the killing.

"Someone trying to frame me. All these murders— the generals, the police, the senator, the two guards— they're all related somehow to something that happened in Afghanistan."

"Maybe they bad people and deserve killing," Monisha said.

"Maybe so," Harwood agreed. "But that doesn't make it right."

"Was it right what you did to save me?"

He looked at her and a thought crystallized. He powered the phone back on and called the sergeant major, who answered abruptly.

"Operational security is another lesson you need to teach your trainees," he said.

"Roger that, Sergeant Major. As I talk to my trainees, I'm telling them that they may have a single adversary that becomes a nemesis for them. And to beat that adversary, the sniper needs to know everything about him, including his personal life. For example, is he married, children, and so on?"

After a short pause, the sergeant major said, "That's an excellent instructional point, Sergeant. Let me do some thinking on it and I'll get back to you."

"You're speaking in code to him, ain't you? Asking him to do stuff for you," Monisha said, smiling again.

"Maybe," Harwood said.

The sun had fully risen. Harwood saw that the time was almost 9 A.M. He had maybe today to resolve the situation. The phone rang again much sooner than he expected.

"Sergeant, two things. I need you to recall a search mission you had when you were a private. Second, I suggest you teach your trainees to build the most complete target folders and to know where those folders are located always, even maintaining access while deployed in the field. And I suggest you instruct your students on that, right now, because you never know when there will be no time left to train and fighting is the only option."

The sergeant major clicked off and Harwood wondered if he would ever talk to him again. He immediately hit the Google home button, and typed in his

Gmail password, which gave him access to a joint account the sergeant major had created for him two years ago to study unclassified information when training to be the best Ranger and best sniper he could be.

He eyed the emails containing sniper manuals, lessons learned from the wars in Iraq and Afghanistan, and blogs from combat veterans the sergeant major trusted and respected. Then Harwood noticed a bold number "1" on the draft folder icon.

Clicking on the drafts icon, he found an unsent, draft email, which he opened.

There he saw a picture of a woman, dark hair, green eyes, fair skin, next to a businessman dressed in a pin-striped suit. They were in a casino, probably in one of the places Harwood knew his life would never take him, like Monaco or Casablanca. It was the same photo he had seen in Kandahar as he had built a target folder on the Chechen.

The dapper man was unmistakably the man who had ridden in the elevator with him. The note contained in the folder read:

TS/SPECAT//This is the Chechen and his wife, Nina Moreau. Three months ago, Moreau was reported kidnapped on the battlefield and has not been seen since. Moreau is DGSE, French CIA equivalent, and a trained registered nurse, but we believe that is a legend. We do not assess her relationship with Basayev to be related to her DGSE official duties. The French government seeks her safe return, though they would prefer not disclosing her links to Basayev. Crater analysis and Q-36 confirms Basayev did not fire mortars. PMC suspected of running drug and sex trafficking ring also on battlefield. Basayev believes U.S. military involved in PMC activities. Basayev possibly the fourth man in 2010. Moreau possibly rogue with Basayev to complete 2010 mission. Russian government believed to be financing. //TS/SPECAT

Harwood immediately deleted the file from the drafts folder. The sergeant major had risked his career by placing top-secret, special-category information in an unclassified email draft folder. Technically, he had not sent the email, so there was no transaction other than the uploading of the photo of Basayev and Moreau.

What he and Samuelson had seen directly before Basayev had held up his "Bring her back! Trade?" sign was the kidnapping of three women by MLQM contractors dressed as Taliban. Moreau, it seemed, had defected to support her husband's mercenary activities. The fourth man in 2010 was a bit more confusing. When Harwood had been a private in 2010, he was serving in the 1st Ranger Battalion at Hunter Army Airfield. The "fourth man" referred to a police stop of four "Russians" walking with shovels and rucksacks. The police captured three of the four, two Russians and one from Kazakhstan.

Murdoch was telling him that Basayev, the Chechen, was possibly the fourth man. Based upon the equipment police had discovered, the men had parachuted into the area. Parachute harnesses, kit bags, shovels, and even some hazmat gloves and masks. Those men were ultimately released, because they had green cards and the Department of Justice saw no reason to hold them, despite the outcry from the local and special operations communities. He and his Ranger buddies, though, had plowed through miles of brush around Hunter Army Airfield with mine detectors, night vision goggles, thermal imaging equipment, and so on. They left no stone unturned and found two kit bags with untraceable high-altitude sport parachutes.

What was Command Sergeant Major Murdoch saying? That Basayev was here in 2010? And had come back to finish the job?

Could this be his trade? Harwood wondered.

The worst-case speculation at the time was that they had planted a tactical nuclear device that would incapacitate the Special Operations Aviation Regiment's 3rd Battalion, the Ranger battalion, and a full infantry division thirty miles down the road at Fort Stewart, Georgia, along with one of the busiest ports on the East Coast, in Savannah.

"Whatcha thinking 'bout?" Monisha asked.

Harwood switched gears, tucking away the thoughts and possibilities. He now understood much of what was happening. He was the rabbit that Basayev needed the police to chase while he maneuvered freely.

"Okay, that's it. A guy I was fighting in Afghanistan thinks I kidnapped his wife. I didn't, but I know who did. If I find the guy who did it, then we'll probably find the wife."

"That's why they trying to frame you. Keep the heat off them," Monisha said.

"Maybe. Something like that. Perhaps, they figured my memory would come back eventually and I know too much. The private military contractors know I saw them. They couldn't just outright kill me, but using my rifle is the next best thing. Frame me for the killing of these people. That's half the equation."

Harwood knew he was missing a large piece of the puzzle. Why kill their own people when doing the frame job? Make it more authentic?

Harwood's adrenaline was fading. Exhaustion swept through his body like an ocean wave.

"Tired?" Monisha asked.

"Yeah. Just worn out. Been on the run. My memory's still not right, but it's getting better."

She looked at him. Wide doe eyes that looked innocent and perhaps could be again. It occurred to Harwood in his drowsy state that Monisha had been a catalyst of sorts for him. Her predicament had catapulted him from reactionary and forgetful to proactive and tactical.

"Want to talk about it?"

"About stuff you don't know about?"

"I know more than you think, Reaper."

"Why don't you tell me about you?"

"I'll trade with ya," she said.

"Deal."

"I ain't never known a brother. My mama? She couldn't afford me, I'm told. So I kept getting put in different homes, mostly homeless shelters in downtown Atlanta. They don't watch over us much there. Public school bus picked us up, but we could pretty much go wherever we wanted if we showed up every few days. Once you turned teenager, the men there expected things, ya know?"

"I don't, but I understand what you're saying," Harwood said. "I'm sorry."

"Ain't nothing to be sorry about. Just life. Do what

you gotta do to survive. This one man started posting my picture on Backpage and he'd drive me to different places. He'd take half and I'd get half. Usually a hundred dollars. Fifty for each of us."

"Tell me about school. I don't like hearing about the other stuff. I saw enough. It's not right what happened, you know that, right?"

"I do, Reaper. I know. But what can I do now. I'm ruint."

"You're not ruined, Monisha." This time, Harwood reached across the gearbox and brushed a tear from her face. She was sitting with her back to the door, legs crossed Indian style. "You're a little girl that got pushed into the big world way too soon. But you can overcome that."

"I don't know how. You know, I tried the school thing. Was super good at math. Give me numbers and I can give you answers."

"What's fifty divided by twenty?" Harwood asked.

Monisha rolled her eyes. "Please. Two point five. If we gonna play this game, take it up a notch, Super Mario."

"Nine hundred divided by twelve."

Without hesitation she said, "Seventy-five. We still on level one."

"Okay, I believe you. So, when we're done with this little ordeal, we get you enrolled somewhere. A good school where you can take advanced math. How's your reading?"

"I can read. Damn well read all them tweets about you," Monisha said. She smiled.

Harwood did, too. "Yeah, I guess you did. You've got to get rid of the ghetto talk though, Monisha. It's not your past that defines you, it's what you do with your past to make something of yourself."

"That what you believe? Killing all them people— excuse me, those people—in Afghanistan. You're going to do something with that?"

"Well, that's not all I did, but yes. I do plan to write a book. I'm defending our country. I'm accomplishing my goals. I can help you accomplish yours."

Monisha stared through the windshield. "That'd be real nice," she whispered. "But you'll probably just forget about me once this is all done."

"I can promise you that I won't."

She nodded. "Trade."

"I was passed around some farms in the Maryland countryside. I could lift some heavy stuff so this one farmer kept me the longest. His wife ran the foster kids, took the money from the government. There was this girl, Lindsay. She was about three years older, but like my mother. She cooked, cleaned, and counseled, as I called it."

"That's a good woman. Taking care of you like that."

"She was a good woman," Harwood said.

"Was? What happened?"

Harwood was silent for a long time, looking out the same windshield as Monisha. He thought the windshield might even symbolize that he and Monisha somehow saw life through the same lens. Starting out with little or nothing and not wanting a whole lot more, but just enough. His heart ached for Lindsay and what had happened to her and he realized that his heart ached for Monisha in the same way. A childhood lost. Innocence stolen too soon.

"It's okay, Reaper. We traded."

"She was killed. I was your age. Fourteen. She was seventeen. Our 'mother' dressed her up and sent her to the barn. I became protective and waited one day. She'd had enough. I'd had enough. The man came in, started unzipping his pants. Her back was to him. He walked up to her. She turned around and lashed out with a pitchfork. The man stepped back, pulled a pistol out of his pocket and pumped two rounds into her body. She stood there for a few seconds like nothing had happened. Like a freeze-frame. Then she just crumpled to the ground, like she was trying to lay down."

Harwood coughed. He realized he was remembering something he had tucked away and protected. They were quiet for a long time, until Monisha asked, "What happened to the man?"

"I think you know," Harwood said.

"He met the Reaper. He was the first bad guy you killed?"

Harwood nodded. "The pitchfork ended up in his throat. I checked on Lindsay, but she was gone. One of the bullets passed through her heart. She had always told me to run when I got the chance. Once I was sure he was dead, I ran."

The sun was beginning to beat down on the car. The memories had made Harwood even more exhausted. His eyelids were drooping, heavy with the need to sleep.

"I'm your Lindsay," Monisha said. "You saved me."

Harwood looked at her serious countenance. Face set, lips tight, eyes tearing up.

"Not yet, but I will," Harwood said. "I promise."

"I feel safe with you. Maybe for the first time ever."

Harwood laid his head against the window and

wasn't sure if he had fallen asleep or not when he heard the noise.

"What's that?" Monisha asked, pointing at the river.

"Oh, man. That's an experimental helicopter and they're looking for us. I heard it in Macon."

The twin-bladed helicopter zipped low along the river three hundred yards in front of them. As it passed, it pulled up into the air and slowed to a hover, lifted above the fog, and turned in their direction.

Harwood grabbed Monisha and his ruck, and they raced out of the driver's side toward the warehouse fifty feet away.

The helicopter minigun began spitting a hundred rounds a second as he pulled Monisha toward him to shield her with his bulky frame.

He was too late. One of the rounds pierced her fragile, ninety-pound body, a straight through-and-through. They reached the warehouse and Harwood blew through the door, ran fifty yards inside behind some unused concrete culvert pipes, and laid Monisha on the floor.

"Hurts," she said.

Harwood placed his pistol on the floor then opened his rucksack and retrieved some gauze, quick-clot, and Betadine. He inspected the wound. She was shot in the leg. There was a lot of blood and he prayed her femoral artery hadn't been nicked. He pulled a tourniquet from his aid bag and snapped it above the wound, cranking it down tightly, until the blood flowed to a trickle. He then yanked an IV bag from his ruck and stuck the needle in her arm, placing the bag on a four-foot-high culvert pipe. He poured Betadine on the wound, stuffed the quick-clot in both sides, and then wrapped gauze around her leg.

"Hang in there, Monisha. Come on. Be strong for me," Harwood said.

Her eyes were dim and oddly she had a slight smile on her face, which was when he noticed the other wound. There had been so much blood he hadn't seen the gut shot. He went to work on that quickly, as well, repeating the process. It was a searing, glancing blow that drew blood. He checked his rucksack and found two more IV bags. At this rate, he'd run out in thirty minutes.

Harwood grabbed his pistol and ran back to the door of the warehouse. Staring through the grimy steel mesh window, he saw Ramsey Xanadu standing next to Lanny's now burning Mustang. Xanadu checked inside as best he could, but the heat was too fierce. He looked in the distance, away from Harwood, and quickly began running toward the helicopter. Blades chopping into the sky, the helicopter lifted away and sped to the east.

Harwood returned to Monisha's side, kneeling. She looked at him with weak eyes.

"Happy. For the first time," she muttered, then coughed.

"You're going to be okay, Monisha." *Please don't die.*

"I'm okay," she whispered. Big eyelashes fluttered as she looked him in the eyes and said. "I'm okay. Thanks . . . brother."

"Hang in there, girl. Don't go anywhere on me," Harwood ordered. "Stay with me, girl!"

Monisha's eyes went blank.

CHAPTER 20

General Buzz Markham was not a happy man. Having this morning flown in on his luxury 737 extended-range jet, he had helicoptered to his Tybee Island compound from Hunter Army Airfield. He stood on the back deck and watched one white fishing boat troll amid a flock of seagulls diving on schooling bluefish. Another boat had just sped away to the south and east. The water was churning as if it were beyond boiling temperature. He smelled the musty scent of ocean life mixed with the salty spray of the ocean.

"What you got?" he said into the phone. "I've got two dead guards. Killed by that psychopath you were supposed to kill."

"Heard that. He's better than we thought."

"Or maybe you're just not as good as you believed?"

Static filled the silence.

"So what other news do you have?" Markham asked.

"I'm standing alone in the middle of our warehouse

with the transfer case racks stacked to the ceiling. I'm secure. Got some good news and some not-so-good news," Xanadu said.

"Worse than two dead guards?"

"Maybe yes, maybe no. We can get new guards."

"That's true. Just give it to me."

"We landed back at Hunter about an hour ago," Xanadu said. "Saw a dark blue Mustang parked in a vacant lot by the river. Put several machine-gun rounds in it just for good measure. Landed and did a quick site exploitation. Saw what looked like the Reaper and a little girl run into a warehouse. Saw some blood. Think we hit one of them, but I heard on the police scanner that cops were coming onto the scene so we bugged out. Didn't want to leave a signature with the helicopter. The miniguns worked great and sounded like a zipper closing, that's about it. I'm not worried about any audible signatures. But, no joy on catching the Reaper yet, though we did get eyes on."

"I need some joy," Markham demanded.

"Well, that brings me to my bad news."

"It isn't good news that you saw the Reaper. Everyone has seen him. He's everywhere!" Markham shouted.

"Well, boss. I need to tell you that I'm staring at an IED instead of my 'girlfriend.' Saw this yesterday, but have been too busy chasing Harwood."

Markham knew that Xanadu had kept one of the women for himself. He had not cared. It was Xanadu's job to get the women and the drugs and Markham fully expected the operative to enjoy some spoils of his hard work, like an undisclosed bonus. And he also knew that Xanadu had not told him of her disappearance because he had been trying to find her. He had been around long enough to know to never send bad news up the chain unless you had expended all options. Apparently, Xanadu was out of options.

"I got to Tybee Island about an hour ago to meet with a new group of investors, who are already here," Markham said. "And you're telling me we've got a squirter? Your girl escaped? That's why we box them up and ship them after we're done with them." He looked at the bluefish churning offshore. "You hung on to the bitch for how long? Three months? Whiskey Tango Foxtrot? Ain't no tang that good, my friend."

Markham took a deep breath and thought about the transfer cases. Those had been his idea when he was still active duty. Having heard about so many ramp ceremonies for fallen soldiers, sailors, airmen, and marines he was shipping back home for the final salute, he found his mind wandering to the possibilities, especially if the transfer cases were on a private aircraft.

However, one of the transfer-case girls on the loose was not a good thing. Then he thought about what he considered the lesser threat and asked, "And an IED in MLQM's headquarters? How in the hell did that happen?"

Markham had bid farewell to his five platinum CLEVER sponsors, who had opted for the hunting lodge in Colorado . . . and its amenities. The general was now scheduled to meet with five gold sponsors, who preferred the beach. CLEVER did very little hiring of veterans and retired military personnel, but the organization did go a long way toward enriching the lifestyle of those involved. CLEVER was no different from some of the veteran "charities" that had preyed upon the humanitarian nature of the American people and delivered fat salaries to their CEOs and slim pickings to the vets. A thought piece published every now and then by a veteran under the CLEVER guise went a long way in the positive-publicity department. The rest was just fund-raising, fucking, and firearms, the three *f*'s of life for Markham.

General Markham was enjoying the spoils of his hard-earned high-ranking status.

"I'm not exactly sure how she escaped. I was in Afghanistan until three days ago getting you more women and drugs," Xanadu said. "We had a routine. I chained her to a water pipe in my office and had her gagged when I was there. Then every time I put her back in, threw her however many MREs and water bottles she needed based upon how long I was going to be gone. No way she got out without some inside help."

There was no love lost and very little trust between a bona fide psychopath such as Ramsey Xanadu and a refined, well-trained senior executive such as Markham. Nonetheless, Xanadu had his uses for exactly those reasons. If there was plausible deniability between him and Xanadu, Markham was solid. The phones upon which they spoke were untraceable secure phones developed by MLQM.

"She was in the transfer case when you left?"

"Of course. Like I said. Where I always kept her unless I was there," Xanadu said.

Markham pursed his lips and rubbed his forefinger across them. "So she could be anywhere? Did one of your MLQM Neanderthals take some liberties with her?"

"If they did—and I don't believe they would do so—why would they leave an IED in the transfer case?"

"I agree, that's troubling," Markham said, calculating his distance from Hunter Army Airfield to be about twenty miles' straight-line distance, well out of the range of any artillery shell. "Are you staring at it now? Is it rigged as one of those artillery-shell IEDs that troubled our forces so much?"

Markham had no personal experience with improvised explosive devices, but had heard they were quite deadly. He walked from the deck to his sunroom, the golden rays slicing through the floor-to-ceiling windowpanes that gave him an expansive view southward into the Atlantic Ocean and the wildlife refuge on the islands to the southwest. Sipping his coffee, he thought about his Tybee set of concubines. They were the first ones and he guessed it was about time to rotate them out. Ten girls at each location was the standard. He had hooked them on heroin and then issued them weekly HIV tests just to make sure none of the CLEVER guests had brought an unwanted disease into the "family." The Colorado girls were the most recent and there was nothing like dusting off a young fifteen-year-old girl in Markham's mind. The first time was a bit sloppy, but once trained, there was no better feeling in the world to him. It was just . . . tight. To that point, at least the Tybee girls were dusted and trained. They knew their role and how to perform. After the all-night flight he could use some stress relief, but first he needed to help Xanadu through this meddlesome problem.

"I'm staring at it. It's metal, like a briefcase. There's wires attached to a standard car battery. The battery looks new. The case looks muddy and old. Like ten years old kind of thing."

"Can you snap a picture with your phone? I'll have some of my intel experts analyze it," Markham said.

"Roger. I'm lucky it didn't blow when I opened the case," Xanadu said. "And there's a note on top that says, "Trade.""

"Trade? Who's asking for a trade?"

"It didn't have a question mark. It was a statement. There's an off chance that she might have been Basayev's wife."

"You kidnapped the wife of the most lethal terrorist in the world?"

"It's possible, though I didn't know it at the time."

Markham stepped inside the bulletproof walls of his mansion's sunroom, looked around, suddenly feeling as if there was a bogeyman behind every door.

"Okay, well, this is different," he said, gathering himself. He stared through the bulletproof windows into the ocean.

A flock of pelicans glided low along the water like a squadron of bombers avoiding radar. They cruised past the boat circling the bluefish and continued south. Lifting his face to the sun beaming through the windowpane, he let the stress leave his body. No worries. If Basayev had come for his wife, then he most likely had her. If he wanted to get revenge, well, this was all on Xanadu.

"And word is that Basayev is in country. The Chechen," Xanadu continued.

Markham coughed. The smile faded.

"Say again? Basayev? Here?" Though that thought had occurred to him.

"Yes. He's been reported as having been at the hotel. Lots of moving pieces."

"Well, it sounds like he's got his woman and left you a bomb. Quite the shit show you've created," Markham said, trying to settle down. He didn't want to take a Valium before the stress relief because sometimes that made it difficult to get hard. And taking a Valium and Viagra at the same time seemed counterproductive.

"I have a plan," Xanadu said. "But it involves a lot of the product and many of the girls."

"Do tell," Markham said, taking another sip of his coffee.

Xanadu laid out the plan as Markham paced back and forth along the expansive sunroom. He understood the plan, but didn't necessarily like it.

"Will you get me more girls?" Markham asked.

"Of course, General. I figured you'd be tired of these by now anyway," Xanadu said.

"Well, true. We can go ahead and redeploy these. And the product? You're talking about a couple of million in walking-around money," Markham said.

"Plenty more where that came from. The only thing in the way is Harwood," Xanadu said.

"And maybe that bomb you're looking at," Markham said.

"Well, as I told you, that's part of the plan."

"Approved. Execute and don't fail."

Markham clicked off the phone call and sat in his favorite chair. He pressed a button on his phone and said, "You can come down now."

Pushing the image of Basayev's face out of his mind, Markham licked his lips with anticipation. The young girl's slender hand slid along the railing as she negotiated the steps toward him, her negligee floating above her thighs like a gossamer welcome sign.

CHAPTER 21

Sirens wailed nearby. Tires screeched. People were shouting unintelligible commands that echoed beyond the warehouse walls.

Harwood held Monisha's body close to him with his left arm as he kept his pistol in his right hand, ready to defend himself in case Ramsey Xanadu returned.

Monisha's body was lying across his lap. Her breathing was labored. At least she was still alive, for the moment. The warehouse was a large space, seemingly vacant, and fifty yards wide in each direction. Old, rusty forklifts and motorized dollies for moving large amounts of supplies known as bulk or break bulk hibernated in the corner, dormant. This warehouse had at one time housed an operation that serviced a portion of the Port of Savannah.

In addition to the forklifts, there were dozens of new four-foot concrete culvert pipes, perhaps part of a stalled water or sewer project. He carefully laid Monisha's body in one ten-foot-long section. Its thick concrete would provide ample protection for Monisha in the event of a firefight. He positioned the third IV on the top lip of the pipe, allowing gravity to feed the essential fluids into her body. He zipped his ruck tight and had started to move to another four-foot-high pipe when Monisha spoke.

"Wha' we gonna do, Reaper?" Monisha whispered. He looked down. Her eyes had opened, briefly, and then shut again.

"We're going to be okay, Monisha. Just hang in there. Be strong for me, okay? I made a promise to you and I'm keeping it."

"Okay," she muttered.

He checked her wound again. The bleeding had slowed. His tourniquet and bandages were working. The key was finding her a hospital, soon. He loosened the tourniquet to allow for circulation. The femoral artery had not been severed as best he could tell.

Against the backdrop of the approaching sirens, there was a sudden whistling sound that Harwood— still on one knee tending to Monisha—identified a second too late. It was the sound of nylon rope moving past a metal snap link at a high rate of speed. Someone had been in the rafters stalking him. Harwood pulled his knife from his pocket and flipped open the blade as the man landed on the concrete floor five feet from him, nylon rope smoking in the carabiner. The man was wearing a ski mask with holes for the eyes and mouth. The attacker immediately landed a roundhouse kick to Harwood's head. It was a square impact from a solid wooden heel, the kind they made in Eastern European and former Soviet-bloc countries.

Like Chechnya.

He raised his arms in self-defense, as he saw the man spin again, this time wheeling a left hook into his rib cage, which Harwood partially blocked. He sliced with the knife, narrowly missing the man's neck. The right-handed cross exposed his right side, which the attacker exploited with a steel-toed-boot kick, which sent his knife skidding. He powered through the pain and got inside his attacker, landed four solid punches to the man's face before another boot landed in his chest. He didn't fall, just backed up a few steps, preparing for the next flurry. His assailant stepped back, flashed white teeth through the ski-mask mouth hole, and said, "Good to see you, Reaper."

A weapon fired. A slug impacted his head.

Harwood's body slid down Monisha's concrete pipe before the world went black.

"Reaper," a voice called out. Harwood instinctively tugged at his hands, going for his knife, but someone had bound his wrists with the same rope used to rappel from the rafters.

"Reaper, wake up," the voice called out again. He recognized the inflection and the cadence of the words. They were the same as those of the man from the elevator. *You do the same, Reaper.*

His attacker was Basayev!

All this time he imagined a long-distance duel with state-of-the-art weaponry between himself and his archrival, the Chechen. Instead, he had been tag-teamed. Close fight, deep fight. Hand-to-hand combat with a shooter looking over his shoulder. It violated Harwood's sense of propriety. A duel had certain rules and expectations, and while Harwood was a good insurgent himself, he had come to expect a show-down with the Chechen in a more . . . formal manner, he guessed.

This was a different warehouse. The smells of fried meat and overheated motors permeated the air. The dimensions of the building were more confined. Someone had strapped him to a conveyor of some type, bound his hands and legs. He could marginally turn his head. Monisha was lying on the dusty con-crete floor about ten meters away. She was covered in a painter's tarp, her head tilted away.

"Monisha. Is she okay?"

Basayev removed the ski mask. "I changed her ban-dages. Your medical field craft is decent, Reaper, but you need some retraining. I'm professionally embar-rassed," Basayev said.

"Where are we?" Harwood asked.

"Good question. You are on a conveyor belt in an old hog-processing plant. Old but still functional. You know what happens when your agriculture bureaucrats determine a hog or its pork to be diseased?"

Basayev paused as if he expected Harwood to answer and then continued when Harwood stared daggers at him.

"They put the pigs on this conveyor belt, which feeds into that incinerator."

Harwood hunched up as if he was doing a crunch. About twenty meters away was a spinning spiral blade inside a giant cylindrical tube that looked like a giant jet engine. Harwood was strapped to a metal grate that sat atop a black, rubberized conveyor belt that, when powered, would propel him into the cylinder.

"The hog or pork is fed into the tube, which slowly

turns and burns the flesh and bones until only ash is deposited out of the other side. Apparently, your port at Savannah processes some pigs. Are you a pig, Reaper? Or will you tell me what you know?"

Basayev was a master torture artist. The absence of sirens meant that the police were at the site where Xanadu had used miniguns to destroy Lanny's Mustang and wound Monisha. The windowless slaughterhouse was dimly lit by the sun seeping through the seams of the corrugated metal walls.

"So, my questions," Basayev started. He flipped the switch on the incinerator and walked toward Harwood, kneeling. Heat washed over his body. "The girl. A bit young for you, don't you think, Reaper?"

"I was protecting her. Nothing else. Sort of like you tried to do with Nina, but failed."

Basayev ran a rough-hewn hand over his brown/blond locks, smoothing them back into place. He wore a tight-fitting black athletic shirt with black jeans and tan leather chukkas that had landed the concussive blow to Harwood's head. Basayev spun and landed a roundhouse kick into Harwood's ribs. Harwood grimaced at the sharp pain. Basayev twisted his own neck, cracking it several times.

"Don't mention Nina's name unless you're telling me where she is, Reaper. Understand?"

Spitting up blood, Harwood said, "I had nothing to do with any of that, but I know who does. I've figured it out."

"You really think you're in a position to discuss this with me, Harwood?" Basayev said. "You know very little." He held up a small silicon square in front of Harwood's face. "This is a nonlethal beanbag projectile.

Let me introduce you to the person who fired it at you."

Basayev stepped back and waved his hand forward, saying, "Abrek. He's all yours. The man who left you for dead on the battlefield."

Harwood was unprepared to hear Samuelson's voice, which assaulted him harder than the beanbag his former spotter must have fired.

"Reaper, it's me. Abrek."

He tried to turn his head and catch a glimpse, but he felt a hand ratchet his head downward onto the metal grate that ferried pig flesh into the cooker. Pain ricocheted through his scalp. The serrated steel edges bit into his scalp.

"Samuelson?" He coughed. "Sammie, where did you go when you dropped me off the other day?" The other day? Harwood couldn't remember what day it was.

Samuelson leaned down in front of him, eye-to-eye, hands on the metal grate that could convey him to his death. He was wearing the same stained trucker hat, flannel shirt, jeans, and boots. His hair was wavy and long, almost down to his shoulders and longer on one side than the other. Scars pocked his face beneath the scraggly beard, probably cuts from the mortar shrapnel and rocks that had impacted so closely. His face was pinched in a hateful sneer.

"It's Abrek, to you, Reaper. I left you for maybe a day. Even grabbed your shit from your room, buddy. You? You left me for dead on the battlefield. But guess what? Khasan saved me after the search-and-rescue guys plucked your precious ass out of the rock pile. They never bothered looking fifty meters away for me. Whatever happened to the Ranger creed 'Never leave a fallen comrade'?" Samuelson's voice was a knife opening old wounds that had been healing, like slicing fresh stitches with a razor.

Harwood leaned his head against the grate and stared at the ceiling, a mixture of crisscrossing metal rafters and dilapidated catwalks. He turned his head and looked at Monisha. Coiled on the floor next to her was some leftover rope. Looking back at Samuelson, Harwood saw hesitation in the eyes, as if he was remembering something. How badly had the Chechen brainwashed Samuelson? he wondered. He visualized them back in Afghanistan taking aim at the Chechen, noticing the snatch operation, then seeing the sign—*Bring her back! Trade?*—and then hearing the mortars. After that the next thing he recalled was Command Sergeant Major Murdoch looking at him as he woke up in the Kandahar operating base intensive-care unit.

"I was knocked out, Sammie. You know that," Harwood said.

"I don't know jack shit, buddy. Seems we both had some badass brain injuries. Problem is, you had first-class care. Me? I had our friend, Khasan, who did his best."

"I'm glad you're okay," Harwood said.

"Did you ever give a shit about me, Harwood? Or was it all about being the Reaper?" Samuelson said. "Because I'm thinking it was fame and fortune, my friend. The cover of *Rolling Stone* magazine? Seriously? Meanwhile, I'm left to die?"

"Xanadu from Milk 'Em fired those mortars on us," Harwood said, pushing back. "And they're running a drug- and sex-trafficking ring on their private flights from Afghanistan back to Hunter Army Airfield here in Savannah. Drugs are going to kids on the military bases and the women disappear."

"Really?" Basayev interrupted. "And you're not involved?" Basayev's skepticism was evident in his tone.

"I'm not involved. I've had the cops, everyone breathing down my neck, chasing me. I had to start figuring things out on my own. Even ditched my phone," Harwood said. Then he looked again at Monisha. "And then I got some help from a friend."

Basayev saw the glance and something registered with the Chechen, who said, "It was close. Lucky the femoral artery wasn't cut. She's quite special to you, isn't she, Reaper?"

Basayev wasn't compassionate; rather, Monisha was a card he could play. And Samuelson? Was he corrupted beyond repair by the Chechen? Samuelson's angst was understandable. Had the situation been reversed, Harwood would have been angry. Pissed off with his Ranger buddy, the Rangers, the search-and-rescue team, the army, the Defense Department, everyone whose responsibility it was to bring him home.

The muzzle of a weapon touched his head.

"Tell me about this girl, Reaper." Basayev nodded at Monisha.

"Xanadu shot her like he tried to kill Sammie and me in Kandahar that day. She was just a kid who I saved from being raped and murdered."

Basayev's face softened fractionally. "The two rednecks being reported as killed near Macon? That was you?"

"That was me, but that's all I've done," Harwood said. "Now tell me about Sammie."

"I'm r-right here, Reaper." *No retort that he was Abrek? Something was getting to him.*

"I know. I want to hear it from Basayev."

"I'll play your game for a minute, Reaper. I found him after you ran like a scared goat onto the helicopter. Abrek was barely alive. Your cowardice surprised me, but we all have our priorities."

"You son of a bitch. I didn't jump on any helo. Sammie, he's lying. And your name isn't Abrek. He's brainwashed you!"

"I hear ya b-bud. Must have been h-hell hooking up with Jackie Colt, g-getting laid every night. Fine piece of ass like that, must have been grueling j-just keeping up. Book on her is she's a certified nympho, like card-carrying type. Have to be to hook up with a s-snake like you," Samuelson said.

"I know what you're doing, Sammie. Don't let Basayev trick you," Harwood said. "I didn't abandon you."

Basayev interrupted.

"Let's discuss these excellent kills you've made, Reaper. First, how did you get your rifle back? Because I had secured it from the mortar attack scene where I found Samuelson and had it until about a week ago. Did you steal it? Have a replica? Or are you some kind of magician?"

"Like I said, I didn't kill anyone except the two men who were going to rape and kill her," Harwood said, motioning his chin toward Monisha.

"If you didn't kill the generals and the others—and trust me, I am glad that every one of them is dead—then who did?" Basayev asked.

"I figured it was you," Harwood said. "What would be my motive?"

"I can think of three off the top of my head, Reaper. First, Milk 'Em fired those mortars at you and you know that. Everyone who has been killed has a connection to Milk 'Em. Revenge is always the best motive. Then of course I've done some hacking into your bank account. Seems you've come into some money. After every kill, you receive a one-hundred-thousand-dollar deposit. That's what they call circumstantial evidence, I believe. And I guess if the first two don't work, a good prosecutor could always argue that you've lost your mind: the angry-veteran prosecution. Happens more than people like to think about."

"I don't know anything about the money," Harwood said. If Basayev could hack into his bank account he could also put the money in there to implicate him. "And yeah I'm pissed at Milk 'Em, but I'm specifically pissed at Xanadu. He's the one who was on the battlefield and who I suspect is leading the snatch teams of the missing women."

"Funny. He said the same thing about you. You Americans. Who can I trust?"

"No. It wasn't me. My mission was to kill you and prevent the harvest of poppy."

Basayev stepped back, face blank. "Seems you failed on both counts there."

Samuelson's eyes darted between him and Basayev. Harwood used the indecision as leverage. "And what do you care, Basayev? You're just a combat prostitute. A mercenary. You pimp yourself out to anyone who pays you."

Basayev sneered. "What do you care?"

Harwood managed a chuckle. "Sammie and I have this saying. 'Bros before hos.' Isn't that right, Sammie? Basayev's nothing but a ho. Sells his services to the highest bidder. No loyalty to anyone. He's using you, bro."

Samuelson's eyes locked on to Harwood's. They flickered with recognition. Something registered. Maybe it was their last moments together in the sniper hide position.

Samuelson stepped in front of Basayev and kneeled in front of Harwood, who could smell Samuelson's stale breath.

"Listen to me, V-Vick, Khasan is pissed because he thinks you've kidnapped his wife. And I'm p-pissed because he is the one who saved me on the battlefield. We need to know where Nina is."

There was a change in the inflection of Samuelson's voice, a softened undertone, the sharp edges of anger perhaps dulled by a memory of their code. Harwood let the moment take hold, then said, "How many ways can I say it? I've not killed those people. And I've certainly not seen Nina Moreau."

Basayev's head snapped toward him. "You know her last name? You've got a target folder on her!"

"I've not seen her. I swear," Harwood said. Though, with his faltering memory, he couldn't be sure. He recalled seeing the flash of a face that looked like the picture sent by the sergeant major. When? Running in Forsyth Park?

"What?" Basayev asked. He must have seen the look on Harwood's face.

"Nothing," Harwood said. "I mean. Maybe it's something."

"You've got her and you've been hunting me, Reaper. Now tell me. Where is she?"

"Khasan, I think he's trying to say he's seen her, but I don't believe he's got her. I passed him running and saw him try to remember me. I think he's being legit."

Maybe good cop/bad cop, or was that the second crack in the outer shell of Basayev's indoctrination of Samuelson? Whether Samuelson truly felt allegiance to Basayev remained unclear. Regardless, the outcome was the same. Samuelson was aligned, at least in purpose, with Basayev. Still, he decided to pursue the opening.

"And what is with this 'we' bullshit, Sammie? Since when did you become a traitor?"

"I'm not a traitor, Vick. He saved me. I owe him for that," Samuelson said. *Vick. Good.*

"That doesn't make me your enemy," Harwood said.

"Either tell me where Nina is or you'll soon be ashes, Reaper," Basayev said. The Chechen looked at the flaming cylinder as it spun. All Basayev needed to do was press the button that started the conveyor belt and he was toast.

"I *can* help you find Nina."

The Chechen was silent.

Samuelson was watching Basayev. Harwood believed he had created a fissure in the Stockholm syndrome induced by Basayev's manipulations. He couldn't imagine what the last three months had been like for Samuelson. Primitive care and treatment in one of Afghanistan's poorest provinces, Helmand. The options he faced were daunting. Either Samuelson could try to recover from his wounds in the care of their archrival, who had killed fellow Rangers, or he could try to escape and evade through enemy territory, while severely incapacitated. There was no choice for Samuelson then. The only path forward now was to recognize the psychological connection between Samuelson and Basayev, continue to gingerly pry at that, and then realign Samuelson with him before Basayev fed him to the incinerator.

"Here's the deal," Harwood said to his two captors. "Let me go. I'll call the police and EMS about Monisha once we're all clear from here. She deserves that. Then I'll find Nina."

"You don't deal," Basayev said. He looked at Samuelson and smirked. "It's your call, Abrek. Me or the Reaper." Basayev walked over and punched a button on the wall.

The chains beneath him shook like a hundred rattle-snakes. The conveyor coughed to life. The metal grate began moving him forward toward the incinerator.

A million thoughts sparked in his mind, but he latched on to the fact that Jackie's younger brother had died from an opium overdose at Fort Benning, Georgia. Jackie had used her considerable interpersonal skills to befriend an FBI agent, who had mentioned to her that they had traced the opium to Helmand Province. She had come to believe that MLQM was the culprit. Could she be the assassin? Could she be with Nina?

"I know where they are!" Harwood said.

Basayev was leaning over Monisha. He had removed the painter's tarp. He stood and pressed the stop button.

"Tell me, Reaper. Or I take the girl and you burn."

"No!" Harwood said. He gasped and strained against his bonds. He felt the heat wash over him in continuous waves. He was halfway to the incinerator. Ten meters away. Flames licked out of the cylinder like a serpent's tongue.

"Talk, Reaper! Where's Nina!"

"Leave the girl, Basayev," Harwood said.

"Not your decision, Harwood. It's up to Abrek. His choice. If he chooses you, then you bring me Nina and you can have her back. If not, well then, goodbye."

Basayev looked at the steaming furnace and then the ailing fourteen-year-old with hardened eyes. His hands flexed, as if preparing for torture.

"Just do it, Reaper," Monisha muttered. "I'll be okay. Don't want you burnt. He ain't nothing." She had turned her head and was eyeing Harwood. "We good," she added.

"I know about the nuke," Harwood said. "Sammie, he's got a nuke ready to blow. Today. Tomorrow. I don't know when, but soon. You're one of the good guys, Sammie."

Samuelson eyed Basayev, then Harwood, and went back to Basayev, as if watching a tennis match.

"Is that true, Khasan?" Samuelson asked. He was confused, uncertain.

"Your Reaper is desperate, Abrek. He will say anything. But as I said, it is your choice." Basayev smirked, but it was a less confident sneer. He cradled the girl and pressed the start button again, feeding Harwood to the pig incinerator.

Harwood eyed Samuelson. His spotter stood temporarily frozen. "K-Khasan. Stop!"

Monisha screamed, "No!" Basayev stepped over

the painter's tarp and Harwood's rucksack as he fled with the teenager. Harwood heard the door slam as the chains propelled him toward the fire. A diesel engine fired up outside and the sound of gravel peppering the metal wall echoed inside the warehouse. Monisha was gone and perhaps so was he.

"Sammie!" Harwood shouted.

Maybe it was the absence of Basayev or the presence of Harwood, but Samuelson turned toward Harwood. He dove toward the wall, slammed the button to stop the conveyor, and then ran past Harwood and shut down the incinerator. Reaching Harwood, he began cutting the ropes with his knife, muttering something unintelligible to himself.

"V-Vick, are you okay?"

Samuelson helped Harwood stand. His shoes were barely intact, the rubber soles sizzling on the concrete. He looped his arm around Samuelson's shoulders and they walked away from the heat. Samuelson opened the door, they both looked at the empty lot, and Harwood said, "Monisha's gone."

"We'll find her, bro," Samuelson said.

The irony was not lost on Harwood. Samuelson was saving him when he had been unable to do the same in Afghanistan. Similarly, he had now failed Monisha. Nonetheless, he needed to press ahead.

"Thanks, bro," Harwood said. He hugged his spotter. Held him tight, then pushed away. "Are you seriously connected with Basayev?" he asked.

Samuelson looked away, eyes furtive. He heaved a heavy sigh, frustration leaving the body.

"He saved my life, Vick." Then, after a moment, he asked, "Is there really a nuke?"

"I think so," Harwood said.

The two former teammates squatted against the wall of the corrugated metal building.

"You okay?" Harwood asked.

"I'm like you. Have good days and bad days. Like I said, he thinks you've got Nina. It's the only reason you're alive. While I was recovering in Kandahar, Basayev said we had to find you to find Nina."

Samuelson's stuttering seemed to come and go as stressful memories ebbed and flowed.

"You were in Kandahar all this time?"

"Yeah, Basayev's not stupid. He knew coalition forces would be crawling all over Helmand Province looking for me. He brought me to a safe house a few miles away from the FOB in Kandahar."

"How'd you get here? I mean out of Afghanistan and into the United States?"

"We took a truck from Kandahar into Iran. He's got some credentials there, too. Passed me off as his captive."

"Which you are, by the way," Harwood said.

"I don't know. Maybe . . ."

"Keep going." Samuelson was remembering, and if that memory cycle took him all the way back to being a Ranger, then good.

"An airplane flew us from a dirt strip into Oman where we flew on a private jet to the Bahamas and jumped on a charter yacht up here. Basayev has money, evidently."

"Why here, though? Savannah?"

"We were tracking you," Samuelson said.

"Yeah, I found the tracker. But if I'm not killing these people, then who is? You guys?"

"Not that I've seen. We figured it was you," Samuelson said.

Harwood turned his head to the left, toward a mesh window. A flash of dark blue swept past. They had been in the warehouse for longer than he wanted to stay. The tarp that had covered Monisha lay at their feet like an empty body bag.

"So, where is it?"

"Where is what?" Samuelson asked.

"My rifle."

Samuelson paused, looked away.

"It's m-missing," he said. "I had it for a while, but it's gone."

"You had it here? Brought it here?"

Again, Samuelson looked away, scratched his whiskers, then spoke. "Yeah. It was in a duffel bag with some other stuff."

"Last place we stayed was a Motel 6 near Fort Bragg. Hadn't seen it since then. Maybe a week? That was a different rifle you saw the other night."

"You were at Fort Bragg?"

"Like I said, we've been following you, b-bro."

Harwood's mind flashed. Images of Jackie Colt putting something in her trunk at Fort Bragg. Was it luggage? A rifle?

"Who else is on the kill sheet?" Harwood asked.

"He just told me he had one. Didn't show it to me."

Samuelson's distant stare was interrupted by rapid eye blinking, as if he was searching his mind for answers.

"No, Sammie, think. Help me here. We used to do this in combat. Who else is part of this thing? Did Basayev mention anyone else? Did you drop him off anywhere with some equipment to dig? Did he ever use your car?"

Samuelson scratched his chin. His eyes flicked left and right. He tugged on his cap, thinking.

"General Sampson's dead. General Dillman's dead. Two cops are dead. Senator Kraft is dead," Samuelson said. "Basayev was tracking them. He'd repeat it after he heard it on the news."

"See? He's got a list. If not an actual sheet, he's got one in his mind. Plus, you left off two of General Markham's guards."

"That's it. I remember that name," Samuelson said.

"Okay, this is helpful. We need to get moving," Harwood said.

"Where?"

"Anywhere but here."

Harwood shouldered his ruck, charged his pistol, and directed, "Follow me."

"But where?"

"To find Nina Moreau and Jackie Colt, then get Monisha back."

Harwood had done the math. Basayev didn't have the range to be everywhere he had been and also do the shootings. No single person had that kind of capacity. It was a two-person job. And the only two people with motive and access to his rifle were Jackie and Nina.

"Why?"

"Because they're doing the killing," he said.

Samuelson nodded, looked away, tried to speak, but the words weren't coming.

"What, Sammie? What's in your mind right now? Just grab it."

Samuelson squeezed his eyes shut tight. Tears

flowed. His lips turned downward in a drool-soaked sob. "I . . . I can't remember, but it's important!"

Harwood placed his hand on Samuelson's shoulder. "It's okay, bro. Remember bros before hos." He hugged Samuelson.

"Bros before hos," Samuelson repeated. "That's my line." He chuckled an odd laugh, like a car engine coughing. Harwood cradled the back of his misshapen skull with his hand, feeling for the first time the dent a rock must have caused. Imagining the pain Samuelson endured, he hugged the sobbing Ranger tighter.

Samuelson's heaves slowed and he pulled away from Harwood.

"He mentioned a man named Lunev," Samuelson said. "Not to me, but I overheard him on the boat one day. He was on the radio. Stan Lunev, I think."

Harwood stepped back. He knew the name.

"Are you sure he said Lunev? Stanislav Lunev?"

"Yes, that's it exactly." Samuelson smiled, like a child who had just answered correctly in class.

Lunev was a Russian defector who had briefed the American government on the ease with which the then Soviet Union and present-day Russia could infiltrate tactical nuclear weapons into the United States using spetsnaz high-altitude insertion.

"If he mentioned Lunev, then he definitely has a bomb."

CHAPTER 22

Not once did FBI Special Agent Deke Bronson believe that his Match.com profile would transition from dating mechanism to intelligence source.

But it had.

"Nancy" had connected with him and said she had valuable information about the sex-trafficking ring. That was interesting primarily because the police and FBI had not gone public with the sex-trafficking angle. It was still close hold. So unless there was a leak from a very small group of people, his meeting with Nancy could be a major break. And he needed a break.

Bronson sat inside the Starbucks on Bay Street just north of City Hall. It was bustling with the usual cross section of humanity. Busy college students hammered away on MacBooks, young professionals carrying satchels ordered lattes, dog lovers sat outside sipping chai while their best friends lapped at tin bowls filled with water or snapped treats from their masters' hands, and rushed patrons waited impatiently as the presses and blenders whirred.

Faye Wilde was across the street checking her phone, looking like any attractive millennial doing her thing on a work break. He could smell the burgers frying at Five Guys just up the road. Max Corent was inside the burger joint on his MacBook monitoring the Starbucks security cameras. It was a simple hack into the system and Corent had radioed that he was live. Randy White was on the roof of a brew pub across the street just above Wilde. He had his rifle in a kit bag ready to go, but Bronson had ordered him to use the spotter's scope initially and then to use his judgment on whether to switch to his rifle.

A waif of a woman dressed in black brushed his shoulder as she whisked past him. A piece of paper fell into his lap as she disappeared behind the patrons waiting in line for their orders. Beyond the line was an outdoor seating venue with umbrellas and beyond that was the open street.

Bronson opened the note: *Catch me if you can. Love, Nancy ;)*

He took that as a cue to follow her. Bronson stood and began walking quickly in the woman's direction as he spoke calmly through his earpiece microphone.

"Following suspect out of the side entrance. Looks like she's going right into the alley," he whispered.

"Roger. I've got her," White said from the rooftop. "Skinny black-haired woman dressed in black. Makes for a good target."

"Not that skinny, actually," Bronson said, turning the corner. He saw the toned triceps of his target about twenty-five yards away. She was moving swiftly, black jeans, tight-fitting short-sleeved black shirt, short black boots, all meshing with the long black hair swishing like a mare's tail. She ducked into an alley that Bronson knew that White, Corent, and Wilde could not observe. Then another turn and another.

Soon he was following her along a dark corridor of low live oak trees. It was a running path and it occurred to the marine in Bronson that he was being led into an ambush. The black-haired woman was the rabbit and he was the fox. Only the hunters preferred the fox over the rabbit.

She turned off the asphalt greenway and onto a small footpath into the trees. Damn the torpedoes, Bronson thought. He whispered into his microphone, "In pursuit behind the Starbucks, maybe four blocks. On a greenway and now a small trail."

"Stop, boss," Wilde whispered from somewhere. Her voice was raspy, as if she was running.

"Already committed," he said.

And he was. He stepped into the woods and soon a high kick caught his jaw and he spun, but not before he got a powerful left arm up and twisted the ankle, however briefly. Regardless of that action, she was on top of him after a quick heel pick and a razor-sharp forearm in the throat.

"The killings continue until you arrest General Markham and Vick Harwood. You've got twenty-four hours," she said.

Bronson couldn't make out her face; the long black hair was a veil, shielding her from recognition. He could smell the sweat and filth, as if she hadn't bathed in weeks. Before he could gather any more clues, she was off him and moving quickly to the north, away from him.

"Wait!" he shouted. "Nancy!"

But she was gone like a vanishing ghost, present one second then diminishing into vapor.

A few seconds later, Faye Wilde came running with her pistol drawn. "Was that her?"

Bronson stood, "Had to be." Rubbing his jaw, he remarked, "Damn good roundhouse. That shit wasn't in her profile, was it?"

"No time for joking around, sir," Wilde said. "We've got to find her."

"She's gone. Fast. Strong. No chance," he said.

Wilde looked at the path into the woods. "Why on earth did you follow her in here?"

"I figured she wanted to say something to me. I just didn't realize she would preface her remarks in the manner she did."

"You ripped your three-hundred-dollar Boss shirt," Wilde said, relaxing.

"Felt that. Aren't you going to ask what she said?"

Corent and White appeared on the scene, the four of them standing at the edge of the tree line.

"Randy, Max, you guys go about a hundred yards in there and see if there's anything. Doubtful, but you never know."

"Roger that, boss," White said, gripping his rifle. "Let's go, Max."

The two men walked carefully into the woods as Bronson stood from his one-knee position and said to Wilde, "She said we need to arrest Harwood."

"Well no shit," Wilde said.

"And General Markham."

"Markham? The air force guy? What's he got to do with this?"

"I don't know, but he's got a house about ten miles from here. I fully intend to talk to him ASAP."

"Tread carefully, Deke. He knows people," Wilde said.

"I'm aware of that, Faye, but I can't ignore it, mostly because she just risked capture by the FBI to communicate with me, whoever she is."

"Say anything else?"

"Yeah, we have twenty-four hours," Bronson said.

"Or what?"

"She didn't say, but I don't want to find out."

Corent and White returned. Nothing.

Wilde's phone rang. She answered and listened.

"Oh my God," she said. "An anonymous tip. Harwood is in a warehouse on River and McGuire Streets."

"Let's move. That's not even ten blocks from here," Bronson said.

Harwood needed to contact the FBI, but on his terms, not with his hands clasped atop his head.

He grabbed Samuelson and led him to the side door. About one hundred yards away was Lanny's shot up Mustang. Basayev had moved them to a completely different warehouse opposite where they had ambushed him. Police were milling in the field around the Mustang, making the route a no-go. The other two doors on the building opened simultaneously. At the front of the building were a black man and a redheaded woman, both aiming their pistols at Samuelson and Harwood. Two men entered from the left side, one with a pistol and another with an AR-15 rifle. Each pair was about fifty yards away.

"We're jacked, dude," Samuelson said.

"No. This was your buddy calling us in. He's playing with us. Likes for us to be on the move, not get complacent. It's all about the nuke."

A voice called out from the front. "Vick Harwood!?" It was both a question and an announcement. Like the man was not totally uncertain, but neither was he convinced it was him.

"Who's asking?" Harwood shouted back. They were next to the only escape route. Harwood assumed that the pursuers had banked on the police blocking that avenue of egress.

"FBI!" the man shouted.

"Got nothing to do with any of this," Harwood shouted.

"Then you've got no reason to run. Come talk to us. Help us figure it out," the man said loudly as they advanced at a fast pace.

"Not my job," Harwood shouted. "Do yours and it's plain to see." The FBI had to know about Lunev, because he was in witness protection.

"You're an American," the FBI man said. "It's everybody's job."

"I'll tell you what," Harwood shouted as he grasped the doorknob, looking through the metal mesh window as he kept an eye on the police outside. The FBI continued to advance. "A man named Xanadu is who you're looking for, not me. And while you're at it, you may want to find Stansilav Lunev."

He nodded at Samuelson, then looked at the tarp

where Monisha had been covered. He heard her imaginary voice: "Reaper, what we gonna do now? Cops ever'where."

But that was just his mind playing with him, and now was no time to open any of those trapdoors. He had an escape plan. He needed to survive for at least the next twenty-four hours so he could find Jackie and Nina, which was the only way he could see to also save Monisha.

"You've got a weapon and that's hostile intent, Reaper!" the lead FBI man shouted.

Hostile intent or not, Harwood took another glance at the cops outside and said to Samuelson, "We can do this." Harwood raced out the door with Samuelson on his heels, hooking an immediate right toward the river. Fifty yards from the river, maybe five to ten seconds for him to get around the back side of the building. He prayed that one of the two boats he had seen was operational and had keys tucked away somewhere.

"Where we going, Vick?"

"River. Follow me."

The police were focused inward on the charred Mustang, like a football huddle. As they rounded the corner, Harwood slowed, flipped his rucksack to his front, and began reaching into the outer pockets.

Approaching the ramp to the docks, he leapt three steps at a time until he was on the pier. Shouts and footfalls thundered behind them. He chose the 25 Mako farthest away and nearest the river because it looked older and unkempt.

"Untie the lines. Look for a key," Harwood said. He tossed two gray smoke grenades onto the path they had just taken and then pulled the pin on a stun grenade and heaved it into the smoke. It wouldn't kill anyone unless they were standing on it, but still, he needed to buy some time.

Samuelson was tearing up the cushions while Harwood shifted to looking above the console and slapped the four fishing-pole cones above the shade screen until he heard a rattle on the fourth cone.

Gunfire sounded off nearby and bullets snapped past their heads.

"Got it," he said, tilting the cone downward, the keys sliding into his hand. One bullet shattered the windshield directly to Harwood's front.

"They're coming through the smoke," Samuelson said.

The grenade and smoke had bought them maybe a minute, but it was precious time. He inserted the key into the ignition, ensured the gearshift was in neutral, and then cranked the motor, which started on the first try. He backed the boat out and rammed the gearshift forward, spitting a giant rooster tail onto the law enforcement officials chasing them.

They sped north, passing beneath the Talmadge Memorial Bridge that spanned the Savannah River. Soon they were out of direct fire range of any of the weapons carried by the FBI or Savannah Police Department. However, an SPD helicopter would likely be in the air soon, not to mention that of Ramsey Xanadu and perhaps even the FBI, which meant he needed to downsize his footprint quickly.

Zipping along the smooth brown waters of the Savannah River, they confronted giant merchant ships that were coming into and departing from one of the busiest ports in the country. He bounced through the wakes, which made his teeth chatter. The massive port infrastructure with cranes and containers stacked to the sky loomed ominously above them. A giant dispenser was disgorging a steady stream of corn from one of the berth-side ships into railcars.

"Okay, we're going in here," Harwood said.

He shot the boat into a tailspin and idled it next to the tall berth made for handling large container ships. He nudged the throttle forward until he reached a series of rungs that served as a ladder.

"Tie the boat off here," he directed. Samuelson grabbed the rope and tied a bowline, the basic knot they'd learned in Ranger School. Harwood grabbed his ruck and ascended hand over hand on the rusty cleats until he reached the top of the pier. Above them cranes were moving in and out with large containers swinging beneath like rectangular wrecking balls. He rolled onto the concrete and saw a series of railroad spurs to his left.

"This way," he said when Samuelson reached the top.

They ran along the railroad, leaping from tie to tie, sometimes stumbling on the gravel. After a mile of running, Harwood pulled up short next to a row of stationary railcars. Breathing hard, he knelt over as Samuelson caught up to him.

Helicopter blades chopped in the distance. Whether the helicopter was from the Savannah Police Department, the FBI, or Xanadu, they all amounted to the same thing: lethal. The sun was well overhead by now, beaming at high noon. Steel wheels screamed on iron rails with an ear-piercing pitch. One of the trains loaded with containers was slowly beginning to pull to the west, away from the river and the port.

"That one, Sammie," Harwood said. They raced

across the uneven tracks until they could grab on to metal rungs not unlike those they had climbed on the berth. Harwood slid in between two cars and stood on the tongue of the coupler. Not a hard leap. He helped Samuelson up and they grabbed whatever handholds they could find. They were well concealed and there didn't seem to be anyone who could observe their position. The train picked up speed, gaining from five to maybe fifteen miles an hour.

Another helicopter joined the search, buzzing along the river. Two helicopters, leaving only one remaining. The calculus of who was looking for him didn't matter anymore. If it was the FBI and Savannah Police Department, well okay. If it was Ramsey Xanadu and either of the other two, then maybe something good for him would come of that. Like the FBI shooting down Xanadu's helicopter.

But part of Harwood wanted to come face-to-face with Xanadu since the barbarian had wounded Monisha. Also, the battlefield geometry indicated Harwood might first have to go through Xanadu to ultimately get Basayev. As the train picked up speed, warehouses slipped by in his periphery. Harwood didn't want to get too far away from his main objective, so after a mile he motioned to Samuelson and they jumped and rolled into a ditch at the base of the tracks. Some forward throw, sharp edges and pain, but nothing too bad.

Once the final railcar had passed, Harwood led Samuelson to the wooded area to the east of the rail. He moved to the far edge where they could see the western portion of Forsyth Park. The witch's-hat roof of General Dillman's house poked up beyond the green canopy of the park.

He found a clearing, dropped his ruck, and turned to Samuelson.

"Thanks, brother."

Samuelson stared at him. "No p-problem, Vick. I just get confused sometimes. Khasan really did a number on me."

"I understand. Take off your hat and let me see your head," Harwood asked.

Samuelson's head was grotesque. Harwood picked through the hair. Part of Samuelson's skull had been dented, like an automobile after a fender bender.

"I've seen it, bro. Pretty gross," Samuelson said, holding his stained red and white trucker's hat in his hand.

"What did he do to you?" Harwood asked.

"He just wrapped it, man. Threw some alcohol in there and put a compress on it. Think a doctor stitched it."

"How's your memory?"

"My what?"

After a pause, Harwood said, "Okay, I get it."

Samuelson smiled. "Haven't lost all my brains, Reaper. Just some of them."

"What was that bullshit back there? Abrek? All up in my face? You know I was as knocked out as you."

"I don't know, bro. Super confused sometimes, you know? He said my name was Abrek. Means 'warrior.' But the more you called me 'Sammie,' the more I started to remember. Still, you know, you got picked up by dust-off and I didn't. That's some bullshit."

"I agree."

"But not your fault."

"So, the Chechen?"

"He's working something, man," Samuelson said. "I think you're right about the nuke." The pupils of Samuelson's eyes were normal black circles. His brown irises didn't flinch as he spoke and looked directly at Harwood. Samuelson's face was pockmarked from shrapnel, but didn't twitch with any tell of a mistruth. "I didn't know he was going to tie you up. Try to burn you."

"It's okay, Sammie. I've got a plan."

"So, tell me," Samuelson said.

And the Reaper told his spotter everything a foxhole buddy needed to know.

Samuelson's only reply was "Damn."

CHAPTER 23

They moved cautiously throughout the day. The sun now hung low in the Western sky.

Sirens wailed all around them. Helicopters buzzed the skies. Dog teams barked in the distance.

"They want you pretty bad," Samuelson said. "Ready?"

"Yeah, but thinking. Where's the one place Basayev didn't take you?"

"What do you mean? How am I supposed to know that if he didn't take me?"

"Think about it. He's known where I am the entire time."

"That's right."

"He's got to have a command center somewhere. And it must be portable. Movable like a tactical operations center. You can be here one minute and there the next minute, because you never know where I'm going to pop up."

"But we knew ahead of time," Samuelson said.

"That's right. You knew my sniper training schedule from someone in Special Operations Command, who coughed it up."

"No. Basayev hacked their training schedules. We knew where you were going to be because he easily got through the firewalls."

"Which brings me back to my earlier point. He probably can't hack from a phone, though I suppose it's possible. He needs a computer, Wi-Fi, a satellite, all of the above."

Samuelson nodded. "Yeah, I didn't see that."

"That you know of. What's the name of the boat you guys chartered from the Bahamas?"

Samuelson strained. His eyes focused outward, then inward. He was coming up blank.

"He gave me some sedatives during that part of the trip. Said my head injuries and the swells wouldn't mix well together. Some happy horseshit like that," Samuelson said. "I was peaced out big-time for most of that."

"Right. That's because he's got a command and control ship parked around here somewhere, probably linked to Ku-band satellite for imaging, drone control, and fully functional intelligence. I mean, why come to Savannah if you're not coming by boat. Lots of ingress and egress."

"I can believe that. I never left my quarters. They brought me chow and everything. I had an Xbox in there and my own television and DVD collection. Caught up on movies I hadn't seen."

"That's because he was scheming. He's got one plan to get his wife back and another plan to do some damage."

"Not following you," Samuelson said.

"One thing I know about Basayev is he's never off the clock for long. He's being funded to do something."

Samuelson nodded.

"It's no accident he left you to decide to save me or not. He needed to know where your loyalties were as his endgame approached. Monisha's bait, but she'll be a bargaining chip later. So, we need something to trade."

"Like Nina."

"Like that," Harwood said.

"But what if he's got Jackie?"

"He doesn't have Jackie."

"How can you be sure?"

"I can't. But I can go with probabilities. If he had her he wouldn't have let either of us live. Or needed Monisha, for that matter. Also, I think Jackie has her own agenda and that's where we're going now."

"Where?"

"To find Jackie," Harwood said.

"You know where she is?"

"I believe I do. Follow me."

They stepped from the forested area that had served as a final rally point. It had taken them several hours of sliding through alleys, dense forests, and warehouse districts to find the marina east of Savannah on the Bull River. Now they knelt behind a ten-foot-wide-by-four-foot-high generator that serviced the motorboats and sailboats sitting dormant in their riverfront slips. Beyond the marina were a widening river and marshes that eventually led to the Atlantic Ocean.

The marina's name had been on the floating key chain that Jackie had scooped up at the last second from her nightstand in the downtown Savannah hotel. The rucksack, the rifle barrel, the key chain. It all made sense to him now. As much as it hurt him to admit that he had been played, he had to consider that as the most likely course of action.

Harwood knelt on the wooden pier and scouted the dozens of boats sitting idle in their slips. There was no way to determine which boat was *Ten Meter Lady* other than to check them individually by walking along each pier.

"A lot of boats, brother," Samuelson said.

The marina had ten docks that poked into the water perpendicular to a concrete berth. Each pier had a gate, which required a numeric code. There appeared to be twenty slips along each dock. Two hundred boats.

Jackie's would be a transient boat, though, and she would want a slip that she could easily transit. She would want one that went unnoticed by most passersby and onlookers. Marinas attracted an unusual number of gawkers, who liked to study the boats, dream of their own one day.

The pier farthest to the left had three slips with boats they couldn't see because larger boats dominated the sight line from the main entrance. There was a construction site opposite that pier and it was closed to non-construction personnel. A few backhoes and bulldozers sat idle, as if resting before another hard day's work. The swim from the construction site to the pier was maybe fifty yards.

"Follow me," Harwood said.

They walked around the marina, found the construction site, and scaled the chain-link fence, which had black silt barriers running head high along the entire fence line. They moved through footing trenches three feet deep and piles of rebar until they were crawling under the fence opposite the last row of boats.

Using his spotter scope, Harwood read the names of each of the boats from left to right. *Majestic, Fine Wine, Left Out, Picked Six,* and so on, but no *Ten Meter Lady.*

"I was certain," Harwood muttered.

"Over there," Samuelson said. Harwood readjusted to the direction Samuelson pointed and saw a tall woman who had Jackie Colt's physique standing alongside a large Boston Whaler center console boat that was parked at the end of the pier. Not in a slip, but moored at the T.

Just as he had thought. Easy in. Easy out. Minimal maneuvering. She would be able to get to the T-head from the rolling current of the Bull River and then into the Savannah River in a matter of minutes. The battlefield geometry also made sense. She could get to the intracoastal waterway and the Atlantic Ocean just as easily. The four engines had "Mercury 350cc" written in bold letters on the covers. This was a big boat that could move her quickly up and down the coast. The boat was long, perhaps over fifty feet. It had tall outriggers used for big-game fishing and could easily be mistaken for a deep-sea-fishing vessel. Its shallow draft would allow the vessel to glide through the notably shallow waters of the marshy Savannah River basin. Importantly, there were multiple routes to Tybee Island, which Harwood believed to be her ultimate objective.

The stability of the boat provided the perfect sniper's platform.

Jackie had spoken briefly and obliquely about her

brother's overdose and subsequent painful death. Richard had been on the fringe of the rough crowd in Columbus, Georgia, home of Fort Benning and the U.S. Army's Airborne School. Her investigation led her to a general's son, who had melted pure opium in a spoon and given it to Richard for injection. Eyewitness reports said that they had been sitting on the Airborne School's property beneath the two-hundred-foot towers future paratroopers used for training. After using the needle, Richard had climbed the tower, and shimmied onto the arm of one of the drop mechanisms. From two hundred feet above ground level, he began singing the resurgently popular "Fly Like an Eagle" by the Steve Miller Band.

And he had tried to do so, falling two hundred feet to the ground, landing atop a stack of metal poles used for paratrooper training. The next morning, the class of Airborne students had found him impaled on their equipment. Before too long the class had created what they thought was a darkly humorous cadence about Richard's ordeal.

"C-130 rolling down the strip, airborne junkie on a one-way trip . . . shoot up, stand up, shuffle to the door, fly through the sky . . . poor Richard's brains all over the floor . . ."

Prior to meeting Jackie, Harwood had even heard the Airborne School troops calling that twisted cadence, but had no idea at the time who Richard was or why his name was invoked in a cadence. Jackie mentioned that she and her parents had petitioned the general to get them to forbid the cadence.

General Bishop, he seemed to recall, was the commanding general of Fort Benning.

Yes, Jackie had motive.

Harwood lowered himself over the metal bulkhead and slipped into the warm, dark water. The musky scent of fish spawning permeated the air. Samuelson slipped in behind him. The rucksack mitigated the movement of Harwood's arms, so he mostly did the sidestroke as he was taught in Ranger combat water survival training. Soon he had reached the wooden pier that had moored next to it a seventy-foot boat called *Non Miserables*. The large wood-paneled Chris Craft boat gave him ample room to shimmy on the opposite side of Jackie's sight line.

Lifting himself onto the pier like doing a dip, Harwood knelt and stared directly at Jackie Colt's boat. She was no longer standing on the pier, but a light was on belowdecks. He low-crawled along the pier until he was alongside the hull of the *Ten Meter Lady*. Motioning to Samuelson to provide him cover, he knelt, then stood and walked to the swim platform and quietly boarded the vessel from the rear. Samuelson prone, rifle aimed.

Harwood stood in the rear of the boat, behind the center console. Jackie was working diligently in the sleeping cabin forward of the center console. He eased his way around the bridge. She was typing on a keyboard. Her commands pulled up a screen on the monitor that seemed to be a camera feed, and then she started typing into a dialogue box. She was communicating with someone and perhaps watching their actions.

He held his Beretta pistol in his hand and said, "Good evening, Jackie."

She jumped and leveled a Sig Sauer nine-millimeter pistol at him.

"Too late," he said. "You shoot. I shoot. We both die."

"How did you find me?" she asked.

"Hey, boo, I was sort of expecting, 'So good to see you, bae.' But I guess I can't have everything."

She lowered the pistol.

"It *is* good to see you, Vick. I'm just in the middle of something here."

"Who you killing with my rifle this time?"

She was silent for a long time, maybe minutes that seemed to stretch into hours but were probably only seconds. The emotional connection he had felt with her surged back like a freight train. His heart raced. Palms sweated.

"It's not what you think," she said.

"Pretty lame. It's exactly what I think. I'm sorry about Richard," he said.

"You don't know . . . everything." Jackie flushed.

"I knew enough to find you here. And I know that you're working with Nina Moreau, who is probably the one who keeps sending you instant messages wondering where I am." On the screen behind her, a new dialogue bubble appeared with the question, *Where is the Reaper?*

Then: *I'm set.* They appeared to be using the same Wickr app that Jackie had recommended for their own communication. The messages disappeared moments after being sent or received.

"Then tell me . . . everything," Harwood said.

Jackie paused, turned toward the screen, placed her weapon on the bench seat, and typed, *Stand by.*

She turned and leveled her blue eyes on him. The freckles were prominent in the mellow lighting of the boat. Her blond hair fell across her shoulders in a silky sheen. She was wearing athletic clothing similar to what he had seen her in every time they had been together for the last week.

"If I tell you, it makes you complicit and I do love you, Vick. I don't want that for you," she said.

"Everybody already thinks I'm complicit. Hell, it's my rifle. How could you do this to me? To them?" he said.

"To who? The drug-dealing generals and the sexual predators on the Lolita Express?"

"What are you talking about?"

"Milk 'Em has been dealing ghost girls. They're bringing young Afghan and Iraqi girls—fourteen to seventeen years old—to the United States on their classified milk runs into Hunter Army Airfield. They kidnap them and stash them in caskets for days and then set them up in what they call 'safe houses.' They're also peddling straight opium, the actual resin that comes from the poppy, to dealers who are paying premium prices. We're talking sex-slave trafficking, drug distribution, and blackmail, at a minimum."

Ghost girls. Like the ghost prisoners taken early in the war. Either parents were too scared to report the kidnappings to the authorities or Xanadu killed them as part of the process. Collateral damage. He thought of his foster sister Lindsay and his inability to save her. In their own way, Harwood, Lindsay, and the other foster kids were ghosts themselves, wafting through the system, often disappearing with no account.

"So, just take it into your hands? Vigilante justice? Frame me for everything? I've been on the run for the past two days. Shot at, mugged, nearly killed."

Jackie dropped her head. "I'm sorry, Vick. I didn't

know at first. I tried to warn you. I'm . . . conflicted on this."

"No, you didn't warn me. You put shit in my sports drink that made me go dizzy."

Again, she averted her eyes. "I found out after the fact that Nina had done that. Her husband had some bottles made in Afghanistan with the date-rape drug. I was livid. It wasn't me. I swear."

"You're spotting for her on a target right now. You telling me you have nothing to do with that?" Harwood's neck muscles tensed. His carotid arteries pulsed hard. His heart pumped against his chest.

"I'm involved in this, Nick. But I never meant for you to be."

He said nothing. Tacked on a corkboard behind the monitor was a piece of standard-size printer paper. At the top of the document were the words "Kill Sheet."

Some names were crossed out, some not.

General Sampson, General Dillman, Officer Tommy Blakely, Officer Ken Strong, Senator Kraft—all had their names lined out. Two names were written in ink, Blake and Wercinski, possibly the guards. General Bishop, General Markham, two congressmen and a few names Harwood didn't recognize were still among the living.

"Bishop?"

Jackie nodded. "Tonight. He's speaking to troops at Hunter Army Airfield and then to the law school in downtown Savannah."

"She's in Forsyth Park. What's your feed? Drone?"

"Yes. We have a butterfly drone that pipes back over Ku-band satellite."

"Why Bishop?"

"His son gave Richard the opium. Melted it in the spoon for him. And General Bishop covered it up with the local police. Kid should be doing twenty to life, but Bishop's in with the local Columbus police."

Jackie was being honest and straightforward. She had nowhere and no reason to hide from him.

"The congressmen?"

"Markham has a plane and they take 'flights' with these teenagers they've brought back from Afghanistan and Iraq. They call it the Lolita Express. There are private bedrooms. It's a large Boeing jet, like a triple seven. It sits over there on the runway at Hunter and when it's not going back and forth between Colorado and Georgia, they retrofit it with the Lolita package, as they call it, and invite CEOs and congressmen down for some fun. There's others, but we're only killing those we can confirm."

"Let me guess. Markham videos them and he blackmails them into giving him contracts or voting for his weapons or whatever," Harwood said.

Jackie said nothing for a moment. She looked at the list. Then she stared at the screen. It was obvious to Harwood she was thinking about neither of those things. She looked toward the stern and then the bow of the boat. Tears streamed out of her eyes. Uncontrollably. She used the backs of her hands to brush them away. Like windshield wipers. But they were rivers coursing down her face. She was steady, though, like the shooter she was. No heaving of her body. Controlled. The moment passed and she turned toward Harwood.

"You're back, aren't you? Fully back. No memory issues."

"Maybe not fully, but I'm back. I'm able to do simple math, if that's what you're asking."

"I'm sorry. You know how sometimes you get carried away with your emotions and you have one single goal and that's all you can think of? Like you with this Chechen guy, maybe? Well that's how I was—no, I am—with Richard. These people have to pay," Jackie said.

"You're committing murder on U.S. soil, Jackie. It's vigilante justice. I don't disagree they should pay. But you shouldn't have to suffer any more than you already have. You're an Olympic champion with the whole world ahead of you."

"Killing Markham will be the hardest. He's holed up in his Tybee Island pleasure palace. I won't survive that I don't think. Markham is in charge of the entire operation. He's got a group he calls CLEVER. Something about CEOs helping veterans. It's all bullshit, though. It's a good-old-boys club where they do some drugs, bang some underage kids, and then go hunting or fishing. Disgusting."

She talked as if Harwood were already part of the plan. Even as if he had been all along. As if there were no question that he would go along. They both turned their heads toward the monitor when a whispering voice said, "Here he comes. Where's the Reaper?"

"He's with me. You're cleared hot. Fire."

Jackie's voice was as calm as he knew her shooting composure to be. *He's with me.* Harwood watched the screen. Some type of hover drone was providing real-time video streaming. The picture was black-and-white, but clear, not grainy as in many of the older video feeds showing bomb attacks. This was new technology. Nina

Moreau was dressed in black. She was perched in a tree observing the Savannah Law School building. The drone was behind Moreau, showing her body, the rifle—his rifle—the park, some more trees, and then the steps to the law school. There were two opposing sets of curved stairways that hugged the exterior wall of the building and led to a landing fronted with columns. Moreau's shot would either be frontal as Bishop crested the far stairway or rear, as he came from the less likely near stairway. Either way, it must have been the only clear shot at the front door of the school from the opposite side of the park.

"We worked the angles using 3D imagery to find sight lines. This was the best spot. Get him on either set of stairs. There was one other but it was too close," Jackie said. She spoke as if he were part of the team. Professional. An operations officer providing a situation report, clarifying an issue for a comrade.

The screen showed two black SUVs pulling up to the curb. One was a chase car and the other carried the principal, General Bishop. They were moving toward Moreau on the one-way street.

First out of the SUVs were military police bodyguards who took up posts at the four quadrants within a ten-meter radius of the planned exit door of General Bishop. They were professionals scanning in every direction, but they would do no good against Harwood's weapon if Moreau could shoot. There was a clear field of fire all the way up to the platform. As Bishop ascended the steps, he would be in the sight picture.

Next, two more bodyguards exited Bishop's SUV and took up post on the far side of the road, in the park. They were scanning the park. Six military personnel providing security and they were all useless, Harwood thought. Just down the street, either Jackie or Nina Moreau had shot and killed General Dillman two days ago. Naturally, that explained the tightened security, but where was the creativity? he wondered. No drones. No advance security that he could notice. No head fake to the front door and then enter through the back door. Like Pickett's charge, a brutally stupid advance up the front steps, albeit the far stairway, of the law school where the general had a publicly announced speech to make at 8 P.M. He had three minutes to be inside and in front of the podium if he wanted to keep the military reputation for time discipline and management.

The right rear door opened on the second SUV. That was the traditional seat where the commander sat, Harwood thought, shaking his head.

"Still clear?" Moreau asked.

Jackie looked at Harwood with questioning eyes as if to ask, "Are you in?"

Harwood said nothing. He thought of Lindsay and the man in the barn who wound up with a pitchfork in his neck. How was this any different? Should he give Jackie her due? She might have picked up on an imperceptible nod, because Jackie turned toward the screen and said, "Cleared hot."

Bishop stepped out of the vehicle, and the two nearest guards collapsed on him shoulder-to-shoulder, as if they were marching in parade. It was a tight fit, meant to be. The heightened security made it clear that the general knew he was a target, knew he had done wrong, and knew there was a chance he would die tonight.

As they ascended the far set of steps, two more men collapsed into a diamond wedge around the general. The man in front was tall enough to obscure the general. They were all wearing army blues with the giant saucer hats.

Jackie remained calm, though her fingers twitched, as if she wished she were pulling the trigger. This was a difficult shot for any sniper. Moreau was DGSE, French CIA. If she had killed any of the others, she had to be a decent shot.

The general reached the second-to-last of the marble steps. Like the Supreme Court. Pillars stood tall at the front of the landing, but coincident with Moreau's shot. The guards tightened around the general like legionnaires protecting their commander, which perhaps they were. As they turned toward the front door, the general's head became marginally visible.

On the screen, the rifle jumped. Moreau was quickly disassembling the weapon before she even knew what happened. Within seconds she was out of the tree. At the top of the screen, the general's hat flew against the tall white door of the law school building. A spray of dark liquid briefly appeared; obviously, it was blood. She had shot the general in the head.

Nina Moreau was more than your average nurse.

The guards drew weapons and were on top of the general. The drone appeared to fly close to get a better picture, what the military called battle-damage assessment. The monitor showed an apparently dead man on the steps wearing the uniform of a two-star general. The face and features of the man appeared to be General Bishop. Moreau had accomplished her mission.

Men were on radios, calling for backup and ambulances, most likely. The drone turned around and now followed Nina Moreau several blocks away from the action as she jogged wearing a rucksack in which she had stashed the weapon. She opened the door of an older Honda Civic and began driving.

Jackie Colt stood and grabbed a ruler and a Sharpie. Leaning over the monitor, she crossed General Bishop's name off the kill sheet.

"That feels really, really good," she said.

CHAPTER 24

General Markham stared into the darkness. The moon's yellow semicircle was a knife cut in the black firmament, the leering smile of a jack-o'-lantern.

The phone call had not been a good one. General Bishop was shot dead on the steps of the law school. Just as General Sampson had been killed at Fort Bragg. Just as Senator Kraft had been killed in Macon. Just as Dillman had been killed on his front porch. That moron Dillman had taken one of the women home and now the FBI was sniffing around MLQM's headquarters at Hunter Army Airfield.

He was feeling the squeeze. Markham clutched the tumbler of Macallan Scotch until his fingers hurt. He had built firewalls around himself and the entire operation. MLQM had plausible deniability. Rationally, he had nothing to worry about. Nothing a good lawyer three years out of law school couldn't handle. He didn't want to get rid of the women and had grown accustomed to the occasional opioid high. He had earned this good life. Worked hard for it. Deserved it.

And now he needed Xanadu to execute like he had never executed before, because the Reaper was on his trail. He believed that. Just as the moon was sneering at him right now, he knew the Reaper was searching for him. Might even be out there in a dive suit with his mask hovering just above the meniscus of the ocean, like a gator lying in wait, eyes unblinking.

"Tell me you've got something," Markham said. His earpiece had buzzed with Xanadu's special ring tone.

"I think so. Been busy setting the trap, but one of Bishop's guys called me. Old unit buddy. Said he saw someone running north and east. Got in a Honda Civic and drove toward Tybee. Your direction. I've got a drone doing license-plate scans outward from your house along the main road. It takes pictures, scans the DMV database, and confirms or denies in a matter of seconds. A lot of road to cover, but wanted to make sure you were safe first."

"I'm fine. I need you to find Harwood and kill him."

"The description I got of the person running away from the shooting scene didn't sound like Harwood. Maybe he's got more than one person helping him. I've got the helicopter on standby with a quick-reaction force serving as a snatch team. We see him or whoever is driving the car, we'll be on them in minutes."

"Make it seconds," Markham ordered. He hung up and continued to stare into the ocean through the floor-to-ceiling bulletproof-glass windows. The dim light behind him cast his reflection in the glass. Was he unassailable on this? He had tapes of corporate

CEOs, generals, and the local sheriff having sex with underage girls at one of the safe houses or on the airplane. That ought to count for something, especially with the sheriff.

Xanadu called again.

"We got a hit. Helicopter is launching with me on it. Everything else is in place. We're moving to a warehouse complex on Old Tybee Road. We don't see the shooter, but we have the car. We're close. Wherever he's going has got to be close."

"Unless he changed cars," Markham said.

"There's that, but this feels right. There're some warehouses down there. Lots of restaurants. A marina. And some boats you can charter. Lots of options for someone trying to stay flexible."

About a minute later, Xanadu said, "Okay, we're over it and landing in the back of the warehouses. Using the drone to scout the backside. We're going door-to-door on each warehouse. Wait, they're not warehouses. They're storage units now that I'm seeing them firsthand."

"Cut the locks," Markham said. "Each and every one of them. Smoke them out."

"We've got movement to the north. Stand by," Xanadu said.

The spot reports reminded Markham of his air force days. He would sit in the leather chair of his command suite in Central Command Headquarters in Tampa when he was a three-star general. Occasionally he'd listen in on the combat operations. He found it all very pedestrian, but needed the background so he could be conversant during staff meetings. Unlike those tedious times, Markham did not yawn. He was a ball of energy, feeling the fear begin to creep up his spine.

The Lolita Express, the safe houses, the opium sales. He had plausible deniability on all of it and the power to blackmail the right players. But if it got to the press, then the whole thing would be unmanageable. Even the WikiLeaks releases during the recent election cycles had pushed him toward phone-only communications. Sending an email nowadays was like publishing a blog, almost.

"Jackpot," Xanadu said.

"Talk to me," Markham replied.

"We've got them."

He smiled a thin-lipped lizard grin, lips pulling back into a sneer that said "Fuck you" to the leering moon.

Jackie vectored Nina Moreau back toward the boat. A series of "go left" and "go right" and "hold, okay, go" and "get cover" commands resulted in Nina hiding under a bridge about two hundred yards to the west. The drone showed her kneeling, taking deep breaths, gathering oxygen, preparing to move.

"We're going to get her," Jackie said. She moved to the center console and started the engines. Harwood stepped on the dock and shouted to Samuelson.

"Come on. We're going along for the ride."

There were two options. Go or not go. Not going would result in losing visibility on precisely what was afoot. Jackie Colt and Nina Moreau were the tag-team shooters delivering vigilante justice to an apparent criminal ring. Sex slaves. Opium. The spoils of war? Privileged men using their power to serve themselves. He could get behind defeating that nexus. Going, though, meant being in the mix. Participating in murders. But justified ones, nonetheless. He wasn't concerned about the ramifications.

He would rather die a hero than grow old.

Do the right thing, Command Sergeant Major Murdoch always advised. He thought of Lindsay again. How she had cooked, cleaned, and consoled him and the other foster children. Just seventeen years old, but already an adult mentally, emotionally, and especially physically. And then noticing their foster mother dressing her up and plastering on her makeup before sending her back to the barn apartment where some stranger would be waiting. She'd return an hour later, clutching a few twenties, weeping.

Then the pistol, the pitchfork, and the birth of the Reaper. Yeah, he could do this.

This was no longer about Jackie Colt or Nina Moreau. Plus, there were bigger forces at play. Ultimately, it was about finding the nuke . . . and stopping it, if it existed. Jackie led to Nina, who led to Basayev, who undoubtedly led to the nuke.

Samuelson untied the lines from the pier cleats and hopped into the Boston Whaler.

"Grew up on the Eastern Shore. Fishing was a way of life," Samuelson said.

"Weapons belowdecks, underneath the bench. AR-15s," Jackie said, gesturing to the port side of the boat. "Left side."

Harwood lifted the seat pad, noticing that the middle seat compartment was locked, but the left and right compartments weren't. He extracted two AR-15s and two magazines for each of them.

"Take the right. I've got the left."

"It's called starboard and port in a boat," Samuelson said.

Harwood said nothing, just stared at Samuelson, who nodded and said, "Roger, boss."

Jackie gunned the four Mercury motors as Harwood positioned himself where he could watch Nina Moreau on the monitor while also looking over the bow of the craft. He heard a helicopter pass overhead. It was the same whispering dual-bladed machine he had seen in Macon and that had fired miniguns at Lanny's Mustang. Jackie was at full throttle on the calm river. Rooster tail was spitting high behind the boat. Samuelson instinctively took up a position on the opposite side, rifle at the ready.

The bridge loomed large before them. Nina was thigh-deep in the river beneath the bridge, waving her arms. The helicopter flared and dropped a thick rope. Fast rope. Gloved combatants began sliding down the rope onto the bank next to the river.

It had to be Xanadu, who had shot Monisha. And perhaps had run the kidnap teams in Afghanistan.

The first man off the fast rope was running beneath the bridge. Harwood led him with the iron sights of the AR-15 and snapped off two double-tap rounds. The man dropped. Harwood shifted to the next man. Two more shots. Another man down. The boat slowed beneath the bridge. Harwood lined up on the third guy. But he fell before he could pull the trigger, so he switched to the fourth guy and fired two rounds. They had just dropped the four commandos on the ground. Samuelson had repositioned to the port side. The boat idled in shallow water. Nina Moreau labored toward them, using the sidestroke until she reached the boat. She handed her rucksack over to Jackie, who put it carefully next to her feet as Samuelson and Harwood lifted Moreau over the side. Jackie was quickly on the controls. She gunned the engines to the north side of the bridge. Moreau looked at him and Samuelson, recognizing them. Then she looked at Jackie, questioning. There was no time for debate. They had helped rescue her and that counted. For the moment.

"Helicopter's still there, waiting," Harwood said. "They've got miniguns that will chew us up."

Jackie nodded. He could tell she was ready to run the gauntlet. He could feel the boat idling, like a racehorse in the starting gate.

"Don't do it," he said. "Where are the flares?"

She backed off the throttle, grip loosening. "In there." She nodded at the same bench where she had stored the AR-15s.

Moreau moved to block him, saying, "*No,*" but relented when he opened the bench seat and retrieved the flares and gun. He inserted a flare into the barrel. Snapped it shut.

"Wait for him," Harwood said.

The engines thrummed, impatient, like Jackie. Her eyes were fixed on a point in the distance. She had her kill sheet to get to. More business to be done.

"Xanadu isn't on your kill sheet, but he should be."

"You said the magic word, Vick. It's my kill sheet. I put on it who I want to," she said.

This was a different, more focused Jackie than the luring, seductive woman he had first met and then dated. She was as dialed in as any combat commander he had seen. Mission first.

The pitch of the helicopter blades shifted from a steady hum to a powerful roar. It was inching its way below the bridge to bring the miniguns into play. Harwood balanced into a shooter's stance. His left foot slightly in front of his right foot. The wheels presented themselves first. Harwood was looking east. The river spread out wide and straight for as far as the eye could see. The marina was to their two o'clock at about a half mile. The black bottom of the aircraft entered Harwood's vision. Then he saw the cargo bay and the cockpit, which meant they could see him.

He aimed the flare gun at the crew compartment, where the miniguns would be. He needed the fire inside the aircraft. He pulled the trigger. It was awkward and clumsy. A hollow thunk sounded when the hammer hit the cartridge. The flare began burning as soon as it left the stubby muzzle. The miniguns spat back at him, but the pilot of the aircraft must have seen the flare. The helicopter banked hard left, minigun bullets chewing at the bridge.

Harwood loaded another flare and fired it at the retreating helicopter. The first flare seemed to have either missed or passed through. The second found its way into the cargo compartment and then into the cockpit, bouncing off the windshield as it burned. The aircraft began racing south, toward Hunter Army Airfield.

"Now, Jackie. Let's go wherever you were going next."

"Roger that," she said.

She gunned the boat east. They sped past the marina. The shallow-draft hull glided along the glassy smooth river. The moonlight showed Jackie with her jaw set, eyes focused. She made a series of turns. Left and right and right again, then a final left. She was navigating the Bull River and its estuary. She slowed the boat, searching.

"NVGs in the bench," she said.

Harwood grabbed a pair of night vision goggles from the same bench that supplied the weapons. He held a PVS-14 night vision goggle up to his eye like a pirate searching for land.

"Duck blind and camo net," Jackie said. "GPS has it about twenty meters up on the right."

"I've got it," he said.

She maneuvered the boat inside the netting and shut down the engines. Nobody said anything. The engines ticked as they cooled. The minimal wake diminished into the reeds. Fish smacked at the surface of the river. Jackie stayed at the helm. Nina Moreau remained belowdeck. Samuelson secured the starboard side. Harwood stayed on port.

After five minutes, Harwood asked, "What's above us?"

"Camouflage net and a thermal reflective blanket. Anything that has thermal capabilities will read this small patch of marsh as a small patch of marsh."

"Okay, let's go down below and talk. You owe me an explanation."

CHAPTER 25

Harwood sat on the steps to the small belowdeck cabin. Nina Moreau had stood and was pacing back and forth in the cramped quarters.

Samuelson remained outside by the center console, AR-15 at the ready. The stars were brilliant. It was a perfect night for Harwood to be with his girlfriend in her boat . . . *while she aided an international terrorist.* Gallows humor, he thought. He'd break down without it. Humor aside, what Jackie was too inexperienced to understand was that Basayev and, by extension, Moreau were unstoppable forces. Terrorists with a long list of scalps. Ruthless mercenaries that would do anything to anyone for the right payday.

"Clear her of any weapons," he said to Jackie.

Jackie removed a small pistol from Moreau's pocket and stuffed it in the rucksack that sat to his right on the steps into the cabin. She patted her legs, arms, and back. "Nothing else."

Satisfied, he said, "Sit down, Moreau. Both of you, talk to me, please."

After a deep breath and sincere look that pinched his heart, Jackie said, "Nina was kidnapped by Milk 'Em the same day you were wounded."

"That was you being snatched by Xanadu's team in Sangin." Not a question; a statement.

Moreau's face jerked up at the mention of Xanadu's name. She locked eyes with Harwood and the memory of Xanadu slapping her in Sangin flashed in his mind. A moment passed before he nodded at Jackie.

"Walk me through how you two connected."

The boat was perfectly still. Coastal Georgia was filled with its thrum of insects and wildlife churning nearby. Sound bounced off the glassy river and carried for miles in every direction. The drawbridge two miles away burped every time a car crossed the metal draw span. Waves breaking on Tybee Island a mile to the east rumbled faintly like distant thunder. Harwood spoke in hushed tones, knowing who might be listening and why.

Jackie looked away, toward the monitor, impatient, thumb tapping against the opposing wrist. She owed him this, though, and he knew that she would oblige him with an answer, however imperfect or imprecise.

"For me, I came to Afghanistan for two reasons. First, I'm a patriot and wanted to support you and all the other troops. I had the misfortune of falling in love with you, however."

"Misfortune?"

"Please, just listen to me, Vick. You asked and I'm answering."

He said nothing and nodded.

"Second, this is about Richard, as I've told you. My outrage and inquiries into the local investigation around Columbus, Georgia, and Fort Benning kept leading to rumors of drug smuggling from Kandahar by a private military contractor. I had already joined the USO tour and because of my status as a 'celebrity' I could go places in Kandahar Airfield that perhaps some others couldn't. Cute girl. Olympic champion. The men were happy to show me whatever I wanted to see. Some even tried to corner me for a quickie. I get it. Deployed for a year. Not getting laid. And so on. So I used that testosterone momentum to my advantage. I asked to see the military-contractor portion of the base, saying that they served as well. And I wanted to thank them, which truly I did, because ninety-nine percent of them are good men and women. However, I was looking for the one percent that had supplied the opium to Richard. I asked questions. Was ushered around. Pardoned myself to the ladies' room, which was about a hundred yards away. I was the only female, so I was left pretty much unescorted for about thirty minutes, acting as if I was lost. While I was wandering around I saw a big gray airplane being loaded with military caskets. They call them transfer cases. Some people call them coffins. I snuck over and saw a few that were still open. They didn't have dead bodies in them. There were burlap sacks. I could smell the resin. It was fresh poppy resin. Sweet, floral, and musty all at the same time. I saw the MLQM symbol on the nearest door, like their office. Someone was in the airplane and I could see a loading crew taking a lunch break in a room glassed off with a small window."

Jackie paused. Harwood said nothing. He sat on

the steps into the cabin and watched Moreau as Jackie spoke. Samuelson was covering him from the center console. He had a direct line of fire belowdecks. Moreau was curled up on the small padded bed directly beneath the bow of the boat. Occasionally she would make a furtive glance in his direction. Shifty eyes. Scared? Calculating?

"I saw enough to convince me that Milk 'Em was running drugs. That was right before we met," she said, pointing at him. "I genuinely liked you—still do—I mean I love you, Vick. It totally caught me off guard. When I got back to Columbus, I spent some time scouting out Milk 'Em headquarters here in Savannah. Found that they were run by a guy named Derwood Griffin. Big-time weasel. Lifer in DoD. Sucked up to every boss he ever had. Changed political affiliations as administrations changed. Finally connected with the former chief of staff of the air force, General Buzz Markham, who is the chairman of the board of directors for Milk 'Em. They were going through some tough times with the downsizing of the military and lost some of their contracts. They were thinned out. Lots of people in Afghanistan and Iraq, Syria even. Their staff back here just outside the gate at Hunter Army Airfield was thin. Like five people. For a private military security company, their security back here wasn't great. Very strong on the private side, but not great if you were coming in from Hunter. I came in from Hunter. Same thing. Signed some books at the post exchange and then got myself lost. Got inside their warehouse one night about a week before we met up at Fort Bragg for my book signing and your sniper class. Pain-in-the-ass drive from Columbus, but whatever."

Moreau began shifting in her near-fetal position. Her gaze was locked on to Jackie, perhaps willing her to stop talking. She clung to the bench seat as if it were a life preserver, which it probably was. Beneath the seat was a large storage compartment for things like the anchor, life jackets, and other boat essentials. It was secured with a sturdy brass lock through an industrial hasp.

Jackie continued.

"In the warehouse, my flashlight caught the glint of silver metal boxes the size of coffins. The same ones that I saw in Afghanistan."

"As you said, they're transfer cases," Harwood said. "We send our fallen back in those."

"Right. Did you know Milk 'Em has the contract to fly some of the dead personnel back home? Not many military, but some. DoD civilians, contractors, and some of the military killed or simply just died over there. Milk 'Em flew them back."

"And loaded a few of the transfer cases with drugs," Harwood added. "Markham helped them get the contract. That's an air force job."

"Exactly," she said. She snapped her fingers and pointed at him. "It wasn't a big contract. I mean a few million, which is good, but what it gave Markham and Griffin was a way to move whatever they wanted back. I mean, who's going to question what's in a flag-draped transfer case?"

"Flag-draped?"

"Roger that," she said. "I saw it. That night I opened

several of the cases and all of them had drugs in them except one."

Moreau began shifting again, sitting up. "*Non*," she said. "Stop. Please."

"He needs to hear it all, Nina. We can go from there. I'm having a watershed moment just listening to myself talk."

"Nina was in the last coffin," Harwood said. Not a question. He knew just by their interaction.

Jackie nodded. "Just enough room for some combat rations and water bottles. So maybe some PTSD going on here."

Moreau looked away, embarrassed.

"Xanadu runs that operation," Harwood said.

"*Vous!*" Moreau shouted, and pointed at Harwood.

"No. Not me. I had nothing to do with it," he replied.

"Liar." This time she spoke in accented English. "Every time girls were kidnapped, you were up in the mountains. Khasan tells me so."

"Khasan is wrong. I was doing my job."

But he had a lightbulb moment, as Command Sergeant Major Murdoch called it. Could the Ranger commander or some of the generals have been directing him where to fight based upon Xanadu's snatch teams? Had he been inadvertently providing cover for them?

Moreau must have seen the doubt in his eyes.

"*Oui*. Even if you didn't know. That's right."

"It was Xanadu. Every one of my kills is legit. Taliban commanders. A few Al Qaeda. And unfortunately, I'm missing one foreign fighter from Chechnya."

Moreau leapt at him, but Jackie used her body and strong arms to stop her.

"We don't have time for this bullshit," Jackie said, pushing her into the padded bench. Moreau sat upright on the cushion facing Harwood, eyes boiling.

"Anyway, I agree. It's Xanadu. He's bad. But what Nina saw was other women at the point of kidnap," Jackie said.

"They're smuggling women and drugs. We've established that," Harwood said.

"Right. I went to the local county sheriff. He buried it. I'm guessing Markham paid him off. Then I went to the DoD inspector general hotline. I got some initial interest, but it suddenly got sucked into a black hole. There was no sense of urgency."

"So you develop a kill sheet with Nina Moreau out here on your boat, where she stays while you meet me at Fort Bragg?"

"Yes and no. I had names for the kill sheet and Nina had names. She's the shooter. I'm the logistics."

"You're still an accessory to murder, Jackie."

"So are they," she said, softly. "They killed Richard."

"Why make it look like it's me? I mean, come on. I've been on the run with the police thinking I'm killing all these people."

"Well, that wasn't on purpose, at least from my end," Jackie said, now looking at Moreau with suspicious eyes.

"Oh, please, you knew all along," Moreau said.

"No, I didn't. I didn't know about the sports drink until later. The bottles are different. And I didn't know it was your rifle until after General Sampson was shot and there was all the coverage. Then it was out of my control. Things were moving too fast."

Harwood looked at Moreau and asked, "How did you even get my rifle?"

Moreau shook her head.

Instead, Jackie answered. "I used a drone to follow her the night after I rescued her. We were near here at a marina. She left and went to the Oatland Island Wildlife Refuge."

Moreau's eyes shot daggers at Jackie. "You bitch."

"Vick deserves to know, Nina. Anyway, she went to the aviary where the hawks and falcons are. And she came back with a rucksack. I'm pretty sure the rifle was in there."

Moreau said nothing, but the searing hatred on her face told Harwood everything he needed to know.

"Basayev?"

"Yes. Khasan Basayev left it for me," Moreau said. She was sitting with her arms wrapped around her knees. "He is a great man."

"He's a terrorist, who killed several American soldiers," Harwood snapped. "How'd *he* get my rifle?"

"He rescued your Samuelson," Moreau said, pointing over his shoulder. "And found your rifle."

Smooth inflections of French surrounded her English syntax.

"Where's Basayev now?"

"I don't know, but Khasan is not a terrorist. He is a freedom fighter just like you," Moreau said. "No different. Tell me, Reaper, what is the difference between you shooting Taliban commanders who are growing poppy and me shooting American generals who are stealing and importing that same poppy?"

Harwood paused. It was a good question. With a

few legal distinctions there wasn't much difference, he had to admit. "We're at war in Afghanistan."

"Please, Reaper. The world is at war. There are no front lines, anywhere."

A cloud passed across her eyes, as if she retreated inward to a different place.

"Vick, I didn't know it was your rifle. I did help her get onto Fort Bragg. She found the best position to shoot from. It was purely an accident that you were in the same location when she killed General Sampson."

"I don't think any of this is an accident, Jackie. If you're not completely complicit, you're being used by her," he said.

"It's true," Moreau said. "We are using each other. I kill her enemies. She gets me access."

"Killing your enemies, also, Nina," Harwood said.

"True. Xanadu raped me repeatedly. Nonstop. He came close to killing me many times over the last three months. Thanks to Jackie, I am free now. Her brother was killed by these men. I owe her the retribution she seeks. Nothing more. Nothing less."

Somehow it wasn't that simple. Harwood detected a contrived story. Three months in a coffin gave the mind plenty of time to churn through plans and possibilities . . . unless the plan was to be in the coffin in the first place.

"When I saw you," Harwood said, "you were fighting off Xanadu and his men."

"You mean when you prevented Khasan from coming to rescue me," Moreau countered.

"My duel with Basayev had nothing to do with you," Harwood said, emphasizing Moreau's irrelevance to him at the time. She might be highly relevant today, right now, but at the time she was an interesting mention in an intel report.

"There were four men with rifles raiding our house. The girls they took were fifteen and sixteen years old. Beautiful young women. Both virgins. I seriously doubt they've been able to save themselves for marriage since their abduction." Moreau's accent transitioned from smooth French to a more guttural German or Arabic base.

"But you knew this was happening several weeks prior to your kidnapping. Why place yourself in the line of fire, or abduction as it were?" Harwood asked. "How did you even breathe in there?"

More furtive glances away and back at him. Shifty eyes. The truth lurking out there somewhere, but perhaps not here in the small cabin of a Boston Whaler Outrage.

"They had an oxygen-circulation system. A quite simple modification to carry live cargo as opposed to deceased remains, as you call them. Just enough oxygen, food, and water to survive."

"Your face. Your hair. I remember it now when I was running the other day. You were driving a car near Forsyth Park."

"That was me," Moreau said.

"But why? Why me?"

The million-dollar question. Why him?

Jackie spoke into the silence.

"Nina told me what those men did to her. I know what they did to Richard. They're disgusting, yes, but powerful. No amount of us going to the authorities would have worked. At first I didn't know, Vick. You must believe me. Nina said she was going to confront General Sampson, not shoot him."

"I don't have to do anything, Jackie, but I'm listening. Right now, I'm the number-one wanted man in America. Maybe the world. You've helped kill a senator. You'll get the needle."

"She didn't have anything to do with it," Moreau said. "She drove me into Fort Bragg, sure. But that was it. I was hiding in your buddy's trunk the night I shot the two cops. Right before you got out, I crawled out and set up in the woods. I do what I want. Tracked you to Macon. You're right, though. I wanted into America. I let them kidnap and rape me. I'm here. You wouldn't understand the motivation, Reaper. Things were done years ago that must be completed. That is why I am here. This has nothing to do with her. Your girlfriend is clean."

"But what? And why?" Harwood asked, but he thought he knew and Moreau would not be admitting what he believed was at play. "What about tonight? Jackie, you helped her escape tonight. And she's been staying on your boat."

"No," Moreau said. "For the record, I'm not here. Nobody will testify that they saw me get on this boat. If this boat is tied up at the River Street Market Place by five A.M., no one will know it was ever missing. And by then, I'll either be dead or gone and there will be no trace of Jackie's involvement."

Harwood said, "This is a woman I used to love."

"Used to?" Jackie asked.

"What? You think we're all square?"

"Vick, come on. Yes, this is risky, but it's not any worse than what Milk 'Em's been doing. It's not terrorism."

"That's precisely what it is. You're harboring a terrorist. She may not have a bomb on her, but she's killed six Americans."

He looked at Moreau when he spoke. More furtive glances. There was a bomb, just not on her. Had to be somewhere. That was the play. Get the world focused on him. Use Jackie's painful loss to get her involved. Make her complicit and use her for access. FBI, police, media all looking at him, like a magician's trick. *Hey, look at this hand over here, while I move the coin . . . or bomb . . . in the other.*

"What's next, Nina?" he asked.

Moreau shrugged, pursed her lips, looked away, and said, "Kill sheet isn't done. I'll find a way."

"No more killing," Harwood said. "My dilemma is if I turn you in, Jackie goes down with you. If I let you go, you'll keep killing Americans."

"We all have made difficult decisions, Reaper," Moreau said. "The kill sheet must be finished."

"Not with Jackie involved."

Moreau shrugged. "I will find a way to finish. General Markham is the head of everything. And Ramsey Xanadu raped me every day. So, you tell me. If that was Jackie, would you be okay?"

Harwood paused. No, of course he wouldn't be okay, and he couldn't promise he wouldn't kill everyone associated with the crimes.

"Where's the bomb?" Harwood asked. Time was up. He needed the answer. That was her play; possibly even Basayev's trade.

Bring her back! Trade?

"I will show you the bomb," Moreau said.

Helicopter blades thumped loudly in the distance.

Harwood climbed onto the deck to inspect. Moreau stood abruptly and dashed toward the steps, angled her body to the left, took the stairs two at a time, and bolted onto the deck of the boat.

"Watch her, Sammie," Harwood called over his shoulder.

A small splash accented Samuelson's report. "She's already in the water."

CHAPTER 26

Harwood and Jackie stood on the deck. The helicopter had turned north, away from their position, still searching. Their last sight of Nina Moreau was that of her feet kicking as she disappeared into the murky moonlit estuary.

"She grabbed one of those Sea-Doo diving propellers," Samuelson said. "Thought about shooting her, but didn't want the helicopter to see the flash."

"You did the right thing," Harwood said. He wasn't disappointed that Moreau had escaped.

"I never expected that," Jackie said. "She can go at least two to three miles with that thing."

They watched the bubbles disappear and Harwood imagined she was going to link up with Basayev. He needed to act now.

"Why did she want this boat back at the River Street Market Place?"

"Where my slip is. Security guy is always checking

on me. He comes on duty at five A.M. He sees the boat and there's no issue, no suspicion."

Harwood nodded, thinking. He retrieved his phone from the baggie in his rucksack and put the SIM card in it for the first time in two days. He was beyond caring about being geolocated by MLQM or the FBI. When the phone powered up, he dialed the FBI.

"This is Vick Harwood, the Reaper. Patch me through to Special Agent Deke Bronson."

After some back-and-forth and some switches and clicks, he heard a baritone voice answer.

"Bronson."

"Meet me at the Breakfast Club on Tybee Island in thirty minutes. Don't come in with guns hot. You won't like the result."

"You get religion?" Bronson asked.

"Big-time. You need me. I know everything. Be there."

He hung up and turned to Jackie. "Let's go. You've been there before."

Jackie nodded, unable to hide the fact that she had provided the platform for Moreau to shoot the two guards in the towers of Markham's gated Tybee compound.

"Doesn't matter about Moreau," he said. "You can redeem yourself."

"I'm actually feeling okay with myself. A little guilty, Vick, because I'm truly sorry that you got sucked into this, but she just killed General Bishop, whose kid gave Richard the drugs."

Eye for an eye. He never saw that coming from Jackie Colt when he met her four months ago. "Okay.

Let's go." They moved to the center console and Jackie cranked the engines.

"Was going to shoot her, but wasn't sure," Samuelson said, again.

"You did the right thing, Sammie."

Perhaps Samuelson was still programmed from the Stockholm syndrome. Told to drive to pick up the Reaper and he did. Drop him off at a certain parking lot. Sure thing. Stand watch while they talk. Roger that. He didn't act without instructions, a common result of severe traumatic brain injury and especially brain-washing. The cognitive functions responded better to instructions than independent thought. Confidence in one's own abilities to think and act independently was muted if not lost.

But when it mattered most, Samuelson had acted independently to stop the conveyor belt and save his Ranger buddy.

Harwood patted Samuelson on the shoulder. A tear slid down his spotter's face. The moonlight cast a weak glow and the tear briefly caught the light. Samuelson's eyes were fixed on the distance; he knew he had lost some measure of himself. Perhaps he was wondering if he would ever be fully whole again.

Aided only by a sliver of moonlight, Jackie took forty minutes to navigate the twists and turns that led them to the Atlantic Ocean south of Markham's compound, which stood like a Spanish fortress on the tip of Tybee Island. Blastproof red-tiled shingles and stucco walls, floor-to-ceiling windows that were equally bulletproof, and multiple wings all rose from the sandy point upon which it sat as if it were designed to prevent naval ships from passing. The only things missing were the cannons and firing ports, but more lethal weapons were most likely aimed at them right now.

They docked at the Breakfast Club, where a disheveled but well-built and attractive African American man stood on the pier with his sleeves rolled up and a pistol in plain sight on his hip. A helicopter sat in the parking lot, engine ticking. Only because it was one in the morning was there not a crowd gathering.

"Special Agent," Harwood said as he stepped onto the dock and held out his hand.

"Reaper," Bronson replied. "And I'm assuming that's Jackie Colt driving the boat?"

Harwood looked over his shoulder, realizing that whatever an assassination team might look like, Jackie, Samuelson, and he certainly fit the description.

"Roger."

"And the young man sitting in the front staring out to sea?"

"That's my former spotter, Sammie Samuelson. Traumatic brain injury. Maybe torture at the hands of Basayev."

"The Chechen."

"Yes. The Chechen is here."

"We know that."

"Yes, but you don't know why."

"I think we do. He wants to kill you."

"No. Well, yes, eventually, but he needed me as a distraction."

"A distraction from what?"

"When I was a private, I was stationed here at

Hunter Army Airfield. That was in 2009 and 2010. Lots of rotations in and out of combat. I was out of combat in 2010 when Savannah police caught three Russians walking down the road near Hunter carrying shovels and rucksacks."

"I know about that," Bronson said. "I've got a situation going down on MLQM property right next to Hunter Army Airfield. Now give me something I don't know or I'm firing that puppy up and heading back."

"You don't know shit, Special Agent. So just listen. There were four, not three, and the one that ran was Basayev. And he's here now. To finish the job."

"And you know this how?"

"I saw him the other night in the elevator at the hotel Savannah police raided. I'm sure he called in the police to get me on the move."

"Why did you run?"

"Because I'm a black man who can shoot a rifle and nowadays that's a tough spot to be in," Harwood said. Bronson remained stone-faced, but the words worked.

"The other night when Samuelson dropped me off near where the two police officers were killed I heard digging and scraping. Back in 2010 when I was a private, we helped the Savannah police look for the fourth man. No one told us a name, but the word was that they had parachuted in and buried an RA-115."

"Suitcase nuke?"

"Right, only nobody in U.S. intelligence has really ever seen one. Could be an artillery shell. A briefcase. Who knows. It's just small enough to carry. Supposed to weigh about fifty pounds. We didn't know what we were looking for, but we looked. Scrolls to the road, as we called it." The Ranger insignia was an olive-drab patch designed to look like parchment, with the battalion number embroidered on it. "Stanislov Lunev."

"Officially, I know nothing about Lunev. Unofficially, he allegedly told our government that there were four-man teams that were smuggling tactical nukes into the United States. Unofficially, he's in witness protection somewhere. So I think he's safe."

"But we're not."

"So you're saying Basayev came back, dug up a previously planted nuclear device, and it's somewhere about to blow in Savannah."

"That's half the story. He came back, framed me using his wife, Nina Moreau, and put every law enforcement agency on my trail instead of his. Classic misdirection."

"Moreau is the shooter?"

"Yes. I think you'll find her wherever you can find Ramsey Xanadu or General Markham. They're her next targets."

"Milk 'Em?" Bronson asked. "We're all up in their grille."

"They're either there or getting on the airplane," Harwood said.

"Milk 'Em's airplane?"

"That or Markham has an airplane, too."

"I saw both. They're seven-thirty-sevens."

"Think about it, Special Agent. If he has drugs and women in safe houses what do you think he's got on the airplane?"

They stood there looking across the street at the restaurant. Images of Monisha popped in his mind. Her smart mouth and slanted, knowing grin. Her loud cackle. Thinking of Monisha gave way to images of his foster sister, Lindsay. Both abused by weak men. Markham and Xanadu were morally weak men, as well.

But that didn't mean they were more of a threat than Basayev, who had repeatedly demonstrated his resiliency and strength. Parachuting into the United States, possibly with a nuclear weapon. Fighting alongside the Taliban in austere terrain. Falling in love with a tough woman like Nina Moreau.

"It doesn't really matter where Markham and Xanadu are," Harwood said.

"To me it does," Bronson snapped.

"You should be focused on Basayev. Everything else has been a distraction."

Bronson stopped walking, leveled his eyes even with Harwood's.

"I should arrest you, you know?"

"But you're not going to. You're going to take me to Hunter in your helicopter and we're going to put a full-court press on finding and disarming this nuke. We're going to shut down the Milk 'Em airplane. And then you can focus on Markham and Xanadu."

"We did find an Instagram account that we think Basayev has used to communicate. The account has a picture of a falcon and of the Oatland Island Wildlife Center sign. We've had three or four people say they saw someone fitting Nina Moreau's description walking to and from the center late one evening. And we found disturbed earth near the back of the aviary big enough to hold a duffel bag. We scanned social media using the term Oatland and found that account. Then traced it to a phone. Last-known location was at the hotel where Basayev stayed."

"Sounds about right," Harwood said.

They both turned at the distant sound of a helicopter lifting from the roof of Markham's compound a mile south. The blinking lights showed it banking hard west toward Savannah and then disappearing into the night.

"They know their time is short. Markham's about to board his jet for one of a few countries," Harwood said.

"Jackie has to get that boat back," Samuelson said.

Bronson flinched at Samuelson's voice. The spotter had approached them quietly.

"Tell her—"

It was too late. She and the boat, too, like the helicopter, were disappearing into the night toward Savannah.

"We're with you, Agent," Harwood said.

"Question is, do I put you in cuffs or kit you up," Bronson said.

"You know the answer to that."

They boarded the helicopter and joined the procession.

CHAPTER 27

Khasan Basayev entered the MLQM warehouse through the chain-link fence on the private side, not the military side, of the compound. He used bolt cutters to chop away the rudimentary lock, opened the gate, and then carried the unconscious young girl through the opening.

Time was of the essence. He cradled her in his arms and walked into the warehouse, which was behind the hangar housing the two airplanes. Basayev had been waiting in the woods a hundred meters away. After the burning helicopter limped back to the airfield, Basayev walked through the maze of military transfer cases until he found the right one.

When he had previously planted the device, he had noticed that the container had small ovals of black spray paint on either side. He opened the case and saw that the car battery and the device were still there. Everything looked good.

He laid the girl inside the case and closed the lid.

Harwood had turned out to be a decent adversary and a worthwhile rabbit for the FBI to chase. From the beginning, this was all about the big payday. The one hundred thousand dollars he had placed in the Reaper's bank account after each of the kills was probably unnecessary, but still a worthwhile precaution. He looked down at the girl and then at the other cases strewn about the floor. He thought of Nina being in this very case and the other ghost girls that were transported from Afghanistan and Iraq to service their new masters. He felt nothing for the girl that lay before him next to the car battery, just as he felt nothing for the women who had been abducted, other than Nina. In fact, he was grateful to them for providing him with a portal and the basis for an elaborate plan.

He fixed a timer to the metal briefcase near Monisha's head and pressed a button to begin the countdown. Next, Basayev closed the lid on what would become Monisha's coffin. He didn't care what the military called the caskets, they were coffins. They carried and contained death.

He retraced his steps as he heard the large corrugated metal door lifting, tugged by a chain pulley system. Quietly he filed through the caskets, out the door, and through the gate. He fumbled with the lock so that it looked shut, but a close inspection would reveal that it wasn't.

He drove his Hummer to the Isle of Hope Marina, where he had moored the Marquis 690 yacht that he had chartered from the Bahamas. He parked in a remote portion of the lot and wiped down the Hummer, removing all fingerprints and DNA. He wasn't sure that there hadn't been some radioactive leakage in the back during the short period of time he had the weapon in the rear compartment, but there was very little he cared to do about that.

He was nearly free.

He walked to the end of the pier, noticing the many other yachts lining the docks. He saw the *Breeze Machine* and stepped onto its swim platform, climbed the rail, and stood in the open deck, absorbing the night.

Time to pick up Nina; she had finally contacted him.

Ramsey Xanadu stood inside MLQM's dark hangar adjacent to Hunter Army Airfield. The MLQM Boeing 737 cargo jet and General Markham's 737 luxury jet were in front of him. The open hangar doors beyond the airplanes gave way to a misty darkness filled with drifting fog and stale air. The cargo 737 had its rear ramp resting on the concrete, like an open jaw on a nutcracker.

Markham will crack my nuts if I don't solve this bullshit, Xanadu thought.

He turned in the dim light and stared at the line of twenty women standing in the dark. Markham's executive helicopter had just delivered the last batch of girls from the Tybee Island compound. Now he could fully implement the plan he had briefed to Markham.

Because he had found the bomb, he had decided to prepare these women for movement overseas. He preferred to sell the women in Syria to ISIS, as he had done in the past. Like a pig farmer, Xanadu wasted no part of the product. The women had provided a valuable service to the MLQM and CLEVER employees and members and now it would normally be time to

cycle them to ISIS for sale. But because of the bomb
and the Reaper activity, he had a different plan.

He walked down the line of women, who were
standing with their hands clasped in front of them
in the fig-leaf pose, eyes cast downward at the concrete floor, their humiliation having taken permanent
hold. They were dressed in a variety of Western garb:
dresses, skirts, blouses. To the average onlooker they
could have been Middle Eastern high school students
on a field trip to Hunter Army Airfield—save the
ankle chains binding them together.

Of course, they were captives and sex slaves, not
high school students, or anything remotely close to
what they should have been: young, eager women
ready to challenge the world. Xanadu knew that each
of them was broken in her own way. He'd already had
four suicides over the last six months. But still, they
looked good. Young and innocent, though he knew
they were anything but that. These girls were maybe
seventeen years old. He had personally captured them
within the last month. They were the best of the remaining lot.

He chose five women using the criteria of youngest,
prettiest, and newest. Furrowed brows, wide eyes, and
sobs reflected the fear and confusion of the sex slaves.

He lined up his five picks and led them onto General Markham's Boeing 737, upfit with separate bedrooms and showers for long-distance trips. The double
beds were covered in white down comforters and
Egyptian cotton sheets, with bulbous pillows resting
against the mahogany headboards. He ushered one
woman to each of the bedrooms and locked the door
from the outside.

Xanadu envied the plush carpeting and presidential office flush with state-of-the-art telecommunications for business travel around the world.

Once he had secured the women in the airplane, he walked down the steps of the aircraft and radioed the crew, two pilots and a steward, telling them that General Markham, two congressmen, and two CLEVER CEOs—one a pharmaceutical company chief executive and the other the leader of a major defense contractor—were about to arrive and would be ready for departure in thirty minutes. The helicopter would return after making the final trip from Tybee Island with Markham and his investors.

He then led the remaining fifteen women across the hangar floor, up the tongue of the cargo ramp. They followed Xanadu in single file into the MLQM Boeing 737, which was kitted out as a cargo airplane. In it, he had previously had the MLQM forklift drivers load sixteen transfer cases. The women were shaking, mouths open in silent screams, clutching one another as they feared returning to their coffins. Every one of them had endured the coffin and several appeared to have decided they couldn't go back. The first girl whose ankle chain he unlocked started to run. Xanadu drew his silenced pistol and shot her in the back, to the horror of the remaining fourteen. The dead girl tumbled down the ramp onto the hangar floor.

"You're getting in either dead or alive," Xanadu said. "Doesn't much matter to me."

"We will be okay? Where are we going?" one of the young girls sobbed.

"Of course you'll be okay. You're going home. We

must transport you this way. Just drink the water and eat the food and you'll be fine."

He escorted the women one at a time to the coffins. He'd lift the lid and from there they knew the drill. Step in, don't make a fuss, and lie down like you're sleeping. A couple asked where the food and water was and Xanadu told them that the pallet was late but he would make sure they all got ample supplies before takeoff.

The transfer case containing the bomb was loaded all the way to the front of the aircraft. It would be the last dumped in the ocean and therefore the farthest away from Savannah and MLQM headquarters just in case it was something worse than what he considered it to be. Xanadu believed it was simply an inert bluff, but he wasn't taking a chance.

He had told the pilots that all the cases needed to be dumped out of the airplane once it was one hundred miles over the Atlantic. He explained that the cases were empty and the military had asked that they be disposed of at sea, that the DNA that remained inside was impossible to remove and would conflict with future transports.

Xanadu looked at it like a burial at sea. The pilots would reach ten thousand feet above sea level and slow to 160 knots. Then the loadmaster would lower the ramp so that it dipped slightly down and he would walk to each transfer case and remove a metal snap hook. The snap hook secured the container to the aircraft floor by a short nylon strap. This device served as a stop along the roller rails that would feed the cases into the ocean once the loadmaster gave the word to the pilots that the ramp was prepared for drop operations. As far as the transfer cases went, the perforations for oxygen flow would cause the containers to rapidly fill with water and sink to the bottom of the ocean.

Problem solved. No eyewitnesses. No bomb.

All he needed now was the crew. He had already radioed them, purposefully summoning the crew of Markham's jet for a thirty-minute-later takeoff. The plane was ready. He had personally filed the flight plan to Kuwait, where it would conduct the normal refuel for its leg into Kandahar to continue MLQM operations. Normally he would go on this resupply route, but he figured he would skip this one.

A set of headlights cut across the fence line and it was the Suburban carrying the crew for the cargo plane: two pilots and a loadmaster.

Xanadu had a brief conversation with the cargo plane's pilots as the loadmaster inspected the tie-downs on the coffins. He walked to the aircraft ramp and stood on the concrete floor as the loadmaster donned his crewman's helmet and parachute before shooting Xanadu a Nomex-gloved thumbs-up.

Xanadu returned the gesture, feeling a huge weight begin to lift from his shoulders.

Then, the world crashed down upon him as the FBI helicopter skidded to a hard landing in front of Markham's jet.

CHAPTER 28

Harwood jumped off the helicopter and ran toward Ramsey Xanadu, who drew his pistol and fired.

The shot was wide, and pinged off the FBI helicopter.

On the helicopter flight into Hunter Army Airfield, Harwood saw a Hummer that fit the description provided by Jackie. It was driving rapidly away from the hangar. Based upon that observation, Harwood knew that the Chechen had not lived up to his promise to take care of Monisha, most likely dumping her in the middle of whatever was happening at MLQM.

Like the linebacker that he used to be, he tackled Xanadu—not a small man—with full force and effect. Xanadu's head slapped against the concrete as Harwood retrieved his knife with one hand and used the other to block Xanadu's shooting hand. He locked his left elbow out, used his vise grip around Xanadu's wrist, and then held the knife against Xanadu's throat as he pinned the man with his body weight.

"Where's the girl?" Harwood asked through clenched teeth.

"Fuck you, Harwood."

Harwood stabbed the knife into the side of Xanadu's throat, and the carotid artery sprayed like a broken fire hydrant. He looked over his shoulder and saw the cargo-plane jet turbines turning and a loadmaster standing in the cargo bay, back toward him, pressing a button to raise the ramp. Beyond the loadmaster, he saw transfer cases.

In the transfer cases, he imagined, there might be women, or even Monisha. He instantly sprang from Xanadu's lifeless body and ran toward the now-moving airplane. It was taxiing from the hangar onto the apron under its own power, blowing hot jet wash against his face. The ramp was at a forty-five-degree angle and if he didn't reach it soon, he would forever miss the chance to see what was inside the transfer cases.

The plane was fully onto the tarmac now, Bronson yelling at him to stop, the ramp slowly inching up; he was ten meters away when he put one final burst of energy into his stride and closed on the airplane. He leapt up and grasped the ramp with two hands, performed a pull-up, kicked one leg over the lip, and rolled through a narrowing three-foot gap of the still-closing ramp door.

He fell to the bottom of the cargo-bay floor, smacking against the same ribs the Chechen had injured with his steel-toed boot. He looked up at the space-age face shield of the loadmaster, who was most likely wondering what the hell he was doing. Wasting no time, Harwood sprang to his feet and planted a kick in the solar plexus of the loadmaster. He didn't know if the man was friend or foe, but he didn't have time to find out. Grabbing two twenty-foot-long yellow parachute static lines balled up in the corner, he tied the loadmaster's hands and legs securely, then hooked each of the snap hooks into an anchor point on the rib of the aircraft. The loadmaster was immobilized. Harwood slapped the button that controlled the ramp.

The ramp began to lower as he retrieved his Maglite from his pocket. He had left his rucksack with Bronson on the FBI helicopter, but brought along his phone, knife, Maglite, and pistol as he had charged after Xanadu.

The plane powered up to full throttle and the brakes were off. Harwood opened the first transfer case and saw a young lady lying on her back. She had black hair and almond eyes that shone in the dim glow of the cargo-cabin lights. She was alive. The transfer case was secured on a bed of roller conveyors and fastened on each side by a snap hook and two-inch-wide nylon strap.

He felt the airplane picking up speed. They bumped along the runway. The ramp was halfway down. The engines whined as they spun at full throttle. He looked behind him. Saw at least ten to fifteen other containers. He didn't know where the plane was headed, but there was no food or water in the transfer case he saw.

He thought about his parachute training and the different ways Rangers could receive supplies. One method was to drop supply bundles from an aircraft in flight at one thousand to ten thousand feet. But these transfer cases didn't have parachutes on them. Another method was called LAPES. Low-altitude parachute-extraction system. The air force had pretty much quit doing it because the technique was risky. The aircraft would fly low, like doing a touch-and-go, and a loadmaster would release a pilot parachute that would catch wind out of the rear of the aircraft and then deploy a personnel or cargo parachute. The tank or artillery piece or whatever was being "LAPESed" would roll off the exact same type of conveyor rollers, over the ramp and onto the dirt airfield, and skid along with the parachute slowing its momentum. It was a heavily used practice in Vietnam. After a crash during a demonstration at Fort Bragg twenty years ago, the air force quickly winnowed that technique out of its resupply options.

But Harwood had no choice and he had no parachutes. With the ramp below the lip of the cargo deck, Harwood locked the transfer case he'd just opened, then cut the two straps, and the transfer case shot out of the back of the aircraft onto the runway, creating a fireworks show looking like sparklers lit up around the case.

But it worked.

He quickly moved to the other cases and began cutting and nudging them while the aircraft was still on the runway bouncing and gaining speed. The pilots were probably wondering why the ramp was still open but they were at the point of no return. To throttle down now would probably put them into a fence or river somewhere. That wouldn't look good on their records. Better to take off with a crazy loadmaster jacking with the ramp than to power down mid-takeoff and wreck.

More straps. More cases. Each most likely filled with a young woman. Was Monisha on board? Had he already cut her free? Ten cases. Now eleven. Two more swipes of his knife and he was at twelve. The front wheels of the aircraft were off the runway. Thirteen cases. He felt that smooth glide indicating that the rear wheels were off the ground. Fourteen cases.

The airplane shot up. He was all the way at the bulkhead of the cockpit. One remaining container. He looked back and saw the runway getting smaller. Transfer cases were littered along the concrete, each aimed in a different direction, as if someone had dumped a tub of children's building blocks. He hoped they had all lived, but he knew he couldn't cut the last transfer case free. The occupant would die. They were probably five hundred feet off the ground and climbing. He looked up at the cockpit, thinking.

This plane was unlike a civilian airliner. It was as if he were in the baggage compartment below, but there were no seats above. There was a ladder to the cockpit. He considered climbing up, but since he was now airborne with the last transfer case, he decided to look inside.

He unlatched the hasps, lifted the top, and saw Monisha's limp form lying in about two-thirds of the casket. She was in the fetal position, wearing the same bloodstained clothes from yesterday. A metal briefcase and a battery occupied the rest of the case. There was a timer on the briefcase with red numbers counting down. Less than five minutes before something happened. Was it the RA-115 Russian nuke that Basayev had jumped into America in 2010 with three comrades? Best case, it was an improvised explosive device that would blow up the airplane in less than four minutes and counting.

He looked at the runway through the yawning cargo

ramp of the airplane. Monisha stirred in the transfer case below him. He eyed the loadmaster's parachute, a clear sign these transfer cases were going to be dumped somewhere over the Atlantic Ocean.

"Reaper," Monisha whispered. "Either that's you or you look a lot like Jesus."

"It's me, Monisha. Hold tight. I gotta figure something out."

Her eyes dimmed. She was weak and needed fluids.

"Okay, Reaper."

"I'm going to shut the case so you don't roll or bounce out."

"Okay, Reaper," she said dreamily. Maybe Basayev had given her morphine?

The plane banked to the right and pushed for more altitude. He let the momentum of the turn carry him to the starboard side of the fuselage. He used a series of ribs and web seats to secure his passage to the aft end of the aircraft where he had tied up the loadmaster. After removing the loadmaster's helmet, he slapped his pistol against the man's head, knocking him unconscious. Harwood untied the man, reversing the loops and knots. Freed him up so that he could slip the parachute off the loadmaster and put it on himself. He stepped into the harness and tightened the leg and shoulder straps. Snapped the chest strap. Flexed and then tightened again. He looked around for a reserve. He didn't see one. The plane banked again and he could see ocean beneath him. The fading lights of Tybee Island were visible below him. They were probably approaching ten thousand feet, the altitude where they would need oxygen or to pressurize the cargo

compartment. He saw the yellow static lines and retrieved three, thinking they would be useful.

He handrailed his way up the starboard side again,
like doing the monkey bars. The plane was still angled
up at least twenty degrees. Any misstep would send
him tumbling out of the aircraft.

He reached Monisha's transfer case and opened it.
Less than two minutes. He lifted Monisha out of the
case and said, "Lean back into me, Monisha." Harwood felt the pressure of her small body; he cinched
the yellow static line around her waist and his back
twice, creating a field-expedient tandem jump rig. He
used another static line for good measure around her
chest. He saw a dozen life jackets stacked in a bin to
the rear, probably a mandatory Federal Aviation Ad-
ministration regulation. He grabbed two and handed
them to Monisha.

"Hang on to these, Monisha. We'll need them." He
wrapped another static line around the life jackets in
case her grip became weak. He also figured it would
give her something to do with her arms. He didn't
need her flailing arms destabilizing their descent.

"We jumping into combat, Reaper?" Monisha
asked.

"Jumping away from it, girl. Now work with me."

"I'm working."

"Okay, we gotta walk to the end of the airplane
and then fall into the sky. It will feel weird, but I just
looked at that bomb and we've got fifty-eight seconds
to get off this airplane."

They waddled awkwardly the length of the cargo
bay and he stopped them on the ramp. One hand was

holding Monisha close to him while the other was grasping the starboard hydraulic arm of the ramp.

He figured they had less than thirty seconds. He went through his pre-jump routine. Flared his arms backward, pulling against his powerful pectoral muscles. Squatted a couple of times to maintain flexibility. Monisha would be a new dynamic. He had never controlled a tandem jump. He'd been on the receiving end one time—in the place where Monisha was currently—and then he was hooked on learning the art of skydiving, which was very different from military parachuting.

"Scared, Reaper," Monisha said. He could feel her trembling. Saying his name somehow connected her to him. A cognitive bind that she needed. He was okay with that. It was nice to be needed.

"Ready, Monisha?" He edged them to the lip of the ramp. The unfortunate part was that Monisha was in front of him and while he couldn't see her face, he was sure that her mouth was open and she was aghast. No thrill in this for her. Takeoff speed for a jet was about 150 knots, which fortunately was also about drop speed.

He quit thinking about it and lifted Monisha and they were off, floating through the sky. He counted to thirty in his head, the amount of time for the bomb to explode, but didn't see anything but the diminishing white speck of the airplane.

Monisha screamed, "What you got me into, Reaper!"

The wind buffeted their faces. There was nothing but ocean below them. Thankfully it was August and the Gulf Stream was pushing hard to the north, bringing with it warm water. They could last for several hours, providing they didn't become shark bait. By

Harwood's calculation, it was 2 A.M. and they would have a long four hours until sunrise.

He pulled the ripcord after that thirty-second count, which he figured put him at four thousand feet above sea level. He could see Savannah in the distance as the canopy caught air, popped, and held. He grimaced as the leg straps crushed his manhood. He toggled toward the lights of Tybee Island, maybe three miles away, but there was no way he had enough altitude to glide that far. There was very little wind to propel him, so he and Monisha drifted generally west.

Soon, they splashed into the black ocean and he knew he needed to work quick. He cut the ties between him and Monisha and then put the life vest through each arm and zipped it up for her. He donned his life vest and used one of the static lines to connect them so they wouldn't float apart.

Monisha was already shivering, so he removed his shirt and slipped it over her life jacket and torso, which meant he was bare-chested. He removed his iPhone 7 from his pants pocket, prayed all of the commercials were accurate—that it was waterproof—and then turned on his "location services."

With any luck, they would survive.

He looked over his shoulder at the black sky where the airplane would be. There was no explosion.

At that moment, he knew the bomb was on Jackie's boat.

Khasan Basayev leaned over from the swim platform of his speed yacht and reached out for Nina's hand. She was standing on the gunwale of the *Ten Meter Lady,* her arm outstretched.

They clasped hand to forearm as Basayev used his considerable strength to swing her onto the teak deck. She landed in his arms, smelling musty and dank. On the deck of the *Ten Meter Lady* blond hair was spread like a fan.

They embraced and Nina kissed him.

"Quick. Into the shower. I'll have the captain get us to the ocean."

"We have two hours," Moreau said. Basayev thought about that and it seemed like a lot of time for something to go wrong, but all the modeling they had done showed that the boat needed to be here in downtown Savannah during a busy summer filled with tourists. He also knew that it could take nearly an hour to get to the ocean and he did not want to draw attention to their vessel. He nodded in support of her timing decision.

"The Olympian?"

She nodded beyond the gunwale of the *Breeze Machine* at Jackie Colt's inert form on the floor of the *Ten Meter Lady*. Already the captain was moving toward the river channel. "If anyone arrives before the bomb, they'll blame it all on her and her boyfriend. The computer records. The weapon. It's all there. And the records are in the cloud also, so once the FBI tracks that they'll still blame them. It's done."

"Okay. Shower, my love. We're done here."

Moreau moved swiftly to the master chambers while Basayev climbed the ladder to the bridge and told the captain, "As fast as possible to the ocean. Your life depends on it."

The captain, familiar with the dangers of working with people who wished to stay off the radar, kept his mouth shut and pushed the three diesel engines to half then full throttle as he sped at thirty knots through the winding river. The ocean was seventeen miles away and after fifty minutes of maneuvering, Basayev saw them pass the northern end of Tybee Island. Ten minutes later they were another mile into the ocean when the captain nudged the vessel to the southwest.

Nina joined him on the bow, where Basayev had an ice bucket with a bottle of Goût de Diamants, her family champagne, and two glasses of crystal stemware.

"One more hour. The yield of the weapon is twenty kilotons," Basayev said.

"I think we should be safe soon," she said. She nuzzled tightly into Basayev's chest. He was dressed in black dungarees, a blue cotton T-shirt, and an unbuttoned dress shirt. Moreau was wearing a new set of clothes, navy cropped pants with a pullover sweater and white Vans boat shoes. Basayev ensured they dressed the part of tourists from Europe taking a cruise on a chartered yacht.

"You've done well," Basayev said, ignoring her comment. He never truly felt safe, but didn't want to frighten Moreau, not that she scared easily.

"Thank you, Khasan. We both love a good payday."

"That and fifteen thousand dead with another twenty thousand wounded, Nina."

"If that materializes, then the bonus should kick in, correct?"

Basayev smiled. His Nina was as much of a mercenary as he.

"It should. We must wait, though. The fifty million is in my account now. Our financiers can track where the bomb is and the fact that it is prepared to detonate.

When we go down below to the command center, I will move twenty-six million into your account. When we get to the Caymans, you can choose to stay or go."

"I want to be with you, Khasan. Our marriage was more than a payday. More than a legend."

"I know," he said. He thought of the many times they had made love. Those were good memories. Her body against his was warm and reassuring. Still, Ramsey Xanadu had taken liberties with Nina. While that was part of the plan, he wasn't sure he could continue with her. It made little sense. She had sex with other men before him, but he wasn't sure he wanted Xanadu's leftovers. Not that she had been with Xanadu of her own free will. Or had she? He would never know. That was the rub. She had volunteered for what was tantamount to a suicide mission and survived. Perhaps his affections for her would not, though.

Changing the topic, he said, "Why do you think Harwood and Colt let you go?"

"I was quick. Into the water before they could really think of me escaping."

"You are quick, my love," he said.

The moon glowed low in the sky, casting a skidding reflection of yellow off the ocean's surface. The vessel churned through the calm seas.

Basayev knew Moreau was quick, but didn't believe for a second that Harwood had let her go by accident. Perhaps there was one more hand to be played. He never relied on hope. For example, the decoy bomb on the plane was misdirection. Now all he could do was wait and believe that the confusion at MLQM, the search for Monisha, and ultimately the nuclear blast would distract them, perhaps kill them, so that they could continue their trek toward safety.

He thumbed the Amur falcon medallion hanging around his neck, looked at Nina, decided something, and then said, "I need to make a quick check-in with the captain."

"You're still nervous?"

"Not nervous. Joyful, but cautious. Be back in a sec."

Bronson had a dilemma. Did he stay at Hunter to potentially arrest General Markham, or did he chase after an international terrorist who was escaping? The police had already helped the young women from the caskets littered along the runway. His guess was that Harwood had cut them free.

Each one would be an information treasure trove, but he still had a developing situation. The endgame was at hand, but had not been fully played out.

He sat next to Faye Wilde in the helicopter. Across from him was Corporal Sammie Samuelson, which gave him an idea.

"Can you still shoot, Samuelson?"

"Yes, sir."

They spoke through the headsets. The helicopter blades were spinning. Bronson turned to White and said, "Randy, you and Max stay here. Do not let that airplane leave. Arrest General Markham when he arrives and take him to the conference room. Don't let him near any of the women from the coffins. That's his helicopter coming in right now." He pointed at a white light circling above the runway. "Probably trying to make his getaway."

"Arrest him on what charges, boss?" White asked.

"Human trafficking. Drug distribution. Call the lawyers. They'll give you ten more things you can charge him with."

"Roger that." White and Corent disembarked onto the concrete tarmac just when Wilde's phone chirped.

"Oh my God," she said.

"What?"

"Harwood's phone is sending a signal. He's three miles offshore."

"Got to be a mistake. I saw him get on that airplane."

"Won't hurt to check it out," she countered.

Bronson nodded. "Give the pilot the lat-long and let's go."

Wilde switched channels on the internal communications and gave the pilot the coordinates. Switching back, she said, "They're on it. Less than ten minutes we'll know."

"Roger that."

"C-C-Cold, Reaper." Monisha's voice was a haunting whisper.

Monisha's teeth chattered, which he took as a good sign. Her body was responding to the cold and trying to produce heat. Too much longer in the water might result in hypothermia even though the temperatures were in the mid-seventies. With her wounds, she was already low on fluids. Dehydration contributed to a more rapid onset of hypothermia. She had another thirty minutes, if that.

He held her close with one arm while using his other to lift the phone as high as possible. He wasn't sure if he was sending a signal or not. He scissor-kicked his legs as hard as he could. And while he was breaking a sweat, he knew that Monisha was losing her fight to stay alive.

"Come on, somebody. You've been looking for me for two damn days and now I'm telling you where the hell I am!"

"It-It's okay, Reaper. You did good." Another whisper coming from Monisha. Her voice was like a soft wind, nearly as silent. He took her comment to be a final statement, but he refused to let that stand.

When he began to believe that God had abandoned him and Monisha the way he believed that He had abandoned Lindsay, Harwood saw a light flickering in the distance. Then he heard the soft whoop of a Black Hawk helicopter blade. Gaining hope, he used his thumb to swipe up on the screen and then press the flashlight function. He began waving the phone until he knew that the pilot had a bead on them.

The Black Hawk drew to a hover, and with the prop wash blowing hard on them, he saw his former spotter Samuelson being lowered on a cable hoist. When Samuelson was face-to-face with him, Harwood said, "Thanks, Sammie. Take the girl up and get her warm. Then just drop the hoist back down for me."

"I've got your back, Vick. No worries." Samuelson took the girl and tenderly hugged her to him, cradling her.

"She's in bad shape, Sammie."

Samuelson nodded. The hoist began rising and they disappeared into the helicopter. As directed, Samuelson leaned over and guided the hoist to Harwood, who had to swim about ten meters to grasp it, sit in the metal T seat, and tug on it to indicate he was ready.

Once in the helicopter, he saw Monisha wrapped in a thermal blanket. A young woman was securing her to the floor while looking over her shoulder and shaking her head. Harwood was not going to let Monisha die. He sat across from Bronson and said, "I know how this ends. Let's get the girl to the hospital and then we have to find Jackie Colt."

"What about Basayev?" Bronson asked.

"Just tell the pilots to go to the hospital. Then we can debate," Harwood said.

Bronson nodded, switched to the intercom, and spoke to the pilots. Switching back, he said, "We're on our way. Now talk to me."

CHAPTER 29

The emergency medical personnel swept Monisha onto a stretcher and wheeled her into an elevator on the roof of the regional hospital.

"Now fly the river starting from the north, near I-95," Harwood said.

"Why there?" Bronson asked.

"Because the bomb is on Jackie's boat," Wilde said. "Basayev's Instagram account now has a picture of the marina by the River Street Market Place."

"Like she said," Harwood replied. "The way Nina Moreau was sitting on the bench seat down below on Jackie's boat didn't make sense. The lock on the middle seat. It was like she was protecting something. It's there. Lots of targets. The interstate. The port. The city. Markham's house. That vicinity."

"So it's real? The RA-115?"

"Has to be. I know we looked for it when I was a private. I think Basayev came back and put it in play, used me as a decoy to trick you guys. They went through a lot of trouble to make me the bad guy for all of this. Plus, I saw what looked like a bomb on the airplane. It was in Monisha's casket," Harwood said. "We were in the water for fifteen minutes. The timer on what was probably a decoy showed less than four minutes when we jumped. I never saw an airburst. That either means it was a dud or a fake."

"Why plant a fake?"

"Lots of people were sniffing around me, all these dead generals and senators. It's a big story. Basayev knew people would start looking inside Milk 'Em. So why not plant a fake there to cause every bomb expert in the country to look there instead of where the real bomb is. There's an old saying, 'Among many, one.' If you make people think there are more than one, it will take them time to figure out where the real one is. Basayev is smart. Plus, my sense is that he wanted to scare Milk 'Em, anyway."

Bronson talked to the pilots and they lifted into the sky and banked to the northwest.

"What are we looking for?"

"Big Boston Whaler Outrage called the *Ten Meter Lady*," Harwood said.

They flew across the city at a diagonal until they were north of the port, where they began working their way along the river. The fog rolled along the water like lost ghosts urging them forward.

"Nothing here," Harwood said. "Like she said, let's head for the market." He pointed at Wilde.

The pilot nosed the Black Hawk forward and within minutes they were astride the moorings at the River Street Market Place.

"There it is. That's it," Harwood said. "Just drop me on the pier and I'll climb on that way."

He didn't see Jackie. The boat sat there, inert, dark. As he jumped from the aircraft, he saw a flash of yellow on the deck. Jackie.

"I'm coming with you," Samuelson said.

Harwood didn't argue. His heart sank when he saw a Sea Doo underwater sea scooter discarded on the pier. Leaping onto the boat, he saw blood next to Jackie's face, her blond hair fanned against the white deck, and his sniper rifle lying across her chest at port arms.

"Moreau," Harwood said. "Her escape was a head fake." He found a pulse on her neck. Her eyes were closed and he thought that no matter how bad she wanted revenge for her younger brother's death, it wasn't worth this. He scrambled quickly into the cabin, broke the middle bench lock with the butt of his pistol, and lifted the seat that Moreau had claimed.

Inside was a rectangular metal case. On top of it was a clock with red numbers that showed thirty-seven minutes and seventeen seconds. It was ticking down. Harwood's mind reeled. He looked at Jackie.

"Help me here," he said to Samuelson. "You used to hotwire shit all the time in battalion. Think you can do it to this boat? Keys are gone."

"Got your back, bro," Samuelson said. Harwood lifted Jackie and his rifle in his arms and carried both to the helicopter while Samuelson opened the engine compartment.

"Back to the hospital, Bronson," Harwood said above the din of the helicopter rotors. "Then go to your command center and look for a decent-sized boat heading out of the river in the last hour or two. Every type of video you can find. Get the name of it and then find it on satellite or however you guys do that stuff. Pick Samuelson and me up at the Breakfast Club where we met earlier."

"That's a lot of orders for a sergeant," Bronson said.

"This isn't a time to worry about rank, Bronson. Let's focus and get this done. And keep this in the helicopter." He patted Lindsay.

Bronson stared at him, nodded, and pointed at the boat. "The bomb in there?" Harwood nodded. "We have half an hour to get the boat into the ocean. I'm not even sure we can start it, much less drive it fifty knots through the river. We'll get it as far away from downtown as we can. Now you can either come with me or do what I asked."

"I got it. You got your phone still?"

"Roger. Get moving."

The helicopter lifted away and because of the aircraft noise, he had not heard the boat engines start. Samuelson had figured it out.

Jumping in the boat, he said, "Let's drive this bitch."

Samuelson was at the helm as Harwood went down below and stared at the bomb. He had done some basic improvised explosive device disarming, but nothing of this magnitude. Reaching into the compartment, made for life jackets and fishing gear but now housing a nuclear weapon, Harwood ran his hands along the rim of the metal case. He found two wires and followed them to a seam in the compartment. Probably connected to the boat battery. Did the bomb need the battery or would it hold its charge even if he disconnected? More importantly, he wondered, was there an anti-handling device that would immediately trigger the bomb if manipulated?

All of this was above his pay grade, but he felt the responsibility was his for no reason other than he was the only one now who could do anything about the situation. He felt helpless and decided that there was only one plan he could put in place that would minimize the damage.

He checked the time remaining: seven minutes and three seconds.

"Where we at, Sammie?"

"Approaching Tybee. North side," Samuelson said. Harwood felt a moment of pride that his spotter had risen to the moment.

He slipped into the cockpit next to Samuelson, pulled up the GPS map, and typed in a lat-long destination due east. As they passed the north end of Tybee Island, the boat corrected marginally when Harwood pressed the autopilot function on the display screen. He then secured the bow line and tied the steering wheel to the seat backrest, preventing any major change in direction in the event that the boat hit something and went askew from its now-designated course.

"Push it to full throttle and let's go, Sammie," Harwood said. Samuelson slid the throttle forward to full and the speedometer and tachometer showed 60 knots and 6500 rpms—both needles pegged into the red zones—respectively. Steadying themselves, Harwood and Samuelson held on to each other as they leapt into the ocean, avoiding the four 300hp Mercury motors spinning at full blast.

Harwood skidded into the ocean. His mouth filled with salt water, he went under deep, and he thrashed for a second before finding his bearings and resurfacing. He saw Samuelson about twenty meters away, thrashing as well.

Swimming toward Samuelson, Harwood gauged their distance to Tybee Island as maybe a half mile. That was doable, though he preferred to be out of the ocean when the bomb exploded. He didn't know the chemistry behind a nuclear explosion on the ocean's surface, and preferred to not learn the hard way.

The bomb had less than seven minutes remaining when they jumped. Sixty knots an hour put the boat speed at nearly 55 miles an hour, the math placing the boat at least five miles out to sea when the nuke exploded. They swam with a low tide going to hide tide, a helping current. The island grew larger with each stroke. The two Rangers made sure they were never more than five feet away from each other.

A light reflected off the water, like a flashing strobe. A few seconds later the explosion followed. They kept swimming. Stayed focused on the island. The chopping blades of a helicopter appeared on the horizon. It was Bronson. They were close to the north beach of Tybee and Bronson must have seen them. They emerged from the water and ran to the helicopter, the rotor wash blowing hot air onto them.

After climbing into the helicopter, they each slipped on a set of headphones.

"See that?" Bronson asked.

"Yeah. Saw it. Next item. Got the boat?" Harwood asked.

"I think so," Bronson said. "It's about twenty miles from here. The *Breeze Machine*. I'm making the call that it is within the twelve-mile radius of U.S. control."

Harwood understood. The boat was in international waters, but Bronson wanted Basayev as bad as he did.

"Let's go," Harwood said. He felt his adrenaline pumping. He was going to have his showdown with the Chechen, after all.

CHAPTER 30

Harwood turned to Bronson and said, "Have the pilot hold off at a half mile." He turned and grabbed his rucksack from the cargo webbing. He reached in and handed the thermal spotter scope to Samuelson. It was 5:30 A.M. and the sun, while threatening, was still below the dark horizon. Through the headset he said, "You know what to do."

Samuelson nodded and began preparing the scope for action. Harwood reached onto the floor of the aircraft and lifted Lindsay. He pulled a box of 7.62 mm rounds from his rucksack and slapped it into the magazine well, then mounted an ATN Odin 32DW Micron sight. Extending the bipods, he lay on the floor, causing the woman and Bronson to move their feet and relocate. He charged the weapon, chambering a round.

Samuelson was on his left talking to him through the intercom. The roar of the helicopter engines drowned out any conversation outside of the headsets. Harwood looked through the scope and placed the bipods on the rattling floor of the cargo bay. There was no way he was going to get a decent shot from this vantage, but he did see the yacht cruising on a south-easterly tack. It was nearly a mile away.

Warm night air washed through the open doors. A half-mile shot from a helicopter was no easy task, especially when Basayev would almost certainly be shooting back. Harwood switched his intercom to Bronson and Wilde and asked, "No rockets or missiles on this thing? Just blow up the boat?"

"Nothing. This is a personnel transport, not a gun-ship, Reaper."

Harwood nodded. "You need to rethink that strategy."

He checked the site picture. The rattling floor and rotor wash could direct the round off course when fired.

"You have a monkey harness in here?"

"Roger that," Bronson said. The crew chief ap-peared from the port side and strapped Harwood into a vest that zipped in the front and had a ten-foot nylon anchor line that snapped into a D ring in the floor of the cabin. He tested the strength of the anchor by lean-ing beyond the skin of the aircraft, feeling the slip-stream push against him. He could contend with that better than a jittery floorboard. He had the crew chief tighten the nylon cord as he wedged the heels of his shoes against where the floor of the aircraft met the outer edge. His body mass was taut against the nylon anchor as he was leaning at about a sixty-degree angle into the breeze and beyond the outer skin of the heli-copter.

"More stable?" Samuelson asked.

"Roger. No way to get a shot off that floor."

Harwood had always been a better pure shooter, whether from a standing or kneeling position than from the prone. Sure, the prone was more stable, and hide positions usually resulted in using that skill, but Harwood liked the feel of holding the rifle in its entirety. He trusted everything about his capacity to shoot and relied on nothing else but the spotter's directions.

"Whatcha got, Sammie?"

"We're officially at one kilometer away at the boat's four o'clock. I see two people on the bow of the ship. Woman and man. Fits the profile of Basayev and Moreau. Looks like they're drinking. Just chill. Like they think they've gotten away. One dude in the captain's bridge. Don't see any other deckhands."

"Okay, I'm going for Basayev first, then Moreau. One-two. I need the call on Basayev and then I'm very quickly going for Moreau."

"Roger. Basayev is the far target, though they are intermingled. She's got her back to us. You've got the top of Basayev's head and some of his upper torso for a clean shot. Then you can nail Moreau before she knows what hit her husband."

"Roger." He switched the intercom again. "Bronson, I'm good at a kilometer here. I've got a clean shot. Tell the pilot to get exactly astride the ship, maybe a little bit forward so I can get a better site picture."

"Got it," Bronson replied.

"And does he have chaff on here? Never sure what a magician like Basayev has on hand."

"That we do have."

"Ropes in case we want to board?"

"Those also," Bronson said.

"Okay. We're all set here. Samuelson and I are in charge. This is our sniper hide. Everyone is under my command."

He switched off before Bronson could argue. The helicopter pushed forward. Back to Samuelson, he said, "Focus me, Sammie. I haven't had a chance to zero this weapon, and I'm not sure if Moreau changed the zero. So I'm going with what we've got."

"What are you seeing with borelight and thermal?"

Harwood flipped a switch on the rail of his reliable rifle, and an infrared light emitted from the bore of the weapon. He dialed the ATN Odin 32DW Micron sight from thermal to infrared and clicked the sight aperture until the crosshairs were aligned with the steady beam of the invisible light. He painted the light on the back corner of the boat, there being no other targets in the vicinity. He was using technology to align his scope sight picture with the muzzle of the weapon so the bullet would impact where he aimed.

"I've got the borelight and the scope set. I've got as stable a platform as I'm going to get up here. I now see the Chechen's head. It's a two-thirds shot, but good enough. I think I'm going for a double tap then moving to Moreau. I've got four rounds in the mag."

"Sounds good. They're drinking champagne. Interesting that their nuke went off ten miles into the ocean and they're celebrating. Maybe they get paid no matter what happens," Samuelson said.

"Okay, we are in position. I have the target. It's a valid target. Do you agree, Sammie?"

"Valid target, Reaper. Kill us some bad guys."

Harwood leaned forward, pushing himself outside of

the helicopter as far as possible. He steadied the rifle against his face and immediately knew that he had made the right call. He flexed his upper body to create an ironclad firing platform. With his knees flexed he could diminish most of the rattle. The sight picture jumped marginally. Switching from infrared to thermal settings, the black-and-white world of thermal imagery provided him the best relief even though he couldn't make out the facial features of Basayev or Moreau. The couple on the bow certainly fit the profile, though.

But still, there was something off. Something Samuelson had said, ". . . they're celebrating." Even though the nuke had missed?

"Just a sec, Sammie."

The helicopter was about two hundred meters off the ocean.

He switched intercoms. "Confirm this is the same boat that picked up Nina Moreau from the River Market Place."

"It is. Same name. *Breeze Machine*. Same size. What's the issue?"

"Nothing. Hook up the fast rope just in case we need to confirm the kill," Harwood said. He switched back to his connection with Samuelson.

"What's up?"

"Something doesn't feel right. No way the Chechen would be just lounging on the boat like that. Like you said, a nuke just went off. He had to have seen it if not felt it. He knows something is up."

"I like the countersniper attitude. You thinking he's inside somewhere?"

"Maybe. Let me try something."

He leaned outside of the aircraft and assumed his firing position. Back tight against the nylon cord. Upper body flexed for a stable platform. Through the optic he saw the bucket with a bottle of champagne poking out. He leveled the crosshairs on the bucket, a big enough target, squeezed the trigger, and watched the bucket and champagne explode all over the couple on the bow.

They didn't move.

"If you move you die," Basayev said to the captain and Nina Moreau, his wife. The champagne exploded all over the frozen "couple." He was happy to have Harwood fire first and reveal his position. He had heard the helicopter as it approached, and, as always, had elected to save himself first. Nina was special, but as he had determined, Xanadu had taken the luster off that shine.

He had tied Nina and the captain at the ankles and wrists, and instructed them to face each other with Nina's back to the direction from which the helicopter would be coming. A hand grenade, with pin removed but spoon still intact, was wedged between their feet. Their teamwork in keeping the spoon affixed to the grenade would determine their fate. The grenade also gave Basayev the freedom of maneuver to take aim at the helicopter with the new Russian man-portable air defense weapon called a "Willow," or in American parlance, SA-25. This upgrade had three sensors that were less easily fooled by chaff and flares often fired by aircraft in response to inbound missiles.

He stood half in, half out of the captain's bridge, using the windshield and its frame as cover, took aim, armed the system, looked through the sight, and began tracking the aircraft.

"He's in the bridge. Got a Stinger or some kind of missile," Samuelson said.

Harwood shifted his aim to the highest point on the vessel. Found what Samuelson was calling the bridge, and saw a man inside aiming a surface-to-air missile at them. He leveled the crosshairs center-mass on the man and pulled the trigger. He was more concerned with shattering the windshield the man was using to conceal himself. At a minimum it would disrupt his shot. He never counted on being lucky, so he didn't believe he would kill Basayev on the first shot.

He saw the windshield explode at the same time the missile left the tube and began smoking directly toward them. He took a second shot at Basayev as the helicopter spit chaff and flares and dove toward the water while simultaneously flying at max speed directly at the yacht's nose. Harwood stayed where he was, straining against the nylon cord and feeling the salt water spray into his face.

The pilot was smart. At Samuelson's mention of the word "missile," barely after Harwood had fired his two shots, he dropped flares and got low. Churned up the water and created a cool water mist shield around the aircraft so that the flares would be the hottest particles in the air. The math wasn't in their favor. The missile flew at Mach 2 and they were flying at whatever the max speed might be, close to two hundred miles per hour. In less than ten seconds they would be at the ship. In less than two seconds the missile would know it missed the target. He knew that without contact there would be no detonation. Without detonation, the missile would continue to pursue.

Quickly they passed over the boat, Harwood still straining against the slipstream that threatened to rip him from the anchor bolt in the floorboard. The helicopter flew so low that he saw shards of the metal bucket and shattered champagne bottle as they whipped across the bow.

Moments later, a bright orange fireball erupted to the rear of the helicopter. The missile had returned and sought out the engine room of the yacht instead of the helicopter.

The pilot slowed, no doubt proud that his trickery had worked. Debris littered the ocean beneath them. Samuelson spoke first: "Zodiac at nine o'clock. Moving east. Now turning to get behind the fire. He's got a weapon."

"Roger. I've got it."

They were maybe three hundred meters away. The pilot leveled the aircraft, steadied it so that Harwood could take the shot, almost willing him to finish the job, as if he were saying, "I've done my part, now do yours."

He had Basayev in his crosshairs, the fire wreaking havoc on his ability to focus the thermal scope. With no time to change, he steadied his aim. Saw that the Chechen was doing the same thing, though in the Zodiac he probably had a less stable platform. Didn't matter. He never underestimated his enemy.

Which was why he pulled the trigger until he was out of ammunition.

He waited, hanging from the helicopter, tears sliding down his face from the wind. Heels dug into the cargo bay floor. Smoke drifted across the water. Noxious fumes gagged him as he coughed. The Zodiac boat bobbed in the wreckage. It was the only thing that was whole. If Nina Moreau and the ship captain had been on the bow, they were most likely dead.

"He's down," Samuelson said. His spotter was still there, lying on the floor of the aircraft, talking to him.

"Okay, take me down."

The pilot began to carefully maneuver the aircraft above the Zodiac. Samuelson dropped the fast rope and was first down. Harwood pulled himself inside, unhooked, and followed his teammate into the water. He held his Beretta pistol in his hand, just as Samuelson was doing.

They swam to the Zodiac, some ten meters away. Shining his flashlight into the rubber boat, he quickly scanned and saw nothing.

There was no dead body in the boat.

"He's gone," Samuelson said.

"Lots of blood," Harwood said.

"Roger that."

He tugged on the rope, the crew chief dropped the medevac hoist, and they each rode it back into the Black Hawk.

The pilot flew for an hour with spotlights shining on the wreckage.

"Nothing," Harwood said.

"They're dead, Reaper. Let's go back," Bronson said.

"We're bingo on gas. That's a roger," the pilot added.

Harwood nodded. "Roger."

He and Samuelson fist-bumped, but it was a hollow

gesture. They both needed to see the Chechen dead. Confirmation provided closure.

Instead, they were left to wonder, was he shark bait or was he executing one more escape plan?

The ocean slid beneath them as they returned to Hunter Army Airfield, where blue lights bounced off every building.

"We've arrested ten famous people you've never heard of," Bronson said.

"Markham?" Harwood asked.

Bronson shook his head. "Nothing."

Harwood thought for a moment, looked to the northeast in the direction of Markham's Tybee Island mansion twenty miles away, and said, "What about the women in the caskets?"

"Well . . ."

General Buzz Markham had not made the helicopter ride to Hunter Army Airfield. Knowing the FBI was lying in wait, he instead put his CLEVER associates on the chopper and retreated deep inside the command bunker of his Tybee Island fortress.

Sitting in an executive leather chair, he spun his officer's Beretta nine-millimeter pistol on the freshly waxed mahogany executive conference table. The room was crowding him. Its low ceiling and window-less walls made him feel claustrophobic. While he was used to the inside of a jet cockpit—where he at least had a windshield to see the world—this underground bunker stuff was never for him, despite the safety it might provide.

Sweating and choking on his anxiety, he considered three possible options: let his lawyers try to weasel him out of this tight spot; stick his pistol in his mouth; or get into the forty-one-foot SD GT3 cigarette boat perched on its lift in the cavern, looking like the Batmobile in the Batcave, and make a James Bond getaway through the tunnel that led into the intracoastal waterway.

He always liked James Bond movies. He wasn't much for suicide. And his lawyers, well, Shakespeare had been right, after all. They wouldn't be able to extricate him from this pickle. So why not live to fight another day? He had money stashed away in his offshore accounts. The boat had a full tank of gas. He could make it somewhere.

Markham walked to the stairwell that led to the boat cave, as he called it. He kept the lights off, because he knew that the FBI would soon know that he wasn't on the helicopter. He pressed the button to lower the boat into the water. Once the *Be One Bomber* was resting in the brackish water of Tybee Creek, he stepped into the vessel.

General Markham reached for the ignition and cranked the engine.

In the distance, a bright fireball erupted, boiling upward.

"About right," Harwood whispered, calculating the distance. A few seconds later the boom rolled across the airfield. Harwood nodded imperceptibly and thought, *A little C-4 goes a long way sometimes.* Lanny's kit bag had been full of the explosives.

"What the hell?" Bronson said.

"Not sure," Harwood said. "Markham may have

taken his own life. I think you were telling me about the women."

Shaken, Bronson looked at Harwood, then back at the fireball, and then back at Harwood. He squinted at Harwood's deadpan face and continued, "One of the women in the caskets died, but the rest made it. Initial report was the dead one may have killed herself. We've got them all, though. And they're talking."

"That's something," Harwood replied. "Let's go by the hospital. I've got a couple of people I need to check on."

EPILOGUE

Harwood sat in a beach chair as Monisha built a sand castle, the ocean ebbing and flowing behind her. The beach was scattered with a few sunbathers. The ocean swayed rhythmically, but no waves were breaking. It was a typical Tybee Island September day, with a zephyr—a warm west wind—and flat seas.

It had been a month since a small nuclear weapon had detonated ten miles east in the ocean. The experts all showed both the wind and the sea current taking the radiation north and east, toward the Labrador Sea, where its diminished effect would be insignificant. If Harwood and Samuelson had not been able to get the bomb to sea, the same experts were predicting fifteen thousand dead and twenty thousand more wounded and ill along the eastern seaboard. Thirty-five thousand people. A big town. A small city.

With a month of healing behind Jackie and Monisha—and himself—Harwood wondered what the future held. He loved Jackie, still, despite the knowledge of the role that she had played in the killing of those involved in what the media had labeled the Ghost Girl Scandal.

He had endured countless briefings with Bronson and his own military chain of command. Command Sergeant Major Murdoch had instructed him not to lawyer up and to just lay it out there like a good Ranger, which he did. The one thing he didn't mention, though, was Jackie's role, to the extent that he understood what it had been.

They had visited Richard's grave in Columbus, Georgia, last week and she was contrite, not boastful. Yet Jackie had also been resolute. She had closure. Then she'd hopped on an airplane to the West Coast, and Harwood hadn't heard from her since.

He wondered if he ever would.

General Bishop, who had facilitated and covered up the opium operation at Fort Benning, was dead by Nina Moreau's aim and his son was being prosecuted for felony distribution. The FBI cast their net far and wide and were still turning over suspects in the operation. The ghost girls the Reaper had saved were either returned to their families in Afghanistan and Iraq or given permanent visas in the United States.

Seagulls squawked overhead, breaking his reverie. He looked up and saw Monisha staring at him, smiling. Monisha was wearing a knotted-up white T-shirt that suspiciously showed just enough midriff to display her abdominal scar. Her blue shorts stopped just above the deep, healing gash that Xanadu's minigun had ripped in her leg. He smiled. She was proud and, of course, ever the show-off.

"Just because we're black doesn't mean we don't burn," Harwood said.

"I'm good," Monisha said. "SPF fifty." She held up a tube of Watermans sunscreen.

Harwood smiled. "Okay, kid. Having fun?"

Monisha smiled. "Told you. I love the beach, Reaper."

Samuelson walked over the dunes carrying a cooler. He had reverted to the Ranger haircut, white sidewalls with a tuft on the top. The doctors had placed a plastic liner beneath his scalp where his skull had collapsed. His head looked normal unless someone knew what they were looking for. There was a scar, but like Monisha, Samuelson wore that proudly.

"You know they're calling this Radiation Beach now, right?" Samuelson joked.

"Well, it's only right that we're here on the first day it's open," Harwood said.

Samuelson looked at Monisha. "And here I thought you were all dead and stuff."

"Not me, Frankenstein," Monisha quipped.

They laughed. It felt good and right. Whether Monisha represented Lindsay or his own failures or simply something he'd done right—saving her—Monisha would forever be the catalyst that got the Reaper back on track.

"Good thing you've got the Reaper protecting you with that mouth, girl," Samuelson said.

"Reaper's my brother," Monisha said. "All I need."

At that moment, Harwood knew that what he had done was right. It might have been about Lindsay from the foster home and it might have been about him needing to heal, but he thought it was mostly about helping Monisha.

"That's right," Harwood said. "I've already started the paperwork."

There was a moment of silence. The wind scurried along from west to east. Seagulls hung in the breeze without flapping their wings, as if suspended on a child's mobile.

"What?" Monisha asked.

"You heard me. Making it official. Adopting you. Nobody else can put up with you. Might as well be my burden."

"Say what?"

"That way I can work on your vocabulary and send you to med school or something. You're the smartest, bravest kid I know."

"Med school? Who gonna pay for that?"

Harwood smiled. "Our friend Bronson is letting me keep half the money the Chechen put in my bank account if I set up a college fund for you with it. Two hundred and fifty thousand dollars, young lady."

Monisha started shaking, then gave way to a full onset of tears. She hugged Harwood as he sat in his beach chair. Samuelson knelt next to him and opened two beers.

"That's something to toast to right there," his spotter said.

With Monisha on one side and Samuelson on the other, Harwood looked out at the ocean, thought briefly of the Chechen and whether he was dead or alive, and realized that all that mattered now was within arm's reach.

Read on for an excerpt from REAPER: THREAT ZERO – the next electrifying Sniper Novel by Nicholas Irving with A. J. Tata, coming soon in hardcover from St. Martin's Press!

CHAPTER 1

As it turned sharply uphill toward Camp David, the convoy of black Suburban sport utility vehicles filled with family members of President Bob Smart's cabinet snaked through the shooter's scope.

A single black Dodge Charger led four hulking black armored vehicles ferrying excited men, women, and children to the well-known presidential retreat in western Maryland on a warm May morning. Windows were rolled down. Children's arms hung outside catching the wind and sun. Parents smiled in anticipation of the fun weekend.

As the automobiles made the U-turn, shiny metallic paint winked through the misty air as the sun burned away the dew. The convoy turned off the main road into the Catoctin Mountain Park, leaving behind the grassy fields before ascending into the thick forests. Little publicized, but accessible to the leader of the deadly Threat Zero Team, as the ambush squad called themselves, the itinerary for the annual family day was right on schedule.

As the first vehicle slowed at the hairpin turn, Zero One—the leader—pressed a garage door opener sending unit, which transmitted a signal to a receiving unit antenna sticking up from a faux curbstone. The blown Styrofoam curbstone contained twelve improvised explosive devices called explosively formed penetrators, or six-inch copper plates, that became molten fists when fired from the PVC pipes.

The EFPs fired in a flurry of black smoke and flame. The black rectangular hood of the first Suburban popped off, flew into the air, and bounced off its own windshield. The precisely placed EFPs punched through each of the armored SUVs like rocks through a flimsy porch screen. All four SUVs were hit, two were on fire. Doors opened. Women and children stumbled out. Then two men rolled out of the fourth vehicle, both on fire.

Zero One leveled his scope on the first of the two men, fired. Switched to the second man, fired. Saw the woman in her jeans and five-hundred-dollar shirt, shot her through the head. Two children on the ground, injured. He took them, as well. The other members of his team fired on their targets. Each was assigned a vehicle to avoid squirters that might escape. Zero One eyed the trail vehicle, which he had assigned himself. The fire burned rapidly, flames licking the sky. Anyone inside was incinerated by now.

He moved his scope to monitor vehicle three, which he had assigned to the newest member of the team. Two women were lying on the ground, blood seeping from their heads. Good shots. While that Suburban was not burning, smoke was boiling under the hood. Someone stumbled from the vehicle, gasping. Zero Three nailed the adolescent through the head, spinning the child around. He fell into the open door and slid down, arms and legs splayed open, as if he were making snow angels.

After no further activity on vehicle three, Zero One scanned up to the lead vehicles. Two men from the lead chase car were aiming rifles, scanning for the threat, for them. Zero One fired once, killing the man who was using the open Dodge Charger door as cover. Another team member killed the other man, eliminating the threat. Police sirens screamed in the distance. Time to pack up and move.

"Rally," he said into his microphone. The team executed their well-rehearsed clean-and-collect plan. They then collapsed to an apartment where they had one final task before they would escape and evade in much the same manner that they had entered the ambush location.

The entire attack had taken three minutes.

CHAPTER 2

The charcoal barrel of an SR-25 sniper rifle pressed into the flesh beneath Sammie Samuelson's chin, aiming upward into his skull.

Vick Harwood had been watching one of the cable news shows on his smartphone—some former senator from Virginia named Sloane Brookes was discussing her presidential aspirations—when he got the Facebook Live notice. Brookes had been commenting on the president's latest tweet that referred to her as "Slippery Sloane" and alleged she was conducting shadow diplomacy with Iran in the wake of the cancellation of the nuclear deal. Brookes had quickly pivoted away and reminded the host of her support for free tuition for all college students, paid for by trimming the defense budget.

All that melted away, though, as he stared at his smartphone, watching the Facebook Live feed from Samuelson's Facebook account. He recognized Samuelson's slightly deformed skull. The unmistakable scar from a mortar attack was a bright red four-inch hash mark just below a tuft of hair not much larger than a Mohawk. Samuelson's face was pocked with wounds from rock and shrapnel sustained during the attack in Helmand Province, Afghanistan. His eyes were in their signature half-lidded stare, nearly catatonic. Eyebrows pinched together, making his normal unibrow look even more authentic. This was a pose that Samuelson could conjure whether he was joking or dead serious.

Harwood hoped this was some kind of sick joke.

Thumbs-up, crying face, open-mouthed shock, angry face, and heart emoticons floated across the screen in a steady stream.

"Don't do it, man," Harwood muttered. He quickly fired up his MacBook, clicked onto Samuelson's page, and enlarged the feed to full screen. He pressed off the feed on his smartphone and dialed Samuelson's number.

A few seconds later a phone began playing George Thorogood's "Bad to the Bone," a specialized ring tone that Samuelson had marked just for the Reaper's phone calls. There was no doubt this was Samuelson with the barrel under his chin. His eyes narrowed slightly at the sound of the phone, but he didn't move. His pupils unflinchingly stared into the Facebook Live feed, presumably done so from a smartphone.

"Pick up, Sammie. Been through too much, man," Harwood muttered. The phone clicked through to voice mail with Samuelson's deep voice saying, "Send it," in true spotter parlance.

"Sammie, come on, man, talk to me," Harwood said. The voice mail did not play through Samuelson's smartphone speakers. The computer screen showed

Samuelson's apartment in the background. It was an untidy studio overlooking a windswept valley of green grass and rising, forested hills. A breeze carried debris and traces of smoke. Over Samuelson's right shoulder was a desk with an assortment of newspapers, magazines, and loose-leaf papers. Beneath them there appeared to be a MacBook of some variety, a silver monochrome edge peeking out from beneath the mess.

"I'm sorry, Vick," Samuelson said.

"What are you sorry about?"

Harwood practically shouted at the computer screen. He studied Samuelson's face. The lips moving in slow motion. The high-definition display on the monitor highlighted every scar, every imperfect line, a cut on the lip, the bristles from missing last week's Ranger haircut.

"It's all right in front of you," Samuelson said. Samuelson's chin pressed deeper into the muzzle of the weapon.

"Whatcha watching," Monisha said, opening the door to Harwood's spare bedroom turned makeshift office.

"Get out, now, Monisha!"

Harwood turned his head. Saw the young teenager he had adopted. His promise to her was to mentor her into college and medical school. She was basically a fourteen-year-old orphan when he had saved her from two men who had connected with her on a prostitution web page.

"Don't yell at me, Reaper. I ain't done nothing wrong," Monisha shot back.

Harwood looked at Monisha, her honey-brown skin covered by a gray army running shirt and blue jeans.

She wore black canvas PRO-Keds that were fashionably unlaced. Her eyes grew wide as she gazed over his shoulder at the monitor. Brow furrowed, teeth clenched, Monisha shouted, "No!"

She knew Samuelson as well as anyone in her life. He and Harwood were her role models. Big brothers. All she had.

Standing to block her view, he turned to look at the screen.

The shot rang loud in the small bedroom, echoing from the MacBook speakers. Harwood was caught in between Monisha's horrified stare and the explosion of blood spraying onto Samuelson's screen.

Through the pink haze of the Facebook Live feed, Samuelson's head—what was left of it—hung loosely to the side, blood draining over the ragged edges of his destroyed skull like red wine over a jagged goblet.

As soon as he could refocus, Harwood heard a noise at the back door. It was the slightest tick of a lockpick set. He removed his Beretta pistol from its holster—he always kept the handgun within five feet of him—and whispered to Monisha, "Get in the closet, now. You know where to go."

"I heard it, too," Monisha said. She had excellent instincts and had proven to be an able assistant and spotter on the range. He had taken Monisha to shoot pistols and rifles so that she would be comfortable with his lifestyle as an expert sniper. Still on active duty, Harwood was required to have a "Family Care Plan" for Monisha in the event he was deployed. He had chosen the parents of Command Sergeant Major Murdoch to care for her, and they had gladly accepted the duty, doting on Monisha from the outset.

Glass shattered in the hallway as Harwood locked the closet door behind Monisha. She would take the hidden stairway into the basement as they had rehearsed.

Harwood moved toward the noise, leading with his Beretta. A shadow crossed the floor to his front. Pushing his back against the wall, he heard the intruder snap off two shots. If Harwood had not insulated the house with sheets of metal between the wooden studs and plasterboard, he would be dead or seriously wounded right now. But he had designed their home in Columbus, Georgia, primarily to protect Monisha against the hazards of his life as a renowned army sniper with many enemies.

Swiping his thumb up on his smartphone, he pressed the Kitchen button on his security system. The camera showed a compact man looking directly at the fiber optic camera. Two more shots and the picture went blank on Harwood's phone. He was dealing with a professional marksman if not assassin. Harwood's specialty was as a sniper, earning him the nickname Reaper, for his thirty-three kills in ninety days. A record for the U.S. Army Rangers.

Still, he was more than competent with the basic handgun of the U.S. Army, the Beretta nine-millimeter pistol. He needed to move though, because he could sense the intruder coming toward him.

Harwood did a running baseball slide across the kitchen doorway, firing upward from his back as he slid across the opening. The attacker had closed the distance so that they were less than ten feet apart. Using the kitchen island as cover, the man ducked as Harwood laid down suppressive fire. His intent was to give Monisha time to evacuate and draw the attacker away from her.

Ultimately, he intended to kill the son of a bitch, which would buy them both all the time in the world. Easy fix. No time for that, though. He pushed the images of Samuelson to a compartment in his mind where he stored all the painful memories of his young life. In full combat action mode, Harwood pushed up to one knee, raced through the dining room, dodged the dinner table, and raced headlong into the kitchen.

The attacker's back was facing Harwood. He waited until the man heard him, looked in his direction.

Then the Reaper snapped off three rounds in the center mass of the man's face. Checking to make sure he was accurate, Harwood's concern shifted to the potential for backup intruders and ultimately the mess he was going to have to clean up from this guy's exploded head. He inspected the body for forms of identification or any intelligence. Black pants, black shirt, and black outer tactical vest were all devoid of any helpful information save a small radio connected to a fiber optic earbud stuck in the man's left ear canal.

Harwood removed the earbud, wiped off the blood and wax, and stuck it in his ear, listening. For a few seconds static carried through the small device.

Then: "Zero Five, confirm kill."

Zero Five? The term meant nothing to Harwood. He was an active duty Army Ranger sniper. Call signs and nicknames were a staple of his regiment, but he'd only heard "05" as a suffix to a call sign previously—such as "Eagle 05," which usually indicated the second-in-command. "06" was typically the commander. He removed the small radio from the outer tactical vest and stuffed it into his pocket, immediately focusing outward, away from the growing pool of blood on the kitchen floor.

"Need code word for cleaners," the voice said into his ear.

Deep baritone. Command voice. Like a drill sergeant or captain, someone who was used to barking out orders, making stuff happen. Inflected with the slightest hint of impatience.

Harwood's mind raced with options. None awesome. His favorite thought was to somehow lure the cleaners into the house and kill them. Monisha had enough time to get into the safe room, lock the door, and survive. It was like a nuclear bomb shelter in the backyard. There was no way in or out other than a combination lock and heavy gauge metal blast-proof door. Harwood knew that he had enemies, both foreign and domestic, and as Monisha's surrogate big brother, he had taken the greatest precaution possible. Perhaps extreme, but Harwood had two speeds: on and off. And "on" was 100 mph, always considering the worst thing that could happen.

Harwood moved to the rear door that had been breached. He had triple locks and had been careless this morning when he had looked outside in the backyard. He should have locked all three when he had returned from his security checks before prepping to take Monisha to school. Scanning the backyard, Harwood saw no visible threats. The yard was a well-manicured one-hundred-foot-by-one-hundred-foot square of St. Augustine grass, thick blades providing a level and smooth carpet all the way to the eight-foot-high fence.

Perfect fields of fire for him. The only imperfection

in the backyard was the imperceptible three-foot-by-three-foot square of sheet metal that led into the safe room. It was covered with the same grass and only Harwood could discern it, primarily because he knew it was there. Detecting no threats in the backyard, he moved to the living room, kept low, and took position between the front door and the bay window.

The street featured the usual traffic of parents driving to work or carpooling to school. A yellow school bus stopped at an intersection a half a block away. Monisha's bus. The driver looked over his shoulder at Harwood's house, waited a beat, perhaps expecting Monisha to come sprinting from the door as she had done so many times. After about fifteen seconds, he gave up, and pulled away with one less student than the normal pickup of five.

As the bus pulled away, Harwood saw a gray sedan, maybe a Ford Taurus, parked on the street. Two men sat in the front seat. The car was aimed away from Harwood's modest brick rambler built in the Georgia countryside outside of Columbus and Fort Benning.

Harwood low crawled to the sofa, pulled his SR-25 from beneath the davenport, slid back to the bay window, and used a hand to slowly push open the windowpane, tilting it ninety degrees. He eased the muzzle of the weapon out of the window and lined up behind the scope. Boxwood shrubs were just beneath the window and the barrel of the weapon, masking Harwood's movement. He flicked on the digital recording device in his scope and laid a steady aim on the two men. They were white, broad-shouldered men, not unlike his dead assailant in the kitchen. Likely accomplices. He had never seen this car or these people on his street.

"Send it," Harwood said, pressing the push-to-talk button on the radio.

From the front seat of the car, two heads turned toward the house. That was enough confirmation for Harwood.

His best shot was on the passenger. The driver's head was mostly blocked by the divider between the front and back doors. He leveled the crosshairs. Exhaled slowly. Pulled the trigger.

The man's head erupted, kicked backward. As Harwood was moving the rifle to attempt a shot on the driver, the car sped away.

He was okay with that. Two down, one to go. While he doubted there were more than the three, he couldn't be sure. He inspected the rest of his house. The garage. The side yards. Nothing.

He called Command Sergeant Major Murdoch, his mentor.

"Blue on blue," Harwood said when Murdoch answered.

"Roger that," Murdoch replied.

He pressed End and found the closet, gained access to the stairway, and climbed into the tunnel leading to the safe room. He stooped as he walked twenty meters past concrete blocks on either side and two-by-eight flooring above. He spun the dial on the heavy metal door, opened it, and found Monisha inside working on the computer.

"I watched it all, Reaper," she said.

Harwood had outfitted the entire perimeter with cameras, which Monisha had been monitoring from the basement. "Damn, you good."

"Work on the grammar, will you, Monisha. I'm not raising a hood rat."

Monisha cackled.

"Yes, sir, Reaper. I'm going to be a doctor, for sure. But like you say, you've got to remember where you've been to know where you're going."

Harwood nodded. "That's right. And where you're going is to stay with Minnie and Pops for a few days until we figure this out."

Monisha leapt out of her chair and did a slight moonwalk, spun around, and high-fived the air.

"Yes!"

Harwood nodded.

"Not that I don't love you, Reaper, but they're the best."

Harwood was concerned about the child's apparent unconcern about the events that had just occurred. She compartmentalized too well and needed to be more afraid, or at least more aware of concepts such as danger and risk. When he found her a few months ago, she had been tied to a bed naked by two white supremacists who fully intended to rape and murder her. They ended up dead by his hands and even then, she had responded coolly, as if she was just turning another trick.

"You know we have a dead man in our kitchen, right? And that I just shot a man in the street. These men were trying to kill us."

Monisha's eyes grew wide. She stuttered, then stopped and looked down.

"Yes, I know, Reaper. I'm scared, and I cover that fear with the good stuff."

"As long as you can feel that you're scared, Monisha. Like we talked about. You need to feel that. You need to know it's real." He touched his chest with his hand. "We lost Sammie."

"I know it's real. I watched it too, Reaper."

He had never been married and had no previous children. Adopting Monisha to keep her out of the court system and from being pimped out again was his solution to saving her. The FBI had allowed him to keep half the money that his previous adversary, the Chechen, had deposited into his account in an attempt to frame him for the murders of high-profile generals and politicians. The $250,000 was in a secure investment trust and could only be used for secondary education and associated expenses. Harwood paid for everything else out of his own pocket and meager sergeant's salary. He wrestled with balancing his time between parenting Monisha and doing his soldierly duties. Mostly, though, he struggled with raising a fifteen-year-old girl, a chore for anyone, he presumed.

"How we going to clean up the dead guy?" she asked.

"I'll call the right people," Harwood said.

"The cleaners? I watch TV, movies and stuff," she said.

"No. I'm calling the police. Keep this aboveboard."

"All right. What about school? Is it dangerous for me?"

"We'll probably keep you at Minnie and Pops's place for a few days. Minnie was a teacher, so she can work on things with you."

"Roger that, Reaper man." Monisha smiled. She was a smart child but aged beyond her years from a childhood that no child should have to endure.

The combination lock to the outer door clicked and spun until Command Sergeant Major Murdoch opened the door. A former collegiate heavyweight wrestler, Murdoch had to lean well forward to navigate the low tunnel to the safe room. He popped up and looked every bit the impressive Ranger that he was. White sidewall buzzed haircut. Bulked chest and arms. Square chin and chiseled face.

"Status?" Murdoch asked. "Other than the guest you've got in your kitchen. Looks like he's making himself comfortable."

"Damn, you funny, Sergeant Major," Monisha said.

"Who gave you that mouth, young lady?" Murdoch snapped.

Monisha stepped back, shut her mouth, which was the typical reaction most people had when Murdoch spoke.

"Pretty sure I killed one guy in a four-door Ford Taurus sedan. Got the license plate on my scope video. Samuelson committed suicide."

"Samuelson's *dead*. We know that much. Let's not jump to conclusions about anything else," Murdoch said.

"You saw it?" Harwood asked.

"Son, half the world's seen that by now. It's all over the news. Most of the Rangers in the barracks watched it. It's everywhere. The questions are, why would he do that? And, if he didn't do it, why would someone want him and you dead?"

Harwood flashed back to the Chechen and his need to confirm that kill, but there was no confirmation. Some blood in a life raft was the only indicator that the Chechen had been wounded. Was he still alive?

"Hundred bucks says it's not the Chechen. This feels different," Murdoch said.

"It's got to be something Sammie found."

"In Maryland?"

"He'd gotten a job as a tech guy at a subcontracting company working on defense programs near Frederick, Maryland. Western part of the state. He sent me a bunch of texts."

"Let me see," Murdoch said.

Harwood pulled up the message function of his MacBook and clicked on "Spotter."

DUDE, CHECK THIS OUT
SEND IT
CUT/PASTE FROM DEEP WEB:
FAMILY DAY
AT CD IS BEST LOCATION.
EASY. BLACK SUBURBANS W
DODGE CHARGER CHASE CAR.
HAIRPIN TURN.

"What's CD?" Monisha asked, looking over their shoulders.

"Camp David. He lived in a town just outside of Camp David."

"Look at this," Murdoch said. He pointed at the television monitor tuned to a news program. A news helicopter showed a road with four black Suburbans destroyed and smoking, the Dodge Charger chase car relatively intact. Bodies littered the field on either side of the narrow road.

"Women and children," Harwood said.

"Some look my age," Monisha seconded. Her voice was quiet, subdued.

Harwood pulled up the Facebook video of Samuelson's apparent suicide. The live feed automatically converted to a video on the individual's Facebook page. He fast-forwarded until he could see the window behind Samuelson.

There was a field and a road with a hairpin turn.

"Looks like a good spot to attack the convoy. Right there from his window," Harwood said, pointing at the paused frame of the video. He saw things he hadn't noticed before. The window was half open. A chair sat facing the window. The bottom sill of the window had light scratching. Saw the silver edge of what looked like a MacBook. Harwood could almost smell the acrid aroma of burning gunpowder.

"You don't think Sammie did that, do you?" Monisha asked. Not much was lost on her. She studied the images with Murdoch and Harwood.

Murdoch's phone buzzed.

He answered and muttered a few, "Yes, sirs," before hanging up.

"I've got to send you packing," Murdoch said. He turned from Harwood to Monisha and nodded. "First, I'll take Monisha to my parents. I've already got someone coming to clean up your house. Meet you at the headquarters where I will sign your papers. I'll get next-of-kin notification rolling on Samuelson once we have confirmation. He was out but he's still a Ranger. Always will be."

Harwood nodded. The thought of a mission sent a charge through his body. All he ever wanted to be was an Army Ranger. He was excited, but Murdoch was giving him that stare to keep his mouth shut, a look Harwood knew well.

"Who were next of kin?" he asked anyway. He had spent less than a month in combat with Samuelson as his spotter. They had shared some time convalescing after the Chechen incident in Savannah, but still, they didn't talk about much other than the superficial niceties that prevented them from sinking into the analytical depths of their dangerous profession. He couldn't recall Samuelson mentioning any of his family. Maybe a sister? Or maybe that was a girlfriend.

"His parents are living. And a sibling out there somewhere that they're checking on. They're in his paperwork. I've got it. Meet me in an hour. Pack your shit." Then to Monisha, "Let's go, Monisha."

Monisha hugged Harwood and said, "Don't get killed or nothing, Reaper. Need my brothers. Sucks about Sammie."

Harwood hugged Monisha and watched her exit with Murdoch. He gathered his SR-25 and other tools of war before heading to Fort Benning.